The Extraordinarily Ordinary Life of

Cassandra Jones

Southwest Cougars Year 3: Age 14

D0839391

Southwest Cougars Year 3: Age 14

The Extraordinarily Ordinary Life of Cassandra Jones

Tamara Hart Heiner

paperback edition
copyright 2018 Tamara Hart Heiner
cover art by Tamara Hart Heiner

Also by Tamara Hart Heiner:
Perilous (WiDo Publishing 2010)
Altercation (WiDo Publishing 2012)
Deliverer (Tamark Books 2014)
Priceless (WiDo Publishing 2016)

Goddess of Fate:
Inevitable (Tamark Books 2013)
Entranced (Tamark Books 2017)

Kellam High:
Lay Me Down (Tamark Books 2016)
Reaching Kylee (Tamark Books 2016)

The Extraordinarily Ordinary Life of Cassandra Jones:
Walker Wildcats Year 1: Age 10 (Tamark Books 2015)
Walker Wildcats Year 2: Age 11 (Tamark Books 2016)
Southwest Cougars Year 1: Age 12 (Tamark Books 2017)

Tornado Warning (Dancing Lemur Press 2014)

Table of Contents

Episode 1:

Never Been Kissed

CHAPTER ONE

Barbecue Bash

Cassandra Jones opened her eyes and stared at the ceiling of her bedroom, an excited flutter in her chest. She stretched her toes and pointed them toward the far wall.

Today was the day of the big barbecue.

The anxious excitement grew into an army of singing crickets, and Cassie's limbs bounced and fidgeted in agreement. She couldn't stay in bed any longer. She hopped up and hurried to the bathroom to brush her teeth, widening her eyes and checking out her reflection in the mirror as she did.

What did Josh see in her, exactly? Of all her friends, she felt the plainest. Her dark hair refused to curl and hung in straight sheets past her shoulders. Her skin looked a little washed out after months of cold weather, but now that it was summer, she should get her color back. When she'd met Josh, she'd been standing in the shadow of her beautiful and vivacious friends, Andrea and Amity. Yet somehow, Josh had liked her more, and today he and his friends were making the two-hour drive from Oklahoma to Arkansas so they could have a barbecue party. Cassie and her friends had planned this with eagerness for a week, and she could hardly believe the day was finally here.

Barely had she put her toothbrush down when her phone rang. Cassie paraded from the bathroom and pounced on it, flipping it open as soon as she saw her friend Maureen's name dancing across the front.

"Hi!" Cassie said.

In the bed beside her, Cassie's sister Emily groaned and kicked her legs. "Be quiet, Cassie. It's too early."

Cassie lowered her voice. "What's going on?" she asked Maureen, suddenly afraid the girl was calling with bad news.

"I can't wait for tonight!" Maureen said, her voice breathy. "I hardly slept knowing we would see Josh and Andy soon! Do you think he will bring any other friends?"

"He said he would," Cassie said. "I haven't talked to him yet today, but I'll ask." That warm giddiness filled her chest again. Cassie gave herself a mental pinch, hardly daring to believe that she was the girl Josh had chosen for his girlfriend, and now she was the girl all of her friends envied. Josh was in high school, almost seventeen, and all of his friends were just as cute and mature as he was.

"What should I wear tonight?" Maureen asked.

Cassie entered her own closet and wrinkled her nose. She was the last person ever to give fashion advice. She would much rather read a book than pick out clothes. "I don't know. You look good in whatever you wear." It seemed like a safe answer, though Maureen was slightly on the chunky side with super long hair that she usually kept in a ponytail. Fashion wasn't exactly her forte either.

"You should wear a sundress," Maureen said. "Show off your shoulders. You have such nice skin."

That sounded like a good plan. Cassie fingered the material of several short, sleeveless dresses in her closet. "I think I will!"

Maureen gave a little giggle. "He's not going to be able to resist you!"

Cassie was still smiling after she hung up the phone and changed her clothes. She never would've been able to guess a year ago that her friends would be some of the most popular girls in school and that they would treat her like an equal, even someone enviable.

She pulled out the curling iron, determined to make it curl her hair. She wanted to look her absolute best. Maybe she could even pass for fifteen.

"Come on, Cassie," Mrs. Jones said, poking her head into the bedroom. "We've got to go shopping if we're going to put on that big barbecue tonight."

"Right!" Cassie squealed.

She searched for a pair of shoes under her bed. But now Emily had sat up and was watching her groggily.

"I can't believe Mom is letting you do this."

"Me either," Cassie breathed. She sat up and slid her feet into her sandals. Her parents had made it very clear she wasn't allowed to date until she was sixteen. But since Josh lived in Tahlequah two hours away, Mrs. Jones allowed Cassie to be his girlfriend as long as they were never alone. She fully supported a barbecue with friends and family in attendance.

"Get some cookies for dessert," Emily said, crashing back against her bed.

The two girls had stayed up late into the night talking, but Emily apparently didn't have an adrenaline rush to propel her from her bed this morning.

"I will. Maybe even a pie." And Cassie was going to eat it, too. She had spent the past year struggling with her weight and her attitude about food. She was doing better now, trying to see food as something vital and important that she needed to nourish her body. But sometimes she had to remind herself to eat more than she was inclined.

"I'm in the car, Cassie!" her mom shouted from the kitchen.

"I'm coming!" Cassie called back.

She had just barely exited her bedroom when her cell phone rang. She paused in the kitchen, fishing through the little purse swaying from her shoulder. She found the device, and her heart gave a little tumble when she saw Josh's name. She flipped it open.

"Josh!" she said, trying to sound like a breathy, flirty girlfriend. This all took so much work. "I've been waiting to hear from you! What time will you be here?"

"Hi, Cassie." There was a pause. "There's been a slight problem. I'm not sure if I'm going to make it."

Cassie froze. The world around her froze. She gripped the phone tighter in her hands, refusing to believe his words. "You have to. All my friends are coming. My mom and I are about to buy the food." This couldn't happen. It would be a total catastrophe of Josh and his friends couldn't make it.

"I'm still working on it, okay? I'll let you know."

"No, you have to come," Cassie said. "You have to figure out a way. Whatever it takes." She hung up and dropped her phone into her bag, the worry and fear constricting her heart. Then she shoved it aside. Josh knew how important this was to her. He would get here.

～※～

Cassie tried to focus on her excitement as her mom picked up food item after food item.

"Do you want this at the barbecue?" she would ask after each one.

Cassie pasted on a smile and nodded, but the worry grew bigger in her chest. Andrea and Amity had already called to say how excited they were, and even Cara had sent Cassie a text to say she couldn't wait to meet Josh. Beautiful, quiet Cara, the one whose approval Cassie most craved.

"All right, I think that's everything," Mrs. Jones said. She pushed the cart toward the checkout line. "Can you think of anything we might have forgotten?"

Cassie shook her head. "No, this looks great." She swallowed hard.

Her phone rang, and she looked down at her hand where she still held it cupped in her palm. Her throat tightened. It was Josh.

She took several steps away from her mother and the cart, moving into another aisle before answering. "Hello?"

"Cassie, I'm so sorry," Josh said. "I can't come."

His apology fell on deaf ears. Her face flushed hot with rage and embarrassment. "We've been planning this for over a week! How can you tell me now you can't come?"

"I'm so sorry," he said, and he sounded miserable. "My uncle needs my car today, and I can't find anyone else's. I would rather be there with you, I promise."

The burning had moved to her throat and her eyes, and Cassie blinked rapidly. She took several deep breaths to keep from yelling at him.

"Cassie?" he said.

"It's fine. It's fine. You did what you can."

"Please don't be angry at me."

Cassie felt nothing except anger toward him. But she also knew, logically, that this wasn't his fault. It was just bad luck. Her bad luck.

"It's fine," she repeated. "I better go."

"Call me later?"

"Yeah. Bye." Cassie closed the phone and inhaled deeply, trying to compose herself. Putting a smile on her face, she walked back over to her mother, who was already unloading the cart onto the conveyor belt.

"Was that Josh?" Mrs. Jones asked, glancing at Cassie before returning to the items.

"Yes," she said.

"What did he say?"

This was her chance. This was the moment for Cassie to tell her mother the boys weren't coming. And she would let her friends down and go from being the most important member of their group to the most pathetic.

"He just needed directions," Cassie said, lowering her eyes and smoothing the front of her dress. "They leave in a few hours."

The cashier continued ringing up items, the machine beeping as the total rose. Eighty-two dollars. Eighty-five. Ninety.

Mrs. Jones smiled. "Wonderful. We'll make sure the food is ready by then."

She whipped out her debit card to pay for the barbecue food, totaling more than a hundred dollars. Cassie swallowed hard against the painful knot in her throat. She was committed now.

◎〜※〜◎

Amity and Andrea were the first of Cassie's friends to show up. They arrived at her house in matching tank tops and shorts, wearing their hair in soft waves and a little too much makeup on their faces.

"Hi!" Cassie said, summoning her best acting skills and greeting them with a perky smile.

Amity squeezed her arm. "Aren't you so excited? I can't believe Josh is coming up here just for this!"

"Yeah," Andrea said. "You're so lucky your boyfriend can drive." She rolled her eyes for emphasis. "The rest of us are all stuck dating fourteen-year-olds."

Cassie nodded, her forced smile still pasted on her mouth. "So lucky." And she would be, if she could get her boyfriend to show up. The girls had just finished their eighth-grade year, and Cassie still couldn't believe she had a boyfriend in high school.

"Who is he bringing? Andy? And who else?" Amity said, glancing at her nails and then back to Cassie, not quite hiding the eagerness in her eyes.

Cassie had not forgotten that Amity liked Josh also. The surprising thing was that Josh preferred Cassie over Amity, with her curvy body and greenish eyes. Cassie always felt second next to her.

"Yeah. Andy. And maybe someone else, I can't remember." She was floundering, unable to think of a plausible lie on the tip of her tongue.

But the other girls didn't notice. "Let's put some makeup on you," Andrea said, calling Cassie back to the bedroom she shared with Emily.

Maureen and Cara showed up just as Andrea finished applying the third coat of mascara to Cassie's eyelashes. Cassie's stomach turned so violently she worried she'd be sick. Now they were all here, except Janice, who wasn't coming.

"Don't you look beautiful," Cara said, leaning close to press her cheek against Cassie's in an air kiss. "I can't wait to meet this man of yours."

"I can't wait for that either," Cassie said, certain her smile wobbled on her face. That day would not be today.

The girls' parents were laughing and talking in the living room, and then Mr. Jones called out, "Cassie! It's time to head to the park for the barbecue!"

Deep breath. She would get through this somehow. She stood up, eyes on the carpet as she pushed past her friends. "Coming."

The girls all piled into the Jones' van, leaving their parents to follow them in separate vehicles. Cassie's family lived out in the country, surrounded by seven acres and beautiful trees but not much else. It took at least ten minutes to get anywhere, and that was only to things still out in the country like the park. Everything else of social importance, like church or school or even the grocery store, took at least twenty minutes to get to. Even most of her friends lived in town.

The excitement and anticipation was ripe in the air, and Cassie tried to act as if she expected a happy ending as the girls pushed each other on the swings, heads turning to look at the road every few minutes. Mr. Jones got a fire going on one of the grills, and Mrs. Jones laid out bags of chips and salads and soda.

Cassie told herself to just enjoy this barbecue with her friends, but she knew everyone had gathered under false pretenses. If they knew the truth, they would be furious with her.

CHAPTER TWO

Stood Up

"What time did Josh say they were coming?" Amity asked after the girls had been playing for several minutes. Cassie pulled her phone out and checked the time. A little after four o'clock. "He said he'd arrive between now and five. So they are probably still in route."

Cara clicked her tongue. "So like a boy. He should've called you when he left so you would have a better time. Give him a call and find out where he is."

Crapola. She couldn't call him now because her friends would hear the truth. But she couldn't not call without it looking really strange. Her mind scrambled for an excuse. "He said he doesn't like to talk on the phone when he's driving. I think it might be illegal in Oklahoma."

The other girls made noises of understanding and nodded their heads.

"He's so responsible," Amity said.

"So important to be safe," Cara agreed.

Cassie nodded, greatly relieved to have avoided that issue. "So we'll just wait a little bit more."

The girls went back to playing on the swings and chatting, but Cassie noticed a difference in the air. They were a bit more impatient now, and conversations stalled as they kept looking down the road.

"What's his car look like?" Maureen asked.

That wasn't something she had ever thought to ask. "I don't know. Just normal, I guess. It's a car."

Maureen snorted out a laugh and rolled her eyes. "So like Cassie, to not even know how important a car is!"

The other girls laughed with her, and Cassie's cheeks burned. Once again she was reminded how different she was from them, and how much effort it took to act like one of them. Why was a car important? How did it matter in the least what he drove? But she could never say that.

"Girls," Mrs. Jones said, coming over to join them. "Do we know what time the boys are coming?"

"Sometime between four and five," Amity said, answering for Cassie.

Mrs. Jones checked her watch. "Well, it's four forty-five. So they must be almost here."

The girls smiled, and Cassie's mom walked away. The small talk had nearly died, as none of them had gathered to chat with each other, something they did on a daily basis. They were all here for one reason: to flirt with cute boys.

The minutes ticked by slowly. A little after five, Mr. Jones came over.

"The burgers are ready. Are we waiting for the boys, or shall we go ahead and eat?"

All eyes turned to Cassie, waiting for her to make a decision. "Let's go ahead and get started," she said. "I'll try and call Josh."

Everyone headed for the pavilion except Amity, who hung behind. Cassie turned her back on her and walked several paces away. She pulled her phone out and dialed Josh's number. She only let it ring once before hanging up, glad he hadn't answered. She turned around and returned to the pavilion, kneading her brows together in false consternation.

"Nobody answered. I'm sure it's because they're driving."

The adults and girls alike murmured their agreement and sat at the tables with plates piled high with burgers and chips. The conversation was stilted and dry, and Cassie found she couldn't eat or participate.

"You're really worried, aren't you?" Andrea said, misinterpreting Cassie's actions. "I'm sure they're okay."

"Yeah," Cassie said, glad she didn't have to be so cheerful anymore. "I'm sure they are." She exhaled and picked at her chips.

"Should we try and call someone, Cassie?" Mrs. Jones asked, sitting down across from her.

"I don't have anyone else's number." Thank goodness for that. And thank goodness none of her friends did either.

"Well, let's try and enjoy our time here." Mrs. Jones patted her hand, but her face reflected her worry.

Cassie bit on her lower lip, falling more easily into this role than being the hopeful and excited girl from earlier. "I hope they're okay," she said.

Instantly her friends gathered around her like mother hens.

"Oh, hon, I'm sure they are," Cara said, rubbing her shoulders.

"I'll keep watching the road," Maureen said. "They could show up any moment."

"Let's sing a song," Amity said. "What about the song you danced to the first time?"

"Can you—"Andrea began, belting out the familiar melody.

Cassie buried her face in her hands, guilt making her face hot.

Amity slapped Andrea on the thigh. "Stop singing that! It's making her sad!"

Cassie giggled, but she hid it in her hands. Her friends could be awfully silly.

Her phone rang in her purse, startling her. Cassie jerked up and grabbed at it before anyone could see the caller.

"Is it them? Is it Josh?" Amity leaned in closer, peering around Cassie's shoulder.

It was. Cassie took a deep breath and stepped away from the picnic table. She moved over to the far side of the pavilion, feeling all eyes on her.

"Hello?" she said.

"Hi, Cassie. I missed a call from you."

She turned slightly so none of her friends could read her lips. "I just thought maybe you found a way to get here."

"Oh, man, you're making me feel so bad. I'm sorry. There was no way for me to get there."

"So you're not coming?" She let her voice rise upward on the last word, knowing it would echo through the pavilion.

"I'll make it up to you. Maybe next weekend. Some other time, I promise."

"Yeah. Sure. It's fine." She sniffled, trying to dredge up some real emotion. But she had played too many parts in the past few hours, and there were no tears to cry. "I better go. All my friends are here."

"Tell everyone I'm really sorry."

"Okay." Cassie closed her phone and returned to the group, keeping her eyes down.

"What happened?" Maureen asked.

"That was Josh. They're not coming."

Her statement was met with gasps and cries of disbelief.

"Why not?" Andrea asked, scrunching her brow.

Cassie searched for a likely reason. "His car broke down on the way here. He had to get it towed home and doesn't have another way to get here."

The lie came easily enough.

"That's what you get for having a bad car," Maureen said, and the comic relief brought chuckles from everyone.

Amity took Cassie's hand and sat her down. "I know it's such a disappointment."

"I'm so sorry," Cara said.

The others murmured their consolation, doing their best to comfort Cassie. She kept her head down and pretended to be weepy, but inside she felt relief she had pulled it off. Nobody doubted her. She wasn't the one in their group who lied.

They all believed her.

There was a strange power in that.

CHAPTER THREE

Adventures in Babysitting

Josh called again on Sunday, all apologies over the barbecue. But Cassie was already over it. Things had turned out pretty well for her, considering it all.

"I have a babysitting job this week," she said as she packed her duffel bag. "Some lady from church. She's going to be gone for three days, so I'm staying overnight with the children."

"Wow. Sounds like a real job."

"Yeah. They're great kids, though. It'll be fun."

"Maybe I could come help you. Stay over there with you."

Cassie straightened up and frowned at the clothing she'd already packed. It was one thing to have a long-distance boyfriend, it was quite another to think he might come over to the house when there were no adults around. "They have a definite no-boyfriend rule." Sister Mecham had never said that, but it was probably because she didn't know Cassie had a boyfriend. Cassie knew it was a rule with a lot of families. She'd read the entire Babysitters Club series when she was younger.

"Figures. I'll have to work something out. I'm desperate to see you."

"Yeah. I better go." She hung up and double-checked that she had enough changes of clothing for three days. All the while a thought tickled the back of her mind, unwelcome and heavy.

Maybe it was a good thing her boyfriend lived so far away. She was starting to get the impression he would expect things from her she wasn't quite ready for.

❧

An hour later, Cassie's dad drove her out to Sister Mecham's house. She lived on the complete opposite side of Springdale, a good forty-five minutes away from the Jones' house.

The children greeted Cassie excitedly when she rang the doorbell. Mr. Jones put her duffel bag in the living room and talked to Sister Mecham for a moment while the younger children climbed Cassie's legs and clung to her shoulders.

"We are going to have so much fun!" Lexi said, peering up at Cassie with great big brown eyes. Lexi was the second oldest at six, and she had an older sister Shelby, who was eight. The youngest was a four-year-old little boy, Harrison.

It was Harrison who sat on her foot with his arms around her calf. He smiled up at her, and the adoration in his eyes warmed her. Cassie had started babysitting them just a few months earlier, but she loved them and knew they loved her.

"I'm off, Cassie! You just call if you need anything," her dad said.

Cassie waved, anxious for him to go and leave her on her own. These next few days would be her first experience at adulting it. She could hardly believe the trust Sister Mecham was putting in her.

"I'm so glad you're here, Cassie," Sister Mecham said. "You already know the basics, but let me go over a few extra things with you before I go." She showed Cassie the food menu and where everything was. She gave them permission to go on walks but not to walk to the lake.

And then she pulled a plastic tub from the cabinet. "Now you probably didn't know it, but Harry has asthma. It doesn't happen very often, but if he has an asthma attack, here's his inhaler and here are some medications."

Cassie's heart skipped a beat. She remembered Andrea having an asthma attack the year before and ending up in the hospital. "Do you think I'll have to use that?" She wrapped her fingers across her palm, feeling how they were getting clammy.

"I sure hope not, but it's better to be prepared."

"What does an asthma attack look like?"

Sister Mecham hesitated, and Cassie could sense her sudden nervousness in leaving Cassie alone with the children. "Like gasping for air but not getting any. His sisters will know." Sister Mecham looked at Shelby and Lexi for confirmation, and both girls nodded. "If you have any doubts at all, just call 911."

Cassie tried to look confident as she bobbed her head. "No problem. It's going to be just fine."

"I'm sure it will be. You're going to do great." Sister Mecham nodded as if to reassure herself as well. "I'm off. Call me every morning and every evening and any other time you need to."

Shelby and Lexi slipped their arms around Cassie's waist, and she put an arm around each of their shoulders.

"Don't worry," she said. "Go enjoy your conference. We're going to do great."

⚜

Monday was full of adventure and excitement as the children had the same sense of freedom as Cassie did: no parents.

She made pancakes for breakfast and let them bounce on the couches while they watched cartoons. Then Cassie got everyone dressed and did a load of laundry as the children pulled out all the toys in the playroom.

Cassie didn't care. They didn't need to clean up until right before Sister Mecham got home.

She made grilled cheese sandwiches for lunch, and then she peaked outside at the beautiful sunshine and the lush green trees. "You guys want to go for a walk?"

"Yes, yes!" Lexi said.

"Oh, I love going outside," Harrison said. He slipped his hand into Cassie's and smiled at her.

"Come on, then. It's such a beautiful day."

The Mechams lived out in Sonora, on the very east side of Springdale. The community reflected the country feel without being as isolated as most rural areas. A lake stretched behind the houses across the street, and Cassie kept the children on her side just to be safe.

The sun beat down on them, pleasant on her skin at first but soon too hot. They made it all the way around the second block before the heat began to feel oppressive.

"So shall we go back and have popsicles?" Cassie asked, smiling at them.

"Yes, please!" Shelby said, wiping her forehead with the back of her hand. "I'm so hot!"

"No, not yet," Harrison said. "We haven't been out that long."

Cassie took his little hands. "We can come back out later. Tomorrow, maybe even today."

Harrison slipped his hands away from hers. "I don't want to. I want to stay out now."

"Well, that's not what we're doing," Lexi said, her voice carrying the commanding tone of an older sister. "Cassie said we're going in now, and she's in charge. You have to listen to her."

"No, I don't," Harrison said, and he shocked Cassie by turning around and running the opposite direction.

"Harrison!" Cassie cried, unable to believe he'd just run off. He had never acted this way any other time she babysat.

"Get Harry!" Shelby screamed, charging after him. Lexi joined in hot pursuit, and all Cassie could do was try to keep up. Oh how she hated running.

Harrison glanced over his shoulder and saw them behind him, then he turned and ran straight into the yard between two houses.

Cassie's heart skipped a beat, and she put on a burst of speed. What if he ran to the lake? She had to be faster than a four-year-old.

His two sisters turned as well, and luckily they were faster, because by the time she panted her way into the yard, each sister had Harrison by an arm. He whimpered, his lip jetting out as tears welled in his eyes.

"Harrison!" Cassie exclaimed, trembling with relief when she reached him. She wanted to scream and smack the boy and wrap him in a sobbing hug all at the same time. "You can't do that! We'll have to walk you home right now."

He began to cry, and he struggled against his sisters, screaming and yelling and dragging his feet down the sidewalk. Cassie glanced back and forth as they walked, afraid people would come out of their homes to see the commotion, or worse, call the police and say she was kidnapping him.

"Harrison, stop that," she hissed, taking one arm from his sister. "You're too big for me to carry you. Now come on."

He didn't let up his howling, and they half dragged him to the house. Shelby ran ahead and opened the garage door. Cassie barely pulled Harrison inside before Shelby slapped the button and let the door close again.

"The popsicles are right here," Lexi said brightly, opening a deep freezer by the entrance to the house.

"Come on, Harrison," Cassie said. She let go of him, smiling, hoping to persuade him with a sugary treat. "Let's get a popsicle and cool off."

His face was splotchy from crying, and he took quick, soft breaths. Cassie watched him with a note of panic. He wouldn't have an asthma attack, would he?

"Come on," she said again, holding out a hand.

Harrison reached out like he would grab it, but then he changed his mind. He darted past her and banged his palm on the button to open the garage door.

"No!" Cassie cried. She leaped forward and grabbed him, pulling him back before the door got very high. Shelby quickly hit the button again, and the door closed down to the concrete flooring.

"I guess we're going to have to go into the house," Cassie said, her pulse leaping in her neck. "Bring your popsicles." She didn't relinquish her grip on Harrison's arm, and they trooped inside.

That wasn't Harrison's last bid for freedom.

The moment she let go of him, he raced for the front door. When Lexi beat him there and locked it, he turned around and hurried to the back door. Shelby got there first and glared down at him.

There were no other doors. Cassie stared at him, waiting to see what else he would try.

"I want my mom," Harrison said, and it broke Cassie's heart.

"Why, Harry?" she said. "We've just barely gotten started."

"Because you're mean!" he said.

"What is it you want besides going outside? What can we do in here?"

Harrison turned around and ran to his room, his sobs echoing down the halls.

"I'll go sit with him," Cassie said. Her hands trembled. Nothing like this had ever happened before. What would Sister Mecham say? "Can you girls play a game or watch a movie or something?"

While they settled down agreeably, Cassie went to check on Harrison. Already a headache grew from his antics, and she pressed a palm to her forehead. This better not be an indicator of what was to come.

CHAPTER FOUR

Gig's Up

That evening Cassie called Sister Mecham while they watched a movie.

"How was everything?" Sister Mecham asked.

"Great," Cassie said, trying to sound upbeat. "We had a fun day. Harrison got a little rambunctious on our walk, but he's fine now." She crossed her mental fingers that Sister Mecham wouldn't ask any more about it.

"I'm so glad. Let me talk to the kids."

Cassie handed the phone off, heart pounding in her throat. She eavesdropped on the conversations of Shelby's and Lexi's happy chatter.

And then Lexi said, "Harrison ran away during the walk."

Oh, no.

"We had to run and grab him and then Cassie dragged him back home."

Her mouth went dry. She'd be fired for sure after this.

"Yes. Here he is." Lexi handed the phone to Harrison, oblivious to what she'd done.

"I didn't want to come home," Harrison said. He started to cry. "They grabbed my arms and pulled me home, and then they locked me in the garage!"

Now Cassie knew Sister Mecham was going to report her for child abuse.

Still crying, Harrison handed the phone back to Cassie. "She wants to talk to you."

"Hello?" Cassie asked, her neck throbbing.

"Cassie, what happened?"

"Harrison ran away," Cassie said, wondering how to defend herself. "I got scared he'd run into the lake. Shelby and Lexi helped me catch him. We ate popsicles in the garage but he kept trying to get out, so we came inside. After that he was fine. We didn't have any more incidents." She held her breath and waited for the yelling, for Sister Mecham to end this babysitting gig.

"You need to be firmer with him, Cassie. He needs to respect you and know you mean what you say."

She hadn't expected that. "Okay." How much firmer could she be?

"Let me talk to Harrison again, and if he gives you any more trouble, you call me."

"Yes, ma'm," Cassie said. She handed the phone over, her heart rate just starting to slow as she realized she hadn't been fired.

Harrison talked to his mom a little more before hanging up. Then he crawled into Cassie's lap.

"I won't cause any more trouble," he said.

Cassie squeezed his little body in a hug. "I believe you."

By the afternoon of the next day, Cassie was exhausted. The kids had behaved wonderfully, but this parenting thing was wearing her out. She made everyone lay down for a nap after lunch, and she fell asleep on the bed beside Lexi. The ringing of her phone woke her, and she opened it when she recognized Maureen's number.

"What are you doing?" Maureen asked. "Want to come over?"

"I can't," Cassie said. "I'm babysitting."

"Until what time?"

"Until Thursday." Cassie yawned. This would be a long week.

"Wow! Are you staying overnight?"

"Yes."

"Lucky! That sounds like fun."

"It's awesome." She rubbed her eyes. "I better go. The kids are crazy."

"Call me when you get home. My birthday's coming up, and I want you to spend the night."

"Sure."

"You're such a great writer," Maureen continued, not picking up on Cassie's desire to sleep. "I love to read the note you wrote Cara last year. And the message you put in Andrea's journal."

"Really?" The compliment managed to soak past Cassie's exhaustion. Cassie didn't know which note Maureen meant, but she remembered writing a page in Andrea's journal. "You think so?"

"Yeah. I can tell you write from the heart. I wish you'd say something like that to me."

"Maureen," Cassie said, "you're the person who most caught me by surprise. I didn't think you really liked me at all. But you ended up being one of the kindest, most caring people I know."

"Can you write that down for me?"

Cassie laughed softly. "Okay. I'll talk to you when I get home." She closed the phone and dropped her arm on the bed. An instant later, her eyes closed as well, and she went back to sleep.

❧

Cassie could barely keep her eyes open during the movie after dinner. Who knew little kids could be so draining? She helped the children into pajamas and said prayers with them, and then crawled into her bed in the guest room.

She had just turned out the light when Lexi came tiptoeing in.

"Cassie?"

"Yes, Lexi?" Cassie held back a sigh.

"Can you sleep with me?"

"No, Lexi. I'm so tired. I want to be in my bed."

"Please, Cassie?"

"Just sleep in your bed, Lexi. We'll play again tomorrow."

The six-year-old girl whined and stomped her foot. "I thought you were my friend!"

"I am. But I need to sleep."

"I want my mom!" Lexi began to cry.

Cassie groaned and threw back her blankets. "Fine. I'll sleep with you. But you better hold still."

"I will!" Lexi said, immediately cheerful.

Cassie followed her down the hallway, her head throbbing. What had she gotten herself into? She needed a pay raise.

Lexi did not hold still. She kicked and tossed and turned on the little twin bed, and Cassie held herself on the edge, trying not to fall off. Every time she started to fall asleep, Lexi would move, and Cassie would jerk awake, grabbing the mattress to keep from rolling to the ground.

Her head hurt so bad when morning came she worried she'd puke.

"Breakfast," she said, grabbing a box of cereal and putting it on the table.

"Can you make us pancakes again?" Shelby asked.

"Not today." Cassie added the milk to the table. The room swam around her, and she gripped the back of a chair. She closed her eyes and took a deep breath. Maybe she needed to sit down.

"Are you okay, Cassie?" Shelby asked.

"I'm gonna lay down just for a second," Cassie said. She helped Harrison get his cereal and then rolled onto the couch in the living room. Her head pounded and it hurt to swallow. She didn't feel so great at all.

"We're supposed to call Mom at breakfast," Lexi said, popping her face over the rim of the couch.

"Right," Cassie breathed. She pressed a hand to her forehead as she sat up, trying not to swoon. Where was her phone? She found it in her pocket, and her hand shook when she opened it. She dialed Sister Mecham's number.

"We're doing great," Cassie said in response to the questions.

"You sound different," Sister Mecham said. "Are you okay?"

"A little hoarse." Cassie cleared her throat and spoke around the drumbeat in her head. "But I'm good." She chatted a moment longer before handing the phone off to Shelby, relieved that was over. She closed her eyes and had nearly drifted off when Shelby said, "I don't think Cassie's feeling well."

Cassie's eyes shot open and she pushed herself up. "I'm fine!"

Shelby handed the phone to Lexi and came over. "Mom wants you to take your temperature. I'll get the thermometer."

"I'm not sick!" Cassie protested, but it was no use. In a moment Shelby was back, and Cassie had no choice but to pop the thermometer in her mouth. In less than a minute it beeped the warning signal. Cassie pulled it out, already knowing what she would see: she had a fever.

"She's definitely sick," Shelby said, taking the phone from Lexi. Then she handed it to Cassie. "Mom wants to talk to you."

"Hello?" Cassie said, not trying to hide the weariness in her voice now.

"Cassie, why didn't you tell me you're sick?"

"I didn't know," Cassie said. "I just felt tired."

"Well, I want you to rest until I get there."

"Until you get here?" Cassie's heart sank. "You're not coming home, are you?"

"Absolutely. I can't leave you by yourself when you're not feeling well. I'll take you home right away. I'll be there in a few hours."

"Oh, no, don't do that! I hate for you to leave your conference early! You're supposed to come home tomorrow!"

"It's fine. I'll have Shelby make you a cup of tea. Don't worry about a thing."

Sister Mecham hung up, and Cassie uttered a long sigh. Oh well. She'd almost made it all the way through her babysitting gig.

CHAPTER FIVE

Revival

"I was available on Saturday," Cassie said into her phone. "I'm not next week. I'm gone at church camp all week."

"And last week you were gone babysitting," Josh said, frustration evident in his voice.

Cassie closed her eyes. Having a boyfriend shouldn't be problematic, especially when he lived two hours away. "I told you to come over yesterday. Now you'll have to wait until next weekend." Why wasn't he getting this? "I can't miss church camp. I'm sorry. I'm busy with a lot of stuff."

Josh sighed. "Can't you miss the first day? I have Monday off. I want to see you."

"You were supposed to come a week ago for a big barbecue, remember? And you didn't." She immediately regretted throwing the failed barbecue at him, but he was annoying her.

"You're right. I'm sorry." Josh sighed again. "Write me?"

Cassie glanced at her desk, where Josh's latest letter sat, dripping with sappy sentiment and clingy emotion. His attentions flattered her, but she was still waiting for her heart to skip a beat when she talked to him. "I already did. You'll probably get it tomorrow."

"That gives me something to look forward to, then." Josh sounded more upbeat now. "I'll see you soon, beautiful."

"See you soon," she echoed, and hung up. At least he hadn't said he loved her, not since the first time a few weeks ago. She'd been very honest when she said she wasn't ready for that step.

And now she could focus on church camp. She packed her swimsuit and several pairs of shorts, excited for a few days in the outdoors. And she couldn't wait to see her camp friends, Tesia and Elise.

She bit her lip as she thought of the latter. Elise had been on a weird kick lately, wearing odd clothing and hanging out with a different group. Last year she hadn't even come to camp. Cassie hoped she would this year.

The next morning all of the girls from the Springdale congregation gathered at the chapel to carpool together. Cassie wandered over to Riley, her closest friend from church.

"I wonder what the campsite will be like this year," she said. Last year they'd been in quaint little cabins and she and Riley had fought the entire time. The thought made her giggle. They didn't fight as much anymore.

"As long as there's a pool, I don't care if we're in tents," Riley said. She pushed up on her tiptoes, making herself slightly taller than Cassie. Her short blond hair brushed the tops of her shoulders. "I just want to swim."

"Yeah that," Cassie said.

The caravan made a forty minute trip to a campsite near Huntsville, Arkansas. The parking lot filled with vehicles coming from around the area.

"Girls," a woman called as they unloaded the cars, "I'm Sister Tenney, and I'm responsible for this nature reserve while we're here. Please don't pick the flowers or touch the wildlife. We need to treat everything with respect. Got it?"

Cassie nodded along with the others and pulled her bag out of the car. She joined the huddle of girls around the woman.

"Which unit are you with?" the woman asked Sue, an older girl from the Springdale congregation.

"Springdale," Sue said. Her red-headed friend Michelle hovered behind her.

"Springdale, you're in dorm number three. Follow that trail to the right and you'll see it."

"So all of Springdale is in the same place?" Cassie asked.

"Yes." The woman turned her attention to the next group. "Which unit are you with?"

"Let's go, girls," Sue said, inclining her head and leading the way.

Cassie lagged behind next to Riley and breathed, "This is not going to go good." She didn't get along with the other girls from Springdale and liked it much better when she got to hang out with the girls from Rogers.

"At least you've got me," Riley said.

They stepped inside the dorm, a one-room unit with six bunk beds and a bathroom.

"It's air-conditioned," Riley said.

"One benefit." Cassie dropped her bags next to Riley's. "Let's go find the pool." She opened her bag and pulled out her swimsuit.

"There's no pool here," Sue said in her normal bossy tone.

Cassie lifted her head and looked at her. "What?"

"No pool," Sue repeated.

"How do you know that?"

Sue rolled her eyes and exchanged a look with Michelle. "We've been here before."

No pool. Cassie's heart dropped. If there wasn't a pool, she just wanted to go home.

"Come on," Riley said, tugging on her arm as if she sensed Cassie's mood. "Let's go for a walk. See what's here."

"Fine," she grumbled.

The two girls stepped outside, and immediately the sticky, hot Arkansas air assaulted Cassie.

"No pool!" Cassie groaned. "This bites."

"Yeah," Riley agreed.

"Cassie! Cassandra Jones!"

Cassie turned her head to see Tesia coming up the hill. Tesia dropped her bags and ran to Cassie, throwing her arms around her.

"Tesia!" Cassie cried, pulling back to look at her friend. The skinny, dark-haired girl seemed to have grown about four inches since last summer. "You're so tall!"

"And you cut your hair! And got contacts!"

They grinned at each other before Tesia turned to look over her shoulder. "Look who came with me."

Cassie peered down the hill, and her heart skipped a beat when she saw Elise.

The last time she'd seen her friend, Elise had dyed her blond hair black. Now she had shaved most of it off, leaving only one side with stringy black strands hanging over her shoulder. Did Cassie even know this girl?

Elise spotted her. "Cassie!" She ran forward and hugged Cassie, holding her tight. "You're the only reason I came, you know."

Cassie squeezed her hands. "You're the reason I'm here." And it must be true. Cassie would endure the heat and her unit and no swimming pool if it meant being the person Elise needed.

"It's going to be a hard week," Elise said, rolling her eyes as she pulled away. "I tried to run away from home, but my mom caught me. Last time I ran away, she called the police. This time she went through my room. Total invasion of privacy. I keep trying to join this gang, but I never get the chance because she takes my things!" Elise glanced at Tesia and Riley, then leaned closer and whispered, "She didn't find my gun, though. I keep that safe. And I can get more drugs."

Cassie took a step back, her eyes searching Elise's face. "You're kidding, right? You're not doing drugs, are you?"

Elise waved her off. "Of course not. But you never know when someone else might need some. And it could save your life." She sighed and shouldered her bag. "Come on, Tesia. We may as well set up."

Tesia hovered behind a moment and murmured to Cassie, "Don't believe everything she says. Elise has been lying a lot lately. She's different than she was."

Understatement of the year. But Cassie knew all about lying friends. She could handle untruths. "We'll find you guys later." She gestured to Riley, and they continued exploring.

⚜

"Look at these rollers my mom packed me!" Sue dumped a bag of small foam rollers on the bed. "What was she thinking? I don't curl my hair!" She tossed them in the middle of the floor. "If anyone wants those, you can have them."

Their first day of camp was coming to an end. Cassie had seen Ana Julia and a handful of other people, but mostly camp felt like it would be very boring this year. The evening devotional had gone long, and Cassie wondered what her friends back home were doing without her. At least there would be a stream on the hike in the morning, and the girls were encouraged to wear their swimsuits.

Sue and Michelle went into the bathroom to brush their teeth, and Riley picked up the rollers. "Did anyone want these?"

The other girls shook their heads, and Riley said to Cassie, "We could put these in your hair. It would be really fun."

"My hair won't curl," Cassie said. "I have to use hot rollers."

"Let's get it wet and use hair spray. Maybe it will."

The other girls were asleep by the time Riley finished wrapping Cassie's hair around the foam rollers.

"All done," Riley said with a yawn. "Let's see how that looks in the morning."

"I bet it doesn't do anything." Cassie turned out the light and climbed onto the top bunk. The sounds of heavy breathing filled the dorm, and it wasn't long before Cassie's eyelids closed as well.

⚜

"Cassie, you're still sleeping?"

Cassie squinted one eye open and stared at the face peering down at her from the railing of the top bunk. She blinked twice before Tesia came into focus.

"Hi," Cassie said groggily.

Tesia grinned. "Hi. I wondered where you were at breakfast. It's almost nine. And what's in your hair?"

Cassie sat up, her hand going to her head, where she found all the foam rollers. "Oh, Riley and I just did that for fun." She began pulling them out. "Almost nine? And no one woke me?"

"Yeah, I can't believe your unit just left you here. Uncool."

No kidding. Even Riley left her. Cassie continued pulling on the rollers, and Tesia's eyes moved up and down with her hand.

"You missed breakfast. You even missed the hike."

"I missed the hike?" Cassie paused in her movement and groaned. "That was the only thing I was looking forward to this week!"

Tesia gave her a sympathetic look. "Maybe you need an alarm clock. Although considering last year, maybe it's better you didn't go."

Cassie stuck her tongue out at her. "I do a lot better without you to lay me in poison ivy, thank you very much." Two years earlier Cassie had gotten sick on the hike, and Tesia laid her in poison ivy while Elise ran for help.

Tesia giggled. "Best year ever."

"By far." Cassie smiled back. She came back to camp year after year, but never had she had such a wonderful experience as that first year.

"Why did you do that to your hair?"

Cassie dumped the last roller into the pile on her bed, then reached up and felt the silky curls. "Did it work?"

Tesia arched an eyebrow. "Your hair's as curly as mine."

Tesia's dark hair fell in tight curly cues around her face and neck. It looked good on her, but Cassie suddenly worried the effect wouldn't be as lovely on herself. "I need a mirror," she said, bolting from the bed.

Tesia followed Cassie to the bathroom, where Cassie took one look at her reflection and groaned. "I look like a poodle!" She covered her head with her arms.

"No, not a poodle," Tesia said, lowering her arms. "More like Michael Jackson."

Cassie smashed the curls between her hands. "I've got to hop in the shower."

"You don't have time. I was sent to find you. You've got dish duty. If you don't get down there to help clean up, they're going to bring the dishes to you. Their words, not mine."

Cassie wanted to scream at everyone who had left her behind. She ran back in the room and rummaged through her bag until she found her bandanna. Her mom packed it every year, but this was the first time she'd used it. "Well, I'm not going out there like this." She tied it around her hair. "Let's go." She'd shoot Riley for this.

CHAPTER SIX

Mudding

"I hate this year so far," Cassie said to Riley before evening devotional. "The only thing I've done is clean dishes and make dinner." On top of having dish duty for breakfast, she'd been on the cooking crew that night.

"You curled your hair too," Riley said, and Cassie scowled at her.

"No, you curled my hair," she said. Thankfully the curls hadn't lasted long in the humid summer heat, but she still wore the bandanna. "And you're the reason I missed the hike."

"It's not my fault you didn't wake up," Riley said.

"It is your fault you left without me," Cassie returned.

"Sorry," Riley said, just as she had a few hours earlier when Cassie chastised her.

"Yeah, well." Cassie sighed and told herself to put it behind her.

She fell silent when they reached the meadow. Some of the older girls were doing a skit, and she tried to be interested. Then finally the leader, Sister Tenney, stood up.

"Tomorrow we'll be taking trips to the cave," she said. "This isn't something you want to miss. Be here at nine a.m. or you might not make it!"

Was it Cassie's imagination, or did she look at her?

"I'll lead us in a song and a prayer before we go to bed!"

"Caving sounds fun," Cassie said, latching on to that one idea.

"As long as you don't sleep in," Riley said.

"It was your fault," Cassie growled.

Cassie went right to sleep and got up as soon as she heard girls stirring in the dorm. She ate her oatmeal breakfast quickly (no sugar or butter, just healthy oats), and then went down to the meadow to join the growing group of girls waiting to go caving.

A truck pulled up to the group, and a familiar man got out, wearing a wide-brimmed hat over his dark skin. Cassie recognized Ana Julia's father, the one who had been so kind to her when she forgot her water last summer.

"I can only take fifteen at a time, okay?" Brother Moda said in his heavy accent. "But I come back later."

Girls pushed past Cassie, and as much as she tried to get to the front, she wasn't one of the fifteen chosen. Riley was, and Cassie pouted as she watched her friend climb into the back of the pick-up.

"Don't worry, girls!" Sister Tenney said, coming over to stop the shoving. "Brother Moda will stay at the cave, but we'll shuttle you guys back and forth every hour. Come back in an hour to get in the next group! Everyone will get a chance, I promise!"

Disappointed, Cassie turned around and trudged back to the dorm. There was nothing she wanted to do for the next hour. She lay down on her bed and wished she'd brought a book.

Half an hour later she went back to the pick up site, determined to be one of the first ones there. A few others were ahead of her, apparently thinking the same thing.

"Hi, girls," Sister Tenney said, walking down to them. "The shuttle's running just a little bit late. Looks like we'll do a pick up at ten-fifteen instead of ten. Just come back in forty-five minutes, okay?"

Cassie wandered into the mess hall and watched the crafters. Ana Julia invited Cassie to make bracelets with her, but Cassie declined. Everything Ana Julia touched turned out beautifully, but Cassie had the opposite effect.

"Are you going caving?" Ana asked. Her voice wasn't as accented as her father's, but Cassie still heard the hint of a foreign flavor.

"Yes. Trying to, anyway. Sister Tenney said the shuttle's late. I'll head back down soon."

"I'll come with you. I want to go."

"Thanks," Cassie said, favoring her with a smile.

At 10:05 they left the mess hall, heading down the hill to the pick up spot.

"There's a truck with a bunch of people in it," Ana Julia said.

"They must be coming back," Cassie said, shielding her eyes to see better. But instead of pulling in, the truck drove farther out of camp. "Hey! They're leaving without us!" She spotted Sister Tenney coming up the hill and broke into a jog. "Was that the shuttle for the cave pick-up?"

"Yes," Sister Tenney said.

"But I wanted to go!"

Sister Tenney clicked her tongue. "You just missed them! They'll be back in an hour."

"I was following your schedule!" Cassie exclaimed. "You said to be here at ten-fifteen!"

Sister Tenney lifted her chin, though her cheeks flushed. "Well, they got back early. Maybe you should be here fifteen minutes before pick up just in case."

She walked away, and Cassie sat down on a large rock, blinking back furious tears. First she'd missed the stream hike, and now this?

"It's okay," Ana Julia said, sitting beside her. "We'll sit here and wait and not miss the next one. Tell me what you've been doing this past year."

It was after eleven before Ana Julia and Cassie finally got on the shuttle to go caving. But Cassie was in a much better mood. The hour with Ana had passed quicker than the rest of the morning.

"Hello, girls!" Brother Moda said, greeting them cheerfully. He handed each of them a hardhat. "Ready for this?" He put his hand on Ana Julia's slender shoulder, and she smiled up at her father.

"Ready," Cassie said.

"You're going to get very muddy," he warned.

"So ready," Cassie said. This had to make up for how boring camp had been so far.

Brother Moda led the way into the cave, the cold dank air quickly replacing the hot humidity. Cassie switched on her headlamp, and they had to turn sideways to get through the corridor. Mud came away on Cassie's hands where she touched the wall, and when she brushed a hair from her face, she felt the mud stick to her cheek.

"We have to climb through this passageway," Brother Moda called back. "Hands and knees."

It was slow progress, with all fifteen girls slowly ambling forward. Cassie crawled through and got her feet beneath her before jumping down. Water splashed around her ankles, bitterly cold as she walked through the underground cavern.

Twenty minutes later they reached the exit, and they had to use a rope to pull themselves out of a tiny hole in the ground.

"That wasn't very big," Cassie said, turning to peer back into the hole once she was out.

Ana Julia joined her. "We are so muddy."

Cassie's shoes squished when she leaned forward to study her clothes. The mud had entered her socks around her ankles and squirmed between her toes, rubbing uncomfortably on her skin. "I'm taking my shoes off." She sat down and removed the muddy shoes and filthy socks, shoving them together and holding them in one hand. The rocks and twigs hurt her bare feet, but at least her feet could breathe again.

Several other girls copied her, and they walked barefoot back to the truck.

"If only there were a pool," Cassie sighed as the shuttle headed back to camp.

"Never a good idea to go camping with no pool," Ana Julia agreed.

Cassie spotted Elise and Tesia when they arrived at camp, and she slipped her shoes back on so she could join them.

"Where are you guys going?" she asked, sliding into step beside them.

"Just to the dorm to take a nap," Elise said. Her eyes took in Cassie's muddy clothing. "What have you been doing? Taking a mud bath?"

"I went caving. It was the best part of camp so far. You should have come."

"Yuck." Elise flipped what remained of her hair. "My boyfriend would never kiss me if he knew I'd been in a cave."

"You've already kissed a guy?" Cassie looked at her in surprise.

"She kisses everyone," Tesia said.

"Someday, Cassie, when you get a boyfriend, you'll understand. Kissing's the most wonderful thing on earth. Well, part of it."

"I have a boyfriend," Cassie said, both intrigued by Elise's words and insulted she assumed Cassie wouldn't have a guy.

"You do?" Tesia peered at Cassie.

"Well, yes." Cassie blushed. "But we don't kiss."

Elise scoffed. "Then he's not a real boyfriend."

"He's amazing," Cassie said, not sure why she was speaking Josh up. "He says he loves me. He's in high school. Sixteen. He can even drive. He'll be a junior next year."

Both of them were staring at her. "You have a picture?" Elise asked.

"Come on back to my dorm."

They followed Cassie inside, and she dug around her purse until she found the picture Josh had sent her weeks before. Elise studied it before passing it to Tesia.

"He's cute," she said. "So how come you're not kissing?"

"Well." Cassie hesitated. "We might kiss someday. But I'm not supposed to date until I'm sixteen, you know?"

Elise rolled her eyes. "Stupid rule."

"No, I get the rule," Cassie said. "I know why we have it. So we don't go places alone. And my parents are fine with him as long as we hang out in groups. So someday we might kiss, but not yet."

Elise lowered her voice and leaned forward. "What about more than kissing?"

Cassie's face burned, a bit embarrassed by Elise's insinuation. "No way. Not with Josh. He's not the one I want to marry."

"How do you know? What if he is the one you end up marrying?" Elise pressed.

Cassie couldn't picture that. She wasn't even sure how much she liked him. "Then I guess there would be more than kissing." The thought made her feel gross. She didn't want that with him. "But how can I be sure right now? I'm only fourteen. It could be Josh, or it could be someone I haven't even met yet."

"Sometimes it's hard to say no," Elise said.

"Not if you say no to the kissing, like Cassie," Tesia said. "She's smart. She knows you can like a guy and not give him everything he wants."

Elise fell silent, her fingers picking at her nails. Cassie felt like she should say something, but she wasn't sure what. She wasn't even quite sure what conversation they were having.

"You just keep saying no, then, Cassie," Elise finally said, looking up. "And maybe you'll win a golden boy in the end."

There was something painful and sarcastic in Elise's voice, but also something almost like encouragement. "And you, too, Elise. There's a golden boy for you too."

Elise stood up. "You gotta be the golden girl first."

She walked out of the dorm room, and Cassie looked at Tesia. "I don't understand."

Tesia blinked, and a tear rolled down her cheek. "You're exactly how Elise used to be. Don't ever change."

The girls were invited to share their favorite experiences from camp at the closing ceremonies Thursday night, and Cassie cried as she listened to her friends talk about what they'd learned and who had helped them.

Elise walked over to Cassie and wrapped her arms around her neck. "You always amaze me. You're the one that keeps me grounded."

Cassie hugged her back. "I didn't do anything."

"That's exactly it. You didn't do anything except be you. That's all you have to be." She pressed a kiss to Cassie's cheek. "See you later."

Cassie held on to Elise's words, cherishing them. They made her want to be the kind of person Elise thought she was. They made her want to be better.

CHAPTER SEVEN

Forcing the Heart

"I'm going to be a nicer person," Cassie announced to Riley as they rode back to the chapel to meet their parents. "A more honest person."

"You were always nice until you started hanging out with Amity and Maureen," Riley said.

That stung. Cassie frowned at Riley. "I'm still nice. I just want to be nicer."

"We'll see how long that lasts."

Riley's assessment hurt. Cassie didn't stop thinking about it while Mr. Jones drove her home. Was she not as nice because of her friends? They definitely made her want different things, like expensive clothes and boys and popularity. Maybe she even acted more like them.

She pondered this up until the moment Andrea called. Andrea was Cassie's best friend—most of the time.

"You're finally home!" Andrea squealed. "Come spend the night!"

"I'll ask my mom," Cassie said. "I just got home this morning, so she might not let me."

"Just let me know. We have so much to catch up on!"

Cassie dumped her dirty clothes into the washing machine and found her mom working in the basement. "Can I spend the night at Andrea's house? I haven't seen her in two weeks."

"Yes," Mrs. Jones said without looking up.

Cassie had been prepared to plead her case, and she paused. Could it really be that easy? "Okay, thanks!"

She ran back upstairs and called Andrea back. Andrea didn't answer, so she fired off a text.

My mom said yes! Call me back.

Her eyes drifted to a letter sitting on her desk. Another one from Josh. She hesitated. She didn't want to continue this relationship with him. It had been fun at first, but she didn't want to be his girlfriend. But she was stuck now, wasn't she?

She sat down and read the letter, her eyes roaming over the sappy love note as if it were to someone else. It didn't touch her, didn't affect her.

She put it aside and checked her phone. Still nothing from Andrea. She lay down on her bed.

The sun was high in the sky when Cassie opened her eyes again. She sat up and checked her phone. Almost seven! She flipped it open and called Andrea again.

"Hello?" a giggly, chirpy voice said.

Cassie recognized the voice, but it wasn't Andrea. "Amity?"

"Hey, Cass! We haven't seen you in weeks! How's Josh? Any kissing yet?" Amity made smacking noises on the phone.

"Why are you on Andrea's phone?" Cassie asked.

"I answered it when I saw it was you."

"So you're with Andrea?"

"Yeah, I'm at her house. I'm spending the night."

Ah. That explained why Andrea had quit responding. "Okay. Have fun. I'll talk to you guys later."

"Did you want to talk to Andrea?"

"No. I'm good." She hung up the phone and tapped her nails on the plastic case. Her heart stirred restlessly, warning her that she wouldn't always be satisfied being the one on the outside looking in.

☙✻❧

An insistent chirping fluttered near Cassie's ear, annoying and demanding. Cassie willed it to go away. She wanted to sleep a little longer.

"Cassie!" Emily snapped, lifting her head off her pillow. "Get your phone!"

Her phone. Seriously? Why did people call in the morning? It seemed like everyone wanted to talk before she was awake.

The phone stopped ringing, and she breathed a sigh of relief. Finally. She flopped an arm over her face and closed her eyes.

The reprieve lasted ten seconds before starting up again.

"Argh!" She uttered a groan of frustration before sitting up and grabbing her phone. She froze when she saw Josh's name dancing across the screen. Her heart rate quickening, she flipped it open. "Josh?"

"Cassie." He sounded warm and cheerful. "You said you'd be back from camp today, right?"

"Right." She folded her legs underneath her and leaned against the headboard. "I'm home."

"Great. Because my friend Gage and I are about twenty minutes from your house and need your address."

Cassie gasped and bolted upright. "What?"

"Surprise! I'm coming to see you!"

And what a surprise. Cassie threw her legs over the side of the bed. "Oh, wow, this is, uh, great!" Hairbrush. Where? "Um yeah. Here's my address." She fed him the information and finally found her brush.

"Great. I'll see you soon!"

Oh, crapola. He was coming here. Right now.

She ran into the bathroom to put in her contacts and brush her teeth, and then remembered she'd better tell her parents.

⟡

By the time Josh and Gage arrived twenty minutes later, Cassie had thrown on shorts and a T-shirt and primped the best she could. Her mom stood beside her when Josh rang the doorbell.

"Hi," Cassie said, her heart fluttering anxiously as she opened the door.

Josh beamed at her, just as handsome as ever with short blond hair and light blue eyes behind his wire-framed glasses. He leaned over and hugged her tightly, and Cassie held very still, feeling awkward in the embrace.

His friend Gage stood behind with a baseball cap on, and he waved. "Hi."

Josh turned to her mother. "Hi, I'm Josh," he said, holding out his hand.

Mrs. Jones smiled and gave it a shake. "Nice to meet you. Cassie, want to give them a tour of the house?"

"Yeah, sure." Cassie ran a hand through her hair, then led the boys through the kitchen to her bedroom. Emily had also jumped out of bed when Cassie said Josh was coming over, but Cassie flushed with embarrassment when she saw the pair of underwear on the bedroom floor. She quickly kicked them under the bed and hoped Josh hadn't seen as he followed her inside.

"This is my room," she said.

"Nice," he said. "It's huge."

"Yeah, it's big." She slipped past him out of the room, keeping her hands close to her body to avoid touching him. "My parents' room is here, past the other rooms."

Mr. Jones was just coming out of the bedroom, and he stopped to shake Josh's hand also.

"Oh, Daddy," Cassie said, "before I forget. Maureen's birthday party is coming up, and I need to get her a present. Can I get the money you owe me for working the store?" Mr. Jones owned a soccer store and often employed his daughters for minimal pay.

"You haven't worked at the store since before school got out," he said, frowning behind his mustache.

"I know. And you haven't paid me since before April."

"Why don't you come by when it opens and I'll see what we can do. Bring Josh."

"Oh, but he might not want to—" Cassie began.

"Sure, we'd love to see your store," Josh said. He smiled at Cassie as Mr. Jones walked away. "I'm here for you today. Whatever you want."

She blushed and looked away from his penetrating gaze.

Half an hour later Josh parked the car in front of the soccer store. Gage got out of the back while Josh hurried around the car to open Cassie's door for her, and he jogged ahead to get the store door also.

"Thank you," Cassie said, her face hot.

"Well, you guys made it!" Mr. Jones boomed, coming out of the back. "Now, what did you need, Cassie?"

"I need money so I can buy Maureen a present," Cassie said. "Money I earned working here."

"No, you need a present for Maureen," Mr. Jones said.

Cassie stared at him like he was daft. "Right. Which means you need to give me my money."

"Or you can just pick one of these clothing items and use your money in the store." He gestured to a whole line of soccer shorts.

"I'm not buying Maureen soccer shorts." Maureen didn't dress that way.

"Then get her a nice jersey. A rugby shirt."

Cassie shook her head. "I need the money."

Mr. Jones sighed, his expressing crumpling. "I don't have the cash right now, Cassie. It's all tied up in the store."

"Really?" Cassie cried. "You don't have twenty dollars?"

"I do," Josh said. "I can let you have some, Cassie."

She hesitated, her desires warring against each other. She could accept Josh's money and get Maureen the gift she deserved. But she would always feel she owed him somehow. It would weigh on her and affect her actions.

Or she could take one of these soccer shorts from her dad's store and call it good.

Cassie fingered a pair of pretty purple shorts with a turquoise trim. "Ten dollars and the shorts and we'll call it good."

"Done," Mr. Jones said, beaming.

Cassie accepted the gift bag with the shorts and pocketed the cash.

"Can you take me to a bookstore?" Cassie asked Josh as they climbed back into the car. "I need to buy a journal." Maybe the shorts wouldn't be so bad if they came with a pretty message.

"Sure," he said. "It was nice of you to help your dad out that way."

"Thanks," she murmured, not feeling very nice. She picked up her phone and realized she couldn't let this moment go unknown. She had to tell her friends Josh was with her. She called Andrea.

"Hello?" Andrea purred into the phone.

"Hi," Cassie said. She glanced at Josh beside her in the car. "You won't believe who is sitting next to me."

"Who?" Andrea asked, sounding only mildly curious.

"Josh."

"What?" Andrea squealed. "No way! What's he doing with you?"

"He came up here to see me," Cassie said, pleased at Andrea's reaction. "He brought a friend. It was a surprise."

"And he's sitting by you now?"

"Yeah. I'm in his car."

"Come get me, come get me!"

Cassie grinned. She hadn't intended to do anything besides gloat, but that familiar warmth of acceptance rose in her chest. She was cool again. "Sure. In a bit."

"You don't mind, do you?" she asked Josh after they bought a journal for Maureen and headed toward Andrea's house.

"No, not at all. We can hang out with your friends. I owe you." He grinned at her, and Cassie smiled back.

"Thanks."

They'd barely pulled into the driveway of the large town house before Andrea came flying out the front door.

"Hi, Josh," she greeted, climbing into the back next to Gage. "What are you doing here?"

"I wanted to see Cassie. It's been too long, and it keeps not working out to see each other."

A sudden jolt twisted Cassie's stomach, and she held her breath. He wouldn't say anything about the barbecue, would he? Her lie could be discovered.

"Oh, you're so sweet!" Andrea said, tossing her honey-brown hair and flashing a smile.

Whew. Cassie let out a breath and relaxed.

☙ ❧

By the time they got back to Cassie's house, Andrea had planned out their day for them.

"We can go swimming at Amity's house. She has a pool. Then we can all go out for dinner. Won't that be fun?"

Mrs. Jones had other plans.

"We need to sort the leftover papers first," she said. "Then if you guys want to go play, you can. Josh and Gage, you're big strong guys. Can you carry these into the house?"

"Of course we can," Josh said. He and Gage followed Mrs. Jones to the van, where she showed them the papers.

"Just take them to the dining room. Cassie can show you. I've got to leave for work, Cassie."

Cassie heard the statement for what it was: not a reminder so much as a warning.

"Okay, Mom," she said, giving her a big smile.

Josh obediently wrapped his arms around a load of papers, and Gage did the same.

"Why do your parents have a bunch of newspapers from yesterday in their car?" Josh asked.

"They have a paper route," Cassie said. "All the papers that people don't buy from gas stations and what not, my parents have to cut the dates out and turn them in so they can get reimbursed for what didn't sell."

Josh raised his eyebrows. "That sounds like a lot of work." He quickly thumbed through the papers in his arms. "There must be fifty here."

"Yeah." Cassie led the way into the dining room. "So just set them here."

Josh and Gage put the papers down where Cassie said. Then they and Andrea stood back and watched as Cassie found a razor blade and sat in front of the papers. In a deft movement she'd done hundreds of times, Cassie cut out the date and put it in a pile. Then she moved the newspaper and did the same to the one underneath it.

Josh sat down beside her. "Give me a knife and I'll help."

She looked at him in surprise, then got up and grabbed another one.

"Me too," Gage said.

"I'll sort the ones you've cut," Andrea said.

"Thanks, guys." Cassie handed out the razors, pleased. "This will go a lot faster with help."

An hour later the work was done, and Amity was only too willing to have them over to swim in her pool.

Josh kept trying to get close to Cassie in the pool, but somehow wearing a swimsuit around him only made her feel more awkward. She avoided looking at his body and ended up on a beach chair, curled up with a towel around her.

Andrea came and sat beside her. "Oh, you're so lucky, Cassie. He's so hot. And I can't believe he drove all the way here just to hang out with you."

"I know," Cassie said, wishing she felt something for Josh. She'd tried, really. Maybe the feelings would grow the more she spent time with him.

Andrea lowered her voice. "Has he kissed you yet?"

"No," Cassie answered softly, and she licked her lips, a strange feeling wicking through her tummy.

"I bet it's going to happen soon," Andrea whispered. "Your first kiss." She squeezed Cassie's hands.

Cassie watched Amity flirt with Gage. She made it look so easy. Cassie wanted that first kiss. She didn't want to be the one in the group who had never kissed a guy, even though Janice and Maureen hadn't either. Maybe the feelings would grow after she kissed him. And yet the thought of kissing filled her with intense nervous butterflies, so rabid and strong she thought she might puke.

⟡

They swam for an hour before Amity's mom came home and kicked them out. Then Josh drove them to Wendy's to get a few burgers, and they said hi to Mrs. Jones, since she was working behind the counter.

"Hi, guys!" she said, beaming at all of them in her fast food uniform.

"I'm going to take Cassie home after this," Josh said. "I have to leave soon."

"Can Cassie spend the night?" Andrea asked Mrs. Jones. "Josh can drop her off at my house."

"Not tonight, Andrea."

Cassie elbowed Andrea. "She was going to let me last night."

"Sorry. Amity came over and my mom wouldn't let me have anyone else over."

The excuse sounded plausible, but Cassie wasn't sure she believed it. She'd watched Andrea lie to her over and over again the past few years.

By the time they got Andrea home, Gage was getting quite antsy. Apparently he was afraid he'd be late to work.

Josh walked Cassie up to the front door of her house and glanced back at his friend. "I'd give you a real goodbye but he's in a hurry. And he's watching."

Cassie's stomach doubled up. He meant, he'd kiss her if his friend weren't there. "That's all right, I understand," she said, both relieved and disappointed the first kiss wouldn't happen today.

"But I'll be back," Josh said, his eyes crinkling as he smiled down at her. "And next time I'll make sure we get some time alone." He squeezed her hand.

Cassie nodded and exhaled quietly as he drove away. Her first kiss was right around the corner. She could feel it.

CHAPTER EIGHT

New York New York

Cassie spent all day Monday doing laundry. Between babysitting and camp, she had more dirty clothes than clean ones. And now she needed to pack again, because on Tuesday she was leaving for the most exciting event of the year: her choir trip to New York.

"I put together a snack pack for you," Mrs. Jones said, bringing a bag of goodies into Cassie's room. "You'll be on that bus for two days, both there and back. This way you don't have to buy food at every gas station."

Gas station food was horribly unhealthy, and Cassie hadn't intended to buy any. She flipped though the snacks her mom had packed and frowned. Cookies, chips, flavored popcorn . . . she wasn't sure this stuff was much better. There were a few granola bars and fruit snacks. She could stick with those. "Thanks, Mom."

"Are you excited?" Mrs. Jones asked, plopping herself down on Emily's bed.

"Yes." Even though Cassie wasn't actually going to sing at Carnegie Hall with the rest of the choir, she'd never been to New York City, and especially not without her parents. "I can't wait."

Tuesday morning her parents drove her to the art center where the choir was gathering. A large charter bus already parked at the curb, and the kids dumped their luggage beside it. She studied the other singers and felt a flutter of nervousness. She didn't actually have any friends in choir. She'd almost quit this year, but the New York trip had kept her going. Who would she talk to for a whole week? If only Andrea were here.

Cassie pulled her bag out of the car and added it to the pile of luggage, then joined the singers fluttering happily around. She kept quiet, listening to their conversations without contributing.

"Hi, I'm a reporter from 40/29 News," a guy in a suit and holding a microphone said to the group. "Could we talk to one of you kids about this trip you're taking?"

A cameraman stood behind him, poised and ready. Cassie looked around for Ms. Vanderwood, certain she would want to talk to the reporter. But instead it was RyAnne Spencer who stepped forward, flashing her white teeth and tossing her dark hair behind her shoulder.

Of *course*. Cassie rolled her eyes. RyAnne was Cassie's age but looked years older. Stunningly gorgeous with dark skin and a strong, Roman nose, she was one of Ms. Vanderwood's favorite singers. And RyAnne knew it. Cassie turned away, not anxious to watch RyAnne's interview. She could have the limelight.

"Cassie, we're leaving." Mrs. Jones leaned against her husband, and they both smiled at her. "You have a wonderful time. Send us pictures."

"Right." To Cassie's surprise, a lump formed in her throat. She hadn't expected to be sad, but suddenly she felt anxious about being left here. "I'll call you." She stepped forward and hugged her mom and dad, not caring if she didn't look cool.

"We'll see you in a week."

She waved until her parents got in their van and drove away. Then she crossed her arms over her chest and faced her peers. Somehow she had to get the guts up to talk to someone.

❦

By the time Cassie got on the bus with her bag of goodies and books, half the seats were taken. She wandered to the back and found an aisle seat next to to a brown-haired girl.

"Is this seat taken?" Cassie asked.

"No," the girl said. "You can sit there. I'm Gabby."

"Hi." Cassie sat beside her and stretched her legs out.

"How old are you?" Gabby asked. "I'm ten."

"Fourteen," Cassie said, and she fell silent. She was one of the older kids in the choir, and it didn't fit her like it had a few years ago.

"Nice to meet you." Gabby pulled out a Stephen King book and buried her face in it.

Seemed like mature reading for such a young kid, but whatever. Cassie pulled out her own book, shoving her hair away from her face before starting to read.

The two of them didn't talk as the hours passed by. Cassie read until even the ghost story plot line got boring, and then she put the book away.

Her snacks were calling her name. She opened the bag up, planning to give the chocolate cookies away. But the sight of them made her mouth water, and instead Cassie ate one.

"Trade you a rice crispy treat for a cookie," a boy to her right said.

Cassie swiveled enough in her seat to face him. She recognized him, though they had only spoken a few time. He had flaming red hair, freckles across his nose, and nice green eyes. He smiled, and she returned it, her chest warming slightly.

"Sure," she said, though she didn't even like rice crispy treats.

They made the exchange, and he said, "I'm Chris. You're Cassie, right?"

"Yeah."

He took a bite of the cookie and made a face. "These are like chocolate rocks."

Cassie couldn't help laughing. "They're not so awesome."

He laughed too and then got serious. "I didn't just insult your mom, did I?"

"No, just the Walmart bakery."

"Oh, well, in that case. They're okay. Just not awesome. Sorry, Walmart."

Cassie laughed again and so did he, a nice, rich sound. She turned and faced front, surprised at how his laugh affected her. Like taking a bite of ice cream covered in hot fudge and letting it squish down her throat and into her stomach.

She shouldn't feel this way if she had a boyfriend, right?

The day pressed on, long and boring. Cassie finished one book and started another. Night time came and the singers quieted down, wrapping blankets and pillows around the chairs and going to sleep. Even Gabby leaned her pillow against the window and slept.

Cassie couldn't get comfortable. Now she realized the folly of picking an aisle seat. She put her pillow against the seat in front of her and tried to sleep that way. No good. She put it on her knees and leaned over them. That hurt her back. What were the other aisle kids doing? She looked up and down the bus. Most of them had leaned blankets over the armrest or against their seat buddy.

She hardly knew Gabby and didn't want to intrude that way. Cassie climbed out of the seat and put her blankets on the floor, then put her pillow on her seat. Wrapping herself up in the blankets, she laid her head on the pillow, closed her eyes, and willed herself to sleep. Exhaustion pulled on her eyelids, and the bus rocked her body slightly as it drove onward. Her heart rate slowed, and she felt closer to dream world.

Her calf had fallen asleep. Cassie wiggled her toes, trying to ease the sensation, but it only enhanced it. She shifted her weight a little, and the prickles in her calf exploded. She straightened her leg under the seat in front of her, but now her body was too low to reach her pillow. She sighed and sat up, the sleepiness fading. Giving up, she crawled back to her seat. She dug her book out of her bag and flipped on the tiny overhead light. She would just have to read.

Her eyes grew hot and itchy as the night wore on, and several times her head bobbed and she thought she'd fall asleep. Each time she closed her book and waited for sleep to come, but each time it disappeared again.

When the sun came up, the other kids started to wake also.

"You're up early," Gabby said.

"You were awake every time I looked over there," Chris said. "Did you even sleep?"

"Yeah," said a kid in front of him. "Every time I woke, your eyes were wide open."

"I couldn't get comfortable," Cassie said, annoyed and frustrated she was the only one. Was she such a sissy that she required a comfortable bed while everybody else was fine sleeping hunched over in a chair?

"You'll probably crash tonight when we get to the hotel room," Chris said. He unwrapped a package of blueberry muffins and held one out to her. "Breakfast?"

Cassie gave him a weary smile and accepted. "Thanks."

⟲∽·⟳

Hours later, the bus arrived in New York. In spite of the grogginess that plagued her, Cassie mashed her face against the window like everyone else, peering over Gabby's shoulder to get her first glimpse of the city.

It was hard to see it all. The buildings rose into the air, and the cars just sat in the street, preventing the bus from moving forward. Every vehicle was honking, and people congregated on the corners, congesting every street. Delis, cafés, and restaurants lined the sidewalks underneath high-rise apartments. The sheer enormity of how many people lived here dazzled Cassie.

The bus slowly maneuvered its way around the block and then came to a stop. Miss Vanderwood stood up.

"I'm going into the hotel to get us checked in. All of you stay right here. When I come back, I'll have room assignments and keys, and then you can get your luggage and go to your room."

The bus erupted into chatter as soon as she got off.

"This is our hotel!"

"Can you even see the top?"

Cassie was on the wrong side of the bus to see anything. She crossed the aisle and huddled closer to Chris, peering over his shoulder. She could only see up about ten stories before the window of the bus prevented her from leaning her head back farther. "How tall do you think it is?" she asked him.

"I don't know, but I hope we're on the very top."

She liked the way he said "we're." The thought of having Chris nearby in the same hotel made her a little tingly, and she favored him with a grin.

Only a moment later, Miss Vanderwood was back. "When I call your name, come on up here."

Cassie waited in anticipation. The names were called in alphabetical order, and Gabby went up before her. Then she heard, "Cassandra Jones,"and she shouldered both her bag of books and her bag of goodies.

"Here's your key," Miss Vanderwood said, handing her a small plastic card. "You're in room 3920."

Cassie nodded and stepped off the bus. That was a big number. Who else would be in her room with her?

The bus driver had unloaded the luggage onto the sidewalk, and Cassie quickly found her bag. She spotted Gabby and asked, "What room are you in?"

"Room 3920. You?"

Cassie let out a little breath of relief. "Me too." She couldn't exactly say Gabby was a friend, but at least they tolerated each other. "I wonder who will be in our room with us?"

Gabby grabbed her suitcase and started for the hotel doors. "Well, we know there's an adult chaperone in every room, so there's probably just one other kid with us. Somebody who has a mom here."

Not RyAnne. That was a relief.

The main entrance was congested with kids trying to get inside, and Cassie spotted a door over to the left with no people. She pointed to it. "Let's take that entrance."

"Sure."

She and Gabby made their way over to it, and then they stepped through to a quiet room separated from the main lobby by a glass door. The elevators on the other side had a long line.

"Let's take this elevator over here," Gabby said, pointing. "There's no one waiting."

"Oh, great idea." Cassie followed her, pleased they were smart enough to evade the other singers.

The elevator clanged loudly when they pulled their bags inside, but there was plenty of room. It was long and spacious. A moment later it began to move.

"Oops, sorry," Gabby said. "I pressed down instead of up. Here." She pressed the button for floor three.

Cassie's eyes traveled over the elevator buttons, going all the way to floor forty-two. "Um, Gabby? I think we're on floor thirty-nine, not three."

"Really?" Gabby studied the key card in her hand and gasped. "I think you're right!"

The elevator came to a jarring stop, and the doors slowly slid open.

A loud whirring and humming sound filled the metal room, and lights flickered in the dark corridor in front of them. A sign dangled from an exposed pipe that read, "Warning: High Voltage." Wires sparked around the sign.

Chills rushed over Cassie's body as she remembered every horror movie she'd ever seen. "Close the doors, close the doors!" she screamed.

Gabby's finger stabbed the Close Door button over and over. "I'm trying, I'm trying!"

The doors slid shut and the elevator jerked upward. Cassie took several deep breaths and then looked over at Gabby.

"I don't think that was the right floor," she said, and they both burst out laughing.

⟡

A girl named Tonya and her mother were in the room with Gabby and Cassie.

"I'm Mrs. Bennett. Just drop your bags off and freshen up real quick, girls. I think we're all getting ready to go to Hard Rock Cafe for dinner."

Real food sounded good after having mostly prepackaged food for two days. But what Cassie really wanted was a nap. She lay down on the bed she would be sharing with Gabby and closed her eyes, relishing in the feeling of being horizontal.

"I didn't sleep all night," she said. "Can I just take a quick nap?"

Mrs. Bennett gave her a sympathetic look. "I'm so sorry. I'm sure you'll get to rest tonight. Don't you want to see New York, after being cooped up on that bus for two days?"

She did. But sleep sounded so nice . . . she let her eyelids drag slowly over her eyes.

"Come on," Gabby said, grabbing her arm and pulling her to her feet. "You better get moving or you'll be asleep."

Cassie sighed and allowed herself to be dragged out the door and to the elevator. She texted her mom and told her she'd arrived, then followed Gabby and the Bennetts off the elevator.

The hotel lobby was bigger than Cassie's house. A line of men in black suits stood at the registration desk. Potted plants and fluffy chairs dotted the porcelain floor.

"We definitely came in the wrong way," Cassie said to Gabby.

"Yeah. We won't make that mistake again."

They spotted the red hair of their choir conductor and joined the huddle of kids gathered around her.

"Chaperones, the restaurant is within walking distance," Ms. Vanderwood said. "Every adult has the location. If you can just keep track of your three kids, we should all get there safely."

"Stick with me, girls," Mrs. Bennett said.

She led the way outside, and Cassie kept her eye on Mrs. Bennett's flowery pink blouse as they walked down the congested sidewalk. Cars honked around them, and a vent beneath them shot steam under their feet as they walked by. Music played from an unseen speaker. They walked past an alley, and the stench of rotting garbage reached her nose. Small black patches colored the sidewalk, and men and women sat against buildings with their legs impairing the pedestrians.

"It stinks," Cassie said, wrinkling her nose. "And it's loud."

"So many people," Gabby said, gawking. "Look at that guy!"

Cassie followed her pointing finger to see a man with no shirt walking their direction. His torso was so covered in tattoos that she almost didn't see the three snakes wrapped around his shoulders. She gasped and darted behind Gabby, who giggled at her.

"He's not going to get us," Gabby said.

"These people are crazy," Cassie said. She held her purse closer to her, trying to make herself narrower. There were too many people bumping along beside her, and not a single one met her eyes when she glanced at them. This place was weird.

CHAPTER NINE
Subway Woes

Dinner was a rowdy affair, but Cassie wasn't that impressed with her burger and fries. She thought they tasted better at Wendy's.
Maybe she was just tired. While Tonya and Gabby flipped through TV channels in the hotel room, Cassie curled up under the blankets and fell asleep in minutes.

Even though she was the first to bed, she wasn't the first awake. That would be Tonya. Tonya was twelve, so a little older than Gabby, but still a bit immature. She opened the curtains and bounced around the room.

"Today we're going to the Empire State Building! Up, up, let's get breakfast and go!"

"Not so fast," Mrs. Bennett said, sitting up in bed. "Remember the reason you're here. This whole trip isn't just a sight-seeing trip. It's a choir trip. Today you meet the other two choirs who will be singing at Carnegie Hall. And you practice."

Cassie pulled out the schedule Ms. Vanderwood had given them and groaned. "Practices all morning. Then we break for lunch and practice again. We don't go to the Empire State Building until three o'clock!"
This especially stank for Cassie. But she had promised Ms. Vanderwood she would practice with the choir the same as if she were actually going to perform with them.

She sure didn't want to, though.

All morning they sang, breaking into groups and practicing the music and then coming together again. The more they sang, the more Cassie didn't like it.

"They're all wearing shoes," she overheard a girl from the other choir say. "I thought they didn't wear shoes in Arkansas."

"Yeah. They look kind of normal," a boy said, and he sounded disappointed.

"I'm from Texas!" Cassie wanted to say. But she'd lived in Arkansas for more than four years now. Could she still say she was from Texas? Besides, Arkansas wasn't so bad.

They finally finished with all the practicing and broke into the same groups of four to head to the Empire State Building.

"Just have to follow this map," Mrs. Bennett murmured, staring at the brochure in her hand. "Come on, girls, we get to take the subway."

The subway! Cassie's eyes widened. That sounded scary!

Mrs. Bennett made her way to a subway entrance, and they hurried down the long stairwell. She stopped and read a map on the wall while Cassie put a hand to her nose.

"It stinks like pee down here," she said to Gabby.

"I guess people mark their territory also," Gabby replied.

"Gross!"

"Okay, this line! Our subway will be here in about ten minutes!" Mrs. Bennett put money into a machine and came out with tickets, which she handed to each girl. "Go through the turnstile. Yes, right there. Go on."

They joined the people already forming bunches. Cassie pulled her purse close again and eyed everyone suspiciously, certain someone would try and take her belongings. No one even glanced at her, but she still didn't trust them.

With a whoosh of loud noise and a rush of wind, the large underground train came to a halt in front of them. The doors opened, and people hurried off just as others hurried on.

"Okay, hurry, go go go!" Mrs. Bennett said, pushing the girls onward.

"This is ours?" Cassie said. It had only been two minutes, not ten. But she couldn't argue with the hand pushing her back, and she stumbled onto the train.

"Let's sit . . . here's a spot . . . over here, girls."

Cassie thought Mrs. Bennett called way too much attention to them as she gestured to a few open seats. But Cassie obliged, coming over and sitting down.

They rode for several minutes before Mrs. Bennett abruptly sat up at one of the stops, her eyes glued to something through the window. "Wait a minute," she said, stepping across the aisle.

"Is this our stop, Mom?" Tonya asked.

Mrs. Bennett pulled out her brochure and consulted it. "This isn't right. No!"

The doors closed and the subway moved forward again, and Mrs.

Bennett returned, her lips white as they pressed together.

"We're on the wrong train! We're going the wrong way! We need to get off on the next stop and catch the train going the other direction!"

"How do we do that?" Cassie asked.

"We go to the other side of the platform!"

Ten minutes later they sat on the correct subway, now moving the proper direction. Mrs. Bennett had calmed down, and Cassie was glad she wasn't the one trying to lead everyone to the right place. New York had too many unknowns, too many variables and factors to make the plans go awry.

They didn't see anyone they knew when they finally got off and stood in front of the Empire State building, but that didn't really surprise Cassie. Everyone else had probably arrived twenty minutes earlier.

"It's so tall," Cassie said, craning her neck back to see the top. Their tall hotel would be dwarfed next to this.

"Insanity," Gabby said.

They stepped inside, bypassing a gift shop and getting in line to buy tickets. A title caught Cassie's eye, and she turned her head.

"A bookstore!" she said, pointing across the street. Were bookstores in New York different? Would it have more variety? "Can we go there?"

"Maybe after. We need to hurry so we can catch up to everyone for dinner."

Cassie liked her small group more than the rest of the choir and wished they didn't have to rejoin them.

They walked though the long twisty path that led through a museum exhibit of the Empire State Building, sharing interesting facts and history of the area. Then an elevator took them several stories up before depositing them. They had to take one more elevator to get to the viewing area.

Cassie sucked in a breath when they exited. "We are so high," she gasped. She gripped the handrails and peered over the side at the distant ground. Wind rattled through the outdoor area, chilling Cassie even though it was summertime. She looked out over the ocean and took in the buildings, all of which seemed so much smaller in comparison.

"We're not even at the top," Gabby said, nudging Cassie and pointing. "Look. You can pay extra for an elevator to take you up there."

Cassie shivered. The people up there must feel like they were on top of the world.

Around them families and groups of kids snapped photos, and Cassie heard more languages than she could count.

"This place is like some kind of mecca," she said.

"Yeah. People from all over the world come here."

That was kind of cool.

By the time they got down, Mrs. Bennett said there was no time to stop at the bookstore. Instead she hurried them along to the deli where they would be eating dinner. People still bumped Cassie, not even bothering to apologize. Perfume and body odor mixed together in fleeting moments.

"Marking his territory," Gabby said, pointing across the street.

Cassie bit her lip to keep from laughing as she spotted a guy moving away from a building, zipping up his fly and shaking his leg. "I guess they need more public bathrooms."

"I guess."

"Let's make sure we take the right subway this time, Mom," Tonya said.

"I will," she grumped.

The fast-paced energy infected Cassie. She stood up straighter and matched the pace of the walkers around her, hurrying to their next destination. It was loud and smelly and moving at sonic-speed, but there was something infectious about New York City.

⌒✿⌒

The next day they practiced for six hours. Six hours! Was it possible for a singer to hate singing? She relaxed in her seat when the choir director walked away and just lip-synced, wishing she could bring a book in and hide it behind her music.

They ate sandwiches for lunch and then sang some more.

"It's just eight songs," she overheard someone muttering. "How many times can we sing them?"

Many times, as Ms. Vanderwood proved to them.

Finally, she released them. "Go to your rooms and dress nicely! We're going to Phantom of the Opera tonight!" She caught Cassie's eye as Cassie passed and flashed a smile. "It might seem pointless to be here since you're not performing, Cassie, but you're doing a great job of improving your musical abilities."

Improving her musical abilities. Cassie grumbled to herself as she got on the elevator.

"Cassie!"

She turned her head as Chris hurried into the elevator beside her. "Hi," she said, pleased to see him.

"What floor are you on?" he asked, punching number thirty-six.

"Thirty-nine," she said, and he punched the button.

"Lucky! I wanted one of the higher rooms."

"Yeah, it's pretty cool," she agreed.

"Want to sit by me at the musical tonight?"

"I would love to," she said, relishing the liquid warmth that flooded her chest.

"Great." The elevator zipped to a stop at his floor, and he got out. "I'll meet you in the lobby."

Cassie took extra care pulling her hair into a clip and putting on her makeup. She wasn't sure why it mattered, but she wanted to look good.

They walked as a big mass down the sidewalks to the theater, with Cassie beside Chris and Gabby and Tonya and several other kids. They filed into their seats, loud and rambunctious as they released all the energy they'd had to contain while they sang.

"What do you think of New York so far?" Chris asked, leaning his head toward her to be heard over the other kids.

"You know, at first I didn't like it," Cassie said. "But it's growing on me. It's not so bad now. You probably get pretty comfortable with it if it's your home."

"I would miss the trees."

Cassie pictured the trees in Arkansas, covering every rolling hill, branches with so many leaves they looked like mounds and mounds of broccoli. "I would too."

"Do you think—" Chris began just as she turned to face him.

Their faces were inches apart, and Cassie stopped breathing. Chris didn't speak either. He held her eyes, studying her, and then his gaze flicked to her lips, real quick. Cassie's heart did a little tumble. She wanted to kiss him. It felt like a natural thing to do. He leaned closer, so close, and then Cassie panicked. She pulled back just a bit, putting nearly a foot between them.

Chris smiled as though nothing had happened. "Are you excited for school next year?"

"Yes," she said, heart pounding in her throat. That had nearly happened. "It will be fun to be the oldest in school again."

He gave her a funny look. "What grade are you going into?"

"Ninth."

"Ninth!" His eyebrows went up in surprise. "I thought you were younger."

Everyone did, but Cassie's heart sank. "How old are you?" she asked, already suspecting the answer.

"I'm thirteen," he said, looking as if the words hurt to say. "I'm going into eighth grade."

Younger. He was younger than her. What had she been thinking? "My boyfriend's going into eleventh grade," she said, smiling, and she felt the words like a nail in a coffin.

"Wow. That's old," Chris said.

"Yep."

The lights went down and the group quieted. Chris faced front, and so did Cassie, wishing she could somehow undo the last five minutes of conversation.

⚬๛ฺⴾ⚬

The days of singing and sight-seeing blurred together until Sunday finally arrived. While the choir members got ready to perform on Sunday morning, Cassie called the preacher of the nearby congregation.

"I got your hotel information from your mom," Brother Powell said. "I'll be there soon."

Cassie put on a dress, ready for church. Ms. Vanderwood took Cassie down to the lobby.

"I'm really sorry it worked out this way, Cassie. We would have loved to have you sing with us."

"I know. And it's okay. I've enjoyed New York."

When Brother Powell arrived, he showed his ID to Ms. Vanderwood, and then Cassie left with him.

"My wife's at home," he said, stepping outside.

Cassie followed him out into the sunshine. She expected him to lead her to a car, but instead he started walking. "That's nice. Do you have kids?"

"One, a little girl. She's precious. You'll meet her soon."

They didn't stop walking. Cassie expected any minute that they would turn and enter an apartment building, but instead they walked. And walked. And walked. She was starting to feel like a pioneer crossing the plains when he finally stopped at a four-story building and led the way inside.

"We're on the third floor," he said. He pulled aside an accordion-style metal door in front of the elevator, and they stepped inside. "I'll leave you with my wife. I have to get to the chapel. She'll bring you in a few hours."

"Okay," Cassie said.

He opened the door to an apartment and stepped inside. "Jean!" he called.

A tall woman with thick, curly dark hair came out of the kitchen, drying her hands. "Hi, Brian," she said, giving him a quick kiss. "You must be Cassie!"

"I am," Cassie said, smiling.

"Come on in. Bye, dear!" Jean turned back to Cassie, not waiting for him to leave. "I'm just making some cookies. Would you like some?"

Homemade cookies. Cassie should say no. She'd eaten way too much junk food this week. But the smell of chocolate and melted butter with sugar filled her nostrils, and she couldn't. "Yes."

Jean grinned. "Meet Jessica. Just talk to her while I get the cookies out."

49

Cassie stepped in front of the little girl in the high chair and blinked in surprise. "Hi, Jessica."

Jessica gave a toothless grin, her creamy cocoa-colored skin the perfect match to her short, wiry black hair. Neither Jean nor Brian were black. Cassie couldn't fathom how this little girl was so dark.

"Here's a cookie," Jean said, offering it to Cassie. And then she focused on Jessica. "There's my sweet girl, my little butterscotch."

Jessica's grin went full-blown, and she giggled and blew raspberries, her little feet kicking against the plastic chair.

"Oh, she likes you," Cassie said.

"I'm her mama," Jean said. She looked at Cassie, a slow smile curling her lips. "I'm sure you're wondering how."

"Well," Cassie admitted.

"She's adopted. Brian and I tried for years but couldn't. When we had the opportunity to adopt her, we jumped on it. And you're just the highlight of our lives, aren't you, little butterscotch?"

Jessica squealed, a high-pitched, happy sound.

"All right, well, eat your cookie," Jean said. "And then we'll leave for church." She scooped Jessica out of her chair. "Let's get you all cleaned up, you little munchkin."

Cassie didn't think she'd ever seen a mom love her daughter so much.

⚬～⚘～⚬

Jean pushed Jessica in a stroller to the chapel since it wasn't too far away. Every few feet someone would stop to compliment Jessica, telling Jean what a beautiful baby she was.

"Thank you," Jean would reply every time, positively beaming.

"Everyone adores her," Cassie said.

"She's a happy baby. She loves people, and they love her."

The church building was unlike any Cassie had seen before. It was on a corner with a drugstore beneath it. They took an elevator to the second floor, and Cassie marveled at the set up.

"When land is at a premium, you go up," Jean said, gesturing Cassie into the chapel.

Brother Powell greeted them, but so did everyone else in the small congregation. A tiny black man spoke to them, but his words came out all whistle-y and click-ish, and Cassie could hardly understand him. After he left, Jean leaned over and whispered, "He's from Africa. Used to live in the bush. Just came to America about six years ago and still speaks like that. You know, all the clicks and whistles."

"Oh," Cassie said, nodding, but she hadn't known people could speak that way. Her mind was opening up to all the things she didn't know. Her world was so small. She needed to see more of it, do more.

After church, Jean said, "I feel bad that you're missing your choir performance. Let's go downtown and look at the sites."

"Sure," Cassie said.

They caught a bus to Times Square, and Jean showed Cassie a beautiful cathedral.

"It's the most famous in all New York," she said as she led Cassie up the steps. "It's three hundred years old."

"Wow," Cassie murmured, unable to even fathom that. A large dome sat on top of the pillars, and the cathedral resembled the White House sitting on top of an ancient Greek temple.

A homeless guy sat on the steps shaking a cup at everyone who passed by. "Just a penny. A quarter. Anything."

He shook it at them, but Jean kept on talking. "The wood rotted once a hundred years ago and they had to take half of it out and redo it."

"Uh-huh," Cassie said, but her eyes were on the homeless guy, wearing not much more than rags and watching them with woeful eyes.

"Thank you," he said as they passed.

"So they're always working on something," Jean continued.

Cassie didn't say anything. She kept picturing that man's face in her mind.

"I know what you're thinking," Jean said, lowering her voice. "We all feel that way. But you realize very quickly after you live here that if you gave to all of them, you would have nothing. So we donate to charities and food warehouses and do our part where we can."

Cassie took a deep breath and nodded. She could see Jean's point. But it hurt her heart. She wanted to give something to him. Something to all of them.

By the time Brother Powell took Cassie to the hotel that evening, she felt like Sunday had been the best day of her whole trip.

"You're a pretty amazing girl, Cassie," he said. "Jean had a great time with you today."

"I had a great time with her," Cassie said. "I wasn't sad at all about missing my performance. This was my favorite day."

Brother Powell smiled. "She'll be so happy to know that."

CHAPTER TEN

On the Skinny

There was no adjustment period for Cassie when she got home from New York. The bus pulled up to the curb Tuesday afternoon, and once again Cassie just wanted to sleep. It had not been a great night for her.

Mrs. Jones was nearly an hour later picking Cassie up. Cassie was the only one left next to Ms. Vanderwood when the van arrived. Not even the bus was still there.

"I'm sorry I'm so late," Mrs. Jones said, giving Ms. Vanderwood an apologetic smile.

"It's fine," Ms. Vanderwood said, her tone indicating it was anything but. "Bye, Cassie. See you when we start up again in the fall."

"See you," Cassie said.

"You have a Sunday dress, right?" Mrs. Jones said as Cassie put her duffel bag in the car.

"Yes."

"We can go home, or you can change into it and go with me to Fayetteville."

"I just want to go home," Cassie said. "Tomorrow's Maureen's birthday party, and I need sleep before then."

"I understand. But if I take you home, we'll miss Elek's court date."

Cassie paused right before closing the car door. "His court date?" she said slowly.

In all the excitement of a new boyfriend and camps and the trip to New York, Cassie was ashamed to admit Elek had slipped her mind completely. Elek was practically a brother to her, having lived with her family for a bit. But a few months ago he'd been arrested for stealing a car, and she'd been waiting for weeks to know what was going to happen to him.

"Sleep will have to wait," she said, opening her duffel bag and pulling out the dress she'd used for church. "I'll change in the back seat."

The courtroom was not what Cassie expected. She had expected something like in the movies, with rows of benches and jury and even a balcony for more people. This tiny room only had two rows of seats before the judge's bench. Cassie and her mom slipped into one in the back, and Cassie's hands fluttered nervously. A policeman or security guard or something like that stood in one corner, back straight and hands clasped behind him.

"Hello, hello," a soft voice said, and Cassie lifted her head as a tiny woman with thick dark hair and smile lines around her eyes slipped into the bench beside them.

"Sang," Mrs. Jones said, wrapping an arm around Elek's mom and hugging her tight. "How are you?"

Her only response was to burst into tears, and Cassie's throat ached. She had to look away.

Elek wasn't here yet, and Cassie forced herself to take slow breaths. What would he look like? What would she feel when she saw him?

And then she knew, because a side door opened and another guard walked in, his hand on Elek's elbow. Elek shuffled in beside him, his head down, dressed entirely in a bright orange jumpsuit. It hung off of him, and his frame looked much smaller than before. His shoulders slumped forward, his whole body language like someone who wanted to disappear.

Cassie covered her mouth to hide her cry. The tears came hard and fast, sliding down her face. This couldn't be the same boy who gave her advice and sat on the front porch talking with her at home.

A door opened up in the front of the room, and a man dressed in black robes walked out, stopping behind the judge's bench.

"All rise for the honorable Judge Harris!" the security guard yelled out.

Mrs. Jones stood up, pulling Cassie to her feet also.

"Be seated," the judge said, not even looking up from his paperwork as he shuffled things around. He lifted his eyes and focused on Elek. "Elek Mellas?"

"Yes," Elek said, his voice just barely audible.

"I see here you've been accused of grand theft auto and assault. Your lawyer's drafted out a plea for you."

Cassie tried to focus on the words, but her emotions made it hard to concentrate. The judge's tone was harsh and stern. He didn't know Elek, he didn't know what a kind and gentle soul he was.

"I'm sentencing you to five years in prison. You are eligible for parole and your sentence can be shortened by good behavior. Your lawyer will have all the details. Court dismissed."

And that was it. No trial, no jury, not even asking Elek for his version of events.

The judge disappeared through his door, and Sang leapt to her feet. She ran forward, crying and blabbering in Greek as she threw her arms around her son. He couldn't hug her back because he was handcuffed, but Cassie saw the tears streaming down his face too.

"Go say something to him, Cassie," Mrs. Jones whispered.

"I'm not sure I can," Cassie said, her eyes burning.

"He'll think you hate him if you don't."

Her mom was right. Swallowing her discomfort, Cassie pushed her way down the aisle. She waited until Sang moved away and then reached up and hugged Elek. He had to bend slightly so she could reach him.

"I'm so sorry, Cassie," he whispered.

She didn't even know what to say. So she just squeezed him tight and then walked out of the court room, leaving her mom to say goodbye for her.

⊙↜෴↝⊙

She cried herself to sleep that night, remembering Elek's face in the courtroom. It was like in that moment, he finally understood what he'd done to his life. Would he ever get it back on track? Would this be a minor blip on his future or had it derailed him entirely?

Exhaustion claimed her before long, providing sweet relief.

Maureen called Cassie the next day as Cassie unloaded her New York trip items into the washing machine.

"Happy birthday to me, happy birthday to me," she sang.

Cassie laughed. "I didn't forget. I'll be there tonight."

"I hope you wrote me something pretty."

"I did." Cassie crossed her fingers that her message would be enough. She doubted Maureen would like the soccer shorts. But she couldn't not give them to her.

"Mom, I need wrapping paper," Cassie said, wandering into her parents' room.

"If we have any it will be downstairs." Mrs. Jones didn't look up from the towels she was folding.

Cassie went to the basement and checked the boxes, but all she found was a small roll of Christmas paper. She came back with it in her hand.

"Do we have anything that's not Christmas?" she asked.

"I think that's probably it, honey."

"Then we need to go to the store! I can't use this!"

Finally her mother looked at her. "Maureen's party is here in Tontitown," her mom said, referencing the rural community where they lived. "I'm not driving you to town for wrapping paper. Just use the Christmas paper. She'll think it's funny."

Totally unfair! Cassie stomped away and threw the paper on her bed, pouting. But there wasn't anything else for her to use, so she reluctantly cut and folded the paper around the journal.

Then she turned to the pretty purple soccer shorts. But no matter how she tried, she couldn't get what remained of the paper to wrap around them. Frustrated, she plopped back on the bed with a groan. What would she do now?

She'd figure it out later. She threw the shorts into her duffel bag and packed again, this time for a slumber party.

⚬➤✦⬅⚬

"Cassie!"

Her friends squealed her name and hugged on her like they hadn't seen her in months. Cassie took a quick head count of the girls in the living room. Everyone was there except Janice.

"Tell us all about New York," Amity said, throwing her legs over a chair and smacking her gum loudly.

"And Josh," Maureen said, making kissy faces. "Has that happened yet?"

"Not yet," Cassie said, her face warming. Josh had written her a letter and called a few times, but Cassie didn't feel like talking to him. She'd texted and said she was back but super tired.

"Let's hurry and open the presents," Amity said. "I want to ride the four-wheelers."

"Four-wheelers?" Cassie said. Most people around their town had one, but her mom said they were dangerous.

"Yeah, my dad brought our four-wheelers over," Cara said. "Said we could ride them back to my house."

"Then my mom will come get us and bring us home," Maureen said.

"So presents!" Amity howled. "I want cake!"

"You'll never lose weight the way you eat," Maureen said.

"Speak for yourself, heifer!" Amity said, and she started a thigh-slapping fight with Maureen.

"I'll eat cake if Cassie eats cake," Andrea said.

Cassie rolled her eyes. Her friends' over-protectiveness of her eating habits had gotten old. "Guys, come on. I've been eating normal for months." It was still a bit of a mental struggle, if she was perfectly honest, but she was doing it.

"Great," Amity said. "We're all eating cake. After we open the presents!" She swung around and glared at Maureen.

"All right, then," Maureen said, and Cassie's mind raced as Maureen opened every else's presents. The shorts were still sitting in her duffel bag. No wrapper. Nothing. Everyone else got her cool things like nice clothes, card games, gag gifts. Cassie's cool factor was about to go way down.

"Okay," Cassie said, taking a deep breath when Maureen turned to her. "I have two things for you. The first one, you just have to reach inside my duffel bag and find it."

Maureen lifted an eyebrow. "I'm not gonna find a pair of your granny underwear, am I?"

All the girls laughed, and Cassie tried to smile past the insult. "If you're lucky."

They hooted at Cassie's response, and Maureen's eyes sparkled. She stuck her hand in Cassie's bag.

"Close your eyes and I'll tell you when you've got it," Cassie said. She watched Maureen's fingers sift through clothes until they touched the shorts. "There."

Maureen closed her first and pulled the shorts from the bag. "Oo, pretty," she said, but her expression remained blank.

"That's not all," Cassie said hurriedly. She reached into her purse and pulled out the journal. "Here."

Now Maureen's eyes lit up, and she grinned. "This is what I was waiting for." She tore open the paper, revealing the flowery diary. "I need a Cassie moment, guys, to go read my message."

They laughed and joked and teased while Maureen disappeared into her room, but Cassie's heart warmed.

❦

They rode the four-wheelers to Cara's house, only a few miles down the road. Cassie sat with Cara and Maureen, clinging tightly to the other girls as the wind whipped through their hair and the four-wheelers dipped and bounced with every rise and fall of the road. It was exhilarating and terrifying, and Cassie prayed they wouldn't crash and die because they hadn't put on helmets.

They were all giggly and hyper as they parked the four-wheelers behind Cara's house.

"Oh, Cara!" Amity exclaimed, spotting the above ground pool. "Your pool is up."

"Yep," Cara said.

"Ah, man," Maureen said. "Too bad none of us brought swimsuits."

"I have a few extra in my room," Cara said.

But Amity was already hauling her shirt over her head, followed by her bra. "Who needs a swimsuit? It's just us!" Her shorts and underwear followed, and then she dove into the water.

Cassie realized her mouth was hanging open. She couldn't believe Amity had just done that.

Cara laughed. "You're right." And then she also stripped down, giggling as she did so.

Cassie's cheeks burned, even though it was too dark to see any of her friends clearly. "I'm not doing that."

"It's all right, Cassie," Maureen said, also removing her clothes. "No one will see us."

Was she the only one who didn't want to? Even Andrea had complied, her clothes falling into a pile at her feet before she jumped into the pool.

They shrieked and laughed and giggled, splashing water as they ran in circles in the pool. A part of Cassie yearned to join them. But a different part of her cowed away from it. She didn't want to be naked in front of them, didn't feel comfortable being outside where anyone might see them. What if Cara's dad came out to investigate the noise? Once again she felt that distance between them. She was different. She wished Janice were here. Janice would stay out with Cassie.

A few minutes later Andrea climbed out, putting her clothes back on and joining Cassie at a chair on the side. "Why won't you come in?"

Cassie shrugged. "I just don't feel great about it."

"It's not a big deal. You wouldn't have to take it all off if you didn't want to."

Cassie folded her arms over her body, wishing she could disappear. Maybe she shouldn't have come. "That's okay."

"What are you girls doing?"

The adult voice that penetrated the darkness sent the three girls in the pool screaming and scurrying to the side, trying to hide their bodies. But then Maureen laughed.

"Mom! You scared us!"

"Good thing there are no boys at this party," her mom said, amusement in her voice. "Best get your clothes on. I've got the truck here to take y'all home."

The girls giggled as Maureen's mom walked away, a bit of nervous energy rippling off them.

"Lucky it wasn't your dad," Amity said to Cara as she pulled her clothes back on.

Cara shivered and huddled close to Maureen. "Now everything's wet."

Maureen shoved her off. "So go inside and get something warm! Your house is right here!"

"Oh, yeah." Cara disappeared inside. She came back out with five sweatshirts, which she handed around. Cassie wasn't wet or cold, but she accepted one.

"Now you can lean on me," Maureen said, pulling Cara's head to her shoulder.

"Now I don't want to," Cara said, sticking out her tongue. But they were playing, joking, and Cassie lagged behind as they went to the truck.

"Lean on me," Maureen sang, turning around and cupping Cassie's chin. "When—"

"Stand," Amity interrupted, singing louder than Maureen. She stood beside her and sang at Cassie. "By me."

"Into the truck, girls!" Maureen's mom hollered.

Maureen pulled down the hatch, and they all climbed in. Maureen faced Amity and scream-sang, "Just to be the man—"

"DA-DA-DA-DA!" Cara shouted.

Cassie giggled. "I'll be—"

"There for you!" Andrea finished, which wasn't even the song Cassie had been singing, but she was laughing too hard to correct her.

"This is the ocean!" Cara sang.

"A big ole city!" Maureen shouted.

"It's all right—" Amity tried, but Maureen sang over her.

"Gone country!"

Cassie joined in, because she knew this song, and she and Maureen drowned Amity out with their scream-singing.

By the time the girls reached Maureen's house, they were a giggling, wet, weepy mess, drunk on goofiness and friendship.

CHAPTER ELEVEN

Double Time

Cassie went home with Amity the next day, and the two girls spent the day swimming. In their swimsuits.

"What did you think of New York?" Amity asked, lounging on the side of the pool and resting her head on her arms. She faced Cassie, her expression serious.

"It was fine. Loud and smelly. I didn't like it at first but it grew on me."

Amity sighed. "I want to get out of Arkansas. I want to be a famous singer someday and go to New York."

"You could. You made Unison this year. So you know you're a good singer."

Amity favored Cassie with a smile. "You just say that because you're nice. There's no mean bone in you."

"Sure there is." Cassie shrugged. "You should see me fight with my sister."

"You should see me fight with mine," Amity said.

"I have," Cassie said. "It's ugly."

They both laughed, and then Cassie said, "I just remembered I have a church dance this weekend. Want to come?"

"Yes!" Amity squealed, pushing off the side and dunking under water. She came back up, dark hair floating past her shoulders. "You don't get to hog all the cute guys, Cassandra Jones!"

"I'm not trying to," Cassie said, laughing, and then she quieted. Josh would be there.

"What's wrong?" Amity asked, picking up on her mood.

"Nothing," Cassie said, shaking it off. "I just get nervous around Josh sometimes, that's all."

Amity gave her an understanding look. "Oh, sweetie, that's normal. You're so new at this girlfriend thing. It gets more natural."

Amity would know. Cassie let out a deep breath. "You're right. It's all going to be fine."

"Come on." Amity pushed out of the pool. "I'll get my mom to take us out for Chinese food."

⟨◦∗◦⟩

On Saturday, Amity, Andrea, and Maureen rode up to the dance with Cassie. They bounced with breathless anticipation, finally getting the chance to see all the hot Tahlequah boys they hadn't seen since May.

"I sure hope Andy's here," Maureen said.

"I get the first dance if he is," Amity said.

"There they are!" Andrea cried, pointing.

Cassie followed her finger, her stomach somersaulting, hoping she'd feel fireworks in her heart when she saw him.

Leaning against the brick wall outside the church were Andy, Josh, and Gage.

Seeing Josh did nothing for her. Nothing good, anyway. She felt a little sick with anxiety.

The boys grinned and mosied over to the car, waiting as the girls climbed out.

"You look beautiful," Josh said, bending over to hug Cassie. He whipped something out from behind his back, presenting her with a box of chocolates and two roses.

"Awww," Cassie's friends chorused.

"Where's mine, Josh?" Mrs. Jones asked from the van window.

He grinned and approached the window. "The chocolates are for you. The roses are for Cassie. But I figured you might share." He winked at Cassie.

"He's so sweet," Maureen gushed.

"Just perfect," Amity agreed.

Cassie worked on her smile, forcing it upward while she handed the gifts to her mom. But she didn't meet her mom's eyes, certain she'd read the truth in them.

The group wandered inside, and Cassie spotted Riley talking to Tyler and Jason Reeves. Relief flooded her at the familiar faces, and she walked over to say hi. A few years ago she couldn't stand Tyler, but last year they'd become sort of friends. Plus Riley had a crazy crush on him.

"Hi, you guys," Cassie said.

"Someone's looking for you," Riley said.

"Yeah, I found him." She turned and gestured to where Josh still chatted with Andrea and Amity.

"That's not who I meant."

Before Cassie could ask, soft, skinny arms wrapped around her waist from behind. Cassie swiveled her head and saw Elise.

"Hey! Elise!"

"Oh, I'm so glad you're here," Elise said, rocking her back and forth.

Cassie squirmed out of the embrace. "How are you?"

"Dance with me." A song was playing, and Elise pulled Cassie to the dance floor. She clasped her hands around Cassie's neck, and Cassie awkwardly moved in time to the music with her.

"Are you all right?" Cassie asked.

"Ah, well." Elise shrugged. "As well as can be. Better now that you're here. You're just so good." She patted Cassie's cheek. "I always feel better when I see you."

"Thanks," Cassie said.

Elise glanced over her shoulder. "Is one of those guys your boyfriend?"

"Yes," Cassie said, and she couldn't help the annoyance that entered her tone. "The one with glasses."

"Looks better in real life than in the picture." Elise turned back to Cassie and appraised her. "But you're not interested in him anymore, are you."

Cassie's face warmed under the words. "Yes, I am," she stuttered.

"Hmm." Elise smiled. "That's okay. It's okay to break up. None of these relationships last forever, you know."

The song ended, and Elise slid her hands away from Cassie, stroking her forearm before letting go. "Thanks for the dance."

Riley was by herself when Cassie returned, and Cassie saw her other friends were dancing.

"That was weird," Riley said.

"What was weird?" Cassie asked, scanning the room for Josh.

"She was all over you."

Cassie focused on Riley. "She was just being friendly."

Riley cocked her head. "Jason and Tyler thought it was weird also."

"She's going through a hard time."

Riley shrugged. "I guess so."

"Dance, Cassie?" Josh said, appearing suddenly beside her. He held out his hand, and Cassie bit back a sigh.

"Of course."

She danced nearly every song with Josh, which just left her feeling disappointed. Her favorite thing about these dances was meeting other guys, getting to know who was here. But all of them seemed to think she belonged to Josh, and only a few asked her to dance.

The dance ended, and the girls once again piled into the car with

Mrs. Jones.

"I'm totally in love with Andy," Maureen said, sighing and fanning her face. "All those crazy blond curls!"

"And Gage." Amity made a soft growl in the back of her throat. "So, so hot!"

"Did you meet James?" Andrea heaved a sigh and tossed her head back. "He had the most perfect eyes!"

"Sounds like you girls are all twitter-pated," Mrs. Jones laughed.

"Mom, we don't use words like that," Cassie said, irritated.

"Oh, Cassie, you and Josh are the cutest couple," Amity said.

"Yeah, everyone said that," Maureen said. "You just fit together."

Cassie didn't say a word. She didn't want to tell them what she'd realized: that she didn't like him anymore.

It doesn't matter, she told herself. *Relationships don't last forever.* This one would end soon, and then she could find someone who actually made her feel something.

It wasn't like she'd have to see Josh for awhile, anyway.

Josh called Cassie the next day after church.

"I loved seeing you yesterday," he said.

"Yeah, it was great," Cassie said, concentrating on painting her toes.

"It's like, all the time apart, when I'm finally with you, it's so worth it."

"Yep."

"But I don't like being apart. And tomorrow's the Fourth of July, so I got the day off. I thought I'd come see you."

Cassie nearly dropped the paint brush. "Already?" she croaked. "I mean, I didn't expect this. We just saw each other yesterday."

"I know. We can almost be like a normal couple, seeing each other every few days."

She ground her teeth together. "Great."

"I'll see you tomorrow, then."

"Yep." Cassie groaned after she hung up. "No!"

"What is it?" her sister Emily asked.

"It's Josh!" Cassie put her head in her hands. "He's coming over tomorrow!"

"Isn't that a good thing?"

Cassie couldn't tell her. She couldn't tell anyone she didn't like him anymore, or it might somehow get back to him. And if they broke up too soon . . . Well, she'd lose her social status. "Yeah. It's a great thing. I just need to tell Mom."

CHAPTER TWELVE

Great Expectations

J osh arrived a little before lunch the next day. He ate sandwiches with Cassie's family, and then Mrs. Jones asked him what his plans were.

"I don't know," Josh said. "I thought we'd hang out for a bit, set off fireworks tonight. Do you want to go anywhere, Cassie?"

"Cara invited me over to do fireworks tonight," Cassie said. "My friends might be there."

"We can do that."

"You guys could go to the mall," Mrs. Jones said. "But you have to bring Annette with you."

Going to the mall sounded better than trying to entertain Josh here at her house. "Yeah. That sounds fun. Want to, Josh?"

"Whatever you want, beautiful."

Cassie's teeth ground together, and she turned away. She did not like it when he called her that.

Annette sat in the back seat and giggled while they drove to the mall, twenty minutes away from the Jones' house. Josh parked the car and opened the door for Cassie. She walked beside him through the parking lot and up to the entrance, and then Josh surprised her by taking her hand as he pulled her inside. His warm flesh felt foreign and soft in her hand, and she wanted to shake the feeling off. But of course she couldn't.

He stopped at a stationary store. "I bet you'd like one of those journals," he said, pointing at a row of books with metallic embossing. "I saw how carefully you picked one out for Maureen."

"They are nice," Cassie admitted. "I do like to write." Stories, letters, journals, whatever came to mind.

"Go pick one and I'll buy it for you."

"No, you don't have to—" Cassie began.

"Go on. If you don't pick one I will, and it's better if you get the one you want."

Her cheeks flamed as she stepped forward and studied the journals. At least it gave her a chance to free her hand. Would this journal always remind her of Josh? She hoped not. She picked a pink one with a silver tree on it. He paid for it, then handed it to her and took her hand again.

How much longer was this day?

They roamed the mall for a few hours with Annette in tow, and then Cassie said, "Can we go to Cara's house? I know it's not dark yet, but we can hang out before we set off fireworks."

"Sure. I'm excited to meet her."

Maureen was with Cara in the front yard, and they both stared as Josh's car rumbled down the drive. Cassie suddenly wondered what Maureen thought of his car. Old, dusty, noisy. Maybe this was a bad idea.

Then Josh opened the door and climbed out, and Maureen's face broke into a smile.

"Josh!" she ran over and hugged him, then turned to the passenger window. "Cassie, you brought Josh! Is Andy here?"

Cassie climbed out and shook her head. "Sorry. No Andy." She turned to face Cara. "Hi, Cara. This is Josh."

"Hi, Josh," Cara said.

"She gets shy around new people," Maureen said to him. She tugged Josh over to Cara while Cassie got her little sister out.

"Are we going to do fireworks here?" Annette asked.

"Yes," Cassie said. "It's going to be terrific fun."

She relaxed in a lawn chair next to Cara and let Maureen talk Josh's ear off. Cara didn't say much, either.

"He seems nice enough," she finally said.

"He is," Cassie said, and then they both drifted into silence.

"Who's ready to light some fire?" Mr. Barnes asked, coming into the front yard with several rocket-shaped devices. Cara's mom followed behind and joined the girls on the lawn.

"This is the fun part," Mrs. Barnes said.

"Come on, you strapping young man, come help me," Mr. Barnes said.

Cassie didn't know Cara's parents well. They often weren't home when the girls had slumber parties, and even when they were, they stayed out of sight. She hadn't known her dad could be funny.

Josh joined Mr. Barnes, holding the light stick, and they set it to the wick before running and howling for the house, covering their heads. Cassie and Cara laughed as the rocket shot into the air.

Annette curled up beside Cassie and yawned. "I'm getting sleepy."

"Yeah, me too," Cassie said. "We should probably go home."

"Thanks for coming," Cara said. "It was nice to meet Josh."

"Oh, don't leave!" Maureen pouted.

"I've got to get my sister to bed," Cassie said, grateful for the excuse. "Come on, Josh."

"We'll see you guys later," Josh said, opening the car door for Cassie. She ignored it and helped Annette into the back, wishing she could crawl back there with her.

"Well, thanks for the nice day," she said to Josh as they drove the curvy roads back to her house.

"It was great. I'll plan another time to come see you."

He parked the car in the driveway, and Annette climbed out.

"Good night, guys!" she called.

Cassie watched her sister go into the house, then turned to say goodnight to Josh. She took a step back when she realized he'd come around the car and stood beside her.

He smiled at her, and then he gripped her shoulders and bent forward. Cassie's heart tumbled into her throat, and she whipped her head to the side without thinking. Josh's lips grazed her cheek.

"Oh, um." Crapola. Nothing could be more embarrassing than that missed moment. She ducked her head, face flaming. "I'm so sorry." She exhaled, noting how her hands shook. "I've never done this before," she said in a rush, deciding honesty was the best policy.

"That's okay." Josh smiled tenderly at her. "Just let it come naturally."

He leaned forward again, and Cassie willed herself to be still, even though her whole body trembled when he finally pressed his lips to hers. The skin was soft and fleshy, a bit moist, and not at all pleasant.

Josh pulled back. "That was nice," he said softly, and then he bent his head and kissed her again. This time, his tongue poked into her mouth, probing around her teeth and touching her own tongue, and Cassie thought she'd gag.

This was kissing? This was what she'd been waiting for?

He stepped back and she tried to smile, but she felt so jittery she was afraid she'd puke.

"See? You're a natural."

She tried not to flinch when he touched her lips. "Yeah. Thanks for that. Thanks for coming."

His eyes never left her lips, and she knew he wanted to kiss her again. "I'll see you soon."

He went around the car and drove away, and Cassie hurried inside to

brush her teeth. Oh gross! That was disgusting!
She never wanted to kiss another person again.

Episode 2:

Rebound and Glory

CHAPTER THIRTEEN
On the Inside

"**Y**ou had your first kiss!"

Andrea's shriek escaped from the tiny flip-phone speaker and filled Cassandra Jones' entire bedroom.

"Hush!" Cassie exclaimed, still jittery from what had just happened. Only moments ago, her boyfriend Josh had planted a kiss on her mouth. While Cassie hadn't felt anything sparking in her heart, she couldn't deny how proud she was to have had her first kiss. "I don't want my whole family to know!"

"Tell me everything," Andrea breathed. "How did it happen? What did he say? How did you feel?"

Cassie's mind reverted momentarily to that instant when Josh's lips had brushed hers. She'd felt—gross. It had taken all of one touch for her to know she really, truly, was not interested in him anymore. Somehow she'd thought kissing would be more exciting, more fun, more exhilarating.

"It was great," she lied. "He surprised me. I wasn't sure what to do."

"Did he use his tongue?" Andrea gasped.

"Yes," Cassie said, suppressing a shudder. "Not the first time he kissed me. But definitely the second time."

"Oh, he shouldn't have done that," Andrea said. "The first kiss should be soft and gentle. Otherwise it's a little weird."

Cassie felt a bit better. Maybe it wasn't her fault. "Really?"

"Sounds like he was in a hurry to move to other things." Andrea giggled. "Hey, I'm having a birthday party next week. Come?"

"Of course," Cassie said, tossing the thoughts of her failed first kiss into the back of her mind. It might not have lived up to expectations, but at least it increased her cool-factor in the eyes of her friends. She couldn't wait to see them and play up the event for their benefit.

Andrea had her birthday party a few days later.

"Come on in," Andrea said, holding the front door for her. "You're the last one here."

"Thanks," Cassie said. She followed Andrea to her bedroom and was surprised when she walked in and only saw Janice.

"Janice!" She hugged the other girl, who she hadn't seen all summer.

"How are you?" Janice asked, returning the embrace. "How's your summer been? Anything new and exciting?"

About that. Cassie didn't answer at first, instead turning to Andrea. "Where's everyone else?"

Andrea shrugged. "They're all fake. I only wanted you two."

Cassie looked at Janice and Janice shrugged. Cassie exhaled and sat down on the bed, her heart pounding with anticipation. She'd expected to have a bigger audience, but this would have to do. "Well, since you wanted to know . . . Josh kissed me."

"What?" Janice shrieked.

"Tell us everything again," Andrea said. Both girls piled on the bed beside Cassie.

"You've had your first kiss," Janice said, and Cassie thought she detected a look of envy in her eyes.

"He came over for the Fourth of July," Cassie said. "We went to Cara's house and watched fireworks. Then he took me home. Right before he left he took me to the driveway and . . . he kissed me."

"How was it?" Janice squealed. "Did it feel amazing?"

If it were just Janice, Cassie thought she might tell the truth. But the way Andrea looked at her with a knowing glint in her eye, as if she suspected Cassie was a horrible kisser, she couldn't. "Yes. It was so amazing. I felt all tingly inside and thought I'd explode like one of the fireworks."

"Oh, that's so romantic!" Janice hugged her pillow and fell back against the bed. "You must really like him."

Cassie's face warmed, and she picked at the bedspread. "Yeah. He's great."

"What about you?" Andrea raised her eyebrows. "Were you any good?" She smirked at her own brazenness.

"He said so," Cassie said, lifting her eyes. "He said I was a natural."

"Well, that definitely means something," Andrea said. "I think we need to watch a romance movie to celebrate. Come on, girls."

⟡

Cassie's phone rang partway though the movie, and Cassie picked it up. "It's Maureen."

Andrea paused the movie. "Don't tell her you're over here!"

Of course. What would their little group be without the secrets? "Hey," Cassie said, answering.

"Hey, Cassie," Maureen said. "Cara and I are having a slumber party tomorrow night. Want to come?"

"Yes," Cassie said, but her heart sank. She already knew her mom wouldn't let her. Two sleepovers in a row? No way. "I'll have to ask my mom, though."

"Just ask her right now."

"She's in bed." Back to the lying. "She works early." All her friends knew Mrs. Jones worked the breakfast shift at Wendy's, so that part would be believable.

"Oh, right. Well, let me know. It'll be so much fun, just the three of us."

"So fun. I'll call you back tomorrow." She hung up and sighed, wishing she could go. Cara was the one person she wanted to get to know better. But she was lucky her mom let her stay at Andrea's, since Cassie was leaving again this Sunday for Camp Splendor and then a creative arts camp and wouldn't be back for three weeks.

"I don't know why you want to hang out with her," Andrea said. "Maureen is such a liar. And she just wants people to feel bad about themselves."

"No, she's not," Cassie said. "Maureen's so sweet."

"You don't know her, Cassie," Janice said, like she and Andrea were the final authority. "Maureen will stab you in the back."

"She's worse when she's with Amity. The two of them just feed off each other. They think they're such a riot." Andrea rolled her eyes.

Cassie knew better than to buy into this. The girls must be fighting.

"Cara surprises me, though," Janice said. "I expect more from her, but then I hear about things she's doing, and I realize she's just as fake as Maureen and Amity."

Cassie blinked at her, hardly believing Janice would say that. "Cara?" Cara was the best of them all. She never lied and never made fun of people.

"Yeah." Janice sighed. "She's changed since she made cheerleading. Already those girls are having an influence on her."

"Hmm," Cassie said, not wanting to commit to the conversation either way. She hadn't noticed any changes, but maybe she needed to pay more attention.

As if reading her mind, Janice said, "You wouldn't notice, Cassie. You only see the best in everyone."

"Yeah," Andrea said. "You're the easiest person to be around."

Well, at least no one was mad at her. That was something. Cassie put the rest out of her mind and enjoyed the movie.

CHAPTER FOURTEEN
Boys and Girls

J ust as Cassie expected, Mrs. Jones said no to having a sleepover with Maureen and Cara. Cassie concealed her disappointment, focusing instead on her upcoming week at Camp Splendor. She and Riley had decided to do the "Roughin' It" camp, where they would have the opportunity to live in primitive camping conditions for a week.

Cassie was a bundle of nerves as Mrs. Jones drove her and Emily to Camp Splendor on Sunday. Cassie loved the Girls Club camp, but this year she'd only get to stay for half the time since she had an art camp that started midway through. She couldn't wait to see old friends and sing all the songs. Camp Splendor was the one place on earth where she felt like someone important. Everyone here liked her.

Except Riley. The past two summers the girls had gone together, Riley and Cassie had fought the entire time.

And that was why Cassie was nervous. If Riley made this week miserable for her, she'd be so mad.

Mrs. Jones dropped Cassie off at her campsite first. Cassie waved goodbye to her mom and sister as they drove to a different campsite. Then Cassie dragged her bags toward the platform tents.

"Hello, Cassandra!" Skippy, a counselor from the year before, waved to Cassie. "Great to see you here again!"

Cassie grinned and waved back. All of the counselors took fake names for camp. Having the counselors remember her filled Cassie with warmth and pride. "Can't keep me away," she said. "I love it here."

"Rainbow's your counselor again this year," Skippy said.

"Awesome." She and Rainbow hadn't gotten along the first year, but last year they'd done great together.

"Cassie's here!" Riley flew out of the tent, followed by two familiar faces: Ashley and Tina, girls Cassie knew already.

Riley nearly knocked her over with her hug. "Come on, there's one bed left for you. Is it all right if Ashley and Tina bunk with us?"

"Sure, of course." Cassie put her sleeping bag on the remaining mattress and glanced around. She loved the platform tents with their rolling canvas sides, pinned up in hot weather but dropping down in the rain. She breathed deeply, smelling the fresh air. "We're not too close to the latrine this year!"

"It's over there," Ashley said. She wore her short hair in pigtails.

"But it's not too far either," Riley said.

"Oh, good. Then no one will mind being my night buddy," Cassie said.

The girls laughed at her joke, just as Cassie had expected them to.

Skippy called all the campers up to the pavilion and gave the usual speech about using the buddy system anytime they went somewhere. She pulled the lid off a large plastic bin.

"And these are our snack bins," she said. "I need all food put in here. Otherwise you'll attract all kinds of critters!"

Cassie lifted an eyebrow at Riley, who always had food in her tent.

Riley waved her off. "Nothing's ever happened before, it's not going to happen now!"

Maybe Riley was right. "I won't tell as long as you share with me," Cassie whispered, leaning her head toward Riley.

"You can have as much as you want."

Cassie grinned and looped an arm over Riley's shoulders, her spirits soaring. They were off to a good start.

❦

"There's a boy at camp."

"There's a boy at camp."

"There's a boy at camp."

The whisper spread like wild fire among the girls, who giggled and chirped as excitedly as little birds.

"Is he the dishwasher?" Cassie asked Tina as they hiked to the mess hall for dinner. The first day at camp, and already thoughts of boys were ruining the atmosphere. Couldn't they forget about the opposite gender for a few days?

"He's the owner's son. I think he does whatever job they want him to do."

Cassie nodded. "I've met him. He was here last year."

"You've met him?" Tina's eyes just about bugged out of her head.

"Yeah. He liked my friend Tiffany." Tiffany hadn't come this year, Cassie noted. She missed seeing her bubbly friend.

"What's he look like?"

"Um . . ." Cassie narrowed her eyes in thought. "I'm not too sure. I can't remember him very well." He'd been interested in Tiffany, and Cassie had only noticed him in passing.

All the girls tried to catch glimpses of him as they delivered their dirty dinner dishes to the window. Cassie didn't.

"You girls are silly," she said when they sat down at her table again. "Did you come to a girls' camp to meet a guy?"

"You tell them, Cassie," Rainbow said.

That didn't stop them all from trying to see him.

The next morning brought a heat wave and thick, humid air.

"Put your swimsuits on," Skippy said, pausing at each tent. "After breakfast we'll ride over to the pool for swim tests."

The girls cheered.

Cassie picked at her breakfast, reminding herself that food was good fuel for a growing body. She settled on the eggs and cantaloupe. It was her turn to hop the table, but all the other campers fought over who got to turn the dishes in. Cassie sat back and watched.

"Did you see him?" she asked Tina when the girl returned to the table.

"No," Tina sighed. "Just his hands. But they look so manly."

Cassie giggled. "I'm sure."

Tina looked annoyed but didn't say anything else.

The girls rode the bus over to the pool so they could do their swim tests, which would allow them to jump off the diving board if they passed. Cassie gathered in the dressing room with everyone else and shoved her clothes into her bag. She spotted Emily and waved, then walked onto the pool deck just as a flurry of girls crowded around each other.

"He's here! He's here!" they giggled, pointing toward the diving well.

Cassie stood on tiptoes and lifted her head above them. A boy stood beside the diving board. The gaggle of girls approached him, and she examined him as she sat next to Ashley and Riley around the diving well. He had to be about her age with straight dark hair and a skinny body. A chain of dog tags rested against his chest.

He was kind of cute, she had to admit. But there was too much competition here. He would never notice someone like Cassie. She wasn't pretty and bubbly like Tiffany had been or flirtatious like Amity or sophisticated like Cara.

"Okay, anyone who wants to use the diving board has to pass the swim test!" Skippy said, marching in front of them and tearing the girls' eyes away from the boy. "You just dive in and swim to the side, and you pass. Ben, can you demonstrate?"

"Sure," he said. He climbed up on the board, his ribcage showing as he lifted his hands above his head. He took a deep breath, dipped his arms toward the water, and dove in.

A splash echoed behind him, and Cassie said, "Why does everyone like him? He's so bony."

All of the girls burst our laughing. Ben's head surfaced from the water, and his eyes flashed over the laughing crowd. For some reason they landed on Cassie, and he gave her a confused smile.

"What's so funny?"

"Oh, nothing." Cassie lifted her eyebrows, feeling guilty for making fun of him. "Just admiring your dive. Nicely done."

Around her the girls buried their faces in their knees, still laughing. He studied her a moment longer before swimming to the middle of the pool.

"Now you know how it's done," Skippy said. She tossed a lifeguard float to Ben. "If anyone needs help, Ben's there to save you."

"I so need help," Ashley said beside Cassie, and Ben's gaze turned their direction for a second. Just long enough for her to see the blue water reflecting in his light eyes.

Cassie stood up, trying to maintain her confident air. "Let's go diving."

CHAPTER FIFTEEN

Secret Crush

Swimming continued without any further excitement. Cassie passed her swim test, and she didn't need Ben to save her, even though he swam out to meet her and treaded water nearby until she climbed out.

They returned to their campsite and changed, then Rainbow sat them down and explained the prep work they would start for their primitive camp.

"In just a few days, we'll be sleeping at our primitive site," she said with a smile. "So enjoy the latrines while you can."

Cassie let out a noise that was a combination of a groan and a laugh.

"I can't believe you talked me into doing this unit," Riley complained as they walked back to their tent. "We actually have hot showers this year."

"Ironic." Cassie sat on her bed and pulled out a notebook. A letter from Josh fell out and fluttered to the ground, and she stared at it.

"What's this?" Riley picked it up.

"A letter from Josh." Cassie reached over and took it, not liking the heavy feeling in her chest.

"Can I read it?"

Cassie shrugged. "He's just all mushy." She lowered her voice. "We've kissed."

Riley's hand fluttered by her mouth. "You kissed someone!"

Cassie nodded. "But." She sighed. "You can't tell this to anyone."

Riley bobbed her head, eyes going wide. "I promise."

"I don't really like him anymore." Cassie spoke in a hush, as if afraid the trees would hear her secret and carry it back to Josh's ears. "I feel like I'm stuck, though. I can't break up with him."

"Why not?"

How could Cassie explain that her cool status was directly tied to Josh? "He likes me too much."

Riley shook her head. "That's not good enough if you don't like him."

No, it wasn't.

Cassie was still pondering those words when the girls began the long walk to the mess hall.

"Hey, Cassie?"

Skippy moved to the front of the line and beckoned to Cassie just as she was about to go inside. Cassie let go of the screen door and let it swing shut, then followed Skippy over to the grass.

"Yes?" Her stomach clenched nervously. Was she about to get in trouble for something? Maybe making fun of Ben?

"I just wanted you to know . . . Ben has a crush on you."

"What?" Cassie crinkled her nose. "No, he doesn't."

"He does. He asked me who you were and told me." Skippy grinned. "And he has no idea you said what you did."

Cassie put her hands to her mouth, horrified. "Are you serious?"

"Yes. But don't tell anyone."

"Me?" No way. Her? He liked her! Of all the girls here, he liked Cassie?

Skippy patted her on the shoulder. "Let's get some lunch."

Cassie's mind reeled as she sat down to eat. What did this mean? How could he like her?

"Can you be a hopper, Cassie?" Rainbow asked.

"Oh, yes." Cassie got up and went through the kitchen to get the vegetable dish.

A large woman and Ben stood behind the counter, handing over dishes as the girls walked through. Ben spotted her, and a smile lit his face, crinkling the corners of his eyes. He pushed a green bean platter toward her.

Cassie's face flushed, and something tickled her chest. "Thank you." She delivered the vegetables to her table, then went back to get the main dish.

Ben was waiting for her, catching her eye when she entered and grinning at her the whole time. Cassie couldn't help it. She smiled back. She grabbed the plate of patties and hurried out.

After lunch the girls gathered around the hearth and sang songs, and thoughts of Ben and his smile kept creeping up on Cassie. She hadn't expected to be affected by his attention this way, but she wondered about him now. What kind of a person was he? What would they say to each other if they talked?

A light sprinkle started as the girls began the walk back to their unit. The morning had been unbearably muggy, and the rain brought a cool relief to the air. Skippy gathered them under the pavilion.

"So this will be our schedule most days," she said. "Breakfast, swim, prep time, lunch, and now quiet time. You can use this time to write letters, read, take a nap, anything that's quiet."

A crash of thunder startled Cassie enough that she jumped, and several of the girls actually screamed. As if the thunder had ripped open the sky, sheets of water cascaded down on the campsite.

"Go close your tents!" Skippy yelled, her voice barely audible over the racket of the rain. "Remember this is quiet time!"

Cassie bolted from the pavilion, trying to protect her head from the torrential downpour. It was no use; she was soaked before she even made it to her tent. She ran around the outside, her fingers struggling with the rope now saturated with water. She had to untie the knots so the canvas walls could come down!

A pick-up truck careened into the campground, and the girls turned to watch as Ben jumped out of the passenger side as it ground to a halt, followed by his dad on the other side.

"We'll help!" Ben shouted. Water streamed from the bill of his baseball cap. His eyes scanned the girls and landed on Cassie, and then he ran toward her tent.

"Saw the rain coming," his dad was saying to Skippy. "We were closest to your unit."

"Come on," Ben said, his fingers deftly untying the canvas flaps. Cassie raced to the next one and managed to loosen it before he came over, his hands gliding over hers as he undid the knot.

In a moment their flaps were down, and Ashley and Tina ducked inside. Cassie glanced around and saw many girls still struggling with their knots. The rope got harder to maneuver as it got wet, the fibers becoming thick and heavy.

"We have to help the others," Cassie said, and she darted away.

Ben chased after her. "You take that side, I'll take this one."

"Get in the tent," Cassie told the girls who had been trying. They were shaking and soaked to the bone.

The cold rain chilled her too, but she managed to get the knot undone. Ben beat her to the fourth flap, and then the tent was enclosed.

Cassie turned around, brushing water from her face, her hair clinging to her neck.

"They're all good," Ben said, stepping up to her. His hand brushed her wrist, his fingers glancing over her skin, and a rush of warmth shivered up her arm, bringing goosebumps to her flesh.

"My dad and I have to help the other units," he said. "You're freezing.

Go get dry!"

"Yeah," Cassie said with a nod. She ran back to her tent and stepped inside the canvas, immediately wrapped in the darkness. Her body shook as she knelt by her suitcase and searched for a towel.

"It's raining hard," Tina said.

"Good thing Ben came by," Ashley said. "That was good timing."

"I don't think it was an accident," Riley said, her tone meaningful.

Cassie said nothing as she stripped out of her wet clothes and hauled on some dry ones. Then she crawled into her sleeping bag.

"Where did you go, Cassie?" Tina asked.

"To help some of the other girls get their tents closed," Cassie responded, staring up at the darkened tent ceiling. Her eyes were adjusting to the dimness now, and she could make out the wooden rafter in the middle.

"Did Ben go with you?"

"Yes," she said without thinking. And then she amended, "He wanted to help also."

"He wanted to help you," Riley said.

Cassie sat up and looked at her friend, sitting on the bed adjacent to Cassie's. "He wanted to help everyone."

Ashley and Tina watched their conversation like it was a volleyball match. Cassie lay back on the bed, unable to banish from her mind Ben's expression when he told her to get dry, or the feeling when his hand had touched hers.

⁂

The rain stopped half an hour later.

"Time to go to the trading post and see if we got mail!" Rainbow said, poking her head into Cassie's tent.

"I won't have anything yet," Cassie said to Riley as they trooped through the mud back to the trading post. "My mom might not write at all, since I'm only here for one week."

"Yeah," Riley said. "My mom's not so good at that either."

The trading post was next to the dining hall, and only a ten-minute walk from the campsite. The girls went around the back where the mailbox was, and Cassie pulled up short when she saw Ben at the box, holding a stack of envelopes in his hand.

"What are you doing here?" she blurted, immediately drawing the attention of every girl in her unit.

His cheeks colored. "Just helping. Sometimes they ask me to sort mail for the units."

"Oh." Could it be that coincidental? She watched him put letters into the different unit boxes, then he handed a stack to Rainbow.

"This is for your group." He glanced at Cassie again and gave her a smile before walking away.

There was no hiding that, and a circle formed around her, the girls more interested in finding out what was going on between them than getting letters from home.

"He likes you!" Ashley breathed.

"I knew it," Riley said.

"He's so cute!" another girl said.

"Do you like him?" Tina asked. "Because if you don't, I'm all over that . . ."

"I have a boyfriend," Cassie said. Dully. Regretfully. Because she didn't want to be Josh's girlfriend anymore.

Cassie wasn't asked to hop tables at dinner, and she wondered if Ben was behind the counter, watching for her.

The counselors gathered the girls around the hearth after dinner for singing time. Then Skippy said, "Cassie, can you come up and lead us in a few songs? You've been coming for years. I bet you know almost all of them."

"Sure," Cassie said. She stood up and made her way up to the hearth by the counselors. There weren't a lot of things Cassie considered herself good at, but she excelled at singing. She took a deep breath, then confidently sang songs she knew the girls would recognize and could sing along to.

A head poked out the kitchen doors during the second song, and then it disappeared just as quickly. She thought she recognized the baseball cap as the same one Ben had been wearing when he helped them take down their tent sides.

The head appeared again during the fourth song, and this time she knew it was Ben. He hovered in the kitchen doorway before disappearing again.

Her heart pounded so hard she almost forgot the words. What did all of this mean?

Several songs later, the girls grouped according to units and headed for the doors.

"Hey," Ben said, popping out of the kitchen just as she walked by. "You have a really beautiful voice."

"Thank you," Cassie said, the compliment filling her with a strange glowing feeling.

She looked down to hide her smile as she walked with Riley and Ashley to the closing flag ceremony, but she couldn't keep it off her lips.

CHAPTER SIXTEEN
Desire and Want

The next day dawned bright and warm, and the girls took the time to tie up their canvases. Cassie felt the water evaporating from the earth like an organic steam bath, sticking to her skin and forming droplets on her upper lip.

"Don't forget to put your swimsuits on, we'll go to the pool right after we eat!" Rainbow told them.

For some reason Cassie's thoughts immediately flashed to Ben. Would he be there?

Why did she even care? Her stomach tightened, and she tried not to analyze her motives.

She couldn't help glancing around as she entered the dining hall, her eyes scanning the open entrance to the kitchen, but only the cook was there, filling plates with pancakes and fruit.

"Want to be a food hopper, Cassie?" Rainbow asked.

"Sure," Cassie said. Maybe he just hadn't come yet.

But Ben didn't show up all through breakfast, and by the time they left for swimming, Cassie had swallowed her disappointment and shoved him from her mind. Ah, well. It was better this way, anyway.

Skippy handed out colored bracelets as the girls wandered over to the pool. "Cassie, you're an intermediate swimming level," she said, handing her a green one.

"Yay," Cassie murmured, wrapping it around her wrist. At least she wasn't a beginner.

She found a chair and dropped her towel on it, then headed for the line forming behind the diving board.

A low murmur rose and carried across the pool deck, and Cassie turned her head to see Ben and his dad walking in, both in flip-flops and with towels over their shoulders. She stopped moving as a gooey fluttery feeling started in her abdomen and tickled her belly.

Ben put his towel on a chair and kicked off his flip-flops, then walked straight to her.

"Hi," he said.

"Hi," Cassie replied. Her eyes traveled over his bare torso with only the dog tags, the summer tan on his skin. Then they landed on his face, on the bluish-gold eyes framed by long, dark lashes. She was aware of the silence on deck, of every single eye focused on them.

"Are you going to dive?" he asked.

"I was," she said.

"Keep going. I'll lifeguard the diving well."

The thought of him watching her swim made her throat tighten, and Cassie had half a mind to turn back to the swimming pool instead. But she gathered her courage. "Okay."

She told herself he wasn't in the water watching her. That all the other girls weren't staring at her. But she felt their eyes like a hundred pinpricks on her skin.

She got to the edge of the diving board and paused. The blue water sparkled back at her, beckoning her. She pictured herself doing a graceful swan dive, parting the liquid like an Olympic athlete. In reality, she'd probably belly flop. Cassie decided to skip the dive and just jump.

She hit the water feet first, and when she came up, she felt, with a sense of relief, that the spell was broken. Chatter had resumed on the pool deck. Ben swam over to her, pulling her arms unto the red flotation device.

"I got it," she said, embarrassed. "I can swim to the side."

"That's okay," Ben said. "I don't mind helping." But he didn't kick them over to the wall. Instead he treaded water in place beside her, his arms loped over the flotation device from the other side.

"So you like coming here?" he said. "You know a lot of the songs."

Cassie nodded, her own legs spinning circles to keep her upright. "This is my third summer." And then she added, before she could think better of it, "I met you last year."

"You did?" His eyebrows lifted in surprise.

"You liked my friend, Tiffany. I met you when you asked her out."

"Oh." His cheeks reddened. "I thought you looked kind of familiar."

Cassie's face warmed too. "But you're not still going out with her, are you?"

"No," he said quickly. "No, we broke up a long time ago."

So you're free, Cassie thought.

What a nice feeling that must be.

Cassie didn't see Ben at lunch. Skippy and Rainbow led the girls to the primitive site, deep in the forest, where they'd be setting up their tents and making a minimal campsite.

"First we have to do a few essential things," Skippy said. "Like make a toilet." She showed them a diagram in a book of a toilet stand, which consisted of tree trunks with branches stretched between them to form a seat, a toilet paper holder made of sticks, and a hole dug in the ground between the branches.

"There are sixteen of us," Skippy said. "So we need at least four of these toilets."

"And are they just going to be out in the open?" a girl named Jennifer asked.

"Yep," Skippy said, grinning. "That's why we call this roughing it! So put your toilet somewhere private!"

The girls tittered nervously, and Tina asked, "What if Ben or his dad come by?" She shot a look at Cassie like that would be her fault.

"They won't. Once we move over here, we'll be completely isolated from the rest of the camp. We won't eat with them or swim with them or see them. It will just be us."

It sounded both liberating and suffocating. Cassie hoped this was a good idea.

"You'll need to chop a few trees down to make your toilet seat. Now, when you're chopping, you want to have what we call a blood circle. Hold your hatchet out like this—" Skippy gripped the small ax in her hand and hefted it straight in front of her, "and move in a slow circle. Anyone within that circle is in danger. Stay clear of each other. And that's what you yell when your tree is coming down. 'Clear!' If you hear that, stop what you're doing and check the sky so no trees land on you!"

Crapola. This kept getting more complicated.

"So grab your hatchets and go fell trees! Don't pick the giant ones, we want the ones with tree trunks as thick as your arm."

The bin of hatchets was at Skippy's feet. Cassie waited in line behind Riley, then she grabbed one and headed after her friend.

"How hard do you think it is to chop down a tree?" Cassie asked, selecting a slender trunk and checking her blood circle. All safe.

"Doesn't seem like it would be too hard." Riley spun in a circle. She came to a stop and began hacking at her own tree trunk. Cassie followed suit.

Twenty minutes later, Cassie's arm ached. She didn't feel she could lift it one more time. Sweat dripped from her forehead and into her eyes.

And yet all she'd made was a tiny inch of an indentation in the tree trunk.

"I gotta take a break," she said, slapping at a mosquito that buzzed around her face.

"These trees are like super dense," Riley said, crouching beside Cassie.

"It's like they're made of wood or something," Cassie said, and they both chuckled.

Cassie didn't want to lift her hatchet any more, but after about five minutes, she stood. "I guess we should get these trees down."

"Yeah," Riley sighed, and they both went back to hacking.

The burn traveled from Cassie's arm all the way up to her shoulder. Then it moved across her shoulder blades and down the side of her back. The tree began to shudder with each hack, the leaves trembling and swaying.

"I think I've almost got it," Cassie said. Less than an inch remained to chop through.

Riley looked over. "Give it a good push. It'll come down."

Anything to not lift the hatchet again. Cassie put it down and shoved her body against the trunk. It gave a loud snap, and Cassie barely had time to yell, "Clear!" before it bent at a ninety degree angle and crashed to the ground.

"Yay! Our first tree down!" Riley said, doing a happy jig.

"Are you close?" Cassie asked.

"Nearly."

Cassie grabbed the tree trunk and grunted with the effort of trying to lift it. "This is really heavy."

"I'll help." Riley grabbed the other end. "Where do we want our toilet to be?"

They needed something to lash their branches to and make the seat, and Cassie spotted two trees about three feet apart. "Let's just do it right here. Then we don't have to go so far."

"This is going to be really interesting," Riley muttered.

Five minutes later Riley had her tree down.

"We need a shovel and the rope now," Cassie said.

The two of them returned to the clearing and retrieved the necessary items from Skippy's bins of supplies, then returned to build their toilet.

Cassie dug the hole, saving the dirt so they could cover the waste when they finished, just as instructed. "Do you think this is deep enough?"

"Oh, this is so sick," Riley said, her face a little green.

"For real," Cassie agreed. She had a sudden mental image of Amity or Andrea trying to do this, and she laughed. "I'm really glad I'm here with you."

"I definitely would not feel this comfortable with anyone else," Riley said.

They exchanged a smile and Cassie finished digging while Riley ran the twine around the standing trees. They hefted one they'd downed into position, Cassie trembling under the strain of holding it in place while Riley secured it to the trees. One log they put in front of the tree trunks, and the other they put behind them, slightly higher so it could act like a seat back.

"So we have something to lean on while we poop," Cassie said, and she and Riley collapsed into giggles.

"We need a sign we can put right here," Riley said, stepping back a few feet. "With a warning on it. And we can flip it over when the toilet's not in use."

"Warning: hazardous material," Cassie said, and the two of them were still laughing when they made their way back to the clearing.

Cassie volunteered to be food hopper for the third time that day at dinner, even though she hadn't seen Ben the other two meals.

This time she was rewarded. She felt a spike of pleasure in her stomach when she walked into the kitchen and saw him loading up serving trays.

"It's you," he said.

"It's me," she confirmed, grabbing the tray of okra.

"Wait." Ben grabbed two more okras from the skillet and added them to her plate. "Your table gets extra okra. Because they have you."

Her face grew hot. "Thanks."

She delivered the plate of okra and went back into the kitchen for the main dish. Ben smiled when he saw her, and she smiled back, picking one of the plates of fried chicken.

"Hang on," he said, and Cassie waited while he grabbed up a few more okras. He dumped them on the plate of chicken. "In case you need more."

She looked at them and laughed. "I'm not sure anyone at my table loves okra that much."

"What?" He looked offended. "Okra is manna from heaven. It's soul food. I love it." He cocked his head at her. "Don't you?"

"I do now," she said, and he laughed.

Cassie delivered the plate of chicken, her chest tingling. Then she returned to the kitchen for the last dish, a bowl of mashed potatoes.

She didn't see Ben when she stepped inside, but she knew instantly which bowl was for her table.

The mashed potatoes had been piled high into a mountain, and two okra sat on top.

The counselors didn't ask Cassie to lead the songs after dinner, which disappointed her a little bit. But she was a good sport about it, singing enthusiastically even if the songs they picked weren't always the ones she would have chosen.

And then after several songs, Rainbow said, "Cassie, can you sing a song for us?"

"Sure," Cassie said, surprised and delighted. "A Girls Club song?"

Rainbow shrugged. "Any song you like."

Cassie thought of a song she loved from a musical that had been in the theater a few months ago. Miss Malcolm had even gotten the music for her so Cassie could practice it during voice lessons. Feeling confident in her choice, Cassie stood up in front of everyone and started singing.

She was only a few stanzas into the song when Ben stepped out of the kitchen again. He had the same baseball cap on his head, which seemed to emphasize the dark lashes around his eyes. And the look he gave her was so intense that Cassie had to turn her gaze elsewhere or she wouldn't be able to concentrate.

She finished the song to cheers and claps from the girls. Ben cupped his hands around his mouth and shouted, "Encore! Encore!"

"We have to head back to our units now," Skippy said. "But we'll definitely let Cassie sing for us again. It's such a nice experience."

"Time for the flag ceremony!" the camp leader, Zelda, said.

The girls obediently straightened up and exited the mess hall in a single file line, heading for the meadow where the flagpole was. Flag ceremony was something they did every morning and every evening, honoring the national emblem by raising and lowering it at light and dark.

Cassie ended up at the back of the group, and a moment later Ben joined her.

"Wow," he said. "I knew there was something really neat about you, but I didn't know you could sing like that."

She tried not to look too proud. She lowered her eyes and smiled at his praise. "I love to sing. I think it's the one thing I do really well."

"I'll say. You're a natural with a voice like that."

"Well," Cassie said, "I have had training." She couldn't accept all of his praise. Ms. Malcolm deserved some of the credit.

"You can't train what isn't there. Someone could try to teach me to sing all day long and all they would get is a croaking frog."

"But it would be a very lovely croaking frog," Cassie said, doing her best to look consolatory.

Ben chuckled and shook his head. "I guess if you're into that sort of thing." He winked at her, and Cassie flushed warm. Nobody had ever embarrassed her as much as he did. He must think she was really weird.

"Well, I better get going to flag ceremony," she said, unsure how else to finish the conversation. They were the only people left in the mess hall; the other girls were spread out across the meadow.

"Yeah. I'll see you later."

His foot nudged hers before he walked away. Cassie went outside, wondering the whole time how someone's shoe touching hers could leave her insides feeling all jittery.

CHAPTER SEVENTEEN

Night Time Visitor

On Wednesday no one even batted an eye when Ben joined Cassie at the big pool.

"Diving today?"

"Maybe later," Cassie said. "Right now I'm just enjoying the warm sunshine."

Ben sprawled out on a pool chair beside her. "It is a beautiful day, isn't it?"

Cassie tipped her head back and squinted toward the sky. "It's not hot yet and it's not raining. That makes it perfect." The warm rays of the sun caressed her skin like gentle kisses, and she gave a delicious shiver. "I love summertime."

"Looks like summertime loves you. You're so tan. You spend a lot of time in the sun?"

Cassie held her arm out in front of her, examining the darker skin tone. "My mom said once she thinks we have Native American blood. Nobody else in my family is this dark, though. I'm the only one."

"That explains it. I met your sister yesterday, and she looks nothing like you."

He'd met Emily? Cassie wondered how that conversation had gone. "Yeah, she looks more like my dad."

Ben straightened his arm and pressed it beside hers. "I'm a white boy next to you."

Cassie laughed. He really was, even though he had a bit of a tan compared to some of the girls here. "Oh, well. I won't hold it against you."

He bumped her shoulder with his. "That's nice of you."

His dog tags rattled when he moved, and Cassie touched one with her finger. "Why do you wear these? Is it army related?"

"Oh, no." He laughed and held up one for her to see. "All staffers got one. It's like a status thing for volunteering at camp."

"Cool," Cassie said, reading his name inscribed in the metal. Ben Graves.

She never did make it to the diving well. In fact, for the first time ever, she didn't swim at all.

After lunch it was her unit's turn to do crafts. They followed the path through the forest away from the mess hall and gathered in the lodge at the bottom of the hill. Cassie did not enjoy crafts and could never think of anything cool to do. While the other girls went through boxes of paper and glue and wax and leftover wood, Cassie found skeins of string and decided to make bracelets. That was one thing she knew how to do. And what better than friendship bracelets to give to her friends at camp?

Cassie looked over at Riley and tried to think what her favorite colors were. She wore a lot of orange and blue. Maybe those were her favorites.

Cassie started braiding the colors but thought that was rather boring, so she switched to doing a braid with four strands, which was just complicated enough to give it a different look. And then she took a bead and strung it on as well, adding more dimension to the bracelet.

She couldn't help thinking of Ben while she braided. Something inside of her lit up every time he was near her, and she felt such happiness she was afraid she would burst. No one had ever made her feel this way before.

She added another bead, a blue one this time. She tilted her head, studying the bracelet. She had thought she was making it for Riley, but the shades of blue and orange were rather masculine. In fact, this bracelet would look much better on a boy than a girl.

Cassie smiled and continued with her braiding. She knew who this bracelet was for, and it wasn't Riley.

❦

Ben was at the trading post again when Cassie's unit went to pick up their mail. This time he was behind the concessions window where the girls could buy sodas and snacks with their own money.

"You got a letter," he said to Cassie.

"I did? I didn't expect my mom to write me!"

"It's not from your mom," he said, and then he turned his attention to the girl behind her.

Something about his demeanor felt a little distant. Cassie tilted her head and stepped to the side, watching him interact with the other girls from her unit. Then she went over to Skippy to wait for her letter.

"Cassandra!" Skippy crowed, holding the letter out to Cassie.

Cassie accepted it, taking a few steps away from the group to examine it.

It was from Josh. Her heart tumbled into her stomach, making her feel slightly ill. He had actually put hearts around her name.

No wonder Ben was acting cold. She couldn't even defend herself. She wandered over to a fallen log some distance away and opened the envelope.

"You okay?" Riley settled down beside her, sipping a soda she had probably purchased from Ben. "I haven't seen you looking down this whole week."

Cassie waved the envelope at her. "It's from Josh."

"Oh. Your boyfriend." Riley raised an eyebrow. "I almost forgot you have one."

"Yeah." Cassie swallowed hard. "Me too." She pulled the paper out and read through it.

Dear Cassie,

I was really worried when you quit texting me back. I was afraid maybe I crossed a line by kissing you.

Ah. Cassie shuddered as she remembered that ill-fated kiss.

I hope you don't mind, I called your house line and was so relieved when your mom told me you're at camp and you're not allowed to have your phone. So I got your camp address and wrote you.

I know you love camping, so I'm sure you're having fun. At least I don't have to worry about there being any guys hitting on you when you're at a girls camp.

If he only knew.

I can't stop thinking about you. Your hot lips. I keep remembering the feel of your soft, perfect—

Stomach acid burned the back of her throat. "Oh, I can't read anymore." Cassie tossed the paper aside.

Riley picked it up. "Mind if I do?"

Cassie waved a hand. "I don't care."

Riley gave a little giggle also. "'Your soft perfect mouth'?"

"Oh please! Don't torture me!" Cassie put her face in her hands.

"Well, that's what you get for kissing him!" Riley handed the envelope back and lowered her voice. "Ben's watching you."

"This is bad," Cassie whispered. "I really like him."

"What are you going to do?"

Cassie sat up and took a deep breath. "I'll have to tell him about Josh. And then I'll have to break up with Josh just as soon as I can." But would it be soon enough? Once Cassie left camp, would she even be able to see Ben?

Cassie hopped tables again at dinner, but Ben wasn't there, and it hurt her heart not to see him. Was he avoiding her? Did he think she was a horrible person?

She volunteered to clear the dishes and was rewarded when she saw Ben behind the small opening, accepting the dirty plates. He saw her also, met her eyes, but his expression was more wary than anything else.

"Oh, hey," Cassie said. "Can I talk to you after singing time?"

"I'll be here," he said.

She nodded and returned to her table, feeling a bit relieved. At least he hadn't said no.

The thought of their impending conversation left Cassie more nervous than getting ready for All-Region choir tryouts, and she could hardly sing as Skippy led the girls through a bunch of songs. She saw Emily glance at her when she wasn't singing, but Emily was sitting with her group of friends and she stayed with them.

Once again the girls lined up to do the closing flag ceremony, and once again Cassie lagged behind. She stood by the window watching the campers file out to the meadow, twisting her fingers around each other.

"Hey."

Cassie spun around to see Ben there, his eyes appraising. She gave a weak smile. "Thanks for hearing me out."

He put his hands in his pockets and shrugged. "Sure. What's up?"

She took a deep breath. "I know you saw the letter I got. I just wanted to explain it."

He tilted his head and didn't say anything.

Cassie opened her mouth to spill everything, but instead of the truth, another story tumbled out. "That's from my ex-boyfriend. He was kind of obsessive crazy about me, and he got my address from my mom. I didn't even tell him I was going to be here."

She watched as Ben's shoulders relaxed, and he gave a slow nod. "Well, I'm not surprised he can't get over you. You're one of a kind."

That delicious feeling returned to Cassie's chest, and she reached out a hand, wanting physical contact with Ben. He met her halfway, grasping her fingers with his. The sensation left Cassie warm and giddy, and she never wanted him to let go.

"I'm sorry you had to find out that way," she said.

He shook his head. "I shouldn't even have worried about it. I just thought maybe you had a boyfriend you hadn't told me about."

The contact between their fingers suddenly felt hot and oppressive, and Cassie fought the urge to pull her hand back. "No. Nothing like that."

Crapola. She was in hot water.

"I can't believe you didn't tell him the truth," Riley said.

"It's practically the truth! I don't like Josh anymore and I'm going to break up with him!"

The two girls stood at the water spigot by the pavilion at their campsite, brushing their teeth before bed. Cassie's hand trembled with a nervous desperation to make Riley understand. "You won't say anything to him, will you?"

"No. What would I say? I don't want him to hate you."

"Ha, yeah, that's what I'm trying to avoid also."

They used their flashlights to shine the way back to their tent. Inside, Ashley and Tina were sharing a bag of chips.

"You said we could have this one, right?" Tina asked, lifting the bag.

Riley waved a hand. "Yeah, that's fine. I have lots."

So unlike the Riley of previous years, when she practically made Cassie beg and grovel to get a treat.

Cassie climbed into her sleeping bag and listened to the girls make small talk. Ashley asked about Ben once, but Riley changed the subject, saying they weren't supposed to talk about him.

Cassie closed her eyes and played out in her head how she would break up with Josh. It would be an uncomfortable conversation, even if it was nothing more than a phone call.

She drifted off to sleep and dreamed she sat with Josh in the kitchen while Ben was at the table.

"I'm going to break up with him, I promise," she tried to reassure Ben.

"Something's on me! Something's on me!"

The girly cry broke through Cassie's sleep, and she sat up, opening her eyes to the darkness. "What is it?" She fumbled for her flashlight and shone it in Ashley's direction.

Ashley was sitting up on her bed, running her hands all over her body. "It was on me!"

"What was it?" Cassie asked.

Riley's light flipped on also, and she sat up.

"You're imagining it," Tina said, her voice drunk with sleepiness. "It was a dream. Just go back to sleep."

Ashley hesitated, still running her hands over her clothes and her sleeping bag. "I guess so," she murmured.

Cassie turned the light out and fell back on her sleeping bag. But a moment later, Tina let out a shriek.

"Ahh!"

The lights came back on as Tina whacked something off her cot. It flew to the floor of the platform tent and scurried under Ashley's bed.

Now all the girls were up, slipping out of their sleeping bags.

"What was it?" Riley cried.

Cassie crouched on the ground, peering under the bed. "I don't know. But it was small."

Ashley climbed into her cot and pulled her knees up to her chest, breathing hard. "I'm not going back to sleep until we get rid of it."

A small, furry creature with a long tail scurried in the path of Cassie's light before disappearing under Riley's bed.

"It's a mouse!" Cassie said, relieved it wasn't something worse.

"I can't sleep with it under my bed!" Riley said.

Cassie agreed. She wasn't going back to sleep with the little critter running around their tent, possibly climbing on top of her sleeping bag. She could just imagine it burying itself in her hair or nibbling on her toes. "Move everything to the center of the tent."

The girls climbed off their beds and began putting everything in the middle of the platform.

"There it is, there it is!" Tina shouted, pointing under Riley's bed.

Cassie was amazed the counselors hadn't woken up. She shone her light on the mouse, which quickly scurried from Riley's bed to Cassie's.

"How do we get it out of here?" Ashley asked, looking petrified of the little rodent.

"We can't catch it," Riley said.

"We have to scare it away," Cassie said.

"If we have a broom we can try and shove him off," Tina said.

"They have brooms at the pavilion," Riley said.

Cassie jammed her feet into her shoes. "Come on. Let's get some brooms."

Five minutes later, each of them armed with a broom, the four girls manage to evict the mouse from their tent.

"I can't even believe that happened," Tina gasped, still looked petrified.

Cassie arched an eyebrow and looked over at Riley. "I can. It's been a long time coming."

"Yes," Riley said. She bent over and picked up a handful of chips and cookies and other snacks. "It's time we locked these things up in a bin."

Once again the girls trekked up to the pavilion. This time they left behind the brooms and all of their snack food safely shut in a plastic tub.

⚬⟳⟲⚬

Cassie woke up headachy and grumpy. It hadn't been the best night for her. To make things worse, it was raining, and as the girls donned ponchos for the walk to the mess hall, she knew they wouldn't be swimming.

That meant she wouldn't get the chance to talk with Ben.

Instead the girls were assigned cleanup duty, and after all the other units trudged back in the rain to their campsites, Cassie and her friends got out the brooms and mops and started cleaning the mess hall.

"This feels familiar," Cassie said, taking the broom.

"At least we're not chasing mice this time," Riley said.

"No swimming. And it's raining, so I don't think we'll get to work on our primitive campsite," Cassie said, sweeping crumbs and items that had fallen off the table from breakfast into the dust pan. "We'll probably spend the day making crafts again."

"Cheer up," Riley said. "I'm sure you'll see Ben at some point today."

Cassie favored her with a grin. "I'm sure you're right," she said, trying to focus on that.

Cassie didn't see Ben at lunch, even though she volunteered to hop tables again. It was still raining outside, and the rain contributed to a rather long, boring day at camp.

"Cassie, will you lead us in a song?" Skippy asked when they gathered for singing time. "Something upbeat."

That she could do. She stayed at the front of the group and began the song by clapping her hand to one thigh and then the other, followed by tapping the elbow before her hands came together. Then she repeated it on the other side. The girls immediately followed suit, recognizing the song. They clapped out the rhythm for several beats before Cassie began to sing.

"There are suitors at my door," she sang, and the others joined in.

A head poked out of the little window where the dirty dishes went. Ben. Cassie smiled at him as she sang, and he made faces at her. She nearly giggled but didn't tear her eyes away from his face.

Some of the other girls swiveled their heads to see what she was looking at and then turned back to face her. They looked at her knowingly, conspiratorially, but also with camaraderie, and Cassie realized they were enjoying her and Ben's relationship almost as much as she was.

CHAPTER EIGHTEEN

The Morning After

Cassie expected to see Ben at the trading post that afternoon, but he wasn't there. Zelda, the camp leader was, though, and she pulled Skippy aside, where they had what looked like an uncomfortable discussion. Zelda's arms gesticulated emphatically, and Skippy didn't look happy as she listened.

Cassie stayed under the eaves to avoid the rain drops and watched them, an uneasy feeling forming in her chest. One time Skippy's eyes slipped toward Cassie, and that feeling solidified. They had to be talking about her.

Zelda walked away and Skippy returned to the trading post, but she didn't look at Cassie or say a word about the conversation. Cassie tried to shrug it off, but Ben's absence suddenly felt more conspicuous.

When the girls began the trek back to the campsite, ponchos over their heads to shield them from the rain, Skippy called Cassie to the back of the line.

"What is it?" Cassie asked, that knot of dread returning.

Skippy spoke in a low voice so that Cassie had to strain to hear over the raindrops. "Zelda isn't happy that we've been letting Ben talk to you. She feels like it's not an appropriate activity for Girls Club camp."

The sick feeling intensified, and a lump formed in her throat. "But we're not doing anything wrong. We just talk to each other."

Skippy gave her a sympathetic smile. "I know. But she's coming down hard on the counselors, telling them not to let you two talk to each other."

Cassie fought back tears. If she didn't talk to Ben here and now, when would she?

Skippy squeezed her shoulder and then let go. "So what you need to do is be more discrete. If you see Zelda around, don't talk to him."

Cassie blinked, and then she looked up at Skippy. She understood immediately what her counselor was saying: she could talk to Ben as long as nobody else noticed. Nobody who mattered, anyway.

"Do you think you can do that?"

Cassie smiled, the tears already drying up. "I think I can manage that."

⁂

The rain cleared up in the early afternoon, so Skippy and Rainbow took the girls out to the primitive campsite.

"It's time to set up our tents," Skippy said. "These aren't the kind of tents you're used to. There are no poles to help this thing stay up." She opened the bag and pulled out a green canvas. "These are old school tents, the kind you've probably only seen in movies."

She then proceeded to demonstrate how to put up an A-frame tent. She flattened the canvas across the rocky ground. "These pegs are your stakes. Secure them through the loops found on the corners of the tents." Using a hammer, Skippy pounded the pegs through the appointed loops. "Then you connect your metal poles together—like this—and insert it here to hold your tent up." The canvas lifted from the ground as Skippy wedged the poles against the dirt, and the proper A-frame appeared. "Make sure you use your rope to hold it upright." Skippy dusted her hands off and smiled at the erected tent. "There."

Cassie replayed the steps in her head. It hadn't looked too hard.

"Now get your buddy, find a tent site, and start putting up your tent. Don't forget to lay down a tarp first!"

"The tarp goes under the tent, right?" Cassie said.

"Yes, we have rainflies for the top," Skippy said. "You don't want to be sleeping on wet ground!"

Cassie rolled her eyes, remembering a camp out she had taken years ago when she couldn't figure out whether the tarp went under or on top. She'd actually guessed wrong, and she and Janice had ended up soaking wet by morning.

"Come on, buddy," Riley said, grabbing one of the bags. "Let's put up this tent."

She and Riley tried to find a less-rocky spot, but their choices were rocks or tiny shrubs, so they chose the rocks. Cassie looked at the ground where they had laid the tarp and where they planned on putting the tent. The tent was open, no zippers to close it. "I think if it rains, we're going to be very uncomfortable." She could imagine all of the water collecting on the tarp and the two of them sitting in it.

"Let's pray it doesn't rain."

Riley put the poles together for the canvases, and Cassie pulled the rainfly over the top of the tent. She started staking the sides down through the loops, using a large rock as a hammer to pound the metal stakes into the ground.

Riley stood inside the tent and put the last pole up at the front. The tent was slightly lopsided, though. Cassie cocked her head, examining it, and then she yanked hard on the side of the canvas to straighten it.

"Cassie! What are you doing?" Riley only managed a yell before the entire tent collapsed on her.

Cassie let out a worried yelp and hurried to the front, pulling the canvas off the ground. "Riley! Are you okay?"

The only response was what sounded like a gasp, and Cassie tried not to panic as she peeled back layers of canvas. And then the noise was followed by a low giggle, and Cassie took another breath.

"You collapsed the tent on me!" Riley cried.

"I'm so sorry!" Cassie said, still trying to find Riley beneath the folds of the tent. She managed to grasp her hand and retrieve her out of the canvas.

"Lucky the side beams fell a different direction," Riley said, laughing.

A red pick-up truck pulled into the campsite, and Riley and Cassie both turned to stare at it. Cassie's heart gave a little drum roll. It was Mr. Fix-it's truck. Would Ben be there? Was he in that truck?

He was. The doors opened, and both Ben and his father sprang out. His dad wandered off to talk to Skippy while Ben came over to Cassie and Riley, smiling so hard his eyes squinted.

"Need some help with your tent?"

Cassie looked at the pile of fabric heaped on the ground. "Whatever makes you think that?"

"Yes," Riley said. "Cassie made the whole thing fall on me."

"Well, we knew she couldn't be good at everything," Ben said.

His eyes crinkled when he looked at Cassie, and she knew she must be turning pink.

"Come on," Ben said. "Let's get this tent up."

As soon as they got the canvas unfolded, Riley went back inside to lift the poles again, and Ben stayed next to Cassie, helping her keep the poles steady.

"It really is easier with three people," he said. "Whenever it's just me and my dad trying to put up the tent, we have a harder time."

"The two of you go camping a lot?" Cassie said.

"Sure. We live at a campground."

"Yeah, that's kind of why I thought maybe you wouldn't. Because you'd get sick of it."

Ben shook his head. "You never get sick of what you love."

The look he shot her made her think he meant something else by that.

"Okay, the poles are in and sturdy!" Riley said, crawling out of the tent. "I don't think you'll be able to make it fall this time."

"Is that a challenge?" Cassie teased. "Should I give it a try?"

"Whoa, a girl who likes a challenge," Ben said. He rubbed his hands together.

Why did Cassie feel like she was constantly blushing around him?

Leaves wrestled near their feet, and all three of them looked down to see a brown snake slithering in front of their shoes.

"Ahhh!" Cassie shrieked and hopped up and down, doing a quick little jig with her feet. There was nothing to climb onto, but that didn't prevent her from spinning around and looking for an escape.

"Wow!" Ben said.

"Cassie, it's okay. It's just a little snake." Riley put her hand on Cassie's shoulder, holding her in place.

Cassie's breathing came in too quick, the way it did sometimes when she went hiking and didn't get enough air.

Another pair of hands took her hand, squeezing it and rubbing the fingers.

"Breathe," Ben said, his larger fingers enveloping hers. "Deep breath."

Cassie tried to focus on his words, but she was scanning the ground, looking for that snake.

"Cassie." Ben dipped his head to peer into her face, forcing her to look into his eyes. "You've got to slow down or you're going to hyperventilate."

She knew that word also. She did not want to hyperventilate, especially in front of Ben. Some of her rational self returned, and she forced herself to relax.

"Good." Ben's hands were working over her fingers, massaging between the knuckles, smoothing the skin on her palm. "Keep breathing. It's okay."

"Should I get help?" Riley asked, her tone apprehensive.

"I don't think so. She's calming down. Does this happen often?"

Cassie shook her head as Riley explained, "She was bit by a snake a few years ago. So she has kind of a snake thing."

Cassie swallowed hard and found her tongue. It felt dry and thick in her mouth. "It's all right." She swallowed again. "I'm okay. Sorry for freaking out."

"Hey, no worries." Ben's voice was gentle as he put an arm around Cassie and moved her away from the leaves. He sat down and pulled her into a sitting position next to him, keeping his arm around her shoulders. "Just take a moment."

She hoped this would last longer than a moment. Her fears of the snake were quickly fading, replaced by a hyper awareness of the warmth of Ben's arm around her and the tender touch of his hand on hers. She moved her fingers around and looped them through his, feeling a tingle travel up her forearm and straight to her chest.

"I'm all right," Cassie said, giving Ben a squeeze. She didn't want to let go, though.

Riley hopped about like a nervous bird, her eyes scanning the meadow around them. The other girls were putting up their tents not too far away, but if anybody had noticed Cassie's antics, they must've assumed it was in jest.

"Ben!"

His dad called from somewhere nearby, and Ben pulled his hand away from Cassie and stood up, leaving her shoulders cold and longing for his touch. He cast her a quick smile before calling, "Coming!" and walking away.

She felt like a piece of her walked away with him. Cassie stood up, keeping her eyes on his back, fighting the urge to follow him like a shadow.

CHAPTER NINETEEN

Bad Vibes

"Cassie." Rainbow came up to Cassie as the girls started the hike to the mess hall for dinner. She took Cassie's arm and pulled her off to the side. "Were you and Ben kissing over by your tent?"

Cassie felt the blood drain from her face. "What? No!" How could someone say that? All he'd done was hold her hand.

Rainbow did not look appeased. "Two of the girls said they saw you."

Cassie's eyes went wide, and she hurried to defend herself. "I saw a snake and I kind of freaked out. Ben was helping me breathe."

"With his mouth?" Rainbow asked sarcastically.

"No," Cassie snapped. "All he did was touch my shoulders and tell me to breathe." She shook her hand out of Rainbow's. She didn't like being accused.

"You're making it difficult for Ben. He's always been able to be at camp, but now Zelda isn't sure he should be here with you girls."

"I didn't do anything," Cassie said. "He was just helping me and Riley put up our tent. Nothing else happened."

Rainbow glanced toward the other girls where they continued down the road toward the mess hall without the two of them. "Don't sit with Riley at lunch or dinner. I think the two of you together is causing problems."

And then she walked ahead of Cassie, leaving Cassie picking her jaw off the ground in disbelief. Like she and Riley were the instigators of trouble here? How could anyone even think that about them? She brushed hot tears from her cheeks, determined not to let anyone see her upset by this.

Cassie sat down at a table in the mess hall, making sure it wasn't by Riley. She sensed Riley's eyes on her and turned around to see her looking at her from across the room. "Talk later," Cassie mouthed.

"What's going on?" Jennifer asked. "Are you and Riley fighting?"

"No." Cassie didn't say anything else. It might come back to bite her.

Skippy sat down at their table. "You okay, Cassie?"

Cassie's eyes shot to her counselor, wondering how much she knew. Did she agree with what Rainbow had said?

Skippy said, "I think you're a very mature young lady, Cassie. But that doesn't mean all of your friends are."

Which friends was Skippy talking about? Not Riley, who, if anything, had been urging Cassie to not get involved. Was it one of the mystery campers who Rainbow said told rumors about her and Ben? Which one of her camp mates was secretly a gossip and a spy? Cassie decided she would have to be more careful who she opened up to.

She didn't volunteer to hop tables. If Ben was in the kitchen, it might just cause more trouble.

But when they gathered around the hearth and Skippy asked her to sing, Cassie couldn't resist.

And when Ben poked his head out the dishwashing window and grinned at her, Cassie's heart felt lighter.

☙❧

They held the Thursday evening luau that night. Having been several years before, Riley and Cassie were both prepared with flower shirts and leis. And they brought extra for their tentmates so nobody had to feel like they weren't ready for the dance.

All of the campers showed up at the mess hall to participate in the dance. Hawaiian music pumped from a stereo system set up in one of the windows, and Skippy promised they would do the limbo later.

That only made Cassie think of last year, when Ben came to the dance and asked out her friend Tiffany. A stab of jealousy wormed through her heart. She might not ever get that opportunity. She walked over to the refreshment table and poured a cup of punch.

Her younger sister Emily came over, a lei of flowers adorning her long brown hair. "Are you doing okay? Some of the girls in my unit were talking about you and Ben earlier."

Cassie smiled at her sister. "Yeah, I'm doing okay. What are they saying about us?"

Emily shrugged. "Things about how he's your boyfriend and you're not allowed to talk to each other."

Cassie's throat closed, and she swallowed hard. "He's not my boyfriend. But there are some people trying to make it so he can't talk to me."

"Emily, Emily!" A huddle of several girls Emily's age crowded around her, hovering just behind her shoulders and peering at Cassie.

"This is your sister?" one of them said in a loud whisper.

"Yeah, this is her."

"Hi," one of the girls said to Cassie.

"Hi," Cassie said back.

Emily gave an eye roll. "I'll have to talk to you later." She lowered her voice and said, "You're kind of famous. They all want to meet you."

Cassie picked up a handful of grapes from the table and popped one in her mouth. Her, famous? For what?

A movement out of the corner of her eye caught her attention, and Cassie turned to see Ben. He was plastered against the wall next to the kitchen door, barely moving. He met Cassie's gaze and pressed a finger to his lips.

She narrowed her eyes at him. What was he doing?

Ben moved another foot toward the mess hall exit.

Cassie glanced around. Nobody had noticed him. Would they notice her if she went to talk to him? She pulled a grape off the clump in her hands and rolled it across the floor in Ben's general direction. Then she walked after it, picked it up, and threw it in the trashcan two feet from him.

"What are you doing here?" she asked, keeping her eyes on the trashcan.

"I couldn't resist the chance to see you. But you weren't supposed to see me."

"How can I not see you?" Her whole soul lit up every time he was near. But she didn't say that, of course.

"I was hiding."

She laughed. "Not very well." She tilted her head. "What are you going to do now?"

"Well, I guess I'll go. I just came to see you and now I have."

Cassie hoped he hadn't heard the rumors about them. "When will I see you again?"

"As soon as possible. Maybe tomorrow when we go swimming. We have a week left, at least."

Cassie's stomach knotted. Oh. Ben thought she was staying for the full two weeks. "I'm leaving Sunday," she said carefully.

He paused, a frown creasing his brows. "What do you mean? Where are you going?"

Cassie realized she was no longer staring at the trashcan. She had also moved closer to him. She didn't dare glance around to see if anyone had noticed. "I have another camp to go to. It starts on Sunday. So I'm leaving here and going there."

Ben blinked several times, and he looked stunned. "I didn't know."

Cassie reached a hand into her pocket and felt the bracelet she'd made him a few days ago. She didn't know when she'd get the chance to give it to him, so she pulled it out and thrust it at him.

"Here. I made this for you."

He accepted it, cupping the bracelet in the palm of his hand. He gave her a half smile. "Thanks." He put it in his pocket and lifted a shoulder toward the door. "I better go before someone sees us talking."

"Yeah." Cassie backed away from him, giving him the space he would need to make his getaway. But she kept her eyes on him as he slinked out the door.

She wandered back toward the group of girls, wondering if he thought she was stupid for the bracelet. If only she had more time.

"Cassie!"

Cassie turned around at the loud whisper and saw Ben waving at her. He had stepped back inside and stood just in the doorway.

Cassie glanced toward her counselors, but they all seemed too involved with the limbo and talking to each other to notice her.

The same could not be said for her peers. Several of the girls closest to her also swung their heads in Ben's direction when he called her. Cassie shot them a look, trying to get them to act normal, and then she slipped to the back of the room where Ben stood waiting.

"What is it? Did you forget something?"

He shook his head. "I didn't forget, I just, I don't know, chickened out."

Now Cassie was confused. "I don't understand."

Ben shrugged. He shoved his hands in his pockets and glanced behind Cassie, then he murmured, "We have a bit of an audience."

Cassie swiveled to see five or six girls moving their direction. "Go back!" Cassie hissed, motioning with her hands.

"Look." Ben took a deep breath. "I better just do this fast before somebody gets us in trouble. Cassie, will you go out with me?"

She spun back to him. She forgot to breathe. Everything inside her chest froze. Somehow, she had not been expecting this. She didn't have to move her head to see the girls around her standing on tiptoes, waiting with bated breath for her response.

Cassie swallowed against her suddenly dry throat. She knew what she wanted, but she couldn't stop the horrible nagging in her head. Reminding her she had a boyfriend.

And then she threw that voice out the window. She wasn't interested in Josh anymore, and she couldn't let this chance go.

"Yes. I'll go out with you."

CHAPTER TWENTY

Dear Josh

A s soon as Cassie said yes, the girls erupted into clapping and cheering. Ben gave her such a big grin that her heart felt near to bursting, but he didn't come close to her.

"Great. I'll have to talk to you later about the details, though. I think we've been spotted." He gave her one last, long look before hurrying out of the mess hall.

The campers crowded around her then, asking questions, squealing, wanting to know how she felt, what she thought. But Cassie didn't answer any of them. She turned around and made her way back into the crowd until she found Riley. She grabbed Riley's hands and pressed her forehead against her shoulder.

"He asked me out. And I said yes," she whispered.

"What are you going to do?" Riley asked.

"I'll think of something."

By the time Cassie left the dance, she knew what she was going to do. The ten-minute trek back to the campsite flew by under her feet as she rehearsed again and again the words in her mind. While everyone else got ready for bed, Cassie sat down on her bunk, pulled out the flashlight, and began writing.

Dear Josh, she began, *thank you so much for your letter. It was very sweet of you to write me here at camp.*

It's been a good time for me to be away from home and away from everyone and just be able to think. Nature has always been a good thinking spot for me, and there's something I'm realizing.

I'm too young to be your girlfriend. I'm only fourteen and in junior high. We can't see each other because of the distance, and our age difference makes it so I feel very young next to you. I think it is for the best for both of us if we break up.

Cassie tapped the pen to her lips, wanting to make sure she worded this just right so Josh wouldn't be angry at her.

You're such a great guy and I really had a lot of fun getting to know you. I know you'll find another girl who is even better for you than I am.

She exhaled and read through the letter. It sounded good to her. Polite, apologetic, and a bit flattering. She signed her name, put the letter in an envelope, and stuck a stamp on it. She would mail it in the morning. A flutter of relief rushed through her as some of her guilt dissipated. As soon as she mailed the letter, it was as good as done. She was a free woman.

❦

The next morning the counselors had the girls gather their overnight gear before they even left for breakfast.

"We're moving over to the rough unit!" Skippy said, an exuberant smile on her face. "That's where we will be for the next two days! Enjoy your meals in the mess hall today, because tomorrow and Sunday we will be eating there at our unit!"

Some of the girls groaned, but Cassie wished she were staying longer. The whole roughing it experience felt like a grand adventure to her.

As they left their tents, Cassie checked to make sure she had the break up letter in her pocket. She had to get that into the mailbox before breakfast. It was the only thing that would relieve her conscience. Today was Friday. Josh should get the letter by Saturday, Monday at the very latest.

The girls packed up their sleeping gear and started the hike to the primitive unit before going to the mess hall. When they arrived, they split up and went to their individual campsites. Riley and Cassie entered the tent they had put up and borrowed the broom to sweep any debris off the tarp. Riley returned the broom to the supply bin and came back to Cassie.

"Don't go out there," Riley said. "Rainbow's yelling at everybody."

Cassie unrolled her sleeping bag and set her toiletries on top of it. "No problem. I'm totally content to stay here until we leave for breakfast."

Ben wasn't at breakfast or at the pool. Cassie put the letter to Josh in the mailbox and hoped his absence wasn't her fault.

The girls returned to the primitive unit, and Skippy called them over to the clearing with the supply bins.

"We need to make our cooking area. I've made assignments for each of you. Come on up here to get yours."

Cassie joined the line of girls and waited her turn. Skippy handed her a card that said, "Spit support."

"Spit support?" Cassie said, wondering if she was supposed to make some kind of spittoon, or a bowl for spitting, in the dirt. "What is that?"

"The spit is what we'll use for roasting food," Skippy said. "You're in charge of making the support. So you'll need two sticks with a fork in each one so we can rest the spit between them."

"Oh." Cassie nodded as her mental image clarified. "Does it matter how I make them?"

"No. Just as long as they work."

Cassie stepped out of line and waited while Riley got her assignment.

"What did you get?" Riley asked Cassie.

"Spit support," Cassie said. "You?"

"I'm making the spits. So the thing that goes between your supports. How hard can that be?"

"Not hard," Cassie agreed. "We should work together so you can make sure your spit fits in my supports."

"Sounds like a plan."

Cassie wandered through the woods until she found a few limbs on a tree that looked to be the proper thickness. The point where another branch took off would be the fork.

Even though they weren't very thick, it still took a lot of effort to cut the branches off.

"How are these for spits?" Riley asked, stomping over.

Cassie gladly put down the hatchet and hefted each of Riley's spits one by one.

"This one feels nice and sturdy, but it's not very long. The others are long but I think they're too thin. If we put food on them, they'll probably break."

Riley nodded. "How thick should they be?"

"I think the sticks have to stretch past the edges of the support so we can turn the spit. And it has to be strong enough to hold whatever food we put on it."

"Which is what? Chickens? Squirrels? Fish?"

"I don't know."

Riley brought up a good point. Cassie knew they'd be cooking their own food. Would they be catching it also? Suddenly this felt more like "Survivor" than roughing it.

Before Cassie could ponder on it more, the purr of a car engine rumbled through the woods. She lifted her head, eyes scanning the road just beyond the campsite.

Sure enough, a very familiar pick-up pulled into the meadow.

Cassie's eyes shot to the passenger side. Ben emerged, pulling a baseball cap over his hair and slamming the door. He lifted his head and met her gaze, and Cassie couldn't help the smile that stole across her face.

A little shiver of giddiness went down her spine, something she had never felt before. This was her boyfriend.

Ben's dad left to find the counselors, and Ben stepped over to Cassie and Riley.

"Hi,"Cassie said.

"Hi," he responded. He nodded at the sticks in her hands. "Can I help you guys?"

Cassie glanced over her shoulder at the branches she was still trying to chop off. "Well, I'm trying to get those branches down so we can make supports for the fire spit. But I'm struggling to get them cut off. It's harder when you're short."

"No problem." Ben picked up the hatchet and moved toward the tree. "Go get the twine for the lashing."

Cassie headed back toward Skippy and the supplies. Riley stepped in beside her.

"Can you believe the way he jumps in and does it all?" Riley said. "He's such a Boy Scout!"

"He's so hot," Cassie said. Ben was smart and motivated and not afraid to do hard work. He had all the qualities she never knew she was looking for in a guy.

She and Riley retrieved the twine and rope from Skippy and then returned to Ben. In that brief amount of time, he had climbed the tree and chopped the branches from above. He jumped down when he saw them.

"Just give me a minute to trim the branches and I'll show you how to lash them."

Riley and Cassie watched Ben lift the hatchet again and again, the muscles bulging in his forearms as he slammed the blade into the branches. For a skinny guy, he was sure strong.

Ben removed his hat and wiped the sweat from his brow. "Here, Cassie." He pulled out a pocket knife and cut off a long piece of the rope Riley had brought. He beckoned her closer. "I'll show you how to do this."

Cassie stepped up to him. He placed the rope in her hands, his fingers covering hers. "Secure it like this, see? You can wrap it around . . ."

The rope glided between their fingers, and Cassie was aware of him giving instructions, of his fingers moving with that rope, but she couldn't focus on anything beyond the pressure of his hand against hers.

Ben glanced at Riley, who was busy using his pocket knife to make pointed ends on her spit. He lowered his voice and whispered near Cassie's ear, "Are you okay?"

Cassie let out a breath. "I guess some people don't like the idea of you and me together," she admitted. She didn't dare tell him about yesterday's rumors. "Where were you today? Are you in trouble? Is that why you weren't at the pool or breakfast?"

Ben hesitated, apparently thinking carefully before responding. "Zelda asked my parents to let me take a break." He gave an eye roll. "I don't need a break, though, so my dad said I could come back to work now."

"I'm so sorry." Guilt tripped Cassie's conscience. "It's not fair that you should be punished because of me."

"Hey." Ben gripped her hand, stopping her motions with the rope. He gave her wrist a squeeze, and she lifted her eyes to meet his.

"This isn't your fault." His blue eyes with hints of golden brown captivated her, holding her in place while he spoke. "How was I to know you were going to be here? And I wouldn't change a thing. Meeting you has been like magic."

His eyes fixed on her mouth, and he licked his lips. One hand moved from her wrist to her waist, and he drew her near.

Cassie knew what would happen next. He would kiss her. The thrill of anticipation whispered through her, but also a seed of fear. Her last kiss hadn't been so awesome, and what if this one wasn't either? What if it ruined what they had?

The next thought hit her even harder. If anyone saw them kissing, they'd be in trouble. And she would have no defense if she was actually doing with they accused her of.

Cassie broke their connection, turning her head and calling out to Riley, "Do you need any help over there?"

Riley lifted her eyes. "No, I think I've got it."

Ben moved his hand away from Cassie's waist and she sighed, wishing they could have maintained the contact, wishing something more could've happened. "Awesome. Well, just let me know if you need something!"

She turned back to the lashing, and Ben gave her a crooked smile. Heat flooded her chest. Surely he knew she had evaded his kiss, but he didn't seem mad about it.

Rainbow came over to check on their progress just a few minutes later, and Cassie was glad by then they had finished the lashings and were assembling the spit with Riley. No funny business going on, and Cassie wasn't even standing next to Ben.

Rainbow still didn't like it. Her eyes narrowed as she studied them. "Ben, you're done over here. Go find your father."

Ben pulled on the bill of his hat and nodded, then walked away.

Rainbow turned to Riley and Cassie. "Girls, finish this up on your own. It's almost time to go to lunch."

Cassie bit back her frustration. There was no reason for Rainbow to be rude. She met Riley's eyes, and Riley rolled her eyes heavenward. Cassie smiled, glad at least her friend understood.

They walked to lunch at the mess hall shortly thereafter. Cassie had seen Ben and his dad drive away from the primitive site, and her eyes scanned the lot behind the mess hall, looking for the truck. She didn't see it, and her heart sank. Maybe they hadn't let Ben come back to work after all.

She focused on her food, though the situation had her stressed out. When the meal finished, she took the dirty dishes to the window. She dropped them off and was about to leave when she spotted her bracelet. The one she made for Ben. It was around the wrist of the pair of hands accepting dirty dishes.

Cassie pushed the plates through the window and whispered, "Ben?"

His face appeared in the opening, and he gave her a big smile. "I told them you wouldn't even see me."

"I don't see you," she confirmed, handing over the dishes.

He disappeared again. Cassie returned to the table, a smile pulling on her lips with each step. She made several trips to the window, and each time, the sight of Ben's wrist wearing her bracelet made her want to sing.

The counselors might have separated them, but they couldn't keep them apart.

The girls went back to their unit, and everyone finished up their assignments. With the campsite ready, Skippy and Rainbow told the girls to take a quiet time.

Cassie crawled into the tent she shared with Riley, grateful for a moment to be away from everyone else. She lay on her sleeping bag, cradling her pillow to her chest and staring at the angled ceiling.

"You're just thinking about Ben, aren't you," Riley said, and Cassie couldn't tell if her tone was teasing or chastising.

Cassie responded with a sigh and turned her head to look at Riley. Even with the canvases pulled to the ground, it was not dark in the tent. She could see her friend quite clearly, also looking at her.

"I've never liked anyone so much," Cassie admitted. "Everything about him is amazing." She sighed again. "I never thought something like this could happen to me. Out of all the girls here, Ben likes me!"

"And what about Josh?"

"I broke up with him. I wrote him a letter last night and mailed it this morning. By tomorrow, he'll know we are through."

"Did you tell Ben?"

Cassie shook her head. "No. Ben doesn't need to know about Josh. It's totally in my past."

"You realize that tomorrow is your last full day here, right?"

Cassie didn't want to leave. What would she do when she couldn't see Ben every day?

The rest of the day passed without any drama. Rainbow seemed in a better mood, and Cassie suspected it was because Ben was gone. They made a fire in the fire pit and sat around joking and telling stories and planning how they would cook food the next day from the tripod someone had built and the spits Cassie and Riley had made. They wouldn't even have to hunt. The food was ready-to-cook in cans and a cooler full of meat and dry ice.

And no one was required to take their buddy with them to the bathroom. They just had to make sure they let their buddy know.

Cassie laughed along with everyone else at the funny stories they told, but her thoughts kept turning back to Ben. She missed him. How could someone she had only known for four days have such an impact on her life?

The hours slipped by until it was finally time to go to the mess hall for dinner. Cassie walked silently beside the other girls, her insides a jumble of nerves. Would Ben be there? Her eyes jumped to the parking lot behind the mess hall as they approached. The truck was there. She let out a slow breath.

She ended up sitting at a table with a counselor she didn't know, and nobody complained when Riley sat with her. "I'll hop tables," Cassie volunteered, and the counselor nodded. Good. Maybe she didn't know about the orders to keep Cassie away from Ben.

Cassie went through the kitchen doors to get the plates of food. Sure enough, Ben was behind the counter serving up platters. His eyes crinkled when he saw her.

"They make you get the food every night?" he said.

"I volunteer," Cassie replied. "I like walking through the kitchen." She grabbed a plate of meatloaf.

"Hang on," Ben said, turning around. He took something off the stove. "I don't have any okra tonight, so an extra roll will have to do. Hopefully your table likes bread."

"I love bread," Cassie said.

"Then that one's for you."

She ducked her head and hurried out, pleasure rippling through her veins like a heady elixir.

She placed the plate on the table and headed back into the kitchen and this time received a plate of green beans. She didn't see Ben, but she knew this was the one for her because it had an extra roll on it.

He was there when she came through the last time, this time to get the plate of rolls. He spotted her and leaned across the counter, getting her attention before she could walk out. "Hey."

Cassie paused and stepped closer, holding the plate of hot rolls in her hands. "Hey," she replied.

"Am I doing anything wrong?"

She tilted her head. "Wrong?"

"You know." Ben gestured between the two of them. "With us. Am I being the right kind of boyfriend?"

His eyes looked so open and concerned. Cassie smiled. "Of course. How could you do something wrong when we're barely allowed to speak to each other? You're doing all right."

At that moment Skippy walked through the kitchen. Cassie and Ben both jerked away from the countertop, but Skippy just made kissing noises and continued on through. Cassie and Ben burst out laughing. She cradled the plate of rolls in her arms, her heart full as she hurried back to the table. At least not everyone was against them.

CHAPTER TWENTY-ONE

Sweet Partings

They slept at the primitive campsite that night. It didn't rain, and the hard ground didn't bother Cassie as much as she had worried it would. But she woke with a lump in her throat, realizing this was her last full day at Camp Splendor. Tomorrow her mom would pick her up and she would leave for the government-funded art camp. How would she possibly be able to say goodbye to everyone here?

The girls got a fire going in the morning and used their tripod to support a Dutch oven full of oatmeal. No one had slept that well, and they were quiet at first. Then the normal giggles and chatter that Cassie associated with camp erupted, and her heart tightened a little more to know the others had another week together without her. She blinked back the tears that pricked her eyes, determined not to spend the day crying.

They heated water so they could wash the dishes. Cassie was helping clean out the bottom of the Dutch oven when a familiar pick-up truck pulled into the campsite. All of the girls lifted their heads to look at it and then swiveled to Cassie as if this were her doing.

Cassie could only blink in surprise as Ben and his dad got out.

"Hey," Ben said, grinning broadly as he shoved his hands into the pockets of his jeans. "Thought you guys could use some help washing dishes. I am the dishwasher, after all."

The girls giggled shamelessly, but Rainbow scowled.

"The girls are managing just fine. This is their camp out. I don't think boys should be here." She looked to Skippy, but Skippy shrugged.

"It's just one day. I don't think any of the girls are going to care if somebody helps them wash the dishes."

Cassie's throat tightened as she heard what Skippy didn't say. This was Cassie's last day. Let them wash dishes together. She flashed Skippy a grateful smile.

Rainbow didn't look too thrilled, but she walked away with only one final comment. "They'll have to leave soon because we're going swimming."

Ben didn't waste any time joining Cassie where she stood cleaning the Dutch oven. He took the scrubber brush from her and began scraping at the pan. "How are you?" he asked.

Cassie lifted one shoulder. "I'm all right. I'm a little bit sad."

He paused, his eyes scanning her face. "Why are you sad? It's not me, is it?"

She laughed and touched his arm. "No, silly. You're doing everything perfectly. I'm just sad to leave you."

He frowned, his expression clouding. "I've been trying not to think about that. Let's just enjoy today." He pulled something out of his pocket and handed it to her. "Open that later. When you're alone."

Cassie looked down at the notebook paper folded into a rectangle. It felt thick in her hand, like several pages. Something metallic clinked inside. She ran her fingers over it, feeling a series of tiny balls just beneath the paper. She lifted her face. "You wrote me a note?" She was dying to open it right now and read it.

"A letter. The first of many, I'm sure. So now you don't have to think about your ex-boyfriend's letter anymore." He glowered at her, but his eyes still held a smile in them.

Cassie sighed wistfully in her mind. This boy was perfect. She gave him a little shove. "Go. You have to go now so I can read this."

He laughed, so soft she almost didn't hear. He did not touch her, but he held her gaze with such intensity that Cassie could feel him as if he had his arms wrapped around her. She wanted so badly for him to kiss her, but they were surrounded by people.

Ben turned away, breaking the contact between them. "I'll see you at the pool."

Cassie waited until the pick-up truck pulled away. She carefully dried the Dutch oven pot and set it on the bench. Then she dashed off to her tent and opened the papers.

A set of dog tags fell out from between the sheets, and she caught them in one hand. She gasped as she looked at them. Ben's staff dog tags! She turned them over, reading his name and the dates on them. Then she turned to the letter.

Dear Cassie,

Meeting you this summer has been the best part of my year. People come and go at camp, and I'm used to meeting lots of girls, but I've never met someone like you. I'm a little embarrassed you remember me liking Tiffany last year, but I was just a kid then, and I don't know how I even noticed her when you were there. You're amazing. Everyone here adores you because you're so sweet and friendly and have the most beautiful voice.

I wish we had met somewhere else, where we weren't constantly being told we couldn't talk to each other. I want to talk to you all the time, I want to get to know everything about you. I think you're an angel, and I hate that you're leaving tomorrow. But you don't live that far away, and I'm going to make sure we have opportunities to see each other.

Until then, I'm giving you my staff dog tags. When you wear these, you'll have me close to your heart, and I'll know that you have me there. When you eat okra, think of me.

Always yours, Ben.

Cassie lifted up the dog tags and held them solemnly. She slipped the chain over her neck and felt the weight against her chest. No one had ever been as good and kind to her as Ben.

～·◈·～

After they finished cleaning up from breakfast, Rainbow sent the girls to change into their swimsuits. Cassie heard her and Skippy talking, and then the walkie-talkie buzzed.

"New plans, girls!" Rainbow called, her voice ringing out across the clearing. She set the walkie-talkie down on the picnic table. "We're going to go to the creek instead of the pool today!"

Cassie pulled her shirt on over her swimsuit, a rush of panic filling her chest. She looked at Riley. "Does that mean Ben won't be there?"

"I don't know."

Well, of course she didn't know. But Cassie wanted her to guess, to say something to make her feel better. Rainbow wouldn't make her miss her last chance to be with Ben, would she?

Maybe she would.

They didn't have to take the bus to the creek. Instead they put on their hiking shoes and trekked through the forest. It took about twenty minutes before they got to the shallow river. Cassie had been here before the previous year. It was quite wide, ten to twenty feet in some places, but it never got more than three feet deep. The sun shone brilliantly down on the water, which was clear enough to see the orange- and cream-colored rocks beneath the surface.

Cassie slipped her water shoes on and dipped a toe into the water. Colder than the pool, but not too bad.

The girls from the other units were arriving, and they splashed into the water around her. Cassie followed as they moved downstream, trying to enjoy the beautiful day and ignore the heaviness in her heart. At least Ben had given her his note. That would have to do for a goodbye.

A large rock formation jetted out in the water close to the bank up ahead, and Cassie joined the girls climbing on top of it. The sun had already warmed the rock, and the radiant heat sent little shivers down Cassie's spine. She crouched at the top and tilted her head toward the sky, the sun hot on her face.

Cassie opened her eyes when several of the girls gave an audible gasp, right before a male voice called out, "What are you doing up there, Cassie?"

She looked down toward the water, a delightful feeling rushing up through her stomach. "Ben! You came!"

He beamed up at her, his dark hair falling away from his face with no baseball cap to hide it. "I told you I would see you later."

Cassie scrambled off the rock. She slipped near the bottom and tumbled toward the water, but Ben caught her. His bare skin was hot against her shoulders, and she sank against him, wanting him to hold her closer. But people were watching, and he helped steady her on her feet before letting go. His eyes crinkled as he smiled at her, his hand trailing down her arm to give her fingers a squeeze. Then he let go.

"What were you doing up there? Are you queen of the rock?"

She hoped she hadn't looked too silly. "I love the sunshine. I love how it feels on my face."

"I think the sunshine loves your face."

Cassie wasn't exactly sure what that meant, but it sounded like a compliment.

Ben started walking down the creek bed, and Cassie followed.

"I see you're wearing the dog tags," he said softly.

She glanced down at the chain around her neck and gripped the metal tags in one palm. "I love them. I'll keep them forever."

Ben didn't say anything, and they strode through the water in silence, picking their way over pebbles and rocks. A few times Cassie slipped, and Ben instantly reached out to her. And a few times, she slipped on purpose, just so she could feel his arms around her.

"I loved your letter," she said. "I'll write you as soon as I get to my next camp and send you my address. Will you write?"

He nodded. "Of course. I'll think about you every day."

"And I'll think about you . . . and okra."

"Okra. It's our thing."

The dazzling sunlight hit the water through the tree leaves, casting dappling shadows and highlighting the water bugs as they glided across the surface. Cassie wished they could be alone just for a minute. Just for a second.

But they weren't alone, and they couldn't be alone. They walked through the water with dozens of other girls around them, and all of the words Cassie wanted to say stayed firmly tucked into her throat.

⟨∘⟩~⚮~⟨∘⟩

Mrs. Jones picked Cassie up so early Sunday morning that nobody else was awake. Cassie woke Riley to tell her bye, and Riley wrapped her arms around her neck and held tight.

"Tell Ben I miss him already," Cassie said.

"I will. I'll keep an eye on him for you."

Cassie bundled her things into her mom's van and then climbed into the passenger seat beside her, her stomach clenching as they drove out of Camp Splendor.

"Well, how was camp?" Mrs. Jones asked. "Was it everything you hoped it would be?"

"Oh, Mom," Cassie sighed, and something unraveled in her throat. "You won't even believe everything that happened. It was the most amazing week ever." And she proceeded to tell her mom over the next four hours while they drove to Mena, Arkansas, all about Ben and the week.

"Wow, I can't believe it!" Mrs. Jones said after Cassie finished. "I send you away to Girls Club camp and you come back with a boyfriend? How does that even happen?"

Cassie closed her eyes. "I don't know, Mom, but of all the girls there, out of all the people he could've chosen, he picked me!"

"I don't know why you're so surprised," her mom said, smiling. "I keep telling you what a beautiful girl you are."

Cassie wouldn't have believed her mom a year ago. She felt like the ugly duckling next to all of her friends. But maybe there was something special about her, even if she was as flat-chested as a boy. "I hope I see him again soon. I already miss him."

"Well, as long as you're not alone, I'm sure we can arrange for you to meet up with him. Huntsville isn't as far away as Tahlequah." Mrs. Jones wrinkled her nose. "Josh was getting a little obsessed with you anyway. You know he called me while you were at camp?"

Cassie bobbed her head. "Yeah, I know. He wrote me a letter."

"When did you guys break up? I didn't know you had."

Cassie fidgeted, not wanting to admit the truth to her mom. "In the letter. He just recently broke up with me."

"Oh, well, isn't that lucky?"

She shot Cassie a smile before facing the road, and Cassie pushed aside any uneasiness. She had gotten what she wanted. Josh wasn't her boyfriend anymore. It didn't really matter how she'd accomplished it, did it?

But she made a mental note to avoid getting herself into something like that in the future.

CHAPTER TWENTY-TWO
Creative Content

C assie had been super excited for this art camp all summer. It was a government-sponsored camp where students across the state of Arkansas could apply and then attend for free if they were accepted. Cassie had been accepted based on her exceptional writing skills. But as her mom pulled up to the check-in desk by a row of dorms, uneasiness rolled through Cassie. She stepped into the line of students and glanced around for a familiar face, but she knew no one here. Maybe she'd made a mistake leaving Camp Splendor.

"You're all checked in and ready to go," Mrs. Jones said, an exuberant smile on her face. "I dropped your phone off, but they have it if you need it. Write me, and have a wonderful time. I'll see you in two weeks."

"Okay, Mom." Cassie tolerated the hug and then stood stiffly with the other kids waiting for their dorm assignments.

Two of the girls in front of her turned around and looked her up and down.

"Hi," one said. She had flaming orangish-red hair and a tall, petite frame. "I'm Tyra. What group are you in?"

"I'm in the writing group," Cassie said, hooking her fingers together and twisting them. "Cassie."

"Nice," Tyra said. "This is Nikki." She inclined her head at the taller girl next to her with brown hair pulled into a ponytail. "We're both in the performing arts group."

Cassie recognized Nikki. "Hey, I know you! We did soccer camp together a few summers ago!"

"Hey, yeah!" Nikki smiled and offered her a hug. "I had red hair back then."

Cassie had noticed that. "Did you dye it?"

She shook her head. "No, it got darker. You still playing soccer?"

"No." Cassie hated to admit how bad she'd been at the sport. "You?"

"Yeah, but I spend more time on the stage. So I chose drama camp instead of soccer camp."

"I almost did that one," Cassie said. "But I wrote a book last year and decided to do the writing track instead."

Tyra popped a big bubble and then smacked her coral-colored lips together. "That's awesome that you wrote a book." She snapped her bubblegum again. "You must be very smart."

Cassie relaxed under the praise. "Probably could be said of everyone here."

"Probably," Nikki said. "I think only the smart people get invited to these camps."

The line shuffled forward, and each of them was handed a bunk number in the girls' dorm.

The boys and girls dorms were both across the street from the mess hall, and the campers began to trek toward the dorms. The girls entered through one end, walking past a communal bathroom to two rows of bunk beds, one row against each wall.

Cassie glanced down at the slip of paper in her hand. Bunk bed number 36. She counted as she walked down the aisle and turned to her left at the last bunk bed. "Number thirty-six," she said, staring at the bottom bunk.

"Are you right here?"

Cassie swiveled as Tyra dumped a bag on the bunk next to her. "Yes," she said.

"Awesome. I'm number thirty-four."

"I'm right across from you." Nikki plopped her suitcase on a bunk across the aisle.

"Excuse me. Excuse me." A thicker girl with curly hair cut close to her head threaded her way through the throng of girls. Her brown eyes scanned the bunks, and she stopped next to Tyra and Cassie. "Sorry, I've got bunk thirty-three."

"I guess you're up there," Tyra said, pointing to the bunk above hers. "I'm Tyra. I'm in the drama program. You?"

"Lydia." The girl threw her bag on the top bunk and gave a graceful curtsy to Tyra. "I'm in the writing program." She spoke with an airy tone, as if something distracted her from giving the girls her complete attention.

"Cool beans," Nikki said. "So is Cassie."

They included Cassie, as if she were one of them. Cassie moved closer to the them, hardly noticing when another girl came to occupy the bunk above her.

"We should be getting ready for the costume contest," Tyra said, opening her suitcase and digging through it.

"Oh, wait till you see my costume!" Nikki said.

"Costume contest?" How had she not known about this?

"Yeah, it's before dinner," Tyra said. "You knew, right?"

"I must've missed the memo," Cassie murmured, feeling nauseous. Her mind flashed to the rough-in camp she'd left behind, to Riley and Ben and all her friends. This place was already off to a bad start.

"That's all right," Lydia said. "We'll fix you up." She pulled an Egyptian headdress from her bag and placed it on her head.

Tyra gasped. "That's fantastic. Can I do your makeup?"

"Sure," Lydia said.

Nikki's ensemble was an old-fashioned giant telephone, made out of foam. She stepped inside it so the telephone receiver sat on her head. Tyra put on a slinky cocktail dress, then turned her attention to Cassie.

"What can we do with her, girls?"

They studied her in silence for a moment, and Cassie shifted restlessly.

"Hillbilly," Nikki said. "I've got hankies we can use."

"And I've got overalls," Lydia said.

"Pig tails." Tyra already had Cassie's hair in her hands as she worked it into two ponytails.

"Lots of freckles." Nikki the telephone held a black eyeliner pencil in her fingers, and she poked Cassie's cheeks with it.

When they finished and put Cassie in front of a mirror, she thought she looked ridiculous. Eyeliner freckles dotted her face, and she looked ten years old. But at least she had a costume.

After the girls paraded in front of the camp leaders, they gathered with the other campers to hear the prize winners. Even though Cassie knew her costume was lackluster and last minute, she couldn't help hoping something about her might impress the judges. She clapped politely at third place, though she didn't know the person.

"Second place: Lydia Marsh as the Egyptian!"

Cassie arched an eyebrow and clapped for her new friend.

"And finally: first place goes to Nikki Woods!"

Nikki deserved that. Her phone costume was unique and cool. The girls took a few pictures before being shepherded into the dining hall.

"We're eating in our costumes?" Cassie said, embarrassed everyone would see her like this for a little longer.

"Hey, at least you're not a big telephone," Nikki said.

Tyra peered over the serving counter. "I need the vegetarian entree, please."

Cassie watched with interest as the plate of sloppy joes and bun was replaced with broccoli and rice. "Why do you get that?" she asked Tyra.

"I'm a vegetarian," Tyra said. "I don't eat meat."

Her food looked much healthier, also. Cassie had spent the past year struggling with her weight and self-image. Being a vegetarian suddenly seemed like a good way to control her eating while being healthy. "Me too."

"You're a vegetarian?" Tyra said, appraising her.

"Yes," Cassie said.

Tyra turned to the serving lady. "She's a vegetarian also. So one more vegetarian entree."

The lady handed over the rice and broccoli tray, and Cassie practically skipped to the table behind her new friends, freckles and all.

⸙

The next morning Cassie and Lydia headed to the writing lodge after breakfast.

"What do you like to write?" Cassie asked.

"I'm a poet," Lydia said in that airy tone of hers. "I love to create imagery about the world around me using the written medium."

"Oh," Cassie said. She waited for Lydia to ask what she wrote. When she didn't, Cassie said, "I'm a novelist."

"Fancy. So you want to write books one day?"

"I've already written one," Cassie said, feeling proud. "I'm working on the sequel." She held up the jump drive she'd brought from home. "It's all here so I can work on it."

"That's fun. We'll see what they have us do today."

"Come on in and find a computer, guys!" a woman with glasses and bushy brown hair said as they entered.

A table lined with computers took up most of the room. Cassie seated herself in front of one, and Lydia sat beside her.

"That's right, that's right." The woman walked around the table, making sure they were all sitting. "I'm Mrs. Miller and I'll help you with your writing projects over the next two weeks!"

Writing projects. Cassie squirmed with excitement. This was where she excelled.

"Your first assignment this morning is to create a character. I don't want to just know this character's hair color and favorite food. I want to know who they are. I want you to come up with their whole backstory, family life, characteristics. Then you'll spend the morning writing a one-page biography about your character. Go on, get started."

Cassie turned and faced the computer. Was it cheating if she used a character she had already created? She had no need to make a new one. What she really wanted was to make some headway with her sequel.

She chose Joyce, the main character from her book, and began writing down everything she knew about Joyce. Which was quite a lot, since she'd been working on this character for over a year.

But still, she was surprised how much she didn't know. When she started the biographical essay, she discovered she didn't even know where Joyce was born. She wrote some more, coming up with the background for her character and loving this discovery process. When she finished, she sat back and re-read her words, checking for errors. It sounded like a real person, and Cassie was amazed at how real this character had become.

"Has everyone written their biographies?" Mrs. Miller asked.

Everyone nodded, except Lydia, who had her head bent over a notepad. She raised one hand without lifting her head.

"I'm not quite done," she said.

"Maybe if you typed on the computer instead of writing on the notepad," a boy said, and the group laughed softly.

Lydia lifted her face. "I think better when I'm writing by hand," she said in a frosty, even voice.

"You do whatever you feel is best," Mrs. Miller said, her tone encouraging. "We'll wait for you."

Cassie turned back to her computer and read through the biography again. Succinct, factual, informational. It looked good.

"Finished," Lydia said.

"Great. Now, since everyone's biography is a page or less, I would like for us to read them to each other. This should only take us ten or fifteen minutes. I want everyone to find something positive and constructive to say about each one, which should take us about as long as it took to read the biography out loud. So this is a half hour exercise. Let's settle in."

Cassie leaned back in her chair and waited for her turn. She listened to the others share their biographies and provided feedback. Sometimes the character seemed like someone she would be interested in learning about or meeting. Other times, she couldn't get a clear picture of who it was, and nothing about their personality structure seemed interesting. Her shoulders straightened. Hers was definitely one of the better ones.

Finally it was her turn. Cassie faced the computer and read Joyce's biography, then waited for the praise. She knew she had an extremely cohesive understanding of Joyce's life since she had known this character for so long, and she had an adept way of describing things.

"I liked it," a girl said. "She sounds like someone I might be friends with."

"It was pretty cool," a boy said. "I wanted to know more about what makes her tick, what kinds of things make her angry."

Cassie nodded. She hadn't considered that.

Mrs. Miller nodded as each camper said a few things about Cassie's biography, and then Cassie looked at her expectantly.

"Looks like your peers gave you plenty of feedback. Time to make your character more well-rounded." Mrs. Miller turned her face. "Lydia? Are you ready to share?"

That was it? Mrs. Miller had nothing else to say? Cassie struggled in silence for a moment before she realized Lydia had almost finished reading what sounded like a poem. It only took her two minutes to read it, and then she lifted her face and peeked timidly out from under her eyelashes.

Cassie also peeked at Mrs. Miller. How could a poem possibly fit the parameters? She waited for their instructor to gently chastise Lydia.

"What creativity, what originality!" Mrs. Miller gushed. "To put your biography into poetic form!"

Cassie wrinkled her nose. She couldn't help saying, "Were we supposed to write poetry? I thought we were writing biographies."

"Of course, that was the assignment," Mrs. Miller said. "But anytime you see the opportunity to do something outside the box, take it." She beamed. "I can already tell which ones of you have extra talent."

Cassie's face flushed with indignation. Mrs. Miller gave them instructions for the next part of their assignment, but Cassie barely heard. Lydia had extraordinary talent? Because she wrote her biography in five little lines that happened to rhyme? She took a deep breath and let it out slowly. Ms. Talo, her English teacher, thought she was extraordinary, and that was why she was here. Cassie reminded herself she didn't have to be the most important to everyone.

She would just spend her time working on her book and get what she wanted out of this camp.

⚬⟋⟍⚬☀⚬⟋⟍⚬

Cassie and Tyra got the vegetarian meal again at lunch. She found she actually enjoyed the culinary creativity of meatless protein. They finished lunch, then headed with Lydia and Nikki to the pool for break time. Cassie settled into a lounge chair next to Tyra, feeling stubby and unsophisticated in her one-piece next to Tyra's long, slender torso on display in her bikini. She pulled out her notebook and wrote a letter to Ben, hoping she sounded upbeat and flirty while begging him to write her.

"What are you doing, Cassie?" Tyra asked. "Writing your boyfriend?"

Cassie's face grew hot. "Yes." She had told Tyra a little about Ben the day before, but not the other girls.

Tyra leaned forward, her wavy red hair falling over her shoulders. "Really? Are you telling him about us?"

"Cassie," Nikki said, "can you run back to the dorm and get my gum? I'll share it with you."

"Sure," Cassie said, happy to feel useful. "Which bag is yours?"

"It looks like a little backpack, kind of green. It's hanging on my bedpost. The gum's in the middle pocket."

"Yeah, I'll grab it." Cassie stood up and pulled her cover-up over her swimsuit. If only Ben were here. She never felt self-conscious around him. Her fingers came up and stroked the dog tags dangling around her neck.

She walked across the road to the girls' dorm. A few people were inside, taking a quiet time to write letters or take a nap. Right away Cassie spotted a backpack hanging on the post next to her bed. She stepped up to it and started digging through it, searching for the pack of gum.

Cassie's bunkmate sat up from where she'd been resting on the top bunk. "What are you doing?" she asked, her voice a little sleepy.

"I'm looking for Nikki's gum," Cassie said, trying to sound confident. It felt awkward to be caught digging through somebody else's bag. "She sent me to get it."

"You're looking for Nikki's gum?"

"Yes." Did she think Cassie was lying?

"In my bag?"

"Oh!" Cassie yanked her hand out and looked at the bag as if it had suddenly become a ball of fire. She stared at the little purse shaped like a backpack. "This is your bag? I'm so sorry!"

To her relief, her bunkmate began to laugh. "I was like, what is she doing?"

Cassie gave a laugh also. "Yeah. Totally embarrassing."

"Nikki's bag is hanging off of her bed." She pointed to the bed across the aisle where a little green backpack sat, which made sense to Cassie, since that was where Nikki's bed was.

"Thanks. I don't know why I didn't see it before." Cassie moved over to that pack, more nervous than she had been before accidentally sifting through someone else's bag. She must look like such an idiot.

But Nikki and Tyra died laughing when Cassie told them about it, and then she didn't feel so stupid. In fact, she even told Ben about it in her letter, able to laugh at herself as well.

⟡

By Wednesday Cassie was feeling quite comfortable with her new group of friends. She didn't mind vegetarian food at all, and in fact it made her feel a little bit healthier than everything else she had been eating. The portions felt smaller, so that helped.

Her mom had already written her saying Josh had sent her a letter and also called the house. She asked if there was anything specific Cassie wanted her to say to him. She also mentioned that Cassie's friends had called, wondering when Cassie would be home.

Her friends! She had almost forgotten about them in all of the excitement of dating Ben and going to a new camp. She felt a rush of anxiety at the thought of what they would say if they knew she had started dating Ben before breaking up with Josh.

She could never tell them.

The one person she hadn't heard from was Ben. It had only been four days since she'd seen him, but she already missed him terribly. Didn't he miss her? Why hadn't he written? He hadn't forgotten her already, had he?

The thought filled her with panic.

They got on the bus after breakfast for the two-hour drive to the state capital, Little Rock, where they were going to watch a Broadway play. Cassie suspected normally this would be very exciting for her, but as she had spent a week in New York earlier in the summer and seen two, this was just one more.

Cassie wanted to sit by Tyra on the bus, but Lydia was always hanging on her, so Cassie sat with Nikki. As soon as the bus got going, Tyra swiveled around in her seat in front of Cassie, looping her arms over the top and resting her chin on them.

"So, Cassie. Have you heard anything from your boyfriend yet?"

Cassie's cheeks warmed. "Not yet. I'm sure he'll write soon."

"Did she show you the note he wrote her before she left?" Lydia said, joining Tyra on the back of the seat. She offered a dramatic sigh. "It was so romantic. And the way they met." Lydia clasped her hands to her heart. "It's something out of a romance novel."

"Wait a minute, I don't know the story," Nikki said, tilting her head to look at Cassie.

"You don't know the story?" Tyra said, widening her blue-green eyes. "About how Cassie goes away to an all-girls camp and comes back with a boyfriend?"

Now Cassie knew her face must be flaming. "I didn't do it on purpose."

Which just made Tyra laugh harder. "Makes it even better!"

"So you haven't been dating this guy very long, then, have you?" Nikki asked.

Cassie shook her head. "Just five days."

"They're still in the honeymoon stage," Tyra said, grinning.

"What happened?" a new voice said.

The four girls turned to see the speaker. It was a boy in the music program. Cassie didn't know his name, but he was tall with thick brown hair.

Tyra gave a wave of her hand. "Hey, John. Cassie was just telling us all the crazy story about how she went away to an all-girls camp and managed to come back with a significant other."

John's eyebrows rose up into his hairline, and he turned to stare at Cassie. "At an all-girls camp?" He sounded confused, like he wasn't quite sure how to interpret the information.

Nikki giggled. "I think you better tell the story, Cassie, John is getting strange ideas about you."

"What?" Cassie gasped as it dawned on her what John must be thinking. She wanted to sink into her seat in embarrassment. "Crapola, no! No, there was a boy there, he worked in the kitchen!"

Lydia and Tyra broke into peals of laughter, and Nikki clapped in delight.

"Oh," John said, his cheeks reddening also. "That makes more sense."

"So what happened?" Nikki asked. "You saw him and he saw you and you guys just fell in love?"

"Um, something like that." Cassie wouldn't call it love, as much as she liked him. Thinking about Ben gave her a warm delicious feeling inside, but she barely knew him. She couldn't say she loved him. "Actually he liked me right away, but I made fun of him and told everyone I thought he was too skinny."

That brought more laughter, and Cassie hadn't realized how her audience had grown until she glanced around and saw several kids hanging over their seats, listening to her.

"So how did he win you over?" Tyra asked.

Cassie thought about all the ways Ben had won her over. Talking to her, teasing her, giving her his dog tags, complimenting her singing. But one memory stuck out more than the others. "Okra," she said, unable to keep the smile from spreading across her face. "He won me over with okra."

That brought more questions, but Tyra was studying Cassie's face, and she said, "All right, guys, that's enough. Cassie is lost in her memories now. Let's let her dream about okra." She gave Cassie a wink. And Cassie smiled back.

CHAPTER TWENTY-THREE
Neanderthal Lock-in

Cassie tried to get some good headway on her sequel at camp, but she found it hard to concentrate. Lydia whispered to herself as she wrote, and other story ideas intruded on Cassie's mind. She found herself wanting to write about a girl who went to summer camp, and then the summer camp was invaded by an army and the girl had to hide and help her captured campmates. That sounded much more exciting than her sequel.

Maybe she just didn't have any more ideas.

She followed the writing prompts from Mrs. Miller and wrote poems and short stories that didn't satisfy her. Every time she shared them with the others in the group, they gave her run-of-the-mill feedback. But everyone seemed to have caught on to Mrs. Miller's fervor about Lydia's work, and they praised everything she did. Cassie was so over it.

On Friday, the group took a four-hour bus ride to Dallas for a few museum tours. One of them, the Perot Museum of Nature and Science, had arranged for the kids to stay after it closed and have a lock-in.

The camp director handed each camper their cell phone in a plastic bag as they got off the bus.

"You're allowed to use your phones while we're here at the museum. Get the most out of them as you can because I'm collecting them when we get back on the bus!"

Cassie did a little happy dance, and she flipped her phone open. She could call Ben! She didn't have his number memorized, but that didn't matter. She always had his letter with her. She dug it out of her purse, then leaned up against the wall outside the museum as nearly every other camper did the same, too excited about being able to call someone to even go inside.

Her phone lit up as new text messages rolled in, but she ignored them, instead punching in the digits written on the notebook paper.

The phone rang for one minute, and then a woman answered. "Hello?"

Cassie straightened. "Oh. Hi." She paused, suddenly flustered. She hadn't expected someone besides Ben to answer. "Is Ben there?"

"He's at work right now," the woman said, her tone friendly. "Can I have him call you back?"

Cassie's heart sank a little. But then she brightened. She would have her phone for the next twelve hours. "Yes, please. This is Cassie. Cassie Jones."

"Oh, Cassie!" The woman's voice warmed. "This is Ben's mother. I've heard so much about you! He'll be so happy you called."

Ben talked about her? The thought made her feel all light and floaty inside. "If he gets a chance to call me, I'll have my cell phone for the next few hours. I'd love to talk to him."

"Let me write your number down and I'll tell him to call."

Cassie gave her number and then hung up, letting out an exhale. It was disappointing not to talk to him, but at least she could still feel secure in their relationship. She had started to worry, since he hadn't written her.

The mob of students had moved into the museum, and she followed, giving her name at the desk and receiving a wristband. She checked her text messages as she did so, feeling that needling thread of guilt as her friends began to ask why she had broken up with Josh. How could she throw suspicion off the real reason?

She texted Andrea, the only person she felt she could trust. *I'm dating someone else now. But don't tell anyone else. I want to tell them.*

"Come on!" Tyra said, wrapping her fingers around Cassie's wrist and pulling her up the stairs before Andrea had responded. "Let's go watch the movie in the IMAX theater!"

"I love these theaters," Nikki said, following close behind. "It always feels like you're right there."

"I'm coming," Cassie said. "I just need to call my mom." She followed behind Tyra, her phone pressed to her ear as it dialed.

"Hello?"

Instead of her mother, Cassie recognized her younger sister Emily. "Emily, it's me, Cassie."

"Hi, Cassie!" Emily said. "How's your week of camp going?"

"It's halfway over," Cassie said. "I can hardly believe it. How was Girls Club camp?" Cassie clutched the phone tighter, suddenly wanting to know everything, wanting to live that last week of camp vicariously through Emily.

"It wasn't as much fun without you, that's for sure. I just got home this morning. Everyone missed you so much. Especially Ben. He wouldn't stop talking about you."

Ben. Cassie closed her eyes. There it was again, proof that he liked her.

"Cassie!" Tyra said, poking her head out of the theater and hollering.

Cassie straightened. "I've got to go, Emily. Tell mom I called, would you?"

"Sure," Emily said.

Cassie silenced her phone before entering the theater and joining Tyra and her friends. Even with her phone on silent, she couldn't help checking it every few minutes just to see if Ben had called her back. Nothing so far.

After the movie they wandered through the rest of the museum, and when Cassie looked at the display of the baby growing in the womb, she had a sudden feeling of déjà vu.

"I'm pretty sure I've been to this museum," she said.

"You've been to a museum in Texas before?" Lydia asked.

"I used to live in Texas," Cassie said, although it felt so long ago that her life in Texas seemed like a dream she'd had once.

"This is such a big city," Nikki said. "It must've been awesome."

"I loved it," Cassie said. "But I'm really happy in Arkansas now." The words struck Cassie as they left her mouth. It was true. Arkansas had become her home even more than Texas. She never would have believed that a few years ago.

Partway through the next exhibit, Cassie's phone began to make that peculiar squeal it made when the battery was dying. "Oh no!" she gasped. She pulled it out. Sure enough, it only had ten percent left. She'd forgotten her charger at home, and now there would be no way for Ben to call her.

She glanced around at her friends, wondering if anyone had a charger she could use. She didn't get the chance to ask, though, before the camp leader was gathering all of the kids into the kitchen.

"The museum officially closes in ten minutes. We're having dinner catered to us here, so we'll just sit here for a bit until the other patrons are out."

"And then what do we do after it closes?" John asked.

"Hang out with your friends. Look at all the exhibits you didn't see. Watch movies all night long." The director shrugged. "It's really up to you."

Cassie and Tyra took apart their sub sandwiches, tossing the meat but eating the tomatoes and cheese on the bread. The whole time

Cassie had her eyes on the phone, watching mournfully as the battery counted down. This was Ben's fault. If he would have called her back earlier . . . or he could've written her a letter . . .

Her phone finished dying while she ate her sandwich, and Cassie dropped it into her purse. She would just have to wait to talk to Ben.

The girls found a section in the Neanderthal exhibit, in a small corner next to barely dressed cavemen squatting over a pile of wood.

"Just what I asked for," Tyra said, putting down her pillow and blanket. "We have a nice private area here."

"Let's go watch that other movie at the IMAX theater," Nikki said. "The one about the mountains that makes you feel like you're on top of the world."

"Oh, I loved the other one!" Lydia said. "Every time the camera rolled down the mountainside into the valleys, I felt like I was an eagle flying!"

"Yeah, but we don't need to see it again," Tyra said, and Cassie agreed with her.

"Let's watch the space one," she said.

"Sure." Nikki shrugged. "I liked that one also."

They watched the space movie again, and Cassie marveled at how the camera angle made her feel as if she were moving. By the end of it, though, she was nodding off, and the girls wandered back to the Neanderthal exhibit where they had set up their things. A few adult leaders walked back and forth, making sure none of the kids were doing anything inappropriate, but the girls didn't worry about them. They snuggled into their blankets and leaned their heads close together.

"Okay, I'm dying to know," Tyra said. "Who here hasn't had their first kiss?"

Cassie felt a stab of relief that she had crossed that rite of passage, thanks to Josh. "I have," she said, in case anyone had any doubts.

"We know you have," Nikki said. "You have a boyfriend."

"I haven't actually kissed him yet," Cassie said, her face growing hot. "It was someone else." Kissing Ben would be a totally different experience. She hoped.

"Oo, I want to know about this," Tyra said, leaning closer.

"I haven't," Lydia said, redirecting the conversation. "I'm still waiting for that first kiss."

"What about you, Tyra?" Nikki said. "Or should the question be, how many guys have you kissed?"

Tyra opened her mouth to answer, just as a group of three giggly girls burst around the corner of their exhibit.

"Hello!" one of them said, throwing a bundle of blankets down near them and sitting on it. "Mind if we join you?" She didn't wait for an answer before tugging on her friends' hands and pulling the other girls onto the blankets with her.

"We were having a private conversation," Tyra said, the annoyance evident in her voice. "I'm sure you can find somewhere else to settle down."

The three girls leaned toward her. "Oh, girl talk?" another said, and all three tittered. "We want to join."

They weren't going to leave. Cassie could see that realization dawning on Tyra as well, who heaved out a breath and lay down.

"You guys can talk, just don't be too loud. We were just getting ready for bed."

Cassie, Lydia, and Nikki followed Tyra's example, snuggling into their blankets.

Though Cassie couldn't help wondering exactly how many boys Tyra had kissed.

On Saturday Cassie turned in her dead cell phone before getting on the bus for the return trip to the art camp. She couldn't shake the sadness that she hadn't been able to talk to Ben and told herself it was just one more week. One more week, and she would be able to call him and talk to him.

The kids took a break on Sunday and didn't participate in any activities, instead attending a nondenominational worship session at the chapel by the dorms.

Monday morning Cassie found herself back in front of the computer for her writing class.

"Today I want you to take a food item and describe it without using your sense of taste," Mrs. Miller said. "Think of it as something different than food, maybe a landscape. Let's see how creative we can get here."

Lydia already had her notebook out and was scribbling what Cassie assumed could only be another poem. But she could not bring herself to be excited about describing food. She stood up, getting Mrs. Miller's attention.

"I'm running to the restroom."

Mrs. Miller waved her off without a second glance, and Cassie hurried off to the dorms. She used the restroom and then stepped into the sleeping area.

"Nikki," she said, surprised to find her friend laying on the bed. "What are you doing?"

Nikki sat up. "Oh, taking a little nap. What about you?"

"Writing class is really boring today," Cassie said. "I wish they would just let us write about what interests us and not stupid things like food."

"You have to write about food?"

"Totally lame, right?"

"How about you eat food instead?" Nikki pulled out a bag of chocolate caramels.

The temptation was too much. Chocolate was not a healthy food, but Cassie's mouth watered at the sight. "That sounds much better," she agreed. She plopped down beside Nikki and took a foil square. She unwrapped it, then nibbled at the chocolate. She sighed as it melted on her tongue. "So good."

"Right?" Nikki handed her the bag. "Help yourself."

Cassie did, selecting another foil-wrapped candy. "I think I'll skip class today."

"I think that's totally fine."

❦

"For your final project here at camp," Mrs. Miller said the next day, "I would like you to write a letter to your family from beyond the grave."

"Beyond the grave? Like, if we were dead?" a girl named Melissa said.

Seemed self-explanatory to Cassie. And this might actually be exciting to write. She brainstormed what she would like to say to her family and her friends, even Ben. This would be a rather emotional assignment, and Cassie can hardly wait to dig in.

Lydia raised her hand. "Do we have to sit at the computer?"

"Only if you're typing," Mrs. Miller said, favoring her with a smile.

Cassie didn't feel like sitting at the computer either. She picked up the yellow notebook beside her and stepped through the doors in the computer room to the lounge area in the next room, with the little yellow couches and chairs. Cassie curled up in one of the chairs and began her fictional postmortem goodbye letter. She addressed each family member by name and then her friends, praising their strengths and giving them hope for their faults. She felt benevolent and mature as she forgave them any injury they might have caused her during life. She even sniffled a little as she thought of how much they would miss her.

Two hours passed before Mrs. Miller called them back in.

"We won't have time to read everyone's entire letter," she said. "But I would love to hear excerpts from anyone who would like to share."

Cassie didn't hesitate before shooting her hand into the air. Surely this would be where she would shine.

She wasn't at all surprised to see Lydia's hand also in the air.

This time Lydia went before Cassie. She cleared her throat and then read short lyrical phrases. "Goodbye, fair earth, goodbye gentle sky, hello soft ground and deep deep green grass," she said slowly, enunciating each word as she completed her poem. Lydia finished reading and lifted her expectant face to Mrs. Miller's.

Mrs. Miller clapped, along with most of the rest of the students.

Cassie refrained from rolling her eyes.

"As always, Lydia, you've managed to capture the essence of a farewell with beautiful imagery and poetic language. You are an extremely gifted writer."

Blah blah blah. Cassie wanted to stick her finger in the back of her throat and gag.

Mrs. Miller finally turned to her. "Go ahead, Cassie. Share something."

Cassie cleared her throat and turned to the paragraphs she had written to her friends where she praised their kindness and other attributes while gently chastising the selfishness and the cruelty they were sometimes prone to.

She finished speaking and waited. Her peers also looked toward Mrs. Miller, taking their cue from her as to how to respond.

Mrs. Miller nodded. "I can see you put a lot of thought into this. You've addressed the letter to the people important to you. You sound a little self-serving, though, in your assumptions and your judgments of them. Maybe your friends would have the same sorts of things to say about you."

Cassie nodded and bit her tongue. *That wasn't with this assignment was about!* she wanted to say. She wasn't supposed to be imagining how other people saw her or censoring her thoughts. She was writing a goodbye letter and putting all of her feelings into it because she was dead already! It didn't matter what people thought; this was her last chance to say what *she* thought!

Mrs. Miller had already moved on, and Cassie put the letter aside. Camp would be over soon, and she wouldn't have to feel like second-best—or fifth-best—anymore.

They worked on a few more writing projects after lunch, and then Cassie and Lydia left the classroom for break time before dinner.

"This has been such a wonderful experience for me," Lydia said. "I can't wait to see what next year brings for my writing."

"I'm going to finish my sequel and then try to get both books published," Cassie said. She only half believed that, though. She had struggled on her sequel this week, not even quite sure where the plot was going. She had her doubts she could create another story with these characters.

Lydia opened her mouth to say something, but before she could, a water balloon smacked into the ground at her feet, bursting open and shooting water all over their shoes and legs.

"Oh my goodness," Lydia shrieked, and Cassie immediately began looking for their attacker. A water balloon whipped past her face, and she ducked.

"Incoming!" a boy shouted, and a balloon smacked her in the chest before plummeting to the ground.

Now Cassie spotted boys running through the camp, tossing balloons at unsuspecting females. Oh no. They were not going to win this war. She ran into the dorm and fished through her suitcase until she found the water bottle she had used at Camp Splendor. She filled it up with water and headed back outside.

The camp had erupted into chaos. Shrieking and laughing campers darted behind trees and buildings, throwing balloons and tossing containers full of water at those walking by. It looked like guys against girls, and when Cassie spotted John and his friend Mitchell walking by, she tossed the contents of her bottle of water at them.

Mitchell stopped in his tracks and wailed like a girl, while John whipped around and started laughing when he saw her. He ran the opposite direction, and Cassie gave chase. John stopped at the water fountain and began pouring water into his hands and splashing it at her as quickly as he could. She dodged the sprinkling droplets and dumped the rest of her water bottle on his head, then turned so she could refill it.

She ended up in the mess hall, and she had to hide behind the wall as kids ran in and out. She hurried to the sink and filled up her water bottle, then turned around and came face-to-face with John and a bowl of water. She ducked, but was unable to avoid the waterfall that cascaded down her shoulders. Cassie let out a guttural cry and grabbed the bowl. A tug-of-war ensued, and John pulled back hard just as Cassie let go. He stumbled, his feet cartwheeling underneath him before he fell flat on his bum.

"Are you okay?" Cassie cried just as several other girls raced to his aid.

He brushed them off and got his feet. "This isn't over," he said, then darted past her to the sink.

Cassie look down at the water bottle in her hands, already full. She took the two steps to close the distance between her and John and then tipped the water bottle upside down on his neck.

"ARGH!" He whirled around with his bowl half full of water, but Cassie danced out of the way, and another boy took the water in the face.

"That was meant for you!" John didn't hesitate before immediately refilling the water bowl.

Uh-oh. The glint in his eye meant trouble, and Cassie swiveled to make her get away. She slipped in the water mess and almost went down, but managed to grab a table first.

A glance behind her showed John's water bowl was nearly full again.

She pushed off the table and bolted outside, high-tailing it for the safety of the girls' dorm.

"I'll be here when you get out, Cassie!" John hollered, running after her.

Cassie laughed all the way inside, where she stripped out of her wet clothes and stepped into the hot shower. She had no idea who had won the water fight, but she'd gotten him good.

CHAPTER TWENTY-FOUR
First Date

C assie never thought she would miss home. She never thought she'd be happy to see her sisters and her brother. She never thought she would be anxious to talk to her mom and dad, to see her own bedroom, to feed her cats and do her chores.

But she was happy to be home.

Art camp had ended that morning, and she only had two weeks now until school started. She stuck her cell phone—still dead—into the charger and unpacked her clothes from the past three weeks, all the time wondering why Ben hadn't written her. Had he forgotten her? Was she still his girlfriend?

There was another letter waiting for Cassie on her desk, though. A letter from Josh. She picked it up, her stomach knotting up. It was postmarked the same day she sent her break up letter to him, which meant at this point he still thought she was his girlfriend.

She tapped the envelope in the palm of her hand. Did she even want to open this? She forced herself to rip open the flap.

Josh's loopy handwriting greeted her, whining about how he didn't like her talking to other boys and how he wished he could be with Cassie. He mentioned calling Andrea and Amity because he missed her so much, but that Amity wasn't very nice to him. Then he went on to talk about how soft their kiss had been, and he couldn't wait to kiss her again.

Ugh! Just the memory made Cassie nauseous. Why had she kissed him? Because she had thought it be something amazing, and it wasn't.

Never again, she told herself. *If I don't like a guy, we are breaking up before I ever have to kiss him.*

She knew when her phone was fully charged because it powered on, and one by one became flooded with text messages and voicemails. Cassie sat down at her desk and scrolled through them. Her heart gave a little flip of joy when she saw that she had missed several calls from Ben. Then she felt a pang of worry. What if he kept calling to break up with her?

She had a few voicemails. Her finger was hovering over the button to listen to them when her phone rang. She gave a groan when she saw Josh's name on the screen. She was sorely tempted to ignore it, but then she shoved aside the desire. Time to man up.

"Hello?" she said cautiously.

"Hi, Cassie," his tenor voice said on the line. "You're back!"

"Yep. I'm back," she said. She sat at her desk and picked up a bottle of nail polish, turning it so the light reflected off of the contents, making them look shimmery and sparkly. "What's up?"

"I—" he hesitated, and Cassie got a knot of dread in her stomach. She did not want to talk about what he wanted to talk about. "I don't quite understand what happened between us. I thought things were going so well?"

Cassie shifted uncomfortably. "Things were going well. It just wasn't working." At all. She hadn't felt anything for him and hadn't wanted to keep up the charade of being the happy girlfriend. Not after she met someone she really did like.

"What do you mean, things weren't working? I'm sorry I didn't come to visit more often, it's just not that easy to get away."

"Oh no, it wasn't that! I just felt like there's a much bigger difference between us than I first realized. I mean, you're in high school. You graduate next year. And then what? I'm only fourteen."

"That doesn't matter," he said, and his voice sounded a little raw. "We could make it work, Cassie. Hi—"

Cassie interrupted before he could say anything more. "I'm so sorry, Josh. I know you'll find the right girl for you. I've got to go."

He made noises on the other end as if attempting to say more, maybe searching for the right argument to convince her, but nothing could. Cassie was done with that relationship. She didn't wait for him to find his words before closing her phone, ending the call.

Guilt twisted her insides at how she had handled that, but she pushed it aside. Josh would be fine.

She flipped through her text messages, this time stopping to read a few from her friends. Half of them demanding more information about their breakup. Cassie chewed on her lower lip, realizing she would have to continue the lie to her friends that she had broken up with Josh because it wasn't working. And she'd met Ben shortly thereafter.

Her phone rang again, and this time a smile lit Cassie's face when she saw Ben's name. The worry returned, though, and she wished she'd listened to his voicemails before he called. She flipped the phone open and couldn't even keep the joy from her voice. "Hi!"

"Cassie!" Ben's voice also sounded happy. "I thought you got home today!"

She squeezed the phone in her hand, relief flooding her. "I'm back. Did you get my letter?" Had he possibly missed her as much as she had missed him?

"I did, and I'm so sorry I didn't write you. Things are so busy at the camp right now. But I should have more time, because the last girls went home yesterday, and the counselors will be gone by today."

The tension eased out of her shoulders. "Oh good, because I started to worry you'd forgotten me," Cassie teased.

Ben made a sound like a cough and a choke at the same time. "Are you kidding? No way. I just wish I could see you again."

"I want to see you too," Cassie breathed, flashing back to the moments at camp where Ben had sat next to her or held her hand or made her laugh. And then, without thinking, she blurted out, "I miss you so much. I couldn't stop talking about you."

"Really?" Ben laughed, such a light and joyful sound. "I'm so glad it wasn't just me! I kept talking to your friends about you, and finally they were giving me these looks and I was like, Ben, shut up, they don't want to talk about her anymore!" He laughed again. "You are the most amazing person I've ever met."

His words enveloped her. How could he possibly think such wonderful things about her? She was just Cassie. She wasn't anyone special. "I think you're pretty amazing also."

A woman's voice said something in the background, and Ben said, "Hang on a second."

Cassie waited, wondering if he'd even heard what she said. Then Ben's voice was back.

"Hey, my mom had this idea. She said she would drive me to Springdale, and we can meet for dinner. Would you like to meet?"

Would she like to? Was he crazy? "Of course!" But then she thought of her parents. Would they agree to let her go to dinner with Ben and his mom? "When? I'll have to ask my parents."

"How about tomorrow night?"

Cassie's stomach did a little tumble. He was really serious. "Let me ask my mom."

She left her phone in her bedroom so Ben wouldn't overhear any conversation. She found her mom in the kitchen, putting away the dishes. "I've got Ben on the phone," she said, grabbing a handful of forks and helping her mom put them away.

"Oh? How is he?" Her mom gave her a sideways look.

"He wants to meet for dinner tomorrow night. With his mom." Cassie winced as soon as she said the words. She'd meant to warm her mother up to the idea, but she wasn't very good about beating around the bush.

"Where?"

"His mom said they would come to Springdale." Cassie lived in Springdale, a good forty minutes away from Ben's house in Huntsville.

"His mom is coming too?"

"Well, of course," Cassie said, getting a bit anxious. "Ben can't drive."

Mrs. Jones look thoughtful as she paused to dry her hands on a rag. "I think that's okay. Do you want me to come?"

Cassie could only imagine how much more anxious she would be if her mother were there also, watching her and Ben. But she didn't want to hurt her mother's feelings. "If you want to."

Mrs. Jones gave a slight smile. "Go ahead and tell him yes. I'll decide later if I'm going or not."

"Thank you!" Cassie threw her arms around her mother, unable to hold back her excitement. Then she ran to her bedroom and picked up the phone left open on the desk.

"Ben?" she said.

"I'm still here," he said. "What did your mom say?"

"She said yes!"

"That's great!"

They made plans for what time and where, and then Ben said, "I'll see you tomorrow."

"Yes," Cassie said, squirming in her chair at the desk. "I can't wait. See you tomorrow."

"Tomorrow," Ben repeated. "I love you."

And then he hung up.

Cassie stared at the phone as his last words registered in her head, and a giddiness rose up in her chest. He loved her. Josh had said those words too, and they had terrified Cassie. But coming from Ben, they made her feel happy and secure.

At the same time, she was glad he had hung up right away, because she couldn't say the words back. She wasn't going to say she loved someone until she was one hundred percent sure she did. She knew for sure she liked Ben—a lot—but she didn't know for sure that she loved him.

What she did know was she was excited to see him tomorrow.

Episode 3:

Kiss and Tell

CHAPTER TWENTY-FIVE

Gummy Bears and Okra

Cassie looked through the shirts in her closet, a nervous energy flowing through her veins. In less than an hour she would be having dinner with Ben and his mom, and she had no idea what to wear. She pulled out a T-shirt she'd bought in New York. Was it nice enough? She didn't want to look like she was still camping.

Mrs. Jones stepped into the walk-in closet behind Cassie. "How about this shirt?" She pulled a dark blue one with a high neckline and short, fluttery sleeves off the hanger. "Put it with a silver necklace and it will look nice."

Cassie grabbed the shirt like it was a lifeline and let out a sigh of relief. "This will be great. Thanks, Mom." She changed into the shirt and found a delicate silver cord to wear with it, tucking Ben's dog tags underneath the fabric.

She looked at herself in the mirror, but her stomach was so tied up in knots that all she saw was a wide-eyed little girl. She brushed some mascara on her lashes, not wanting to look like a child.

"You have such pretty eyes," her sister Emily said, watching her from the bedroom.

"Thanks," Cassie breathed. She brought her hands down the jeans and turned sideways, making a face at her thin body. At least she had a padded bra so she didn't look so flat. Would Ben think she was pretty?

She hoped so.

Half an hour later, she and her mom parked in front of the restaurant in Fayetteville that Ben's mom had chosen.

Cassie clutched her mom's hand, too nervous to get out of the car. "Come in with me?" She couldn't deny the painful butterfly attack going on in her chest. Butterflies? More like a hornet's nest.

"I'll walk in with you," Mrs. Jones said, a slight smile on her face. She squeezed Cassie's hand in response. "You don't need to be nervous, sweetie. This isn't a date. You're going to dinner with the boy you like and his mom."

What about this situation was supposed to not make Cassie nervous? What if she and Ben didn't know what to say to each other? What if he just didn't like her anymore?

She held onto her mom's hand until they walked through the doors of the restaurant, then she let go, her hands dropping by her sides. She spotted Ben and his mom right away, at a booth next to a window. Cassie stepped forward, trying to put a big, confident smile on her face. Ben's mother's back was to Cassie, but Ben spotted her. He wore a gray T-shirt and his usual baseball cap. He lifted his face, his eyes catching hers, and a wide grin split his face.

"Well, look who's here," he said, pushing off the bench and coming to her side. He reached over and pulled her into a hug, and Cassie's shoulders relaxed, immediately feeling at ease with his arms around her. He released her with a reassuring smile and slid back into the booth across from his mother.

His mom craned her head over. She had dark hair, cut short and wavy, and wore glasses. She stood up, a pleasant smile on her face. "Well, hello, Cassie! How wonderful to meet you!"

"Hi," Mrs. Jones said, sticking her hand out in front of Cassie. "I'm Cassie's mom, Karen."

Cassie turned her attention away from the adults as they introduced each other, and Ben scooted over in the booth.

"Sit by me?" he said.

Cassie had a split moment of panic. She thought she'd sit across from Ben where she could look at him, not next to him. But she needed to sit down now or he would think she was weird. So she slid into the booth beside him. Her body felt stiff and tense, and she froze when Ben reached over to take a sip of his soda, afraid he would put his arm around her.

But he didn't. Instead he gave her a smile around his straw and said, "You look really pretty. Even prettier than you do when you've been roughing it in a tent for two days."

Cassie laughed. She waved bye to her mom as Mrs. Jones left. What had she been so nervous about? This was Ben. They knew each other. They were friends. More than friends.

"Well. Let's get Cassie's drink ordered and then we can get some food," Ben's mom said, gesturing to the all-you-could-eat buffet behind them.

Ben's hand slid down next to his leg. He found Cassie's fingers and squeezed them before she had the chance to get worked up about it. Warm tingles floated up her arm, and surprisingly they flowed through her navel also. She tightened her grip on his fingers when he started to let go, marveling at how the simple touch of his hand could make her feel like she was floating. Then she let go, almost embarrassed of her actions, until she saw the way Ben looked at her with his intense blue eyes. Whatever she felt, he felt it too.

Cassie followed Ben to the buffet line after her mother left. She took a plate and stared at the food options, trying not to think about the fact that she would be sitting next to him and his mother while he watched her eat.

Something jostled her arm, and she turned her head slightly to see what it was. She laughed in surprise and delight when Ben placed another spoonful of okra on her plate.

"That's enough!" she said, sliding her plate away from him. "I won't have room for anything else!"

"I know how you love okra," Ben said with a grin that sent her insides bubbling up like lava from a volcano.

I love you, Cassie thought. But she bit back the words. Whatever she felt for him, she wasn't ready to say she loved him. "Okra is great," she said. "But so is mashed potatoes and broccoli and spaghetti . . ." She gestured to the other food items on the buffet line.

"And gummy bears."

She didn't see any gummy bears in sight, but she agreed with another laugh. "Yes. And gummy bears."

They filled their plates and returned to the table, where Ben's mom already sat with an enormous salad in front of her.

"What were you guys giggling about over there?"

"Oh, nothing. Cassie just has a fondness for okra and gummy bears," Ben said with a straight face.

The heat rushed up to her ears, but she found all she could do was giggle.

"Not at the same time, I hope," his mom said.

"No," Cassie choked out. "I manage to keep them separate."

"I hear there's gummy bears on the dessert bar," Mrs. Graves continued as she buttered her bread.

"Oh yes, we'll definitely have to check that out." Ben shot Cassie a grin.

She stuffed herself on all of the food, gigglier and happier than she could ever remember being. She went back to the buffet to get it another roll. When she returned to the booth, a little plastic bowl shaped like a tulip sat in front of her at the table. Inside were dozens of multi-colored gummy bears.

Cassie looked at Ben, who lifted his shoulder.

"I thought I'd let you get a head start."

That gooey feeling filled her body, all the way to the tips of her fingers. An insane part of her wanted to grab his face and kiss him, right there on the lips, right in front of his mom. But she restrained herself. Her last experience with kissing had not been awesome, and she didn't want to ruin her relationship with Ben by kissing him.

⚬～⚬※⚬～⚬

After dinner Ben's mom drove them across the street to the mall. Cassie's nerves returned full force as she walked beside him and his mom through the parking lot. She hardly knew how to act at the mall when she was with her friends. What was she supposed to do with a boy?

She was so distracted by her thoughts that she walked into the bumper of a car and nearly fell over.

"Careful!" Ben said, grasping her by the shoulders and keeping her from toppling. "There's a car there, you know."

Cassie tried to laugh through her embarrassment as she rubbed her side. "Now I do."

"It's not the only one. There's lots of them."

"You're so helpful," she said.

"I try to be." The smile never left his face, but he moved his hands from Cassie's shoulders and put them in his pockets. She instantly missed their weight.

"Well, guys," his mom said as they entered the mall, "I'm going to sit down on this bench and read my book. Why don't you walk around together and meet back here in an hour?"

"Sure," Ben said like it was no big deal, while Cassie's heart suddenly started up a double time beat. Leave the two of them alone together? What if they ran out of things to say?

Ben didn't give her a chance to voice her fears, though. He walked through the food court, slow enough for Cassie to keep up.

"Where do you want to go?" he asked.

The only place she really enjoyed at the mall was the bookstore, and they closed it down a few years ago. So she shrugged. "I don't really care. I'm just glad to be here with you. I missed you so much." That was the truth.

Ben stopped walking and turned to face her, his expression suddenly quite serious. "You have no idea. I couldn't stop talking about you. Everyone at camp was like, shut up, Ben! I just wanted to see you again."

Cassie stared back at him, unable to tear her gaze from the pull of his eyes. She reached one hand out, and Ben took it, clasping her fingers in his. The biggest smile split his face, and he turned around and kept walking, this time his hand holding hers.

They wandered aimlessly through the mall, occasionally ducking into a store. Cassie got Ben back for teasing her about bumping into a car when he bumped into a clothing rack and turned around to apologize to it.

"Now we're even," she said.

"Not even close," he said. "You didn't apologize to the car."

"I'll make sure to do that on the way out."

They passed a display of televisions, and Cassie touched the corner of one, expecting to feel the cold, hard edge of metal. Instead it was light and flimsy beneath her fingertips, and the whole TV set wiggled.

"Well," Cassie said. "That's not a regular television."

Ben stepped over and poked it. "It's made of cardboard!"

She tilted her head and studied it. "It looks so real."

"Are they all made of cardboard?" Ben stepped up to another television set and stuck his finger in it. Or tried. "Nope. That one was real."

Laughing, Cassie joined him, and they poked their fingers at different appliances to see which was real and which wasn't. They reached a small couch, and Ben collapsed into the corner.

"This one's real," he said, and he pulled Cassie down to sit next to him.

The sudden contact of his thigh against hers and the length of his torso against her rib cage sent hot flashes all the way up to her face. Ben took her hand again, and if he noticed her sudden fever, he didn't comment.

"This is nice," was what he said instead.

You're nice, Cassie wanted to say, but she lacked the ability to say anything at all, so she just sat in silence next to him, feeling the warmth of his fingers around hers.

A woman walked by with a chest so large it looked like she would topple forward. Cassie didn't mean to stare, but she couldn't tear her eyes away. She didn't dare look at Ben, certain the woman wouldn't have escaped his attention either. Only after she had walked by did Cassie sneak a glance at him, and from the way his lips were clasped together, she knew he was trying not to laugh. He met her eyes, and then Cassie couldn't contain herself, and they both erupted into giggles.

"I'm sorry," Ben said. "I didn't mean to look."

"I think it was impossible not to," Cassie said, trying hard to contain her embarrassed laughter for her gender. The next words escaped her mouth before she could contain them. "Do you think they were real?"

With a straight face, Ben said, "Maybe they were cardboard."

They headed back to Ben's mom a little while later, still walking hand-in-hand through the mall.

She glanced at him once and caught him staring at her. "What?" One hand came up and brushed her hair back.

"You look so pretty tonight."

Her face warmed. "Thanks."

"So," Ben said, his tone casual, "what are the rules about kissing?"

Kissing. The word conjured up thoughts of his mouth on hers, and a little flame ignited in her chest and fired through her belly. "Rules?"

"Yeah." Ben sneaked a glance at her. "Is it allowed?"

He wanted to kiss her! Cassie fought the desire to grab him by the shoulders and pull him into a corner and tell him to kiss her already. "Yeah, it's allowed. My parents are fine with it."

"Oh. That's cool," Ben said, and Cassie's stomach twisted around. Now she would spend every moment wondering if this was the time he would kiss her.

But it wasn't going to be right now. They turned the corner to the food court and spotted his mother, still sitting on the bench reading her book.

She looked up and smiled. "Hi, guys. Did you have a nice time?"

"Yes," Ben said. "Right, Cassie?"

"Yes," she agreed. "A great time."

Ben's mom drove Cassie home, and Ben held her hand the entire twenty-minute journey from Fayetteville out into the country, holding his up against hers and admiring the size differences.

"Your hand is so tiny," he whispered.

She lifted her shoulders. "I'm a small person."

"Is this it?" his mom asked as she turned into the circle drive in front of Cassie's house.

Cassie looked up at the plantation-style one-story house with blue shutters and four white pillars. "Yes." She turned to Ben, dreading the moment when their non-date would end. "Do you want to come in?"

"Of course."

His mom parked the car and pulled the key out. Then she and Ben followed Cassie into the house.

"Hello!" Mrs. Jones said, smiling as she appeared in the entry hall.

"Hi," Ben's mom said, her expression brightening.

Immediately their moms started up a lively conversation. Cassie left them, pulling Ben through the kitchen.

"This is my room," she said, pushing open the door. Her face flushed with shame when she spotted the huge pile of clothes on the floor. "Um, that's my sister's pile. I think she's hiding a pig under there."

Ben laughed and shook his head. "I like rooms where you can't see the carpet. Mine usually looks like this too."

That made Cassie feel a little better.

"Ben!" His mom called from the entryway. "It's time to go!"

Ben turned around and looked at Cassie. She swallowed hard, her heart sticking in her throat. Would this be when he kissed her?

He put his arms around her shoulders and pulled her into a hug. He didn't let go for long moment, but finally he did.

"I'll write you, I promise."

"You better," she said, trying to glare at him.

With a final glance at her, he went back through the kitchen to the front door. Cassie trailed behind, forcing back both the relief and disappointment that he hadn't tried to kiss her.

CHAPTER TWENTY-SIX

Hands and Lips

C assie watched Ben's car pull away, and then ran to her bedroom to call Riley.

"You won't believe who was just here!" Cassie squealed into the phone.

"Who?" Riley asked, sounding just as excited as Cassie.

"Ben!" Cassie said, and they both shrieked into the phone. Cassie marveled at how close she felt to Riley these days. She'd really turned into a good friend.

"Did he kiss you?" Riley asked.

"Not yet," Cassie said, squirming on her chair as a tickle filled her tummy. "But I'm sure he will soon."

Another call dinged on her phone, and Cassie pulled it from her ear to check the caller. Maureen. Even though she'd gotten home the day before, she hadn't told any of her other friends.

It was time.

"Riley, I've got to go. I'll talk to you later."

"Okay," Riley said, and Cassie clicked over.

"Hey, Maureen," she said, tempering her excitement. She couldn't tell her about her date with Ben. None of them even knew about him yet except Andrea.

"Hey," Maureen said. "I hear you have a new boyfriend."

Cassie winced. So much for keeping it a secret. "Yes," she said. What else had Maureen heard? "He was just here, actually."

"He was at your house? Who is he?"

How much should she say? "His name is Ben. We just met."

"You know, Josh is telling everybody you cheated on him."

"What?" Prickles ran up and down Cassie's spine. How could he possibly know that? Cassie had not told anyone.

"Yeah, we told him it's not true and to stop being such a baby about your break up. We all know you wouldn't do that."

"Of course not!" Cassie said. She crossed her mental fingers. If she had ever considered telling them the truth, now she knew she couldn't. While she had sent Josh a break up letter the very night Ben asked her out, she hadn't waited for him to get it before saying yes.

What difference did a couple of days make, anyway?

Ben called her the next day.

"I just have to tell you," he said, "how pretty you looked yesterday."

"Thanks," Cassie said. "I think you said that yesterday."

"You really did. Not that you don't always look pretty, but yesterday, wow. You were amazing."

"It's the first time you've seen me in make-up."

"I noticed that, but it didn't bother me. You're still pretty."

"You're funny," she said, wishing she did something besides laugh on the phone with him.

"My mom said you could come over this weekend," Ben said. "If you want. We can have dinner with my family, spend some time together."

"Really?" Cassie said, surprised and a little worried. Were things moving too quickly?

"Yeah."

"Well, I don't know," she hedged, feeling nervous all over again. "We just saw each other."

"We used to see each other every day. And school starts in a week, and then I don't know when we'll have the chance. Can you ask your parents?"

He made a good point. They might not have very many chances after this week. "Sure, I'll ask."

Cassie wandered into the living room where her parents and younger siblings watched a movie. "Mom? It's Ben. He wants to know if I can come over next Saturday."

Mr. and Mrs. Jones slowly rotated their heads to stare at her. Cassie blushed. Maybe she was asking too much.

"Who else will be there?" her mom asked.

Cassie shrugged. "His whole family."

"And what will you be doing?"

Well, this seemed like a silly question. "Hanging out with them. Eating dinner."

"Do you think it's a good idea to let her go over to a boy's house by herself?" her dad muttered.

"We won't be by ourselves," Cassie said.

Mrs. Jones waved a hand at her husband, then looked back at Cassie. "We'll have to establish some rules. Like you can't be alone with him. But I'm fine with you going to his house."

"Really?" Cassie gasped out. She hadn't expected her mother to say yes. She couldn't believe it! She was going over to Ben's! "I'll go tell him!" She ran back to her bedroom.

"Yes! They said yes!" Cassie said into the phone, unable to contain her excitement. She fervently hoped Ben didn't know how giddy she was.

"That's fantastic!" he said. "I'll see you Saturday, then."

☙ ❧

The days couldn't pass quickly enough. On Wednesday Cassie returned to voice lessons, where Ms. Malcolm told her she could tell Cassie hadn't practiced all summer, and Cassie felt frustrated and unnoticed. She's sung plenty of times at Camp Splendor!

Maureen and Amity both called on Thursday, pumping her for details about Ben and how they'd met. Cassie hedged, not wanting to give too much away, but she felt like they were trying to catch her in a lie.

And then on Friday, Cassie got a letter from Ben.

Her hand trembled as she opened it, and she exhaled in disappointment when she saw it was only a few paragraphs long. Then she smiled at the sight of his boyish handwriting. He mentioned how much fun he'd had at the mall and that he couldn't wait to see her on Saturday.

He added at the end, "You looked good Tuesday night. I mean that."

The comment lifted her lips, and she tucked the letter away in a drawer. Tomorrow she would see him.

Cassie told herself not to be nervous when Saturday morning arrived, but she couldn't help it.

"Just remember the rules," her mom said as she should pulled up the driveway to the small house situated at Camp Splendor. "No being alone with him."

"I know, I know," Cassie said, annoyed by the reminder. What did her mom think was going to happen, anyway?

A sudden bout of nerves seized Cassie when she got to the front door, and she stood directly in front of it, unable to lift her hand to ring the doorbell.

"You ring it," she told her mom.

Mrs. Jones laughed at her. "This is your boyfriend, not mine." Still, her mom obliged her and pressed the button.

Immediately voices came from the other side. "Is that her? Is she here?"

It was Ben's voice, and Cassie smiled in anticipation of seeing his face. Then the door swung open, and Ben stood there.

"You're here!"

"I'm here," Cassie echoed.

"Well, let her in, Ben," his mom said, appearing over his shoulder. A small redheaded girl with springy curls flounced to Ben's side.

"Is this your girlfriend?" she said.

"Go away, Lucy," Ben growled, sending the little girl a dark glare. He stepped out of the doorway. "Come on in." He gestured Cassie forward, almost touching her but not quite. "This is my house. And that's my annoying little sister."

Cassie stepped inside, taking in the orange kitchen, long pendant lights, and wood paneling. It didn't look like it had changed much during the past few decades.

"Hello!" Lucy said.

"I'll pick you up after dinner, Cassie!" Mrs. Jones' said, interrupting them with a wave.

"Ben, why don't you show Cassie around?" his mom said as soon as Mrs. Jones was gone.

"Come on, I'll show you my room," Ben said. "I cleaned it up just for you. So you can see the carpet."

Cassie laughed, marveling at how Ben put her at ease with his casual smile and joking.

He led her through the living room and a hallway covered with more wood paneling. A bedroom door was ajar. Ben pushed it the rest of the way open and tugged her inside. A dresser and mirror sat against one wall, and a twin bed was pushed against the other wall. Lucy followed them in, giggling.

"Get out, Lucy!" Ben said.

"I don't have to," Lucy said. "Mom said I could go wherever you go."

"Only when we get on the jeep!"

"No," Lucy said, arguing like any younger sister would.

Ben poked his head into the hallway. "Mom! Lucy won't leave us alone!"

"Lucy!" Mrs. Graves called. "Get out of there!"

Lucy stuck out her tongue and left the room.

"Sorry." Ben gave an eye roll. "She's so annoying."

"I know how it is," Cassie said. "I have younger sisters."

"Yeah, but I met your sisters. They're nice, not annoying."

"You don't have to live with them."

Ben took Cassie's hand and pulled her over to his bed. He sat down, and she lowered herself beside him, a whisper of awkwardness settling around her shoulders again. They sat side by side, facing the mirror. Cassie watched Ben's expression in the reflection as he took her hand in his, playing with her fingers and turning them over with his own. His touch sent goosebumps up her arm. She liked the sensation of his skin brushing hers.

"Do you think you'll come to camp again next year?" Ben asked.

"I hope to," Cassie said. "Will you be there?"

"I'm planning on it."

"Good. I'm going to need my okra fix."

Ben snorted and squeezed her fingers. "You're funny."

"I am?" Cassie raised an eyebrow. No one had ever said that about her before. That description went to Maureen.

"Yeah. It's one of my favorite things about you."

"Really?" The thought pleased her. And here she thought he was the funny one.

Ben rested his head against hers, and then he met her eyes in the mirror. He wrinkled his nose and stuck his tongue out at her, and Cassie found herself giggling like a silly girl again. She stood up and moved over to the dresser, rifling through the books and combs and other things he had on top before stopping to stare at her own reflection. A plain girl with almond shaped brown eyes, bangs pushed to the side, and dark brown hair pulled into a ponytail was what she saw. Was that what Ben saw? Nothing spectacular or special. She pulled out the rubber band, letting the hair fall across her shoulders.

"You're so pretty," Ben said, and Cassie's face warmed at the praise.

"You really think so?" *Say it again.* She would never get tired of hearing it.

"It's one of my other favorite things about you," he said. "Don't you know that? You're beautiful."

She shook her head.

"And you don't act all silly around me. I can actually talk to you. I like that a lot." He flashed her a smile.

Cassie smiled back and then pulled her hair into the ponytail.

"Oh," Ben said, letting out a soft sigh.

"You don't like it up?"

"You're pretty no matter what. But when you wear it down . . . well, I just really like it."

The dark locks had a crease in them from the ponytail holder, but she obliged him and took it down again.

"Yeah. I like that." Ben stepped up to the dresser beside her and ran his fingers through her hair. That same feeling from before shivered down her spine. His touch was electric.

"Let's look at pictures from camp." He took a photo album from his bookshelf and returned to the bed. Cassie followed, and they laughed over familiar counselors and girls acting goofy or looking ridiculous.

Ben lifted his gaze, his eyes trailing over her face before meeting her eyes. "So. Have you ever kissed anyone?"

The kissing talk again. It got Cassie's heart pounding a double time rhythm. "Yes," she admitted. "But I didn't like him very much. So it was pretty gross."

Ben threw back his head in laughter. "Was it your ex-boyfriend?"

She'd forgotten that she'd mentioned Josh to him. "Yes."

"I've kissed a girl before too." His expression turned serious, and he focused on her. One hand came out and grazed her cheek before cupping the back of her jaw.

Cassie didn't move. She didn't breathe. She even forgot to close her eyes when his face dipped to hers. His lips touched her mouth, and an odd, bubbly feeling sprouted in her chest. Ben pushed her lips open with his, deepening the kiss, and now her eyes closed as her arms went around him, the bubbly feeling turning into a full-body tingle.

This was how kissing was meant to feel. This was nothing like when Josh kissed her.

Ben pulled back, studying her face cautiously. "Was that okay?"

She took a short breath and nodded. "Yes," she said, her voice cracking. "Yes, that was nice." *Very* nice. Cassie wouldn't mind at all if they did that again.

CHAPTER TWENTY-SEVEN

Kissing Mania

"**H**ey, I know." Ben's eyes lit up, and he pulled Cassie to her feet. "Let's go for a drive around the campsite."

"You drive?" She let him guide her into the hallway.

"We have an ATV. I can drive it."

His mom listened while Ben asked permission to take Cassie to the campground.

"You can go," she said.

"Yes!" Ben didn't try to hide his fist pump.

"But you have to take Lucy with you."

Ben groaned. "Mom. Really?"

She gave him a no-nonsense look. "You think I would let you drive Cassie off into the campsite alone?"

He rolled his eyes, but Lucy perked right up from where she colored at the kitchen table. "I can go?"

"Better hurry up," he growled at her.

Mrs. Graves smiled and pulled a key ring from a hook above the stove. "Be back in time for dinner."

Ben led them outside to a carport, and Cassie spotted what looked like a small jeep.

"Sit in the back, Lucy," Ben called, and she climbed right over the door to get in. Ben opened Cassie's door for her.

"Sorry she has to come," he said.

"It's all right," she said, and she meant it. She didn't mind having his little sister there.

Ben drove the ATV with Lucy in the back over to the mess hall, just a short two minutes from his house. They bumped over the ruts and grooves in the dirt road, the green wilderness encroaching on them.

"Look." Ben slowed the vehicle and pointed into the woods. "Two fawns."

Cassie peered over his arm, following his finger. She let out a small gasp when she spotted the baby deer, still with their little white spots on the rump. "They're beautiful!"

He grinned at her. "Yeah, they are."

He parked in front of the familiar mess hall. As soon as he turned off the rumbling engine, the sounds of birds chirping high in the trees echoed around them. The three of them got out and wondered through the empty building.

"This is where we cook the food," Ben joked, leading her into the kitchen. He glanced over his shoulder, and Cassie followed his gaze to where Lucy was messing with the windows. Ben grabbed Cassie's hand and pulled her around the corner, out of sight. He yanked her body close to his and dropped his mouth on hers, kissing her again. The same pleasant thrill as before warmed her, and Cassie leaned into him. His hand went to her waist, and he squeezed her hip, and the sudden, hungry desire to pull his body closer surprised her.

Ben broke away just as Lucy scampered into the kitchen.

"It's different when there are no campers here," Cassie said, her lips still tingling from the touch of his mouth.

"Yeah. It's so quiet." Ben squeezed her hand and walked over to a giant metal door. "Here is the big freezer where we keep all the food. Want to see it?"

Cassie couldn't imagine what would be exciting about the deep freezer. But Ben already had the door open, so she shrugged. "Sure."

He tugged her inside, and then he let the door swing shot.

A rush of alarm rippled through Cassie. "We can't get stuck in here, can we?"

"No, Lucy isn't tall enough to lock us in." And then his hands were looping around her again, pulling her body close to his. His mouth found Cassie's, prying her lips open with his.

He'd pulled her in here so they could kiss some more? It was too cold to enjoy the activity. She returned the kiss for a few seconds before breaking away and saying, "I'm freezing." She added a shiver for good measure.

"Yeah, let's get out of here." Ben pushed the door open, and she welcomed the hot, humid air that greeted her from the kitchen.

"Finally!" Lucy exclaimed. "I thought maybe you got stuck in there! What were you doing?"

"Just cooling off," Ben said. "Let's go look at one of the campsites."

"That sounds fun," Cassie said. "I have so many memories of camping here."

"Yeah, it'll be great."

Ben drove the ATV again, sitting close to Cassie while Lucy hung over the front seats from the back. A minute later they arrived at the campsite Cassie had stayed at during her first year at Camp Splendor, when she arrived on crutches. The familiar platform tents had all been stripped of their canvases in preparation for winter.

"It looks so bare and skeletal," she said.

"It's always like this when everyone leaves. Kind of sad." Ben hopped out of the vehicle, followed by Lucy. Cassie took her time climbing over, and by then Lucy had already bolted away.

Ben arrived at her side and took her hand as she jumped to the ground. Before she could step away from the ATV, he put an arm around her waist. Suddenly he was kissing her again, one hand squeezing her hip while the other remained firmly planted on her back.

A seed of annoyance sprouted in her chest. Was he going to make every moment an excuse to kiss her? She tried to enjoy it, to put some feeling into kissing him back, but she was tired of his mouth on hers, tired of the kissing.

"Ben! Come on!" Lucy's voice came closer, and she popped out from behind the pavilion.

Ben broke away, his hands sliding down Cassie's waist. "Coming!" he said, securing Cassie's hand and following Lucy.

He didn't want to kiss Cassie in front of his sister. Cassie made a mental note to keep Lucy as close by as she could.

By the time they returned to the house for dinner, Cassie was conflicted. She really liked Ben. And she had really liked kissing him— at first. Now she was tired of it and honestly wouldn't care if he never kissed her again. And it made her annoyed with Ben. Was there something wrong with her? Did kissing a guy change her feelings for him?

No, she told herself. *There's nothing wrong with me. I just want to do something besides kiss. Like talk.*

That was the problem. She and Ben had spent so much time laughing and talking and getting to know each other before they started kissing. Now it seemed like that was all he wanted to do.

Dinner was nice because he didn't try to kiss her, and they had a good laugh when they saw his mom had prepared okra just for her. But still, Cassie felt some relief when her mom came.

Ben gave her a brief but strong hug before she left. "I'll write you. And I promise I'll see you soon."

Not too soon, and not alone, Cassie hoped. She really didn't want to spend another day making out.

"Well, how was it?" Mrs. Jones asked as they walked down the driveway to where she had parked. "Did you follow our rules?"

"Yes. We were never alone." Technically.

"Did he kiss you?"

The question surprised Cassie, and she hesitated, suddenly worried about her mother's reaction. But she wasn't in the habit of keeping secrets from her mom, so she answered truthfully. "Yes."

"With tongue?"

Tongue. Now Cassie's face warmed with embarrassment. "Um, yes." Did that make her a bad person?

But her mom didn't chastise her. She just said, "Just remember, when there's tongue involved, boys get a little bit more excited than you might imagine."

Cassie thought she knew what her mom meant. "Yeah, he seemed to really like it."

"And you didn't?"

Her face burns. "I did. Just not as much as him."

"Did he try to do anything else?"

Cassie reared back as if scalded. "No! Mom!"

"Hey, I have to ask, I'm your mom! Just be careful, okay? It can go from kissing to more than that very quickly."

Cassie remembered the hot feeling of desire that had fired up in her during their second kiss. "No need to worry. I don't intend to kiss again anytime soon."

Mrs. Jones only laughed.

⚜

That evening Cassie's parents called her to their room.

"I think we need to lay down more ground rules," her dad said. "It's not okay for you to be kissing boys yet."

Her mouth fell open, and she shot a glance at her mom. "What?"

Mrs. Jones just shook her head, and Mr. Jones continued.

"We let you go over to a boy's house and that was a mistake. You're too young and we should have known better than to trust you to be responsible."

"Responsible?" she sputtered. "We didn't do anything wrong!" Now she glared at her mom.

"You kissed him. That's not appropriate. So no kissing, no dating, no going over to friends' houses or hanging out with them if boys will be there."

"Are you serious?" Her heart pounded with indignation, and she regretted telling her mother the truth.

"Dead serious. You're only fourteen. And these are the rules. Next time you're with that boy, the two of you don't leave my sight."

At least he hadn't told Cassie to break up with him. Her chest puffed out, and she wanted to argue, to tell her dad he had no right. But he could ruin them. So she bit her tongue and nodded before marching out of the room.

She wanted to call Ben, but she couldn't tell him what her parents had said. What if he agreed? What if he thought they shouldn't be together anymore? She put her head in her pillow and cried over the unfairness of it.

On Monday Cassie met up with her friends at the junior high so they could get their school schedules. It had been weeks since she had seen them, and Amity and Andrea squealed over her like it had been months.

"We have so much to get caught up on," Andrea said, hooking her arm through Cassie's.

"Like finding out all about this new guy in your life," Amity said.

Ben. Cassie gave a little sigh as she thought of him. She almost regretted kissing him. Things had been so simple before. Now her parents acted like she was going to get pregnant the next time she saw him or something. And she hadn't done anything wrong!

"Ben's wonderful," Cassie said. "My parents are being a bit weird about him, though." They had been all fine with Ben until Cassie told them they kissed. Now suddenly Ben wasn't appropriate.

Amity nodded in understanding. "My parents do the same thing. I hate it."

The girls continued to the locker hall, where they ran into Janice, Maureen, and Cara, the other girls in their group. The hugging and squealing resumed, and then they scattered to try out their lockers. Although not right next to each other, their lockers were relatively close together. Just a quick spin around the locker hall and they could see each other.

"Hey guys, tonight's one of the last nights the Grape Festival is open," Cara said, referencing the local carnival. Tontitown had been founded by Italians, and they still carried on the tradition of harvesting the grapes. They celebrated the end of the harvest with a spaghetti dinner and grape ice cream and grape soda and plenty of thick-skinned grapes for sale.

"Oh, that sounds like so much fun!" Andrea said. "I'll be there for sure."

"Count me in," Maureen said.

"I'm not sure," Janice said. "My mom has some things she wants me to do."

"You know I'll be there," Amity said. She turned to Cassie. "What about you?"

"Sure, I'd love to be there." This was the first she was hearing about it, though, and she still had to ask her mom. Then she thought of something else. "Will there be boys there?"

The girls cracked up, and Amity elbowed Cassie.

"Your boyfriend going to be jealous?" she said.

"You know it's not a party without boys," Andrea said.

Cassie kept her eyes on Cara and waited for the response.

"Of course there will be boys," Cara said, tilting her head and blinking at Cassie. "It's at the Grape Festival. They'll be lots of people there."

Cassie relaxed a little. Her parents couldn't say no just because there would be boys at the carnival. She had no control over that. "Count me in, then!"

CHAPTER TWENTY-EIGHT

Too Many Boys

C assie searched for Riley as she walked out of the school building, but she didn't see her friend. It surprised her that she missed Riley. She's been excited to see her other friends, but they'd missed out on so much of her life this summer. She felt the distance between them simply because they didn't know what was going on with her. Riley knew.

But she didn't see Riley. She would have to call her later and find out her friend's schedule.

Cassie should've expected the third degree when she told her parents about Cara's invite to the Grape Festival, but somehow she hadn't. She wasn't used to her parents not trusting her, and it annoyed her, especially when she did everything she could to do what was right.

"And there won't be any boys there?" her dad said.

What was Cassie supposed to say? That all boys had been banned from the Grape Festival?

"That's right," Cassie said, allowing herself an eye roll. "It's just me and my friends. We've got the whole Grape Festival to ourselves."

"He means no boys at Cara's house," her mom said.

"Good grief," Cassie snapped. "What do you think we are?"

"Just normal teenage girls, honey. We're just making sure," Mrs. Jones said.

"No, you're not treating me like a normal teenage girl. You're treating me like someone who's already been a rebel and is trying to cause more problems. Haven't I earned any trust and respect?"

Her mother looked properly chastised, but Mr. Jones just puffed out his chest.

"Teenagers don't think properly. So it's our job to think for you."

Cassie's mouth fell open, and she searched for a response, but her mom raised a hand before she could say anything.

"You can go. Go on and get your things ready." She shot Cassie a look that said, "Don't say another word."

Cassie obeyed, standing and marching from the room.

But indignation fired through her chest. One thing had suddenly become very clear to her. She couldn't be honest with her parents about everything. If they flipped out about the little things, there was no telling how they would react to other things.

The girls met by the big white chapel at the festival. A stage had been set up in front of it, and happy cowboys sang ballads for the karaoke machine. Even Janice had come, in spite of thinking she might not be able to. Cassie was glad not to be the one left out.

"Come on!" Andrea grabbed Amity's forearm. "Let's go on the Ferris wheel."

"No way." Amity dug her heels in, refusing to budge. She had filled out more over the summer, Cassie noticed. None of them look like little girls anymore.

Except Cassie. Her hand came up and brushed the surface of the padded bra, giving her more curves than she naturally had. At least she looked normal.

"Chicken," Andrea said, but Amity didn't budge.

"Fine." Andrea turned her attention to Cassie. "Come with me on the Ferris wheel."

Cassie had no problem with the Ferris wheel or any of the rides. "Sure."

They wandered to the other side of the field, past all the little kid rides, where a line of people stood waiting to ride the Ferris wheel.

"Those guys are cute," Andrea said, pointing at some boys a few people in front of them.

Cassie looked them over but didn't see anything appealing about them. Then one of them pulled out a cigarette and began to smoke. "You're kidding, right? They're like old and gross."

"They're not gross just because they're smoking," Andrea said.

Cassie begged to differ. She thought of Ben and wished he were there with her. He might like to kiss a lot, but he was always very respectful and she couldn't imagine him doing something as gross as smoking.

Andrea giggled, and Cassie looked over to see her batting her eyelashes at one of the guys. They leered at her, revealing brown teeth when they smiled. The yuck factor increased. Cassie elbowed Andrea.

"Seriously? Quit looking at them."

Andrea's smile deepened, and she said through clenched teeth,

"Don't be such a child. They're men."

Andrea's dig stung, but not because of what she said. What hurt was how quickly Andrea disregarded her advise.

"Whatever," Cassie said. "You can have them both."

Luckily the guys got on the Ferris wheel several seats in front of Cassie and Andrea, so they weren't forced to make conversation with them. The swinging car stopped in front of Andrea, and both girls moved to get on when Cassie grabbed Andrea's arm.

"Sick," she said, pointing out a pile of vomit on the seat.

"Oh, no way!" Andrea scrunched up her nose and stepped back.

"Sir?" Cassie called to the conductor. "Someone threw up in here."

The man, who wore a vest over his bare chest and cargo pants and sported long hair with a beard, stepped over to investigate. "Ew!" he cried in a surprisingly girly voice when he saw it.

"I don't wanna sit in that one," Andrea said.

He grabbed a handful of paper towels and wiped it down. "That's fine. Wait until the next one arrives."

They did, and Cassie wondered what Ferris wheel rider had thrown up in his seat and then left without saying a word to anyone. Pretty gross.

They got in the next car without incident, and Andrea spent the whole time craning her neck back to look at the guys with the gross teeth. Cassie's gaze wandered out over the horizon to the gently rolling hills and the thick green trees. The Ferris wheel stopped every two seconds to let people on and off, and Cassie wished Andrea would talk to her. It wasn't nearly as much fun without her.

The guys got off the Ferris wheel first, but to Cassie's horror, they stopped a few yards from the wheel and waited. She had no doubt they waited for Andrea.

As soon as the girls stepped out of the seat, Andrea tossed her wavy brown hair over her shoulder and flounced toward them.

"Hey, beautiful," the bigger one said, showing a mouthful of brown teeth as he smiled. "I was hoping we'd get the chance to talk to you."

Andrea giggled like a maniac, and Cassie sure hoped she didn't sound so stupid when Ben made her laugh.

"What ride are you going on next?" Andrea asked them.

"Whichever one you're going on," the bigger dude said. The other one was a bit shorter with dark skin and dark eyes, and so far he hadn't said anything, just stayed in the shadow of his friend. "We'll go on it with you ladies."

Total creep. "I don't think that's a good idea," Cassie said. "We came to ride together."

"Oh, it's no problem," the big guy said to Cassie, as if she'd only voiced a doubt and he needed to reassure her. "It's just one ride. We won't steal your friend away forever." He turned his condescending grin on Cassie.

Cassie refused to give in. She wouldn't leave Andrea with this dude. "She rides with me."

"I don't mind," Andrea said, that ridiculous giggle emerging again. "There's two of them and two of us, Cassie. The other one can ride with you."

Cassie turned a glare on Andrea.

"Yeah," the smaller guy said, speaking up for the first time. The high pitch in his voice startled her, and Cassie gave him her full attention. "I'll make you feel real comfortable."

She doubted that.

They had reached the end of the line, and it was their turn now. Without waiting for permission or saying another word, Andrea scurried into a seat next to the big guy. At a loss as to what else she could do, Cassie followed the other boy into the little car. She scooted as far over to the side as possible, trying to hold her breath and ignore his stench.

The ride powered up, the car lifting into the air from the arms that extended out of the center of the device. The car bounced up and down twice, a tickle forming in Cassie's belly.

Beside her, the boy lifted his arms and squealed like a little girl. "This ride goes so fast!" He followed the observation up with several unnecessary swear words.

His voice came out fast and high pitched, and Cassie couldn't help swiveling her head to stare at him.

"Come on over here, girl," he said, beckoning her closer in a squeaky voice. "We can hold on to each other!"

"I'm good where I am," she said. Would this ride never end?

He kept talking, keeping up a steady stream of high-pitched words, and Cassie ground her teeth.

She'd get Andrea back for this one.

⟡

"Oh my gosh, that was the most fun ever!" Amity couldn't stop giggling as they climbed into Cara's mom's SUV. "So many cute guys!"

"And they all wanted to talk to you," Maureen said, sounding annoyed.

"Yes, well." Amity shrugged. "I'm obviously not a kid anymore." Obviously.

"I got guys to talk to me, also," Andrea said.

"Guys?" Cassie put in, still put out by Andrea's behavior. "Those were a bunch of middle-aged creeps."

"I didn't see you doing any better," Andrea huffed.

"I was doing everything I could to keep their hands off you!" Cassie said.

"Shush," Cara said, glancing toward her mom, who was driving.

Cassie lowered her voice. "It was gross. I'd rather not spend another evening fending off dirty boys."

Amity giggled again. "Sounds like the kind Andrea attracts. Dirty boys."

Andrea glowered, but then Cara's mom pulled into the house, and they all piled out. The customary box of pizza waited at the counter, and they dove in, argument forgotten.

Except Janice. She went to the bathroom and then sat on the couch, studying her hands.

Cassie nibbled on her slice of pizza, as always reminding herself that food was good. She had this insane fear of gaining weight and getting fat, even though she logically knew not only was it unlikely, it wouldn't matter if she did. She put the slice down and joined Janice, sitting cross-legged beside her on the couch.

"You okay?" she asked.

Janice let out a sigh. "Sometimes I feel like the odd one out."

"You?" That surprised Cassie. She often felt like the odd one; she was the newest to their group of friends, and she still felt she had to earn her place.

Janice nodded. "Boys notice all of you, but they never even look at me."

Cassie knew that pain. "Boys didn't notice me until recently."

"But they are now. I might not ever have a boyfriend."

"Of course you will," Cassie scoffed. "We're just kids, Janice. There's lots of time."

"I'd even take the gross guys Andrea gets."

Cassie laughed. "You would not. You're not desperate."

But Janice looked desperate, with the forlorn expression on her round face.

Cassie tried a different tactic. "That boy sitting next to me on the ride? I'm not even sure he was a boy. He could squeak higher than my little sister Annette."

Janice arched an eyebrow. "What do you mean?"

"He was all like, 'oh, look at this ride, we're going so high, it's so amazing, want to sit closer to me, don't you want to cuddle?'" Cassie pitched her voice into a high squeal while she spit out the words.

Janice burst out laughing. "He did not sound like that."

"Yes, he did. He was so girly."

"What are you doing, Cassie?" Amity asked, coming around the couch.

"That's how that stupid guy talked at the fair," Cassie said.

"Do it again," Maureen said. Andrea and Cara crowded behind her.

Cassie imitated him again, this time adding a few ridiculous facial expressions. Amity and Maureen collapsed in peals of laughter.

"He wasn't that bad," Andrea said.

"His hair wasn't as greasy as the one sitting next to you, if that's what you mean," Cassie said.

"I wondered if maybe he didn't have any shampoo," Andrea said, looking slightly embarrassed. "It was gross to touch."

"You touched it?" Cara said, turning to regard Andrea.

"I didn't know it would be that gross!"

"Oh, she flirts with all the boys," Amity said. "Even the nasty ones."

"You're no better!" Andrea snapped back.

"Okay, okay," Cara said, settling down on the floor across from the couch. "Let's all be friends."

"Let's all be friends," Maureen sang. She grabbed a stuffed bear off the couch and sat next to Cara.

Andrea finally relaxed. She sat down next to Cassie on the couch.

"We are friends," Cassie said. "Friends look out for each other."

"But sometimes people make mistakes," Amity said. "Will we still be friends if one of us screws up?"

"Screws up how?" Maureen asked, but Cara elbowed her.

"It doesn't even matter," Cara said. "Of course we'll still be friends."

"What if I never get a boyfriend?" Janice said.

"What does that matter?" Maureen said. "I've never had one either. It doesn't change who you are."

"I promise," Cara said, her light brown eyes meeting Janice's, "that we will always be friends. No matter what." She met each girl's gaze in the circle. "I promise each of you. Friends forever."

"Me too," Cassie said, inspired by the words. "Friends forever. I promise."

"We'll always have each other," Amity said. "Friends forever."

"Friends forever."

The other girls echoed the chant, and as Cassie looked around at all of them, her heart warmed. She truly believed they would be.

✦

No one wanted the sleepover to end, so in the morning the girls got permission to head to Amity's house for a swim. The good feelings from the evening before continued, turning into the usual frivolity of teasing and poking fun. They climbed onto the flotation devices in Amity's pool and tried to knock each other off.

"Don't," Andrea said when Cassie started to splash water on her. "I can't get my head wet."

"Whatever," Amity said. She jumped off her raft and waded over to Andrea, then put both hands on Andrea's float. "You're about to get dunked."

Andrea shied her face away. "No, Amity. I can't."

Amity pushed on the float, and Andrea let out a shriek. "I said no! My head can't get wet!" She got off the float and headed for the steps, then disappeared into the house.

"What's wrong with her?" Amity said, her tone insulted.

"She's been really weird lately," Maureen said.

"She just wants attention," Janice said. "She'll do anything to get it."

Cassie had to agree that Andrea was acting strangely, but she felt bad speaking against her friend. "There's a lot going on with her. We just have to patient."

"Oh, you don't even know, Cassandra," Maureen said importantly. "You haven't been here all summer. You don't know half of what's been going on."

The idea that she was out of the loop stung Cassie. She frowned. "Yes, I do," she said. "Andrea tells me everything."

Amity scoffed. "Yeah, right. You're like the last person she would tell."

"Lay off, guys," Cara said. "Andrea might have told her. You never know."

That silenced them and the subject changed, but the words grated Cassie. She faked a smile and pretended to be involved in the conversations, but she kept replaying what they'd said. They knew something about Andrea and no one was telling. And now she had to pretend like she knew what it was also.

She stayed in the water long enough for everyone to forget about the deal with Andrea. Then she stood up and went into the house.

Andrea sat at the kitchen table, talking into her phone in a low voice. Cassie sat down across from her and stared at her until Andrea hung up.

"I have to go," Andrea said with a sigh. "My mom wants me to come home. She's coming to get me."

"Everyone says you have some crazy secret you're not telling me," Cassie said.

Andrea wrinkled her nose. "What? I don't know what they're talking about."

"I don't know either," Cassie said. "But they said a lot happened with you this summer and I'm the only one who doesn't know."

"What else are they saying?" Andrea asked, her eyes darkening.

Cassie shrugged. "I told them not to talk about you, so they stopped. And I told them I already know everything."

Andrea let out a breath. "Thanks, Cassie. And don't worry about them. There aren't any secrets." She flashed a smile.

Cassie waited with her until Mrs. Wall arrived and took Andrea home, but Cassie couldn't help feeling that Andrea was still lying.

What had happened to her this summer that Cassie didn't know about?

CHAPTER TWENTY-NINE
Secret Keeper

C assie barely slept the night before school started. Ninth grade. This was the year that school actually started to matter. All of her grades would be on a permanent record for whatever college she chose to go to. She got up and dressed carefully, wanting to impress. Cassie studied her reflection in the bathroom mirror, standing on her tiptoes to take in the short, flowery skirt and the matching baby T. She tried to curl her hair, but the stubborn strands refused to cooperate, and she gave up. Fine. She still looked good.

Mrs. Jones was up also, making breakfast and reminding them that this was the only day she'd drive them to school. Cassie's little sister Emily was in seventh grade now, so they'd be at the same school.

"Will we have any classes together?" Emily asked Cassie.

"No," Cassie said. "The seventh graders don't mingle with the ninth graders." Cassie's friends were in her classes, though. She hoped seeing each other multiple times a day would strengthen their friendships.

And help cement Cassie's social status as one of the cool girls. She hated always feeling like she was on the outskirts, trying to fit in.

After dropping Scott and Annette off at the elementary school, Mrs. Jones was almost late to the junior high. Cassie barely had time to shove her stuff into her locker before running to her first hour class. Civics.

Andrea and Janice were also in there, and they stopped talking as Cassie slid into the desk beside Andrea, slightly out of breath.

"You look nice," Janice said.

"Thanks." Cassie ran her fingers through her hair, feeling what remained of the curls. Janice's hair hung straight and dark as usual. Andrea's hair, on the other hand, was coiffed in perfect waves. "You guys do, too."

Coach Benson called the class to attention and started taking roll. Cassie's eyes scanned the classroom, noting other friends like Luke, who she'd eaten lunch with all seventh grade.

Andrea leaned over and whispered, "Guess who I talked to last night."

Cassie hadn't the foggiest idea. She called, "Here," when Coach said her name, and then said, "I have no idea. Who?" Did Andrea have a boyfriend? She couldn't remember one being mentioned.

"Josh." Andrea sat back with a smug look on her face, her eyes roving over Cassie's face.

It took a full second for Cassie to remember Josh was *Cassie's* ex-boyfriend. "Oh. Why were you talking to him?"

"I think he might like me."

Cassie felt a tiny prick of jealousy, but it passed. Following on its heels was relief. If Josh liked Andrea, he'd forget Cassie. "That's nice. I'm happy for you guys."

"He also says he hates you now."

That startled her. Cassie reared back, her face growing hot. "He hates me?"

"Yeah. He says you lied to him and cheated on him."

The temperature in the room increased a few more degrees. He couldn't know that. She hadn't told anyone. "That's not true!"

"Why is he saying that?"

Cassie sputtered. "He's just mad that I broke up with him! And then found someone else!" Not in that order, but Josh didn't know!

"He's just being a jealous ex," Janice put in, rolling her eyes. "Exes can be so vindictive."

"Ugh!" Cassie pushed her hands off her shirt as if brushing off something distasteful. "What a jerk!"

She tried to put the negative thoughts from her mind, but they plagued her all the way until she went to English in third hour. This was her favorite class and her favorite teacher. She sat by her friend Nicole, who was apparently still dating Jimmy, because they passed notes during the class.

Cassie waved to Jaclyn and Leigh Ann, other friends of hers.

"How's your book coming, Cassie?" Ms. Talo asked, reminding Cassie of the book she'd finished writing the year before.

"Good, good," Cassie said. "I'm still making the revisions the editor requested, but then I'll submit it to the publisher again." And at some point, maybe she would finish writing the sequel.

"That's fantastic. We all want to know after you get a contract."

Cassie smiled, and for a while she forgot about Andrea. But when she saw Andrea again in Spanish class, the conversation came flooding back to her mind. Andrea didn't bring it up, and Cassie refused to show it bothered her. When she saw Amity in the locker hall before lunch, though, Cassie rushed over to her. She pulled her slightly off the side.

"Hey, do you still talk to Josh?" she asked. Cassie knew Amity and Josh had become friends after Amity crushed on him.

"Yeah, we still talk," Amity said, her greenish-brown eyes narrowing. "Why? Are you interested in him again?"

"Oh, no," Cassie said. "Not at all. It's just—" She spared a quick glance over her shoulder but didn't see Andrea. "Andrea told me he said he hates me. Is that true?"

"He's never said that to me," Amity said. "He always goes on and on about how much he loves you and he's so heartbroken and he can't understand why you broke up with him. He's like a love-sick dog, actually."

Better than being hated. "Do you think he said that to Andrea?"

"Maybe if he was trying to convince her he's over you." Amity lowered her voice. "But remember what we told you? Andrea's a liar. She'll say anything for attention."

Cassie exhaled, feeling a tad bit better.

Amity tilted her head. "What really happened between you and Josh?"

Cassie stiffened again. "What do you mean?"

"Tell me the truth. You guys were all happy and in love and then you were dumping him. And then just like that, you had a new boyfriend."

"I've told you the truth," Cassie said, glancing down at her hands and noticing a broken nail. She picked at it. "I just thought he seemed too old for me. So we broke up. And then I met Ben."

"Is that everything?"

"Yes!" Cassie snapped, lifting her head. "That's everything."

"You sure?" Amity pressed.

Cassie didn't deign to answer. She waved her hand and stalked toward the cafeteria. Her heart pounded a little too hard in her chest, and she knew she was sweating.

They were watching her. One false move, and her friends would figure out the truth about their break up.

⟡

Cassie was relieved to see Riley when she walked into choir in seventh hour. Maureen and Amity waved Cassie over, but she pretended not to see them. She crossed the room to the alto section and crouched next to Riley.

"How's your day been?" Cassie whispered.

"Fine. Yours?"

Cassie glanced over her shoulder. Maureen and Amity were goofing off and not paying her any attention. Janice was an alto, but she was talking to Sierra. Cassie lowered her voice even more, making Riley lean closer to hear.

"They keep asking me about Ben and Josh. Josh is telling everyone I cheated on him."

Riley gave her a wide-eyed look. "What are you going to do?"

"Nothing." Whatever she did, she had to keep it a secret. What if it got back to Ben? Her blood ran cold at the thought. "You won't tell, will you?"

Riley shook her head. "Your friends don't talk to me. And they don't know I was there."

Good thing. Cassie exhaled slowly. "We'll just have to keep it that way."

⟲⟳⟳✲⟲⟳⟳

"How was the first day of school, Cassandra?" Mrs. Jones asked when Cassie walked in the door behind her siblings.

"Good enough," Cassie said. She surveyed the fruit bowl and selected a peach. "I have classes with all my friends. And I like my teachers so far."

"Hmm," Mrs. Jones said, and something about her tone made Cassie look at her.

"What's that mean?" Cassie asked, watching her mother load the dishes.

Mrs. Jones paused with a plate in her hand, and then she said, "Do you still miss Texas?"

Cassie lifted her eyes toward the ceiling and considered the question. She'd hated Arkansas when they moved here in fifth grade, but that was four years ago. Now she'd grown close to the people and didn't know the ones in Texas at all. "No. I'm happy here."

Mrs. Jones let out a slow breath. "But you could make friends again. Just like you did here."

Cassie put down the peach, growing suspicious of this conversation. "Where's this going, Mom?"

Mrs. Jones finally closed the dishwasher and looked at Cassie. "We're kind of in crisis mode financially. If your dad can't find a job that pays the bills here, we have an offer in Texas."

"No," Cassie said.

"It might be all we have. We'd move back to Texas, you'd see your old friends—"

"No," Cassie said again.

"Come on, honey. Sometimes we have to do—"

"No! I won't go!" Cassie ran to her room, banging the door so hard behind her that it bounced right out of the frame. She threw herself on her bed and stared at the ceiling, trying to calm her breath.

It won't happen, she told herself. *It's all hypothetical.*

Fear gripped her heart, nearly choking her. She had a place here. She had a boyfriend. She loved her school. Suddenly everything about Arkansas felt perfect and amazing. She couldn't go somewhere else.

⚬⚬⚬

Ben called that evening, and Cassie told him her fears about moving.

"Maybe it won't happen," he said. "Maybe your parents are just planning for worst-case scenario."

"I'm sure you're right." Cassie chewed on her lower lip, catching the soft skin. "I don't want to move."

"It would really suck," Ben agreed. "When am I going to see you again? I miss you."

His words warmed her heart and removed some of the anguish. "I don't know. Let's plan something."

"My birthday's next month."

"Come over," Cassie said, getting an idea. "I'll throw you a party, invite my friends. They can all meet you."

"Yeah, that sounds fun."

They made tentative plans, then Cassie hung up and went back to worrying. It couldn't happen. She couldn't bear it.

She didn't tell her friends, keeping her fears to herself. The next day school got harder as all the teachers assigned homework.

"Hey, everyone's coming over for my birthday this Friday, right?" Amity said, glancing up in fourth hour as she penciled the problems over her paper.

"I'll ask my mom, but probably," Cassie said, and the other girls answered similarly.

"Is Todd going to be there?" Andrea asked, a twinkle in her eye.

Cassie swept her gaze back around to Amity, curious. "Todd who?"

"Todd Wilcox," Andrea answered for her.

Amity glared at Andrea. "No. Of course not."

"Why would you want him there?" Cara asked, voicing Cassie's unspoken question.

"She has a crush on him," Andrea said, reminding Cassie again why they didn't tell their secrets to Andrea.

"Andrea!" Amity growled, and then she smiled sweetly at the other girls. "I just think he's cute."

"That's not what you—" Andrea began, but Amity kicked her hard enough that she winced.

Birthday party. Cassie had completely forgotten. But that reminded her of Ben's upcoming birthday, and that reminded her of her dad's possible job change. She still hadn't told her friends. She looked over at

Amity and gave a big smile, then forced herself to focus on math problems.

The rest of the day proceeded smoothly, and Cassie looked for Janice on the way to science class. She didn't see her, so she stepped inside and chose a table next to Jaclyn, leaving a space on her other side for Janice.

"Hi," Jaclyn said, revealing two dimples in her dark skin before returning her attention to a homework assignment.

"Hi," Cassie replied. She pulled out her book and read while she waited for Janice.

Mr. Adams cleared his throat, bringing the class to order, and Cassie looked up. The spot beside her remained empty. Cassie swiveled in her seat, eyes scanning the room. Then she spotted Janice in the back, next to Salley, who had been whispering with her the day before. A lump formed in Cassie's throat, and she pushed down the hurt. Why would Janice snub her? She faced forward again and tried not to feel too wounded.

☙ ❦ ❧

"How's it going with Daddy's job hunt?" Cassie asked Mrs. Jones when she got home. Her mom was in the laundry room this time, sorting darks and whites. "Has he found anything close by?"

"Not yet. He's still looking, but you need to prepare yourself. We might have to move."

Cassie shook her head. She refused to consider that option.

Cassie exhaled in relief and broached another subject. "Ben's birthday is next month. Can he come over? Can we have a party for him?"

"That might be nice. I'll talk to his mom."

"Really?" Cassie beamed. "Oh, and don't forget I've got Amity's party on Friday. I'm going home with her after school."

Mrs. Jones squinted her eyes. "Who will be there?"

"Just the normal people, Mom," Cassie said, annoyance replacing her earlier gratitude. "Me, Andrea, Cara, Janice, Maureen. And Amity, of course."

"Any boys?"

Cassie rolled her eyes. "Mom!"

"I'm serious, Cassie."

"Mother," she said, allowing the full weight of her irritation to tinge the word. "It's a slumber party. Of course not!"

"Well, okay, then. I'm trusting you, Cassie."

She said the sentence with lots of emphasis, as if expecting Cassie's guilty conscience to bend under the implication. But Cassie had no guilty conscience, and it bugged her that her mom kept expecting her to do something wrong. She grumbled under her breath and went to her room.

CHAPTER THIRTY
Birthday Woes

C assie rode home with Amity after school, so she got to hang out with her while they waited for the others to arrive. Cassie set out the birthday plates and filled pitchers with water. The doorbell rang, and Cassie and Amity raced each other to answer it, shoving each other into the door frame as they raced each other to greet their first friend. Amity got the last shove, her hip sending Cassie into the corner, where she giggled so hard that Amity started laughing also. She swung the door open wide.

"Cara!" she cried, smirking as she hugged the other girl and pulled her into the house.

"What's wrong with Cassie?" Cara asked, looking at her in the corner, where Cassie laughed so hard she hardly made a sound.

"She's having a spaz attack," Amity said. "Don't mind her."

The doorbell rang again, and Cassie jumped to her feet. She leaped for the door just as Amity shouted, "Oh, no, you don't!"

They collided in the doorway, and Cassie rubbed her head where she'd bumped Amity's. Amity opened the door, a big smile on her face as she greeted Andrea.

"Come in, come in!" She pushed Andrea toward the kitchen, then looped an arm around Cassie's shoulder. "Don't try too hard. You might hurt yourself."

"Only because your head is so much harder than mine," Cassie returned.

"I think you just insulted me," Amity said, "but I'm not smart enough to get it."

Cassie groaned.

The weather was still warm enough at the end of August that the girls spent the remaining daylight hours in the pool. Mrs. Stafford brought the pizza out to them, and they splashed and ate until Amity's mom returned and called, "Time for cake and presents!"

That brought immediate cheering. They hurried inside, shivering and toweling off as they crowded into the den.

Mrs. Stafford appeared in the kitchen a few steps up from the den, smiling broadly as she carried a two-tier cake in her hands. "Happy birthday to you," she sang. The candles danced in the dim light, and the girls picked up the chorus.

"Happy birthday to you."

Mrs. Stafford took another step, then another. And then she put her foot in a puddle of water pooling on the linoleum floor. Her eyes grew wide, and her mouth morphed into an O only seconds before her feet slid out from under her. Amity shrieked and jumped to her feet, and Cassie leaned forward.

None of them could prevent Mrs. Stafford's fall, or do anything more than stare in horror as the cake dropped face down onto the floor.

For a moment they stared in dreadful silence. And then Maureen shouted, "Cake!" She dove for the mess, digging her hands in and grabbing what she could.

Tears swam in Amity's eyes, but she quickly smiled and shouted, "Save some for me!"

Cassie joined the foray, laughing and wiping cake on Andrea and Maureen when they got too close. Only Cara stayed back, grinning but keeping away from the mess.

Cassie grabbed a handful of cake and turned around. She extended her clean hand, hiding the cake behind her. "Cara, help me up?"

Cara leaned forward and took Cassie's hand, and Cassie whipped out the cake and smeared it up her arm.

"Cassie!" Cara cried, but her eyes twinkled with mirth.

"You have to have cake too, Cara."

"Yeah," Amity said, noticing the two of them. "I'll get you some." Her hand closed around a fistful of fluffy white frosting and thick cake.

"You're too sweet! I'm good." Cara shook her head, smiling.

They ate their fill of cake, and then helped Mrs. Stafford clean up what was left. She couldn't do anything except throw it away, and they pretended to cry while the remains were emptied into the trash. Then they cleaned themselves up and settled down in front of the TV.

"Good night, girls," Mrs. Stafford said, turning out the light in the kitchen.

Amity turned on a movie. She pitched the volume rather high, then settled down in front of her friends.

"Okay, guys," she whispered. "I'm supposed to meet Todd at the corner in twenty minutes."

Cassie straightened up. This was news to her. Amity had told her earlier in the week that she liked Todd Wilcox, but that was it. "You're meeting Todd? Tonight? Is he your boyfriend now?"

"No, you idiot," Amity said, smacking her leg. "But I like him. So he said he'd come over. He can't come here, obviously, so I'm going to meet him at the corner."

Andrea squealed and leaned forward. "Can we come?"

"I need you to cover for me," Amity said. "In case my mom comes to check on us."

"This isn't a good idea, Amity," Cassie said, growing uneasy. She'd told her mom there wouldn't be boys. And it was dark out. "We can't just let you go outside by yourself."

"She's right." Maureen nodded. "We'll have to come."

"Well, you can't all come," Amity said with a huff. "My mom will definitely know something's wrong."

"I'll stay," Cara said.

"I'll stay with Cara," Janice said.

"I'm coming," Andrea said, her eyes gleaming.

"Me too," Cassie said, not about to let her friends walk into trouble without her to protect them.

Amity looked at Maureen, who said, "Don't leave me out."

"Okay, then let's go. We have to sneak out the back door."

Amity led the way through the den to a side door, and the four of them slipped out. Cassie glanced back to see Cara and Janice spreading out blankets and pillows, making it look like there were more people than just two still sitting in front of the TV.

Crickets chirped outside, and the few street lamps cast odd shadows on the gutters and sidewalks. Blackness draped over the houses, and Cassie felt more uneasy. "Are you sure about this, Amity?"

"Quit worrying," Amity snapped.

They stopped on the corner and waited. A few cars drove by and Cassie tensed each time, but none of them stopped. How much did they know about Todd Wilcox? He'd been in Cassie's sixth grade class, but that was forever ago.

"Someone's coming," Andrea hissed, and Cassie straightened.

A male figure approached from down the sidewalk. He seemed too tall to be a teenage boy, and Cassie's heart gave a little thud in her chest. Too tall and too filled out. Much more like a man than a boy.

"Who is that and why is he coming over here?" Maureen murmured.

Cassie turned to Amity, about to suggest they leave, when the man spoke.

"Amity, you get on home. All of you girls get back to the house."

"Dad?" Amity gasped out.

Mr. Stafford stepped into the street light, his lips pressed tight in an unhappy expression. "You're lucky it wasn't your mom who realized you were gone."

Amity's face grew pale. "Okay. I'm coming home."

Mr. Stafford waited.

Amity sighed. "Let's go in." She gestured forward, and Cassie kept pace with Andrea and Maureen. Mr. Stafford nodded and moved ahead of them, turning the corner to the house first.

Amity stopped walking. "Cassie and Maureen, go back to my house. Andrea, wait with me. I know Todd will be here soon."

"But—" Maureen began, but Amity silenced her with a harsh wave of her hand.

"Just go before my dad figures out I'm not coming yet!"

Cassie didn't want to leave Amity either, but at least Amity wasn't alone. "Come on, Maureen."

Maureen screwed her mouth up into an angry pout and stomped back to Amity's house. "We should march straight to her dad and tell him what she's doing."

"I don't think that would go over well."

"Amity's supposed to be my best friend! Why did she ask Andrea to stay?"

"I don't know," Cassie said, a bit surprised by Maureen's declaration. "I thought Cara was your best friend."

Maureen didn't answer.

Cassie wondered who her best friend was. She'd always thought it was Andrea, until recently. Andrea had started acting weird and distant and kept lying, and sometimes the lies were designed to make Cassie feel inferior.

As soon as they walked in, Cara and Janice cornered them.

"Where's Amity?" Janice asked.

"Her dad is going to be so mad if she doesn't get back here," Cara said.

"She's waiting for Todd," Cassie said.

"With Andrea," Maureen added, her displeasure evident.

Janice and Cara exchanged a look.

"Todd's not exactly good boyfriend material," Janice said.

Cara nodded in agreement. "He's been in trouble a lot in school. And some of his ex-girlfriends speak really bad about him."

Alarm shot through Cassie as she considered Amity and Andrea outside by themselves. She gripped Maureen's arm. "We have to go get them."

"We'll make them come back," Maureen said, and they hurried back out into the night.

They went around the house, stumbling over their feet in their rush to get to the corner.

But Andrea and Amity weren't there.

"Maybe it wasn't this corner," Cassie said.

Maureen's breathing came out quick and shaky. "Oh no! Where are they? What if they're in trouble?"

Cassie ignored her and ran down the block, looking into the shadows in case the two girls were hiding there. Adrenaline pumped hot and heavy through her blood. She turned around and grabbed Maureen's arm.

"We better get back and tell Amity's parents."

"Amity will kill us!"

"What else can we do?" Cassie cried. "She's not here. I don't know where she is. I don't care if she's mad. We have to make sure she's safe." What a stupid thing it had been for Amity to do, agree to meet a boy she barely knew outside in the dark. Cassie uttered a silent prayer that Andrea would keep Amity out of any trouble. But she wasn't sure she trusted Andrea any more than she trusted Amity.

Voices met Cassie as she pushed open the door to the den, and she straightened in surprise when Amity turned around.

"There you guys are!" Amity said. "You shouldn't be sneaking around outside!"

Relief filled Cassie at the sight of Amity and Andrea huddled with Janice and Cara. Then her relief morphed into anger. "We were looking for you! What were you doing!"

Amity smiled and pressed a finger to her lips. "I was waiting for Todd. And then he came, and—" she sucked in a breath and then let it out. "He kissed me!"

"Why did you kiss him?" Cara asked.

"Well, that's why we met up! Of course we were going to kiss!"

"Gross," Maureen said. "You shouldn't have kissed him."

Amity narrowed her eyes and sent a dark look Maureen's direction. "Just because you've never kissed a guy doesn't mean you have to be so angry when someone else does."

Maureen's face turned pink. "I'm not angry. I think you were stupid going out and kissing some boy you know nothing about."

Andrea rolled her eyes. "Chill out, Maureen. It's not like anyone got hurt."

"Yeah," Amity said. "Maybe someday you'll get to know what it's like."

Maureen stood up, her eyes crinkling, and then she burst into tears. It was so unexpected that Cassie only stared. Then Maureen ran out of the room. Cassie jumped up and ran after her.

She found Maureen in the bathroom, curled up on the toilet seat and crying into her hands.

"Maureen?" Cassie said, mildly alarmed. She didn't think she'd ever seen Maureen break down.

"Amity can just walk outside and meet up with a stranger and he kisses her," Maureen said. "I've never had a boyfriend. I'm never going to get a guy."

"Maureen, you don't want some strange dude to walk up to you and kiss you," Cassie said.

Maureen waved her hand. "I don't even care! I'd just take the kiss!"

The bathroom door banged open, and the other girls paraded in.

"I wasn't trying to hurt your feelings," Amity said. "I think you're overreacting."

"Yeah. Don't let it be such a touchy subject," Andrea said.

Maureen lifted her face from her hands, glaring at the two of them. "Just go away! You have no idea what it's like to feel unwanted!"

Cassie straightened up. "Out, guys, out. You're not helping. Just give her some time."

The girls eyed Cassie and Maureen but filed out of the bathroom. Cassie turned around and gave Maureen a hug. She held her while Maureen cried, then grabbed a piece of toilet paper and folded it up before handing it to her friend.

Maureen took it and dabbed her eyes. "I love you," she murmured.

Cassie turned around, certain she'd heard wrong. "What?"

"I love you," Maureen whispered. "No one's ever as kind as you are."

Tears pricked Cassie's eyes. She bent and kissed Maureen's cheek, then hurried out of the bathroom before she cried also.

She didn't think any of her friends had ever expressed such affection for her, and it warmed her heart.

The others hadn't gone far. They crowded on the other side of the bathroom door.

"What's wrong with her?" Andrea asked.

"I think it bothers her more than we realized, that she's never had a boyfriend." Cassie couldn't help the smidgen of relief inside that she was no longer in that position.

Amity crossed her arms over her chest. "I don't see what the big deal is. Janice has never had a boyfriend, and you don't see her crying over it."

"Sometimes I do," Janice said.

"You can't understand, Amity," Cara said. "You don't know what it's like to not have a boyfriend. You've always got at least one."

That elicited a smile from Amity, and she dropped her arms.

"You're lucky," Cassie said. "I couldn't wait for my first boyfriend. Sometimes I felt ugly and wrong because no guy liked me."

Janice nodded. "I know how she feels."

"All right," Amity said. "When she comes out, I won't say anything more about it. We'll just drop it."

Amity and Andrea went back to the den. Janice followed and Cassie trailed behind, but then Cara said, "Cassie."

Cassie stopped, giving Cara a chance to walk next to her. "Yeah?"

"Have you kissed Ben?"

Cassie nodded. "Yes."

"And Josh, too, right?"

She tried not to grimace at the memory. "Yes."

Cara looked a little nervous, avoiding Cassie's gaze. "Was it weird?"

Cassie blinked in surprise, and then she laughed. "Yes! I thought it was just me!"

Cara broke into a smile. "No, it's not."

"I get worried every time Ben goes to kiss me," Cassie admitted. "I feel like I don't know what I'm doing and he's going to think I'm an idiot."

"I feel that way too. I keep wondering when it's going to get easier."

Cassie pursued the conversation further, confessing her deepest thoughts. "Sometimes I don't want him to kiss me. I get so anxious about it that it's easier if he doesn't do it."

"I get scared too."

"Do you ever not want to kiss?"

"Sometimes." Cara nodded. "But he likes it a lot."

"Yes," Cassie said, remembering how Ben stole every second to try and kiss her.

"And sometimes I like it too," Cara added.

Cassie wasn't sure about that. She always thought she wanted the kiss —until it happened. "I just need more practice."

Cara giggled. "Practicing can be fun."

Cassie had to laugh. "It can be."

CHAPTER THIRTY-ONE

Harmony

The first weeks of September passed quickly as Cassie fell into a routine.

"Ben's birthday is this weekend," she said to her friends at lunch. "He's coming over for a birthday party on Friday, and I want you guys to meet him. Can you come?"

"Oh, I want to!" Amity said. "Can't wait to meet this famous Ben."

"Me too," Maureen said. "See if he's as cute as you say he is."

"He is," Cassie said, grinning.

"I don't know," Cara said. "But I'll try."

"Same," Janice said.

"Andrea?" Cassie asked, turning to her.

Andrea shrugged, looking uninterested. "Yeah, I guess."

Her response didn't bother Cassie. Now that she wasn't constantly trying to be Andrea's best friend, Andrea's dramatics didn't get under her skin. "Perfect!"

"And we're staying after school to practice for All-Region today, right?" Maureen asked. "We need you so we can stay on pitch."

"Yep, I'm staying," Cassie said. She was bound and determined to make All-Region this year. Last year she'd gotten sick and had sung a bit flat. Nothing would stop her this time.

She looked forward to Unison with Maureen and Amity every day. Sometimes she talked to Riley, also. It was one of her favorite classes.

When class ended, the sopranos crowded around the piano, and Ms. Berry pulled out the music.

"These songs are hard," she said. "You have to pay close attention to your voice. Move with the notes, not behind or ahead of them."

"But they're pretty songs," Cassie said, and Ms. Berry favored her with a smile.

"When sung correctly, yes, they are."

They started practicing the music. It went smoothly enough until the melody jumped up a fifth into a high note.

"We're scooping," Ms. Berry said. "I want you to glide up to that note, nice and gentle. *May the wind*—" Ms. Berry stood on her tiptoes and lifted her hand above her head, then brought it down slowly while lowering her heels. "Let's try again."

Cassie took a deep breath and focused on breathing from her gut, centering the note. Then she released the sound, floating it lightly around the words, careful to stay on pitch.

"Beautiful!" Ms. Berry said, lifting her hands from the piano. "Cassie has it! Everyone listen to Cassie!"

Cassie's face warmed, but she beamed under the praise. Amity scooted closer to her.

"One more time," Ms. Berry said, and they started again. But as they approached that high note, Cassie second-guessed herself. She shied away from going all the way up and ended up coming underneath it. She tried to recover but only managed an awkward scoop.

Oops.

"What was that?" Ms. Berry asked, frowning.

Amity tugged on her ear and then said in a sing-song voice, "Cassie messed up."

The other sopranos burst out laughing, and Cassie did too. "Sorry," she said.

"Let's get it right this time," Ms. Berry said. "Here we go."

Cassie straightened up and concentrated. One mishap like that in the try-outs could cost her All-Region.

⊙──✦──⊙

On Wednesday Cassie took her All-Region music to voice lessons with her. She always had voice lessons before youth group.

"This is a familiar tune," Ms. Malcolm said, playing the notes on the piano. "I'll record it for you so you can practice it whenever you want."

"That sounds great." Cassie stood straight like she'd been taught, one foot slightly in front of the other and hands at her side. "I'm going to make All-Region this year."

"You have a beautiful voice," Ms. Malcolm said. "Just don't get nervous and remember to breathe. You'll do fine."

The next day Cassie's mom took her shopping to buy Ben a birthday present.

"I have no idea what to get him," Cassie said, feeling near a panic as she perused the different aisles of the department store. "What do boys like?"

"He'll like whatever you get him, sweetie."

Completely unhelpful. Cassie picked up a bottle of cologne, then put it back. Felt too presumptuous. Sweater? What if he didn't like that color? She stopped in front of the baseball caps. He always wore one. Surely she couldn't go wrong there. She picked out a blue one and a couple of chocolate bars.

"That looks like a nice, thoughtful gift. And no boy will say no to chocolate."

"I hope you're right."

Friday morning all Cassie could think was that Ben was coming over that evening. It had been weeks since they'd seen each other, and she was more nervous than she wanted to admit. What if he didn't like her anymore? What if he didn't think she was pretty or funny anymore? What if he hated chocolate and the color blue?

She shrugged off her fears and smiled at Andrea and Janice when she sat down in first hour. "Are you guys coming over for Ben's birthday party tonight?"

"I'll be there," Andrea said.

"I don't think I can come," Janice said. "I'll let you know tonight."

Cassie nodded and faced forward, hoping someone besides Andrea would make it.

"We should be finishing up our mosaics today," Coach Benson said, drawing the class's attention as he walked around the room. "Remember this is a representation of your cultural heritage."

Cassie removed from her bag the pieces of her mosaic, just waiting to be glued together. She'd chosen to make it in the shape of a viking helmet, to represent her grandfather's heritage. The other pieces were cut from magazines, slices of terrain and buildings to represent Europe and later New England.

It had taken some work to get her mom to talk about her side, but finally she learned the family had immigrated from the Central American rain forest only two generations earlier. She didn't know many people on her mom's side except one family in Georgia, and they weren't particularly friendly. It explained why Cassie had darker skin, though no one else in her family had pulled that side of the gene pool. So for her mom's side, she had pictures of forests and waterfalls and exotic food dishes. She couldn't be sure what her ancestors had eaten, but this was a decent representation.

"That looks really nice, Cassie," Coach Benson said, stopping beside her desk. "What do the pieces represent?"

The essay that explained the mosaic was due on Monday, so he would be reading all about it soon, but Cassie obliged her teacher. "Some are pictures of Europe and New England to represent my father's line, which came to America hundreds of years ago. Others are from my mom's side, which only came here fifty years ago."

"Fascinating." He nodded as he examined her work. "Great job."

Cassie focused on those words and tried not to worry about Andrea coming over for Ben's birthday.

⟡

Amity called Cassie after school on Friday.

"I'm so sorry," she said into the phone as Cassie finished picking all the clothes off her bedroom floor. "I thought I could come over today. But my mom forgot we have to go to Fayetteville for something."

Cassie surveyed her room with the phone pressed to her ear. At least this time Ben wouldn't think it looked like she was hiding a pig under her clothes. "Really? I wanted you to meet Ben."

"I know. Next time. I'll make sure I can be there."

Cassie sighed. That meant of all her friends, only Andrea was coming. "It's not your fault."

"You have a good time, though, okay? Don't kiss too much!"

Cassie laughed, though that knot of dread returned to her stomach. She hoped there wouldn't be an opportunity for that.

The doorbell rang, and Cassie dropped the phone as a tremor overtook her hands. Was that Ben or Andrea? She wasn't sure who to wish for.

She ran out of the room and through the kitchen, arriving at the front door the same time as her mom. Mrs. Jones glanced at her and then opened the door. "Hello, Ben!" she said. "Come on in!"

Cassie swallowed hard, nerves making her chest contract. Ben stepped into the house, already wearing a big smile, his blue eyes scanning the entry way.

"Cassie!" he exclaimed when he saw her. He strided over to her and wrapped her in a hug.

"Ben!" Cassie returned the hug, relaxing into his embrace. She saw his mom come in next, and the two mothers chatted.

Ben stepped back and held her shoulders, examining her. She met his gaze, and he smiled. She smiled back. His smile, his eyes, his touch, it was all so familiar. What had she been afraid of?

"It's so good to see you," he said, slipping an arm over her shoulder and guiding her to the couch.

Cassie shifted to face him. "My mom baked you a cake. And my friend Andrea is coming also. And I got you a gift."

His cheeks flushed. "You didn't have to do that."

He looked so cute when he blushed. So innocent and vulnerable. Cassie's lips quirked upward. "I know. But I wanted to." He wasn't wearing a baseball cap today, and his dark hair hung straight around his face. Hopefully he'd like the one Cassie had gotten him.

"Let me guess." He swiveled so his body faced hers also. He held her hands in his and closed his eyes. "You got me fried okra."

She burst out laughing and pulled her hands away to swat him. "No."

His lower lip came out, drawing her attention to his mouth. She forgot she didn't want to kiss him and found herself hoping he would. "But I love fried okra," he said.

"Me too," she said, and his eyes met hers. The moment felt thick and heavy with expectation, and Ben leaned toward her.

"Cassie, Andrea's here!" Mrs. Jones called from the entry way, reminding Cassie that they were very much not alone.

"Oh, great," Cassie said, sighing. She stood up. "Sometimes Andrea's a little weird," she whispered to Ben. "Just be polite if she acts odd."

"I have friends like that too."

Cassie went outside to greet Andrea, and Ben followed.

"Hi, Andrea!" Cassie said, waving. "This is Ben!"

Andrea had an expression on her face like she'd just smelled something gross. "Hi."

Mrs. Jones stepped into the doorway. "Why don't you guys go for a walk? We'll have cake when you come back."

That sounded fun. Cassie just wished Andrea didn't have to come. "Yeah, sure."

Ben took her hand, and they started across the yard. The family dog, Pioneer, jogged beside them. Andrea lagged behind and wouldn't catch up, no matter how many times Cassie motioned to her with her hand. Ben paid her no mind, cracking jokes the whole time, and Cassie forgot about Andrea as he made her laugh.

"Hey, look, there's some flowers," Ben said, and he let go of Cassie's hand to run between the long stems.

Cassie turned around, smiling. "Isn't he great?" she said.

But Andrea's look hadn't faded. "He's weird."

Cassie frowned at her. "No, he's not. You're being weird."

Andrea gave an eye roll. "He's not even cute. I can't believe you kissed him."

Ben, not cute? Fury roared up in Cassie's chest. She whipped around, indignant for his sake. He spotted her and came back, his grin a little sheepish as he handed her a bouquet of Queen Anne's lace and black-eyed Susan's.

"If we were alone, I'd kiss you," he whispered, meeting her eyes as she closed her fingers around the stems.

Cassie glanced back at Andrea and suppressed an aggravated sigh. "I wish we were alone." But a small part of her felt relieved, also. At least she didn't have to worry if he was going to kiss her.

CHAPTER THIRTY-TWO
Weird Friends

Andrea stayed long enough for Ben to open his present from Cassie (which he loved, and he immediately donned the baseball cap) and have a piece of cake. Then she waited outside for her dad to pick her up. Cassie and Ben waited with her, but they sat on the porch swing with Ben trying to grab her hand and pretending like he couldn't quite reach it. She tried not to giggle too loudly, certain Andrea would make fun of her.

Andrea's dad arrived, and Andrea said, "Bye, Cassie."

"Bye," Cassie said, her heart giving a little tumble as they drove away. She and Ben were alone. Finally.

Ben turned to face her, his expression more urgent, as if he too sensed this fleeting moment might be one of their last alone. He bent his head and kissed her, his lips gently pressing against hers.

Cassie closed her eyes and sighed when he pulled back. "That felt nice," she said, opening her eyes and smiling.

He grinned. "I thought so." He kissed her again, but this time he opened his mouth against hers, and Cassie felt the familiar stirrings of panic in her chest. She wasn't so good at this kind of kissing.

The front door opened, and he pulled back with a loud *smack*.

"It's time to go, Ben," his mom said, stepping out with a friendly smile on her face.

"Okay," he said. He squeezed Cassie's hand and pushed off the porch swing. "Thanks for the awesome party."

"It was kind of lame," Cassie said. She stood up, brushing her hands on her pants.

Ben shook his head, then tugged on the bill of the baseball cap she'd given him. "See? I love it."

His mom was already walking to the car, and he bent near her to whisper, "And you too."

Cassie watched them leave, then returned to the house, giddy from his visit. And then she thought of Andrea and her reactions, and she scowled. What a strange person Andrea had become.

⌒〜✦〜⌒

"She's so weird," Cassie complained to Amity in choir. "She wouldn't even talk to Ben. It was like, super rude."

"I'm so sorry I couldn't be there," Amity said. "I would have talked to him."

"Oh, I know. But he was a good sport about it."

Maureen cleared her throat. "I would have talked to him also."

Cassie turned slightly to include Maureen in the conversation. "Sorry. I didn't mean to talk so loud."

"No, that's okay, I want to hear also. I can't believe Andrea acted that way."

Cassie rolled her eyes, reliving the aggravation. "So bizarre."

Ms. Berry played a few notes on the piano. "All right, girls, let's warm up."

Amity moved closer to Cassie. "I need to hear you sing or I won't get these notes right."

Cassie's ego puffed up, and she inclined her head Amity's direction so she could hear her better.

"I'm singing to your hair," Amity giggled.

"Oh." Cassie straightened up. "Sorry."

Amity scooped Cassie's hair into her hand and sang her scale toward the dark mass.

Cassie laughed. She pulled her hair away, then turned and sang at Amity's head. "Now I'm singing to your hair," she said, and both girls struggled to keep a straight face as the song continued.

"Call me tonight," Amity said when choir ended and they went their separate ways. "You can tell me more about what happened."

"I will," Cassie said. The smile didn't leave her face as she walked to the bus to meet up with her sister Emily and go home. It was so much easier to get along with Amity, who didn't play as many mind games as Andrea.

⌒〜✦〜⌒

Cassie stayed up too late talking to Amity on the phone and then stumbled through what remained of her homework. She was pretty good at time management and usually got homework done at school, but sometimes there was too much. Plus the Children's Community Choir was supposed to start up again in a week, and a hard rock of dread filled her stomach every time she thought of it. She'd enjoyed the trip to New York, but she didn't want to be in the choir anymore. Ms. Vanderwood insisted on keeping Cassie as a second soprano, and Cassie felt neither valued nor appreciated. It was just one more obligation on her schedule. Her mom had said she didn't have to do it anymore, and Cassie intended to follow through with that.

But what made her even more nervous was that next week she would start a religion class during zero hour. It wasn't offered by her school but through her church. Riley was doing it too, so the two of them had already made plans to ride together to and from church for the class. Cassie did not look forward to the loss of another hour of sleep.

She stopped in the school bathroom to apply makeup under her eyes, which betrayed her exhaustion with deep shadows. Andrea would say she looked "cadiving." One of her made up words.

Thinking of Andrea gave her an unexpected pang of sadness. Their friendship was on the rocks, and only now did Cassie realize she missed her.

A text message came as Cassie stepped out of the bathroom. She flipped her phone open to check it, and her shoulder collided with another person.

"Oh, I'm so sorry," she said, looking up. "I wasn't paying attention." She blinked when she recognized the person in front of her. Miles Hansen.

"Cassie!" He was taller than last year and no longer wore glasses, but the friendly smile that spread across his face was as familiar as the sunrise. "How are you? I haven't seen you all year!"

"I'm great," she said, surprised at how easily she talked to him. Last year he'd had her tongue all in knots when she tried to say a word, but this year he didn't seem to affect her. "Did you get contacts?"

"I did. Finally time to ditch the glasses." He moved with her, walking toward the locker hall. "We still don't have any classes together."

"I know. It's almost like it's intentional." *I don't have a crush on him anymore,* Cassie realized as she stopped at her locker. But she still had feelings for Miles. A rush of warm friendship and appreciation for his presence filled her. "But you're in choir, right?"

"Yeah." Miles leaned against the lockers while she switched out her books.

"So at least we'll see each other at concerts." She closed her locker and faced him. "Great to see you, Miles!"

"You too, Cassie."

He waved as she walked away, and she found her step slightly lighter. All the drama and hurt feelings between them from last year were gone. Now they could just focus on being friends.

Andrea wasn't in class yet. Cassie talked with Janice until Andrea arrived, and then she fell silent. She hadn't forgiven Andrea for her behavior toward Ben.

Class got underway with a reading assignment. Cassie looked up from her text book when Coach Benson stepped to her desk.

"Cassie, I enjoyed your mosaic so much I wondered if I might keep it? It's a great example of what I'm looking for. I would use it for future classes."

Cassie lifted an eyebrow. "Really? You want mine?"

He nodded. "It was one of the best I've seen."

She smiled, flattered by his praise. "Well, yeah, you can keep it."

"You sure? You didn't want it as a keepsake?"

She chuckled. "I'm not in the habit of keeping my schoolwork."

"Maybe you should be. I'm sure you're a very good student." He patted her shoulder.

☙❧

"Amity must be sick," Cara said at lunch. She wore her cheerleading outfit today, a short, pleated white skirt with an orange ribbon around the edge, and a sleeveless, fitted white top with an orange cougar on the front. All the cheerleaders wore their uniforms for the pep rally at end of seventh hour.

"Yeah." Cassie sat by Cara and Maureen. "I haven't seen her today. But I saw Miles this morning. I don't have a crush on him anymore."

"That's because you're so busy with your precious Ben." Janice batted her eyes and made a kissy face.

"Yep," Cassie said, even though heat crept up her neck. "Ben's awesome."

"He was pretty nice," Andrea said, speaking up from the end of the table. "And he's really cute."

Cassie spun around to face her. "You didn't talk to him the whole time. You ignored him and said rude things about him." Her anger from the weekend returned, sweeping over her and making her bold.

Andrea avoided her eyes. "I was in a bad mood. I didn't want to talk to anyone."

Cassie stabbed a straw into her apple juice. "I didn't make you come."

Andrea lifted her head. "You guys have to meet him. He's a great guy."

It wasn't exactly an apology, but Cassie recognized Andrea's intent.

"I'm glad you're so happy with someone, Cassie," Cara said. "I know it's not easy when your boyfriend goes to a different school."

"Yeah." Cassie sighed. "I really miss him when I don't see him. I'm worried we'll drift apart." Even though Ben said he loved her . . . She was only fourteen and he'd barely turned fifteen. How strong could his love be?

"You won't," Andrea said. "You'll make it."

Cassie finally favored her with a smile. "Thanks."

⟡

With no Amity to talk to in class, Cassie was forced to branch out a bit. She took Amity's seat in math so she was beside Cara. Ms. Allred explained the assignment and then left them to it. Cassie started on the problems, determined to get them done before class got out.

"Cassie," Cara whispered. "Look at these pictures." She passed a pile of photographs over to Cassie.

Cassie's mouth fell open when she saw their group hanging out at the Grape Festival. "You were taking pictures?"

Cara nodded. "With my phone. The whole time."

Cassie pressed a hand to her mouth as she saw the gross-haired dude Andrea had been flirting with. "Ew!"

"I know!" Cara giggled.

Cassie leaned in closer, and they tried to laugh quietly, their shoulders shaking with mirth as they relived their time at the fair.

"Cassandra, what are you doing?" Ms. Allred looked up from her desk, and Cassie jerked away from Cara.

"Nothing," she said. Stupid response. Everyone said that. "I mean, Cara was showing me something on her paper. I was checking her work."

"Yep," Cara said, her face a mask of innocence as she held up her notebook. "This one right here." She pointed her pencil at the newest problem.

"Compose yourselves. Help each other without laughing loud enough to distract the whole class," Ms. Allred said in a dry tone.

"Yes, Ma'am," Cara said, and their teacher turned back to her desk.

Cassie faced Cara. "Well," she mouthed. "I better compose myself."

Cara's mouth twisted as she tried to keep a straight face.

Classes ran on a shorter schedule because of the pep rally assembly. Cassie sighed as she walked into seventh hour. It would be a long class without Amity. She nodded at Riley, sitting in the alto section, then sat down in the soprano section. Maureen came in shortly thereafter, and Cassie scooted closer.

"We can try and blend with each other today," Cassie said.

"Yeah," Maureen said. "It would be nice to hear you better."

Maureen sang so quietly that Cassie hadn't even been sure what her voice sounded like. It was pretty, she realized as they sang together.

"You should sing louder," Cassie told her. "You have a nice voice."

"I'll try," Maureen said.

When the sopranos started up again, Cassie elbowed Maureen,

urging her to get louder. Maureen smiled and sang a little more. Cassie elbowed her again, then again, until Maureen had to stop singing because she was laughing.

"That's not helping," Maureen said.

"Just belt it out," Cassie said. "You're doing great."

Maureen's smile fell off her face. "You talk to me when Amity's not here."

"What?" Cassie blinked in confusion.

"You never notice me when she's here."

The words stabbed Cassie and brought a pang of guilt. Riley had said the same thing last year. Was Cassie doing it again, but to Maureen now? "Yes, I do," she said, vowing to make sure she did.

Ms. Berry turned her attention to the altos, and Maureen faced Cassie.

"I'm worried about Andrea."

Cassie's breath went out in a whoosh. "So it's not just me?"

"Not just you?"

"She's been *so* strange lately. Amity and I were just talking about it. Something's really up with her."

Maureen nodded. "We need to talk to someone about her."

"Mr. Adams." Cassie immediately thought of her science teacher. He was the kindest, smartest old man she knew. "He'll help."

"Great idea," Maureen said. "He knows all of us. Let's talk to him tomorrow."

The bell rang early, and Ms. Berry dismissed them for the pep rally. Maureen and Cassie meandered down the hallway to the gym, only a few steps from the choir room. Riley joined them.

"Can I sit with you guys?"

"Of course," Cassie said. Though she and Riley had drifted a bit since school started, she still thought of her as a close friend. And she didn't want to make someone else feel ignored.

"Yeah, that's fine," Maureen said with a shrug. Not exactly inviting, but at least she wasn't rude.

They found Janice and Andrea, and Cassie again missed Amity. Everything was funnier with Amity around.

"Let's watch Cara cheer," Maureen said as they settled onto the bleachers. "See if she's gotten better since the tryout."

Cassie and Janice exchanged a glance. Of their group of friends who tried out, Cara was the only one who made it, which had caused no small amount of ire among them. According to the others, Cara was the worst dancer at the auditions, and it wasn't fair she'd made it.

"Let's see," Cassie agreed. She hadn't seen Cara cheer yet.

The cheerleaders came onto the floor, screaming and yelling and waving pompoms. Then they threw them on the floor and lined up in two rows. Music started, and they launched into a dance routine. Cassie's eyes remained glued to Cara, and she winced as Cara fell out of step, kicked the wrong leg, missed a turn, and then sat down facing the wrong direction.

"She's not very good, is she?" Cassie whispered to Janice.

"Oh, this is an improvement," Maureen said, a malicious glint in her eyes. "You should have seen her before."

"Cheerleading camp must have helped," Andrea added.

This was an improvement? "Well," Cassie said, forcing a smile, "I'm sure she'll continue to improve."

⟨⟩

Cassie told Mr. Adams in sixth hour the next day that she and Maureen needed to talk to him. Seventh hour was his planning period, so he agreed to meet them in the library. He wrote them a note excusing them, and Cassie and Maureen left seventh period to talk to Mr. Adams.

They joined him around one of the round tables. Mr. Adams' portly belly brushed the edge of the table. Though he didn't smile, his light eyes radiated warmth and affection. "What's this about, girls?" he asked.

Cassie looked at Maureen, who took a deep breath.

"We're worried about Andrea. She's been weird lately."

He frowned behind his gray mustache. "She's not in any of my classes this year. What's going on? Is she in trouble?"

"We don't really know," Cassie said. "She's distant. Telling lies. She could be in trouble. We wouldn't even know."

"Does she have a boyfriend?"

"Not at the moment," Maureen said.

"Could it be trouble at home?"

"I don't know," Cassie said. She remember Andrea's weird mood when she'd come over for Ben's birthday. "Maybe."

Mr. Adams sighed and leaned back in his chair. "This is a hard age for youngsters. Most teens go through a rebellious stage as they try and figure out who they are. They quit liking their parents, they experiment with things, sometimes they even abandon their friends."

Ice filled Cassie's stomach. "She can't abandon us. We need to help her."

Mr. Adams nodded. "That's exactly right. I think the best thing you can do—the only thing you can do—is be her friend no matter what. Make sure she knows you're there for her. Even if she gets in trouble or hurts your feelings."

Cassie looked down, afraid he'd see the guilt in her eyes. Andrea had hurt her feelings, all right, and Cassie had immediately shunned her.

"So the whole turn the other cheek thing?"

She felt his eyes studying her. "If necessary, yes."

She looked at Maureen, and understanding passed between them.

"We can do that," Maureen said. "We can be her friend no matter what."

CHAPTER THIRTY-THREE
Back to Work

"I'm really getting nervous for All-Region," Amity said as she and Cassie walked to fourth hour after lunch the following week. "I feel like I've missed a lot of school and practices."

"You have," Cassie said.

Amity bobbed her head. "When can you practice? We only have a few weeks now."

It was true. September had already turned into October, and All-Region tryouts were this month. "I'll talk to Mr. Adams. Maybe he can let us practice during seventh hour."

"That's choir."

"Yes, but Ms. Berry won't spend the whole time going over our notes with us. We can do that on our own."

"Thanks, Cassie." Amity favored her with a smile. "You're the best."

They went inside the room, and Cassie sat down by Andrea. She'd rearranged her seating after the talk with Mr. Adams a week ago. She still preferred sitting by Amity, but she thought it was important to strengthen her friendship with Andrea. They made small talk until class started.

Cassie debated asking Mr. Adams to let Maureen out of class, too. They could all practice together. But she really just wanted to have some time alone with Amity. She stepped up to his desk when sixth hour ended.

"Can I get a note for Amity and I to use your classroom next hour so we can practice for All-Region?"

He looked at her as he put away the grade book. "You won't use it just to goof off and be silly girls?"

She bit her lip to keep from laughing. "No goofing off or being silly. Just practicing."

"Then yes." He pulled out a paper and wrote the note for her. "Just you and Amity. No parties."

"Of course." She breathed out a sigh of relief that he'd given her the perfect excuse not to invite Maureen. She'd understand.

Maureen didn't look too happy about it, but she accepted it when Cassie told her Mr. Adams had said only two people.

"Is that really what he said?" Amity asked as they walked down the hallway together toward the science room.

Cassie was on the verge of telling her she hadn't asked when she remembered that everything she said to one person made it back to the others. *Secrets*, she told herself. The only way to keep something silent was to tell no one. "Yes. He said only you and me."

"Oh, well, that was nice of him to let us use his room."

"Agreed," Cassie said.

She and Amity set up their music and closed the door. They ran through the song a few times, Cassie helping Amity on the transitions and notes she struggled with.

"How are things with Ben?" Amity asked after awhile. "You haven't mentioned him lately."

Ben. Cassie paused. "I don't know." Thinking his name still brought a warm feeling to her belly, but not with the strength of before. "We don't talk every day anymore."

Amity studied her. "Do you like someone else?"

Cassie shook her head. "No. What about you?"

"No, no one." Amity looked disappointed. "It's kind of boring when you don't have a crush."

"And unusual," Cassie added. "You usually have at least three crushes at one time."

"Hey!" Amity tried to smack her, but Cassie easily evaded the movement.

"One more time," she said. "Let's go through the music one more time."

⚬~❄~⚬

Cassie's phone rang as she walked home from the bus, vibrating inside her backpack. She pulled it out, a jolt of surprise going through her at the sight of Ben's name. He hadn't called in nearly a week. It was almost as if he knew she'd been talking about him earlier. She hesitated just a moment before answering.

"Hello?"

"Hi, Cassie!" His cheerful voice came over the line. "How are you?"

"I'm good. Just walking home from school." She evaded her younger sister as Annette and Scott tried to hit each other with their backpacks.

"You walk home?"

"No, from the bus stop, I mean." Had she remembered her civics homework? She paused and did a mental check. She'd opened her locker and pulled out several books. Was her civics book one of them?

" . . . this weekend," Ben said.

What had he said? She hadn't even been paying attention. "This weekend?"

"Yes. Do you think you can?"

Her mind raced. What had he asked her to do this weekend? "I'm not sure. I'll have to ask my mom."

"Yeah, of course. I miss you. I want to see you."

"That would be nice," Cassie agreed. "I'll ask my mom and call you back."

"Great. Talk to you later."

Only after Cassie hung up did she remember she didn't know what he wanted to do.

⚬⟞⟝⟞⟝⚬

Cassie put away her homework and climbed into bed, tucking the blankets around her. Emily was still in the kitchen so she left the light on, knowing her younger sister would turn it off. Her eyelids felt heavy and thick, and she let them droop over her eyes.

The phone rang in the kitchen, but Cassie barely stirred. Emily answered and spoke a few muffled words, then the bedroom door opened and she stepped in.

"Cassie," she said, "It's Ms. Vanderwood. She wants to talk to you."

Cassie pried her eyes open, struggling with the fog in her brain. Ms. Vanderwood. The children's choir director! A surge of panic sent Cassie waking up. She couldn't face her director, couldn't admit she didn't want to do choir anymore. Not after Ms. Vanderwood had made it possible for Cassie to go to New York even though she wasn't singing. "Tell her I'm not doing choir anymore. Tell her I'm sorry."

Emily curled up on her bed. "Tell her yourself."

"Emily!" Cassie put force into the word without getting too loud. "I'm already in bed. Just walk back out there and tell her."

"No."

Seriously? Emily wouldn't do this for her? "You answered the phone. You have to say something to her!"

"No, I don't. She called to talk to you, not me. I'm going to bed."

"I'm in bed!" This time Cassie's voice rose to a shriek, and her heart pounded with indignation. Oh, fine, whatever. She was fully awake now. She thrust her legs over the side of the bed and stomped past her sister, making it clear she was furious. Then she tried to calm her nerves as she stepped into the kitchen and picked up the phone.

"Hello, Ms. Vanderwood?"

A dial tone greeted her. Cassie exhaled, feeling a mixture of guilt and relief. Apparently Cassie had taken too long, and Ms. Vanderwood had hung up. It wasn't the best way to let Ms. Vanderwood know Cassie was quitting choir, but she felt certain her director would get the meaning.

She turned around and went back to bed, still glaring at Emily. Emily didn't even look up from her book.

⚬◦❊◦⚬

The girls' practicing began to pay off.

"You're doing much better today," Cassie told Amity in choir.

"Thanks. It's because I have a good teacher."

"Okay, girls," Ms. Berry said. "I think most of you have it, but I want to listen to your voices individually."

"Not solos!" a girl groaned.

"No, not solos. I'm going to have you sing in pairs, just the first two stanzas. I need to hear how all of you handle that transitional note."

"I'm singing with Cassie," Maureen said.

"No, you're not! I am!" Amity hissed.

They battled back and forth, with Maureen finally saying, "You always get to sing with her! It's my turn!"

Amity crossed her arms over her chest and pouted.

Maureen smiled and stepped closer to Cassie. "I'm just going to follow you."

"I hope I don't lead your astray," Cassie said.

Their turn came, and Maureen's voice blended with Cassie's, gliding right up to the note and then back down.

"Very nice, ladies," Ms. Berry said. She turned to Amity and her partner. "Go ahead."

Their voices wobbled a bit at the top of the note, but they came down smoothly. Ms. Berry gave them a few words of advice, and Amity glared at Maureen.

"That wouldn't have happened if I'd been singing with Cassie."

"I won't be singing with either of you at the tryout," Cassie said. "So you better learn how to do it on your own."

They settled back to listen to the other groups, and Maureen rummaged through her purse. "Here," she said, pulling out a glossy sheet of paper. "I brought this for you." She handed it to Cassie.

"What is it?" Cassie asked, opening the paper. A cut out from a magazine stared back at her.

"It's an article that talks about the different kinds of friends we have. This is you."

Maureen pointed to a paragraph, and Cassie read the words, "Always ready to listen, keeps a secret forever."

"I know you're the one person I can tell anything to," Maureen said. "You're always there for me."

Was Maureen putting her on a guilt trip? Cassie gave her a side hug. "Of course. Always."

Cassie pulled back, but Maureen's eyes didn't leave her face.

"What?" Cassie dragged a hand down her cheek. "Do I have food on me somewhere?"

"No. You're just so pretty." Maureen leaned over Cassie to say to Amity, "Isn't she?"

"Isn't she what?" Amity looked up from her phone.

"So pretty."

Amity didn't even look at Cassie, just returned to her phone. "Yeah, she's pretty."

"Prettiest one of all of us, my dad says," Maureen said, settling back.

The words swelled Cassie's heart. "Thanks, Maureen."

⚜

Cassie walked to the soccer store after school, carefully crossing the four-lane highway and continuing to the shopping complex about two miles from her school. Even though she wanted her dad to succeed, there were days when she cursed this store.

"I'm here," she said as the bell jangled and she walked in.

"I'm doing inventory," he called from the back. "I brought out some new shorts. Please put them on hangers and man the register."

"Got it." Cassie pulled the shorts over to the glass counter and began pegging them onto the hangers, then sorting them by sizes.

"I brought a letter for you. It's from Elek."

"Where?" Cassie's heart raced in anticipation. Elek was her unofficial brother. He'd lived with her family for awhile, but last year he'd stolen a car and gone to jail. They hadn't spoken since his trial, through from time to time she got a letter from him.

"Under the register."

Cassie found it and pulled it open. Her heart rate slowed and disappointment riddled her chest as she read his words. He talked about his cellmate, how he was such a nice guy but needed a good girl, talked about how the system worked against him, talked about the friends he was making in jail. His words and tone felt wrong. Like he was becoming one of them, turning gangster. Like he didn't think it was his fault he was in jail.

The last line asked if it would be all right to give her address to his cellmate so he could write her, and her face went cold. She didn't want to be set up with a jailbird.

The door clanged as a customer walked in. She put the letter down and came around the counter with a smile. "Hi! Can I help you find something?"

"Yes." The man wore glasses and had short-cropped, graying hair, but something about his face seemed familiar. "My son is playing on a traveling team and they need a certain kind of shinguard. I'm just checking to see if you have them in your store."

"Sure, what are you looking for?"

He gave her the specifications and Cassie rummaged through the shinguards, looking for what he needed.

"Do you go to Southwest?" he asked.

"I do," Cassie said, pulling a few over to the counter.

"I think you're friends with my son. He goes there."

"Oh? Who's your son?"

"Miles Hansen."

She froze in the middle of pulling the shinguard from the plastic wrapper. Then she peered up at him, understanding now why he looked familiar. "I know Miles! He's a good friend of mine."

Mr. Hansen smiled, the same easy-going, friendly smile his son had. "He's a good kid. Wish I could get him to play soccer. It's for his older brother."

"Yeah, he's great." Crapola. Cassie's face warmed, and she bit her tongue. What a lame thing to say. She cleared her throat. "Do any of these work?"

He examined them and then selected one. "This will do nicely. What was your name?"

"Cassandra. Cassandra Jones."

"Yes, I'm sure Miles has mentioned you."

"He has?" she blurted, then barely refrained from clapping her hand over her mouth. "Let me ring that up for you." She rang up his purchase and then handed it to him. "Thanks for coming in today."

"I'll let Miles know I saw you."

"Thanks. Tell him I'll see him tomorrow." Was her face bright red? It burned all the way to her hairline.

Mr. Hansen left, and Cassie groaned. What would Miles say to her tomorrow? What an idiot.

Ben called that night, and Cassie gasped as she remembered he'd wanted to do something on Friday. For a brief second she considered not answering, but then she decided to own her mistake.

"Hello?" she said, flipping the phone open.

"Hi, Cassie." He sounded warm and upbeat as always. "So what did your mom say? Are you coming tomorrow?"

She'd planned to tell him the truth, that she'd forgotten to ask, but the words flew from her mind. Instead she said, "I'm so sorry. My mom said I can't." As soon as she said it, she regretted it. She wanted to see Ben. Why couldn't she just admit what happened? She might be able to make it work still.

"Oh. That's too bad." He sounded down, so different from his happiness a moment ago.

"I could ask again," she said, and then she realized she'd have to admit she didn't even know what she was asking for. Disappointment sank in her stomach like a rock. She'd doomed herself. "I better not, though." She heaved a sigh. "Maybe we can do something next weekend?"

"Yeah." He didn't perk back up, though. "Call me and let me know."

"Okay, I will. I'll think of something and call you tomorrow."

Cassie waited for him to say "I love you," like he always did, but all he said was, "I'll talk to you later, then."

She closed her phone and frowned at it. Why did they have to live so far apart?

⁓⁓✧⁓⁓

Cassie stopped on her way to her locker Friday morning, a little alarmed to see Miles standing there.

"Miles," she said, spinning the combination and wondering if she should say something about his dad. "Hi."

"Hi, Cassie," he said, laughter in his voice. "My dad told me he saw you yesterday."

"Oh, yeah." She shrugged like it was no big deal. "He came to buy a few things for your brother." She hefted her backpack again and started down the hall. Miles kept pace with her.

"Do you work there a lot?"

"It's my dad's store, so yeah. A few days a week."

"I didn't know your dad owns a soccer store."

She favored him with a smile. "You would if you played soccer."

"Touche. Maybe I should take it up."

"I bet you'd be good at it."

The look he gave her reminded her of the heart he'd put in her yearbook at the end of eighth grade. Was it possible Miles felt something more than friendship for her?

The warning bell rang, and Cassie nodded at the classroom behind her. "I better get in there."

"Catch you later. At least I know where to find you."

Why exactly would he need to find her?

Andrea was chipper and happy in first hour. "Guess what? There's a dance next weekend!"

"Great," Cassie said, not at all excited. She liked her church dances way more than the school ones.

"Hey," Janice said, leaning forward. "I was talking to my mom last night about how it makes me sad I never get to have friends over because our house is so small. So she said we could do a campout."

"That sounds fun!" Cassie said. "When?"

"Well, she said tonight. Is that late notice?"

"I don't think I have anything else going on." At least, nothing since she'd ditched Ben. She still felt a strange ache in her heart over it, and it was all her fault.

"Me neither," Andrea said. Her eyes glittered. "You've never had a slumber party!"

"I know," Janice said. "I'm so excited to host one."

CHAPTER THIRTY-FOUR

Crushed Plans

F riday evening, Cassie's mom dropped her off in front of Janice's small house. A wide green pasture stretched out around them. Her other friends were already outside, and Cassie jumped out of the car, waving to them.

"I'll pick you up in the morning," Mrs. Jones called, and Cassie barely glanced back before turning to hug the other girls.

Janice's dad stayed outside long enough to get the fire going and make sure the tents were up. Then he disappeared into the house, telling the girls to get him if they needed anything. They gathered around the campfire, roasting hot dogs and marshmallows.

"Everyone's coming to the dance next Friday, right?" Cara asked. "StuCo is putting together a really awesome fall theme."

"Wouldn't miss it," Amity said, and Andrea agreed.

"Maybe," Janice said.

"Yeah," Cassie said. "I'm not sure I'll go."

Maureen poked her. "Why would you not?"

Because it's boring, she thought. But she thought of a better excuse. "My boyfriend doesn't go to school here."

"So invite him," Cara said. "It's the perfect opportunity for us to meet him."

What a splendid idea. Why hadn't Cassie thought of that before? "I'll ask him tomorrow."

"What about the rest of you?" Cara asked. "Anyone have boyfriends they want to tell us about?"

The girls hemmed and hawed, naming various male classmates and talking about the ones they kind of liked and which ones they mostly liked.

Janice sniffed. "Do you guys smell something burning?"

"Yeah, I do," Cara said. "What is that?"

Cassie smelled it, too.

"Cassie!" Andrea shrieked. "Your shoe's on fire!"

"What?" Cassie looked down and saw the tip of her shoe poking a hot ember. Thick black smoke curled away from her foot. She let out a cry and tumbled backward.

"Stick your toe in the dirt!" Janice ordered. "Hurry!"

Cassie did as she was told.

"Does it hurt? Are you on fire?" Cara asked, her face twisted with worry.

"No, I'm fine," Cassie said. "I didn't feel a thing. I didn't even know." She pulled her foot out of the dirt, exposing the darkened surface. "See? It's all good."

Janice pressed a hand to her chest and heaved a sigh. Amity gave a short laugh.

"Leave it to Cassie to catch her shoe on fire," she said, and the other girls laughed with her.

❧

Cassie forgot to call Ben when she got home. It wasn't until Monday when her friends asked if he was coming to the dance that she remembered.

His mom answered the phone, and a moment later Ben came to the line.

"Hi, Cassie. You finally found time to call me, huh?"

He said it jovially, but Cassie detected a wounded note in his voice. Crapola. She'd told him she'd call on Friday. "Things got busy. I was at a camp out all weekend," she said, trying not to sound defensive.

"Sure, that's fine, don't worry about it." His tone said otherwise.

"Did you have a good weekend?" She put enthusiasm in her voice, trying to get the conversation on the path she wanted it to go.

"A little boring, but fine. I didn't go without you."

Go where? But she couldn't ask without revealing that she hadn't paid that much attention to him to begin with. "I'm sorry," she said again. "Let me make it up to you. There's a dance at my school this Friday. Want to come?"

"Hey, that sounds fun." Some energy returned to his tone. "You want me to come with you?"

"Well, yeah, you're my boyfriend."

He laughed. "Yeah, I am. Let me ask my mom."

The phone went silent, and then he returned. "Cassie, my mom said I can't come. She doesn't feel comfortable about school dances. But she said you can come over. We could go to a movie together or something."

Cassie sighed. She really wanted her friends to meet Ben. "Are you sure?"

"Yeah, sorry. I can't change her mind."

"Well, I told my friends I'd go to the dance," Cassie said, stalling. "But maybe I can come up there after."

"Let me know, okay? I'd really love to see you."

"Okay. I really want to see you too. I'll call this time, I promise." She hung up and went off in search of her mom. She found her in the downstairs office, filing paperwork.

"Mom? Ben wants to know if I can come over this Friday, see a movie with him."

Mrs. Jones pursed her lips together, looking thoughtful. "I don't know, Cassie. I'm fine with you having a boyfriend, but going on dates is another matter. I don't really want you to be alone with him."

"I'm sure I wouldn't be. The whole family would go."

But her mom shook her head. "In a few years that will be fine. But not now."

"Okay." Cassie sighed and went back to her room. She'd have to tell Ben she couldn't come, and once again they wouldn't meet up. This long-distance dating thing was hard.

His line was busy when she called back. Not only did he not have a cell phone, but he didn't have call waiting. His parents were even stricter than hers were.

Cassie tried three more times that week to talk to Ben. She left messages with his mom twice, but the third time when he wasn't home, she just said she'd call back later. At least she didn't have to feel guilty this time. It was his turn to call back.

She skipped the dance since Ben couldn't come, and all of her friends understood. Instead she went to Riley's house.

"How are you and Ben?" Riley asked as they spread out across her bed. Riley had moved from the bedroom in the back to the guest room at the front of the apartment, which was much bigger and had room for a full bed.

"Oh, it's been so long since I've talked to you," Cassie said. "We're still together, but things are a bit weird."

"What do you mean?"

Cassie shrugged. "I don't know. We keep having a hard time getting together to see each other. And he doesn't call me as often."

"I'm sure he still likes you. He was crazy about you."

Cassie remembered the time they'd had together at Camp Splendor and smiled, the memory warming her. "Yeah, he was."

"Remember the okra he kept putting on your plate?"

How could Cassie forget? Nostalgia pushed through her veins, and suddenly she wanted to see him more than anything. "I'll call him when I get home. We'll get together next weekend."

"Why don't you call him now?"

She could. He'd wanted to go to the movies tonight; maybe he was home. She pulled out her phone and called his number.

"Hello?" his mom answered.

"Hi, is Ben there?" Cassie said.

"He's not here right now. Can I have him call you back?"

Cassie deflated slightly. That hadn't worked the last few times. "Do you know where he is?"

"He went to the movies with some friends."

He'd gone to the movies without her! The knowledge stung. She had skipped the dance since he couldn't be with her, and she'd just assumed he'd done the same. "Oh."

"Who is this? Can I have him call you?"

His mom didn't even know who she was. Warning bells were going off all over in her head. "This is Cassie. Again."

"Oh, hey, Cassie. Did he never call you back? I'll make sure he does."

Just what she wanted. "No, it's fine. I'll just call later."

Riley watched her, and as soon as she hung up, Riley said, "What's going on?"

"He went to the movies." Cassie shrugged it off. "I'll just try again later." She smiled like it was no big deal, but a cold fist squeezed her heart.

⟨⟩∾✧∾⟨⟩

Ben didn't call back on Saturday or Sunday.

Cassie couldn't spend too much time worrying about it because she had an Algebra test to study for. She was a nervous wreck Monday morning. She reviewed problems all through first hour, but in second hour Ms. Talo made her put them away.

"I'm making a live-video of this class to show my seventh graders. I need you guys to act normal." She glanced around the room, then snapped, "Jimmy! Get your head off your desk!"

"I'm taking a nap," he said, lifting his face. "That's normal for me."

"Cassie needs to fall asleep also," Leigh Ann said, eliciting giggles from the class.

"I don't sleep. I just rest my eyes," Cassie said. Her early morning class left her drained, but she tried to stay awake.

"She needs to be writing," Nicole said. "That's what Cassie does in her spare time."

The class laughed a little, and Cassie grinned, but the truth was she hadn't written anything new in a long time. She hadn't even worked on the book she wrote last year, and that was something she needed to do. The publisher was waiting for the manuscript. She made a mental note to work on that later. She didn't want this window of opportunity to pass her by.

Her nerves returned in full-force after lunch, but when Ms. Allred placed the test in front of Cassie in fourth hour, she relaxed a little.

"That wasn't so hard," she said to Cara when they finished.

"Not so hard for you," Amity said. "I was dying! None of it made sense to me."

"We've gone over those problems," Cassie said. "You know how to do them."

"I forgot."

"Me too," Andrea said. "My mom said she's going to hire a tutor for me if my grades don't start improving."

"Are they bad?" Cassie had three classes with Andrea, and it seemed like she got her work done on time.

"Mostly just my math grade. Spanish and civics are fine."

"Just have Cassie tutor you. She's the smartest at everything," Amity said.

Cassie smiled at the praise, but now that her test was out of the way, she was back to worrying about Ben.

"You're quiet today," Maureen said in choir. "What's going on?"

Cassie sighed. "I'm worried about me and Ben."

"Worried why?" Amity asked, giving the conversation her full attention.

"First he couldn't come to the dance with me. Then he didn't return my calls all week. Then he went to the movies with other people!"

"Another girl?" Maureen asked.

"How many calls?" Amity asked.

Cassie counted them up in her head. "Five calls. There can't be another girl. Ben wouldn't do that to me."

"Yeah, but a girl might have gone to the movies with him," Amity said.

"Someone could be moving in on your turf," Maureen added.

Their words fueled the jealous insecurity in Cassie's chest. Ben was hers. "What do I do if he won't even answer my calls?"

"Break up with him," Maureen said.

"In a letter," Amity said.

"No. Tell his mom."

Both girls laughed at this, but Cassie hardly found it funny. She had to talk to Ben. But she didn't want to leave him another message.

Cassie went to Amity's house after school so they could practice All-Region again, but Amity was in a goofy mood. She kept switching to opera when they went through the notes, and Cassie gave up.

"Are we going to practice or not?"

"Later. I have to water my neighbor's plants. Let's do that now."

They walked down the sidewalk, and Amity said, "Are you going to try calling Ben again?"

Cassie shook her head. "I feel stupid. I called him on Saturday."

"Maybe he's not getting your messages."

"How could he not?"

"Does he have a younger brother? Sister?"

He did. Cassie's eyes went wide as she thought of Ben's little sister. "Yes. Do you think she's not telling him?"

"Have you left any messages with her?"

"Several," Cassie said. Hope lifted in her chest, and then it fell. "But on Friday I talked to his mom."

Amity shrugged. "Maybe give it one more try. Unless you're ready to write off the relationship."

They had reached the neighbor's house now, and Amity used a key under the mat to let them in. She watered the plants while Cassie stood around examining the family photos on the wall.

"Cassie," Amity said. "Catch!"

Cassie whipped around just as Amity threw a sponge at her. Yelping, she ducked her head. The sponge crashed into a plant dangling from the ceiling. The plant wobbled a moment, creaked, and then fell to the floor.

"Crapola," Cassie said.

"You were supposed to catch it, not duck! It wasn't going to hurt you!" Amity ran over and picked up the plant.

"Sorry," Cassie said. "I didn't know what it was."

Amity picked up the chain connected to the plant. "Lift me up and I'll put it back."

Cassie put her hands around Amity's waist and tried to lift her, but nothing happened. She began to giggle inexplicably. "I can't lift you."

"Weakling," Amity huffed. "You do it, then. I'll lift you."

They switched positions, but Amity couldn't lift Cassie, either.

"Get a chair and try and put it back," Cassie said.

Amity dragged a chair under it, but no matter how they tried, they couldn't get the plant back in the ceiling.

"What now?" Amity asked, staring at the forlorn plant.

"Write a note and tell them what happened. I'm sure they can put it back."

Amity grumbled under her breath. "Yeah, I'm sure. But it makes me look irresponsible."

"You can blame me."

"Then I'll look bad for bringing a friend over." Amity wrote her note, then looked at Cassie and laughed. "I never know what's going to happen when I bring you along."

CHAPTER THIRTY-FIVE

Perfect Pitch

C assie worried about Ben all day Tuesday, trying to decide if she should call him again. She spent the evening working in her dad's store. Just as they were locking up, her phone rang. "Oh!" Cassie cried. "It's Ben!" She let her dad finish closing and ran a few paces down the sidewalk.

"Ben, hi!" she said. "I've been trying to call you for days!"

"I know, I'm sorry. Things got busy."

Things got busy. Was he parroting her words back to her? Was this payback?

"How was your weekend?" she asked, more hesitant now.

"It was great. I went to the movies with some friends. Wished you were there."

Well, that last part was good, but it didn't erase the worry from her heart. "I didn't know you'd go without me."

"Did you go the dance?"

She'd considered it, and now she was glad she could truthfully answer, "No."

"Oh, well, I hope your weekend wasn't ruined for that."

"Not ruined. I just wish I could have talked to you."

"Yeah, I know that feeling."

Again she wondered if he was hinting at something, trying to say something to her. "What about this weekend? Are you busy? Can we do something?"

"I'd love to," he said, and then he added, "I miss you a lot. Sometimes I feel like you don't feel the same."

It was a tiny admission, a peek of vulnerability. Cassie bridged the distance between them. "I'm so sorry. I miss you too. I haven't been the best at writing or calling. But I think about you all the time. I really wish we could be together more."

"I'll do better at calling," Ben said. "I like you so much."

He liked her so much.

A few weeks ago he'd loved her.

Had that changed? Or was she reading too much into it?

"I'll ask my mom about Saturday. Maybe we can meet in Fayetteville or something," she said.

"Same. I'll call you later tonight."

"Sounds great!" Cassie hung up and rejoined her father, feeling much better. It wasn't perfect, but she and Ben were still together. They could make this work.

"Ben and I want to meet up in Fayetteville this Saturday," Cassie said to her mom when she got home. "Would that be okay?"

Mrs. Jones pulled the calender from her purse and looked it over. "That's November first. Aren't you forgetting something?"

The day did sound vaguely familiar. "What?"

"That's All-Region tryouts."

Cassie groaned. How could she have forgotten that? "I can't miss it!"

"Why don't you guys get together Friday night? It's Halloween. You could do something fun."

"Great idea."

"Oh, and Cassie, don't let me forget, you have an eye doctor appointment in a week."

"Can I get some colored contacts?" Andrea had some, and they made her eyes a turquoise shade of blue. Cassie so badly wanted blue eyes. Blue eyes and dark hair. Her favorite combination.

Just like Ben.

"They're so expensive," Mrs. Jones said.

"I have my own money. I've been saving it."

"We can look at them. No promises."

"That's all I ask!" Cassie hurried to her room and called Ben, crossing her fingers he would answer. Or at least be home.

She got her wish. His mom called for him, and Ben came to the phone.

"Cassie, you called!" His voice was buoyant and energetic again, just like she remembered it. "My mom said she'll take me to Fayetteville on Saturday!"

She exhaled. "I've got bad news. I can't. I've got a choir thing all day."

"Oh." He sighed, his tone deflating. She could almost feel the energy sapping out of him. "I guess that's just how it goes."

"But she said we can do something Friday," she said, anxious to make this right again. She wanted to hear that happiness in his voice. "It's Halloween. We could do something super fun."

"Let me ask."

Cassie waited, listening to the silence on the phone, before Ben finally returned.

"I can't," he said, sounding totally low now. "We've got some family Halloween thing planned."

Cassie swallowed against a lump in her throat, wanting to cry. "Okay."

"Hey, don't be sad. We'll find another time. Okay?"

"Yes. Okay. Some other time." Why did it feel like they kept saying that?

"Maybe the weekend after."

"Yeah."

"I better go now. Love you, Cassie."

He was saying it again. The words choked in Cassie's throat. She was so close to saying them back. "You too," she managed to get out before hanging up.

⊙ つ፨ ⌒⊙

"We're not allowed to wear costumes to school," Cara said on Thursday. "So I had an awesome idea. What if we all wore poodle skirts tomorrow? It's not a costume, but we'd make a statement." She beamed at everyone over her can of soda.

"I love that idea," Andrea said. "We can do our hair like the fifties also."

"Great idea!" Cassie knew her mom had a poodle skirt. She'd wear her hair up in a high ponytail and look super cute.

Cassie walked to the soccer store after school to find her dad shaking hands with another man.

"Cassie," he said, turning to her with a smile, "soon you won't have to come work here anymore."

"Oh?" Cassie tilted her head, trying not to stare at the other man. "Why?"

"This is Kurt. I just hired him to manage the store. He'll be starting right before Christmas."

The gray-haired man smiled and held out a hand, and Cassie took it. "Congrats." She turned back to her dad. "I thought I was a good employee?"

"You are." He grinned broadly at her. "But now I can afford to hire someone else. Because I got a job."

Her mouth dropped open. "You're not going to just run the store?"

"Nope. Someone else will work the store."

Cassie squealed as another thought occurred to her. "That means

211

we're not moving!"

"That's right. It also means I can quit the paper route. In fact, to celebrate, we're going to Disney World and spending Thanksgiving with your mom's family in Georgia!"

Cassie remembered those cousins, the ones that only wanted to play video games. But Disney World? And no moving? She laughed and hugged her dad. "This is great news!"

❦

Friday morning before school, she dug out the poodle skirt and put it on. It slid down her hips and straight to the floor.

"Mom!" Cassie called, trying not to panic. Why hadn't she tried this on the day before?

"What is it?" Mrs. Jones asked, coming into the hall bathroom.

"I can't get this skirt to stay up!"

Mrs. Jones pulled on it and laughed. "You're much skinnier than I was. Let me pin it."

Ten minutes later Cassie was all pinned up with the pink poodle skirt, a white shirt, a white scarf tied at her neck, and her hair in a ponytail.

"Can I wear one?" Emily asked.

"No," Cassie said. No way was she dressing up to match her sister.

"I don't have another one, Emily," Mrs. Jones said. "I'm sure you can next year."

"You look so cute," Emily said as they walked to the bus. "I bet Ben would love to see you now."

Cassie thought of him with a sad longing. "I wish he could."

The girls gathered in the locker hall before school in their matching poodle skirts, and they laughed at their own cleverness. Cara snapped pictures before they separated for classes. Cassie got compliments everywhere she went, and she almost forgot about All-Region tryouts the next day. Until seventh hour, when Ms. Berry shushed them and reminded them.

"Don't stay out late getting candy, girls. Go home and sleep. Take care of your voices. Tomorrow is an important day. Now, let's go through it."

Amity and Cara leaned in close to Cassie, matching her pitches on every song. Confidence filled Cassie's chest. The music had been hard a few weeks ago, but now it felt familiar and uncomplicated. She would do well tomorrow. As long as she didn't wake up sick.

To Cassie's relief, her throat didn't hurt Saturday morning when she woke. She gargled warm water and practiced her scales all the way to school.

"Good luck today, Cassie!" Mrs. Jones said. "You're going to do great!"

Cassie nodded, too nervous to give a response.

Riley found her before Cassie even went inside.

"I'm so nervous I couldn't eat breakfast," Riley said. "You?"

"Yeah, no way." Cassie shook her head. "I don't think I'll be able to eat all day." She spotted Amity, Janice, and Maureen and peeled away from Riley to sit with them.

"Oh, good, you're here!" Amity latched onto Cassie. "Come on, Maureen. We have to practice."

Cassie's number was one of the first auditioners this year. Her stomach knotted itself up in triple knots, but at least it would all be over soon. She warmed up with Amity and Maureen, and then she went to the audition room and stood outside it, waiting her turn. She heard the girl before her singing for the judges, her voice a little shaky on the ending notes but otherwise on pitch. Then the girl stepped out and Cassie recognized Sierra, another soprano. They gave each other timid smiles before Cassie walked in.

The three judges were still writing on their little sheets of paper. Now they looked up at her.

"You may begin," one said, her eyes keen and sharp.

The music started up. Cassie tapped her foot, counting the measures, and then she came in right on cue. She didn't miss any notes, though she cut off a little too soon at the end. She exhaled, her heart rate slowing, feeling quite pleased with that performance.

The judges were scribbling away. The same one lifted her head again. "Thank you. You may go. Send in the next person."

Cassie stepped into the hallway and smiled at the girl waiting. "Your turn."

"You did so good," the girl said. "I was just in awe."

"Thanks."

Amity was three people away, and she grabbed Cassie's arm. "Cassie, you were perfect! It was great!"

A sure confidence was replacing her earlier nerves. "You're going to do great, also," she said.

"Wait for me," Amity said.

Cassie did. She winced a little when Amity scooped up to the high note, and then she went a bit flat on the way down. She seemed to catch herself, though, and she finished the piece where she needed to be.

Amity stepped out of the room with her chin wobbling. "I messed up."

"You did great." Cassie put an arm around her and led her down the hall. "Don't worry about it now. Let's just wait and see later."

"You're going to make it. I know it."

Cassie sure hoped she was right.

Riley wanted Cassie to come over after the tryouts, so Cassie went home with her and Mrs. Isabel. Cassie's phone started ringing a little before five, and it seemed like half the choir had gotten her phone number.

"I heard your tryout was really good," Bekkah Wilcox said. "I'm sure you made it."

Then Sierra called. "I was so freaking out, I messed up on the last note. But you did great!"

Maureen called, wanting to know if she'd heard yet. "I'm sure you'll make it."

The door to Riley's room opened and Mrs. Isabel came in, waving her phone, her eyes dancing. "Guess what, guess what, guess what?"

Cassie sat up on the bed. Had Ms. Berry called Mrs. Isabel? Did she know if Cassie had made All-Region?

"What?" Riley asked.

"You made All-Region!" Mrs. Isabel threw her arms around Riley.

Cassie blinked. She took a minute to check herself, feeling like she'd entered an alternate reality. Riley made All-Region? But what about Cassie? She forced a smile to her face and ignored her phone as it pinged with another text message.

"Congratulations, Riley." She gave Riley a hug as her friend squealed and wiped away tears of delight.

What about me? Cassie burned with the need to know. She glanced at her phone, glad for an excuse to look away from Riley.

Did you make All-Region? another unknown person asked. Cassie wished she had an answer.

CHAPTER THIRTY-SIX

Jealousy

*H*ve you heard anything? Amity texted, right on the heels of the last message.

Cassie paced the kitchen in the Isabels' apartment, not willing to spend another minute next to Riley and her happiness.

No, nothing, Cassie responded.

And that burned her. If she'd made it, surely she'd have heard by now. But how could she not make it?

I'm going to check. Call you soon, Amity said.

OK, Cassie said, and she told herself to calm down and wait.

Fifteen minutes later Amity called. Cassie stared at the phone, terrified it would bite her like a poisonous snake, and then she flipped it open.

"Cassie?" Mrs. Stafford's voice carried over the line. "I'm so sorry, honey. You didn't make it."

The news hit Cassie like a rock to her head. She grabbed the stove for support, the room spinning. For a moment she only heard buzzing in her ears, and then she registered the sound of someone sobbing while Mrs. Stafford spoke.

"Amity didn't make it either?" Cassie asked, her voice so wooden she hardly recognized it.

"No. She's crying too hard to talk. But she'll call you later."

"Thank you, Mrs. Stafford," Cassie said. She hung up and sank onto the linoleum floor, staring at a spot on the cupboard in shock. She hadn't made it. She felt the tiniest bit better knowing that Amity hadn't either, though she knew she should feel bad for her friend. She couldn't. She was too busy feeling bad for herself.

She'd forgotten to ask about Maureen. Had Maureen made it?

Cassie couldn't go back into the bedroom and be happy for Riley. So she called her mom.

"I need to come home," she said when Mrs. Jones answered. "Come get me."

"All right. I'll be there in half an hour."

Cassie locked herself in the bathroom. She texted Riley to tell her she wasn't feeling well and didn't come out, even when Riley knocked on the door and asked if she was okay.

"I'll be okay," she said, her words nasalized from her stuffy nose. "My mom's coming. I'm just going to go home."

"If you're sure," Riley said. Her voice still had a happy edge to it that her concern for Cassie couldn't stifle.

She heard her mom's knock on the door and bolted from the bathroom, barely saying bye to Riley before jumping into the van.

"Cassie, honey," Mrs. Jones said, following her in. "What's wrong?"

Cassie couldn't keep it in anymore. "I didn't make All-Region!" she sobbed, her shoulders shaking as a gush of emotional anguish flooded out of her.

"Oh, honey, I'm so sorry." Mrs. Jones wrapped her in a hug, holding her close. "It'll be okay. There's always next year."

The disappointment over not making All-Region didn't fade as the weekend drew to an end, and Cassie dreaded going to school on Monday. Hopefully by now everyone knew she hadn't made it and no one would ask her painful questions.

Amity met her in the hallway as she got off the bus. Her eyes were red and her mouth trembled. "Are you okay?" Amity asked.

Cassie's own eyes burned as she struggled with a response. A lump in her throat made it hard to swallow. "Yeah. I'm okay. Are you?"

Amity burst into tears. "I can't believe we didn't make it!"

That set Cassie off. She leaned against Amity, both of them crying.

Cara found them that way and hugged them. "I heard you didn't make it. So sorry."

Maureen joined the huddle, looking annoyed. "I didn't make it either. But I'm not crying."

Amity lifted her face. "Because you didn't care as much!"

"Are you guys okay?" Nicole, Cassie's friend from English class, stopped next to them, her eyes wide with concern.

"They didn't make All-Region." Maureen turned and walked away.

Nicole's face crumpled in understanding. "I'm so sorry. I cried last year when I didn't make All-Region band."

"I'm okay." Cassie wiped the tears, straightening up. "It's okay." She didn't understand why she hadn't made it. She thought for sure she'd done well on her tryout.

Unfortunately all of her friends seemed to think the same thing. Some had assumed she did make it and were shocked to learn she hadn't. Every new question, every expression of surprise and then sympathy, was another dagger to Cassie's heart.

I should have stayed home today, she thought.

She still had to make it through choir, where she'd endure the pitying stares of her classmates while she read the judges' critical feedback.

Cassie waited quietly beside Amity and Maureen as Ms. Berry handed out the judging sheets. She knew the moment Ms. Berry got to Cassie's audition sheet because her eyes lifted and landed on Cassie.

"Cassie," Ms. Berry said, coming over with a gentle smile on her face. "I know you didn't make it, honey, but you should be proud of your chair. You did so well. You worked really hard and deserved to make it. Maybe next year will be your chance."

Cassie swallowed hard and nodded, willing herself not to cry. Hadn't Ms. Berry said the same thing last year? She felt several pairs of eyes on her and she picked up the pink judging sheet, trying to ignore everyone.

#24 was written at the top and circled with a red pen. Chair twenty-four. Cassie nearly cried again. She was only seven chairs away from making All-Region. She went through and read the judges' comments. The first two were full of kind words and encouragement, and one of them praised her voice as "beautiful, melodic, and unique."

That judge gave her a sixth chair rating.

The last judge, however, had not liked Cassie's voice. She said it sounded weak and needed to come in stronger and to hold the notes longer and to keep practicing and round out those vowels. Each critique was a red-hot knife to Cassie's ego.

That judge had rated her number fifty-four.

Curse that judge! Cassie put the paper down with a sigh. The first two judges had rated her high enough to get her into All-Region. The third one blew it for her. Cassie trembled with indignation. To be so close! And yet to not make it. She wiped the corners of her eyes and tried to be happy with the glowing words of the first two judges.

CHAPTER THIRTY-SEVEN

Tipping Cows

"I have to go help at the soccer fields today," Mr. Jones said Tuesday afternoon as Cassie stood helping him sort shoes. "So we're closing the shop early."

"Really?" Cassie scowled at him in displeasure. "If I'd known, I could have ridden the bus home."

"Well, I had no way to tell you. So let's go."

Cassie pulled her cell phone out of her pocket, wondering why he didn't just call her. He probably hadn't thought of that.

"I'll just stay in the car and work on homework," she said.

"That's fine. I'll be working at that white tent over there." He pointed across the fields.

"Great." As he walked away, Cassie thought of something. She opened the door and shouted, "I might go for a walk. If you need me, call me!"

He waved a hand and didn't look back.

Cassie finished up her math assignment and studied her science vocabulary and then got tired of sitting in the little car. Time for that walk. She stepped out and started up the sidewalk before it suddenly occurred to her that she could walk to Andrea's house. It was just up the street.

For a moment, she hesitated. It had been months since she'd gone to Andrea's. Would Andrea want her to come over?

Cassie brushed aside the reluctance. Of course she would.

Ten minutes later, Cassie knocked on Andrea's door. Andrea opened it, and her expression morphed from surprise to delight.

"Cassie! Come on in!"

It was like nothing had ever changed between them. Cassie wondered if Andrea even missed her, even noticed that they hardly talked or hung out anymore. Andrea talked nonstop, not missing a beat as she pulled clothes out of her closet for Cassie to try on.

"Here, this skirt," Andrea said, tossing a short plaid skirt at Cassie that looked like it belonged at a private school. "And this blouse." She added a button-up blouse to the ensemble.

"What are you trying to do, turn me into a prep?" Cassie asked, pulling the clothes on.

"Nah, preps dress like this to show everyone how they belong in a private school instead of a regular school. To show how much better they are than everyone else. We're dressing you up because it will make you look cute."

Cassie accepted the backhanded compliment and then admired how well the clothes fit her body. "They do look nice."

"Makeup and hair next." Andrea went to work curling Cassie's hair and putting makeup on her, until Cassie glanced at her phone and jumped up.

"I better go! My dad said he'd be done at six and that was ten minutes ago!" She peeled the clothes off and pulled her own back on.

"Take these!" Andrea grabbed a plastic bag and shoved the clothes inside. "Wear them tomorrow!"

"I can't wear these to school. It's not my style," Cassie protested.

Andrea fixed her with a dark glower. "They look fantastic on you. You will wear these to school."

"If you're attempting mind control on me, it's working. Fine. I'll wear them to school tomorrow."

"Great." Now Andrea's face lit up in a smile. "You'll be great."

Cassie walked back to the soccer fields, feeling slightly like she'd been sucked into a tornado and emerged covered in new clothing and a new face.

❦

The air took a chilly drop in the beginning of November, and having to wake up early for her religion class meant it was colder than usual. Cassie showered quickly and curled her hair before checking the time. Already six-thirty. Her church class started at seven. At least she already had her clothes picked out, thanks to Andrea. She scowled as she buttoned the plaid skirt and shirt, feeling silly and fake. These clothes belonged on someone else.

Cassie's dad was already in the kitchen, pulling on his jacket. "Go start the car, please," he said, tossing the keys to Cassie. He stopped and gave her another look. "What are you wearing?"

"They're Andrea's clothes. She let me borrow them." Cassie glanced down at the shirt and skirt. He wouldn't make her change, would he?

There wasn't anything wrong with the clothes, that she could tell.

"Hmm," was all he said, and he went back to his jacket.

She started the car, glad she got to sit up front the whole way today. It was Mr. Jones' week to drive Cassie and Riley.

Ice covered the windshield, and Cassie slipped a bit running back into the house.

"It's a little icy out," she said, grabbing her binder and purse.

"Can't be too bad or they would have canceled school."

Cassie followed him back out to the car. She yawned, climbed inside, and leaned her head against the seat, wanting more than ever to go back to sleep.

Riley's dad waited at the bottom of the hill, the designated pick up spot. Cassie didn't even open her eyes as Riley climbed into the back. Silence reigned, with only the pumping heater to fill the car.

Mr. Jones drove down the curvy road. Cassie's body rocked with the gentle rhythm as the vehicle took the switchback curves.

The car jerked to the right so suddenly that Cassie's eyes shot open. She didn't even have time to cry out as they swerved off the road. A horrible scraping, grinding noise sounded around them. Something scratched over the windshield. Cassie's heart leapt in her throat.

The windshield is going to break, she thought. *I'm going to die.*

The car barreled forward, trees whipping past them. Her hands found the edges of the seat, and she held on tight.

Then the car jerked to a halt. Cassie slammed forward before the seatbelt dragged her back. She shook in her seat, unable to think, hardly breathing. What just happened? Where were they?

Mr. Jones undid his seatbelt and got out of the car, and the action pulled Cassie into the present. She took a deep breath, hearing how the oxygen whooshed through her mouth, feeling her lungs expand. She swiveled around and saw Riley, flattened against the backseat and putting her seatbelt on.

Putting her seatbelt on.

Cassie started laughing. She pressed her hand to her head and laughed and laughed. Then she opened the door and got out. Riley followed, and they hugged each other.

"We're alive," Cassie said, holding her friend. "We're okay." She pulled her back and gave her a scolding look. "And you weren't wearing your seatbelt."

"I won't make that mistake again," Riley said.

Mr. Jones went back to the car. He started it up, then looked at them. "Sorry about that. Are you girls okay?"

"I think so." Cassie looked herself over. "Riley?"

"I'm okay."

"All right." Mr. Jones didn't look so happy. "Let's find a way out of here."

They couldn't go back out the way they'd come, under the barb-wire fence that had scraped the car up from hood to trunk. It was obviously made of sturdier stuff than the car. Instead Mr. Jones had to find a gate. He opened it up, drove the car out, then closed it again before they drove onto the road.

"I'll have to come back later and talk to the owner," he said with a sigh. "See if there was any damage. After I find out how much it's going to cost to repair my car."

They were twenty minutes late to their religion class. But as soon as they walked in, Riley announced, "We were in a car accident!"

Ms. Betty stopped teaching as the class let out exclamations of concern and relief.

"We're all okay," Cassie said, finding a seat in the middle and settling down. "Just a bit shook up."

"And the car?" Tyler Reeves asked. His brother Jason poked him.

"The car doesn't matter. We're just glad you two are okay," Jason said.

Jason was always the sweeter of the Reeves brothers, though Cassie had to admit in her more honest moments that something about Tyler attracted her to him.

"I'm not sure how the car is. But thanks for your concern for us." She smiled at them both.

"We're all glad you're fine," Ms. Betty said. "Can we resume class now?"

Cassie pulled out her copy of the Old Testament, ready to read and listen.

When class ended, most of the students followed Cassie to her car, where Mr. Jones showed off the scratches covering every inch from bumper to roof.

"I just got back from a body shop," he said. "Looks like it'll be four thousand dollars to fix it up."

Crapola. Cassie winced, glad she wasn't the one who had caused the incident.

The kids whistled and shook their heads, then began to leave in groups of two or three, heading to different schools.

Jason lingered by the car. "You're sure you're okay, Cassie?"

"Yeah, yeah, I'm good."

"No more car accidents. We'll see you guys tomorrow."

"Tomorrow," Cassie said. She waved, then she and Riley climbed into the car to go to school.

"What a way to start the day," she said to Riley.

"Yeah," Riley said. "It can only get boring from here."

The accident was the only thing on Cassie's mind when she walked into school. She searched out her friends, eager to tell them about the mishap. They spotted her first, and before she could even say a word, Maureen said, "Cassie! You look gorgeous!"

They formed a circle around her, admiring her hair and clothes.

In all the earlier excitement, she'd completely forgotten what she was wearing.

"Told you," Andrea said, her expression smug. "You should dress this way every day."

Cassie wished she could. She wished her family could afford to shop places with clothes like this, that they could afford for her to always look trendy and put together.

Her confidence grew with every step, as classmates noticed her and called out to her. She stepped into first hour and held her head high. Coach Benson called the class to order and gave them an assignment. Then he walked down the aisle, stopping at their desks to check their work. When he got to Cassie's, he said, "You look nice today, Cassie."

She smiled and lowered her eyes. "Thanks."

Even her teachers noticed her.

She walked out of the classroom and headed for her English class. She almost skipped, feeling as if she walked on air. Could she someday be as beautiful as everyone thought she was right now?

"Hey, Cassie," a familiar male voice said, and Cassie stumbled in her skipping. She threw out a hand to catch herself but didn't, and then she landed on the floor on her rump, purse collapsing next to her and binder scattering around the hallway.

She turned her head to see Miles standing there, his expression torn between concern and laughter. "Are you oh—" he tried to say, but then the humorous side won out, and he started laughing.

Cassie did too. She couldn't help it. She must've looked ridiculous, falling in the hallway with these fancy clothes on.

He took her hand and pulled her to her feet.

"I'm okay," she said, brushing herself off. "Thanks, though."

"I was going to ask you something," he said, his eyes sparkling merrily. "But after that spectacular fall, I don't remember what it was."

"Well, if it comes to you," she gathered up her books, "you know where to find me." She walked away, this time careful not to add any skips or jumps to her steps.

CHAPTER THIRTY-EIGHT

Eye Ow

C assie's mom picked her up after school so they could go to the eye doctor. She'd brought Cassie's money box with her, but first Mrs. Jones asked about the accident.

"I had to call the Isabels and tell them what happened. Are you sure you're not hurt?"

"We're okay," Cassie said. "It was a really freak thing. Somehow we weren't hurt at all. And Riley wasn't even wearing her seatbelt!"

Mrs. Jones muttered under her breath. "Well, I'm very grateful it turned out so well. The car's in bad shape, but better the car than one of you." She glanced over at Cassie, her eyes roving over the skirt and blouse. "Where did you get that outfit? It's not yours."

"It's Andrea's. She let me borrow it."

Mrs. Jones didn't say anything for a moment, and Cassie wondered what she was thinking. Then she said, "It looks very nice on you."

"Thanks."

They didn't have to wait long at the eye doctor for her turn. He checked out her eyes and then settled back with a smile.

"Everything looks good. How are they feeling?"

"Great." Cassie pleated her fingers together. "Can I look at the colored lenses?"

He leaned back, rubbing one thumb over his chin. "Your eyes are too dark for tinted lenses. If you want color, you'll have to go with the opaque lenses. They're much thicker and quite a bit more expensive."

"Can I see them?" she begged, looking from the doctor to her mother.

Mrs. Jones shrugged. "If you want, I guess you can. It's your money."

Yes! Cassie did a mental fist bump.

The doctor led her into the small lighted room with all of the contact lenses, reminding Cassie of the year before when she tried on contacts for the first time. She had to smile at the way she'd spazzed out, not wanting to touch her eye but needing to get the lens in.

She'd come a long way since then.

"She wants to try some opaque colored lenses," the doctor said to his assistant. "Can you help her out?"

"Sure!" The woman smiled at Cassie. "What color you want, sweetie?"

"Blue," Cassie said, without hesitation.

"All right, here we have the different shades." She held up a diagram showing an iris with different colors of blue.

"This one," Cassie said. "The light blue."

"That's the baby blue. Very nice. Let me get it." The assistant placed a plastic strip on the counter with two little indentions. Then she dumped a contact lens in each indention. "Go ahead, try them on."

Cassie washed her hands. She already had her normal contacts out, since the doctor required it to do his exam. Now she scooped out the right lens, checked to make sure it wasn't turned wrong, and popped it into her eye. Immediately it began to sting and burn, and she blinked several times to stop the sensation.

"Is everything okay?" the assistant asked.

"Fine." Cassie kept blinking, her eyes tearing up. She dipped her finger into the dish and put the left lens into her eye. The same reaction occurred, burning and stinging. Her eyes filled with water, and she couldn't stop blinking. She lifted the mirror and held it to her face. The baby blue color was stunning, but hard to see with her eyes tearing up the way they were.

"Honey, what's going on?" The assistant leaned over and looked into her face, frowning.

Now Cassie blinked so much that she hardly had her eyes open. "I don't know. They hurt really bad." She'd thought maybe the burning would go away, but it was getting worse.

"Your eyes are bright red. Let's get those lenses out."

Cassie forced her eyes open and gripped the slender plastic lens with her thumb and forefinger, but it wouldn't come off. "I can't get it," she said, slightly panicked. "It's stuck to my eye!"

"Keep trying." The assistant's voice was more urgent now, serious and commanding.

Cassie managed to get her fingers around one lens and pop it out. She let out a cry as her eye seared her, the pain hot and cutting.

"Now the other one. Come on, sweetie. Let's get it out."

The assistant's calm voice soothed her, and Cassie took a deep breath, focusing. There was so much water it was hard to hold her eye open, and her lids kept wanting to close. She gripped the lens and braced herself, knowing it would hurt when she forced it off. But she did. She dropped it back into the dish and shut her eyes, the pain still throbbing beneath her eyelids.

"Open your eyes, please. I need to see."

Cassie felt a hand on her shoulder and knew it was her mom. She opened her eyes, squinting against the bright light. The woman held her chin and studied her eyes.

"I'm going to get the doctor, okay? Just sit tight."

Cassie grabbed a mirror as soon as the woman left. She held it up and examined her reflection. Her eyes were bloodshot, the red veins visible around the iris. A slender raised ring circled the irises, looking as though the contact lenses were still there. But Cassie knew they weren't.

"Are you okay?" her mom asked.

"Yeah, I think so. That was weird."

Dr. Brandon returned, frowning with concern. "Let's take a look." He shown a light in her eyes, and she focused on the wall behind him. "There's no lens in her eye right now?"

"No," the assistant said. "Her eye swelled up beneath the lens. That's the mark it left behind after we got it off."

"Okay." He put the light down and looked directly at Cassie. "I think you had an allergic reaction. You can't have those lenses, unfortunately."

"No colored lenses?" Cassie feared she might cry, and not from the pain in her eyes.

"Not that brand. Jen, wait till her eyes calm down, and then try the hypoallergenic lenses for sensitive eyes. Maybe they'll work."

He walked away, and the assistant smiled at her. "It's okay. We'll try the other brand in a bit and see how it goes."

Fifteen minutes later, they had deemed Cassie's eyes normal enough to try the other lenses.

"I only have one color," Jen said apologetically. "But they come in other colors, so if this one works for you, we can try one of the others."

"Okay," Cassie said.

Jen rinsed and cleaned out the dishes, then put in two colored lenses. Cassie hesitated only a moment, then she plucked one up and put it in.

No pain. Not even a little. She exhaled and smiled. "It worked!"

"Great. Do the other so you can see how they look."

Cassie put the left one in, overjoyed that she could still have colored lenses. She held the mirror up to her face and examined them. They were a deep forest green, and she knew right away she didn't want that color. The lens created the radiating lines of an iris since the color completely concealed her own. But it had worked!

"This is great," Cassie said, blinking several times to check how the lenses felt under her eyelids. "I can use these!"

"Fantastic." The assistant beamed. "I'm so glad we found something that works for you. Here are your color options."

She laid down a laminate sheet. It didn't have as many colors, and there was only one blue. Cassie frowned. It was a darker blue, not the same light sky blue that Cassie so adored on the other lens. But she didn't have any choice. "I'll take the blue one."

"These don't come in disposable," the woman warned. "You'll have to buy the yearly lenses."

"How much is it?"

"Two hundred and fifty dollars. But you probably want to get the insurance on them, in case one tears. Then it's almost three hundred dollars."

Three hundred dollars! Cassie had that much money, thanks to frugally saving her allowance and leftover lunch money for the past two years. But never had she excepted to spend it all on contact lenses! She'd expected it to be half that much.

"Cassie?" Mrs. Jones asked, and Cassie shook off her doubts.

"That's fine," she said, lifting her chin. "I'll do it."

"Okay, then. We'll get these ordered. We'll have them in two days."

⁂

"It's too bad you can't do the Fall Festival this year," Ms. Malcolm said as Cassie put away her music books after voice lessons. "You've improved so much since last fall. You'd have a good chance of taking a place."

"I know. I'm sad too." But Cassie couldn't be too sad about it, since she was getting to go to Disney World instead. Her mind buzzed with anticipation. The last time her family had gone, she'd been ten years old. What a different experience it would be now!

"Well, have a nice time on your trip." Ms. Malcolm smiled at her. "And don't forget to practice your Christmas song. 'O Holy Night' has three verses, and you'll be all of them."

"I'll have it memorized. My dad will make sure of that." Mr. Jones had specifically requested that song for Cassie. It was his favorite, and he really wanted to hear his daughter sing it.

"I'm sure he will."

Cassie headed outside, where her mom's van waited to take her to church. As they approached the signal to turn at Zion's Road, however, a road block of three police cars spanned the way. Mrs. Jones slowed the car and came to a stop as an officer stepped to her window. She rolled it down.

"Is everything okay? Was there an accident?" she asked.

"No, ma'am. But we do have an escaped convict in the area. He was put away for killing three people, so we've blocked off the whole road until he's found."

Cassie let out a gasp. "He's loose somewhere?"

"That's right. So we need you to turn around. If you live over here, find somewhere else to be for the next few hours."

"Thank you very much, sir." Cassie's mom rolled the window up and drummed her fingers on the steering wheel. "Well. I guess you don't get to go to church tonight."

Cassie had extra time on her hands now. She worked on some homework when she got home, and then she thought of Ben, with his blue eyes and dark hair. What would he think about her colored contacts? She pulled her phone out and called him. His mom answered, and Cassie left a message for him to call her.

She put the phone down and chewed on her lower lip. They hadn't seen each other since September and had barely spoken on the phone this month. A gnawing worry festered in her belly. They were supposed to do something this Saturday, but neither one of them had taken the initiative to set something up.

That couldn't be healthy for their relationship.

Ben didn't even know they were leaving to spend Thanksgiving in Florida and Georgia. What was going to happen to them?

Episode 4:

Masquerade

CHAPTER THIRTY-NINE

English Girl

C assie woke up Friday morning with a horrible canker sore in her mouth.

She winced at breakfast as she tried to eat her toast, and brushing her teeth was grueling. She moved the brush gingerly around the sore on her lip, feeling like it was an ineffective cleaning job. How could she go to school like this?

"Why are you talking funny?" Andrea asked in first hour.

"Canker sore," Cassie said, trying to keep her lip away from her teeth while she spoke. "It hurts to talk."

Andrea laughed. "You sound like you have an accent."

Cassie grumbled under her breath and tried to focus on her class assignment. After class, she stopped by Coach Benson's desk and got her homework for the next week.

"Don't cause any trouble at Disney World," he teased, handing her a thick packet.

"I won't," she said, thumbing through the assignments. Especially not if every teacher gave her this much homework.

Mrs. Jones texted at lunch. *Your contacts arrived. I'll pick you up after school to get them.*

Yes! Cassie did a fist pump and gave a little squeal. Finally, she would have blue eyes!

"My contacts are here!" she told her friends at lunch.

"Why are you talking funny?" Maureen asked.

"She's got a cold sore," Andrea giggled.

"You got a cold sore?" Amity gasped. "People get those from kissing too much."

"Canker sore," Cassie growled. "Anyway. I've got my contacts!"

"When do we get to see you in them?" Amity asked. "Don't you leave for Florida tomorrow?"

Cassie nodded. "You could come over."

"Okay. I'll ask my mom."

"I'm so jealous you're going to Florida," Janice said. "I wish I could come."

"I wish you could too!" Cassie said. "It would be so much fun!" Instead of being surrounded by her friends, she'd have to deal with her siblings for an entire week.

But by the end of the day, all Cassie could think about was her contacts. She could barely contain her excitement. As if going to Disney World wasn't enough, now she got to have new colored contacts!

She tapped her fingers on her thighs as her mom drove her to the eye clinic. "I can't wait."

"What's wrong with your mouth?"

Cassie rolled her eyes. She'd heard this question all day. "Canker sore."

"Ah. You must be excited. I get canker sores when I'm stressed or excited."

Cassie suspected all she'd done was poke her lip with the tooth brush, but that took too many words to say, and speaking was painful, so all she did was nod.

"Okay, we're here. Let's check this out."

Mrs. Jones did the talking while Cassie tried to imagine how she'd look with blue eyes. Exotic. Dark skin, dark hair, and crystalline, piercing blue eyes. The kind people couldn't help but notice.

"Here we are, Cassie," Jen the assistant said, leading Cassie back to the lighted room. "Let's make sure these fit you."

She opened the box and deposited the contacts into little dishes.

"They don't look blue," Cassie said, studying the grayish color on the lens.

"That's just the water. Wait till you get them on."

Cassie hoped she was right. She took out the contacts she was wearing and slipped on the colored ones. Then she opened her eyes and looked in the mirror. A sigh escaped her lips. "They're gray."

Both the assistant and her mother leaned over to peer at her.

"They're definitely gray," Mrs. Jones said.

"Hmm. We must have put down the wrong color."

We. As if Cassie had been the one to order the lenses. "These aren't the ones I want." She took them out of her eyes and put her regular ones back in, her chest heavy with disappointment. After all these days of waiting for them to arrive, and the contacts were the wrong color.

"It's a lovely gray," the assistant said.

"She paid three hundred dollars for blue lenses," Mrs. Jones said.

"Yes, of course." Jen boxed the lenses back up. "I'll send these right back and get new ones ordered. Blue this time. I'll have them here by Tuesday at the latest."

"We'll be out of town," Mrs. Jones said. "We leave tomorrow."

"No problem. I'll have them waiting at the desk for you when you get back from your trip."

Cassie turned to her mom. "So I won't get them until after Thanksgiving?" It felt silly to cry over something like this, but she wanted them now!

Mrs. Jones hesitated. "Well, we could have them delivered to my sister's house in Georgia. That's where we'll be for Thanksgiving."

Cassie brightened, hopeful again. "Oh yeah! Can we?"

"I'll ask my sister."

❧

"They didn't have the right color," Cassie told Amity on the phone that evening. "So there's no point in coming over to see them."

"That's too bad. Well, have a great time in Florida. We'll miss you."

"I'll miss you guys, too."

Cassie hung up the phone and surveyed the huge pile of homework she was bringing. It was like her teachers didn't know she'd be on vacation.

She wanted to say Ben would miss her also, but he'd never even called her back. The days of him missing her seemed long past.

She picked the phone up and tried calling him one last time. She held back a sigh when his mom answered. "Is Ben home?" she asked.

"No, he's not. Can I take a message?"

Why was he never home? Why wasn't he returning her calls? None of this sat right. "It's just Cassie again. Just tell him to call me."

"Okay, I will."

Cassie put away the phone, wishing she hadn't called at all.

❧

Cassie alternated between sleeping and reading on the drive to Florida. She spent a decent amount of time texting, also, though her friends didn't seem as bored as she was and didn't respond quite so quickly. It wasn't until a day later that Mr. Jones pulled the van into the same camping resort where they'd stayed last time.

"No tent," Cassie said.

"Yeah, we got rained on last time," Emily agreed.

"That's fine," Mrs. Jones said, emptying the van of food and suitcases. "We got the big RV this time. It has two bedrooms. The girls can have one room and Scott can have the table-bed."

Cassie grabbed her suitcase. A smile touched her lips when she walked inside, though she didn't let it grow too big because it hurt her mouth. She had so many nostalgic memories of these RV houses. She followed Emily into the bedroom at the foot of the RV. It was only big enough for a bed, which she and her sisters would be sharing. A few cupboards lined the walls above.

"This is so fun!" Annette said, coming in behind.

"The fun part is tomorrow," Cassie said. "This is just the arriving."

They helped unpack the van. Cassie had promised Ms. Malcolm she'd memorize the words to her Christmas song, so she spent the evening doing that. Mr. Jones called the family to the kitchen for a quick meeting.

"Tomorrow we'll hit Magic Kingdom, and on Tuesday we'll do EPCOT. Wednesday and Thursday we'll just hang around the camping resort, so you kids can plan those days for homework. Cassie." Mr. Jones looked directly at her. "I know you've been trying to get your book done to resubmit to the publisher. Why don't we work on it together this week?"

To be perfectly honest, she had mostly forgotten about her book. She nodded. "Yeah, that's a good idea."

"And then Friday, as long as it's not too cold, we'll do the water park."

"Let's hope it's warm!" Emily said. "Last time was miserable!"

"We won't go if it's cold like that," Mrs. Jones said.

The next morning was chaos as Mr. Jones shouted orders and urged them out of the RV so they could catch the early monorail to the Magic Kingdom.

"We don't want to waste a single minute! The tickets cost the same whether we're there all day or for just an hour!"

Cassie thought she was too old to get excited about Disney, but her anticipation grew the closer they got to the park. Iconic Disney characters smiled from road signs with fingers and arrows pointing the way. *We're going*, Cassie thought in silent acknowledgment to them.

The weather was breezy but pleasant. Not exactly warm, but definitely not cold. Even though they'd hurried, by the time they got to the front gate, a long line had formed.

"Where do we want to go first?" Mr. Jones asked.

"Space Mountain!" Emily said. "My favorite."

Everyone listed one of their Must-Sees except Cassie, whose attention had been attracted elsewhere. A boy walked by in a baseball cap, looking so much like Ben that her chest squeezed. She took a step closer, ready to call out, when he turned his head. Not him. She shook her head. "Quit being silly," she mumbled.

They split up inside, with Emily and Cassie standing in the one-hour line to ride Space Mountain. The line shuffled forward inch by inch. The walls and hallways were covered with astronaut trivia and things to look at, but that wasn't as exciting as being on the ride. Cassie checked her phone, trying not to wish Ben would call. Did he still like her? At least forty minutes had crept by.

"I hope it's as fun as I remember it being," Emily said.

"Better be, after this long line," Cassie said with a laugh.

A boy in front of them turned around. He had to be about their age, and Cassie eyed him as he looked her over.

"Are you English?" he asked.

Wasn't that obvious? How many people spoke English if they weren't English? "Yes," she said, keeping her voice polite.

"Oh, that's super cool!" His eyes lit up. "I love English accents. What part of England are you from?"

England? And then it dawned on Cassie what he meant. English as in from England! "Oh, um . . ."

Emily giggled beside her, and Cassie didn't know how to get out of this one.

"Tontitown," Cassie blurted out, naming the tiny city next to Springdale where their house sat.

"I've never heard of that one," he said, looking disappointed. "I want to visit York and Bath someday. And London, of course."

"Of course," Cassie echoed. Sweat beaded on her hairline.

"But those are the big cities, everyone wants to go there. Tell me about your city. Maybe I'll add it to my list."

Crapola. "Well, it's pretty small. There's not much to do there."

"What does it look like?"

Emily was still giggling, and Cassie ignored her. "It's very green. Lots of trees. Some rolling hills." She pictured the countryside around their home, the acreage spilling into the forest.

"Sounds like most of England."

He moved up in the line then, and it was his turn to get on. "Nice meeting you. Maybe we'll meet up later and I can get your address! We could write!"

Cassie waved as he got on, and then she sank back into Emily.

"Whatever we do, we can't meet back up with that kid," Cassie said.

"Yes, my lady," Emily said with her best English accent, and Cassie couldn't help laughing.

CHAPTER FORTY

Blue-Eyed

Cassie checked her phone repeatedly throughout the next three days, hoping for a call from Ben. She memorized all three verses to "O Holy Night" on Wednesday, and then on Thursday her dad sat her down at the clubhouse with his computer.

"What more do you need to do?" he asked.

At the end of last year, Cassie had submitted her manuscript to a publisher. They'd responded with a very favorable letter and asked her to make a few changes before resubmitting. Cassie opened the file where she'd made a list of the changes the editor requested. She'd only done the first one: remove the dialect.

"Well, I'm supposed to flesh out the action scenes, add more verbs. Add more setting and description throughout the whole book. Remove the extra points of view scenes and decide which character is the main character, then rewrite the story from her point of view." Ugh. Cassie resisted the urge to close the computer. "It's kind of a lot."

"It sure is. That last one looks the hardest, but it also sounds like you shouldn't proceed with the rest until you've done it. What if you add setting to a scene that you later decide isn't necessary?"

"This is why I'm stuck," Cassie sighed. "It took me a year to write the book the first time. What if it takes me a year to rewrite it?"

"Then you better get started. It's already taken you six months to sit here and do nothing."

Good point. "Which character do I choose to be the main character?"

"Let's discuss your characters. What are their traits?"

"Well, there's Sandy. She's like, the shy girl who doesn't say much. And there's Kendra, the one who's super nice to everyone. And Melissa, the bossy, popular girl. Then there's Joyce. She's smart and headstrong and a leader." Cassie paused, considering her characters. "I kind of think of Joyce as the main character. Her friends look to her for advice. I think most of the story is told through her eyes."

"Sounds like you already know who it should be."

"I think I do." A tiny flicker of anticipation jumped in Cassie's chest, and she pulled the computer closer.

"I'll leave you to it, then."

Cassie didn't even answer as Mr. Jones walked away. She didn't have to rewrite the whole story—just cut some story lines and change a few scenes.

Friday morning Cassie examined the canker sore in her mouth after she brushed her teeth. It had been a week, and though the sore was healing, it stubbornly remained on her lip, painful and taunting. She put on her swimsuit and a sundress over the top, then stepped outside of the RV. The sun shown down pleasantly, prickling the tops of her bare shoulders.

"Remember last time we went to the water park?" Emily said as the family hopped into the car.

How could Cassie forget? Although it had been four years, she still recalled the drizzling rain and the frigid water. "How miserable."

They split into groups again, with Mr. Jones taking the younger children and Cassie and Emily pairing up to go on rides together. They road the lazy river first, then took a tube down the slide.

"Let's go on that one." Emily pointed to a high slide that looked like it dropped straight down into a pool of water.

"No way," Cassie said, turning her back on it.

Emily grabbed her and pulled her around. "Come on, it's not that bad. Look, everyone's laughing."

And picking wedgies. Cassie studied the people getting out of the slide, smiles on their faces as they pulled their swimsuits back into place. "They're laughing because they're embarrassed."

"Come on, Cassie. Please?"

"Fine," Cassie said, relenting. "But if I hate it, I blame you."

They climbed the long switch-back staircase several stories before they ended up in line behind dozens of other slide-goers. A man and his wife talked to their oldest child, trying to convince him the slide would be fun.

"I'm dreading it too," Cassie said, inserting herself into the conversation. "But my sister convinced me we'll be okay."

The man smiled at her and turned back to his son. "See? It's normal to be frightened of new experiences."

And scary things, Cassie thought.

"But we do them anyway, especially when people we trust are telling us it's okay."

"I'll go down if you do," Cassie said to the boy, who looked about ten years old. "You look braver than me."

The boy straightened and puffed out his chest. "Yeah. I can do this."

His father turned to Cassie and mouthed, "Thanks." Then he said, "Where are you girls from?"

"Arkansas," Cassie said.

"Arkansas! But you don't have an Arkansas accent. You sound like you're European."

Cassie looked at Emily, who shrugged helplessly. "Um, well, I guess this is how we talk." Cassie didn't feel like explaining about her stupid canker sore.

"I've been to Arkansas once. We went to Hot Springs. Is that close to where you live?"

Cassie had no idea. "I'm not sure. We haven't lived in Arkansas that long." Just four years.

"Ah. What's the nearest city to you?"

"Fayetteville. The university is there."

"Hmm." He rubbed his chin thoughtfully. "The name is vaguely familiar. Do you remember what highway it's by?"

Why all the hard questions? She didn't drive. She had no idea. She looked again to Emily, who said, "Seventy-one?"

Cassie had heard that number before. "Yes, seventy-one."

His eyes lit up, and he lifted a finger. "That's it! I remember Hot Springs being off of Highway 71. You must live near there. Lovely place!"

"Yeah, it's beautiful."

"Are you Hispanic?" his wife asked.

"Yes." Cassie tried to remember the country in Central America where her mom said their relatives came from. "From El Salvador."

"Oh, well, that explains your accent," the man said. He looked at Emily. "Are you from Arkansas too?"

"We're sisters," Emily said, gesturing to Cassie.

That had the man lifting an eyebrow. "But you don't have an accent."

Crapola. "I hang out with more Hispanic friends than she does," Cassie said. Where were these stories coming from?

"Ah, so you get your accent from your friends. Do you speak Spanish?"

Cassie shook her head. "No, only my dad does. None of the rest of us learned it."

"Your dad and not your mom?"

"Yeah." They were nearly to the top now, to Cassie's relief. "My mom doesn't talk about her family much. I guess some weird stuff happened when they came to America. She only talks to her sister, and they don't speak Spanish."

"That's too bad. How does your dad know Spanish?"

"From when he lived in Venezuela."

The man nodded as if everything made complete sense. "So your dad's Venezuelan and your mom's Salvadorean, but only your dad speaks Spanish and you have an accent because you hang out with your Hispanic friends."

And we live in Hot Springs, Cassie thought, realizing the crazy lie she'd weaved without even meaning to. "That about sums us up."

"Well, that's sure interesting!"

His wife touched his back. "It's our turn, honey. Let's pay attention."

"It was nice meeting you girls. Enjoy your time here!"

They went down the slide, and Cassie could breathe again after they left. "Holy crapola," she murmured.

"Your canker sore is sure giving us an interesting experience."

"Next," the boy manning the slides called.

There were two slides, and Cassie's nerves returned in full-force when she stood behind one and looked at the drop. "I can't do this," she said, panicking.

"Yes, you can," Emily said. "It's fine. Just let go and slide. I'll see you at the bottom."

"No, I—"

"Cassie," Emily interrupted. "Just do it."

"Clear," the boy said, and Emily swung off the bar onto the slide.

Cassie groaned, hating every second of this, and she also pushed off.

The water rushed up around her body as if it wanted to lift her back to the top. The angle was so vertical she feared she would fly right off the slide. She opened her mouth to scream and water rushed in, so she quickly shut it.

She slid into the pool of water at the bottom of the slide with all the grace and force of an elephant, and the sliver of fabric on the bottom of her swimsuit slid right into her butt, giving her the wedgie she'd seen everyone picking out. She thrust her feet down and sputtered to the surface, heart pounding, gasping, terrified and relieved she hadn't died.

Emily waited for her at the side. "You did it!"

Cassie paused to rearrange her suit, then glared at her sister as she climbed out. "I am never ever ever doing anything like that again."

❦

The drive to Georgia from Florida wasn't nearly so long as the drive from Arkansas. Cassie sat in the back with her dad's computer, the time flying as she rearranged the last half of her book into Joyce's point of view. The story felt stronger now, more solid, and she was absolutely certain the publisher would love it.

"We're here," her dad said as they pulled into the long driveway of the house in Georgia.

Their cousins had come out to meet them, taller than last time and unfamiliar after four years apart. They looked similar to each other, short brown hair, fair skin, and light eyes. Cassie didn't see much of Central American blood in them, but then, Scott and Annette were pretty fair, also. She recognized Carla, a girl about her age.

Cassie closed the computer and put it away as she remembered something else. "My contacts!"

Carla waited as she stepped out of the car. "Hi, Cassie."

At least they remembered names this time. "Hi, Carla," Cassie said, trying to be polite. She grabbed a suitcase out of the back. "I'll just take this into the house."

No one stopped her. Cassie crossed through the garage into the kitchen, then turned right and headed for the game room. It doubled as a guest room, and that's where they'd stayed last time, so she assumed they would stay there this time, also. She dumped the bag and returned to the kitchen, where her aunt Jadene was putting away dishes.

"Did a package come for me?" she asked, pulse thrumming anxiously.

Aunt Jadene looked up and considered her as if she wasn't quite sure who she was. "Oh, yes. In the library on the piano."

"Thanks." Cassie walked out of the kitchen and down the hall to the library.

Sure enough, a small box sat on top of the piano. She picked it up and held it in her hands, uttering a quick prayer that they would be the right color and the right kind. Then she ran to the bathroom.

Inside the box were two foil cases. She removed the first one and slowly pried off the foil lid. A small blue half disk lounged in the saline solution within. Cassie pried it up with a finger, lifting the disk to the light and admiring the streaks of color designed to imitate an iris.

She reached her hand toward her eye when suddenly she remembered. She'd almost forgotten to remove her regular lenses! She dropped the lens back, then ran to the guest room to retrieve her lenses case before returning to the bathroom. She plunked her old lenses into the case and carefully removed the blue disk again. Taking a deep breath, she finally placed it in her eye. She blinked, feeling the sphere slide into place over her eye, and let out a breath of relief. No pain.

Don't look, she told herself. *Not until you have the other one in.* Her heart pounded in anticipation, and she unwrapped the second foil tray. An identical blue disk lay there, and she removed it gently before plopping it into her eye.

Only now did she lift her gaze to the mirror in front of her. Deep blue eyes stared back at her, the color of the sky before a storm or the deep part of the ocean. It didn't have the same effect as the light, baby blue color she had so admired, but it was still blue and it was still glamorous. Her heart tightened with joy. Now she couldn't wait to go home and show Ben!

If she ever got a hold of him, anyway.

The thought dampened her excitement, but she quickly cheered up. At least her friends would care.

❦

When Cassie returned to the kitchen, she found everyone still bringing things in. She was surprised to see Carla helping.

"You can stay in my room if you don't want to stay in the guest room," Carla said, putting two sleeping bags in the guest room.

Cassie looked at her in surprise. Carla hadn't been super friendly last time, but Cassie supposed they had all just been kids. "Yeah, sure."

"Okay. Get your bag and come on upstairs."

Cassie followed Carla up the flight of stairs to the second floor, then down the hall to the left. Carla had a bunk bed, and she assigned Cassie the bottom bunk.

"Jennifer's gone to college. You can have the bed."

Cassie put her stuff down. Carla sat on the floor and pulled out a music player.

"What music do you like?"

Cassie joined her. "I don't know. I don't really listen to anything."

"How about some country?" Carla turned on a song full of guitars and twang and sad words. "What grade are you in?"

"Ninth," Cassie said. "You?"

"Tenth. High school's hard, isn't it?"

"I'm still in junior high. But yeah, it's hard."

Carla sighed and rolled her eyes. "My mom wants me to learn Spanish and 'bring the culture back to life.'"

"I'm taking Spanish also. I still can't say much more than, '*hola, como estás*' and '*sí, y tú?*'"

Carla laughed. "If our moms wanted the culture to be alive, they shouldn't have let it die."

"Why did they?" Cassie asked, curious. "My mom never talks about it."

Carla shrugged. "There was some big scandal when they came to America, something that ripped the family apart. I guess we're pretty lucky to even know each other."

"I can't imagine something that would make me stop talking to my mom or siblings. Must've have been awful."

"Yeah." Carla twisted her lip. "Must have been."

239

CHAPTER FORTY-ONE

Cross Roads

Cassie spent the next four days talking with Carla. Sometimes Carla left the house for school events or other commitments, during which time Cassie did her best to finish up her homework assignments. She was almost done. But mostly she bonded with her cousin.

"I wish you lived closer," she said to her Wednesday night as they lay in their beds.

"It would be nice," Carla said from the top bunk. "We only see each other every few years."

"Maybe you guys could come up to Arkansas."

"Maybe. We should convince our moms."

Thanksgiving day arrived with much food and much excitement. Carla and her older brother Braden invited a few friends over for games after the meal.

"Come on, Cassie," Carla said, coming into the bedroom where Cassie lay on the bed, reading a book and digesting her dinner. "You can't just stay in here. We've got friends over."

"But they're your friends," Cassie said.

"And they want to meet you. Come on." She led Cassie down the hall to the study, where her dad usually worked. Today he wasn't in there, and Braden had set up a card table. Two boys and a girl already sat around the table.

"Hey, Cassie!" Braden said cheerfully. "We've got a spot for you right here!" He gestured to an empty chair.

Cassie watched as he dealt cards for five players. "I don't know how to play cards."

"We'll teach you," Carla said, sitting beside her. "We play all the time."

"This is Michael, and this is Matt," Braden said, introducing the boys. The one on Cassie's left nodded at her. "And that's Rachel," he said, indicating the girl.

"Hi," Rachel said.

"Hi," Cassie replied, already feeling nervous and out of her element. She just wanted to return to her room and read her book, but Carla had dragged her here.

Carla leaned over. "So you don't want anyone to know your cards, but I'm going to help you since it's your first time. Go ahead and play this one but hold on to this."

Each time it was Cassie's turn, Carla told her what to do, making Cassie feel extra lame. She was at a table letting someone else play the game for her.

Braden won the first round, and as he dealt again, Cassie said, "I'll try without help this time."

"You got this," Matt said, grinning at her.

His words warmed her, and she blushed under his gaze.

As soon as she had her cards in her hand, she tried to find any winning runs like Carla had explained. This was all luck, mostly, but there was enough skill involved that she didn't want to lose. She played the cards she could spare as each turn came, and then she accidentally put down one she needed.

"No, wait!" she cried as Matt started to play. "I need that card!"

He looked at the card she'd put down and started laughing. "I think it's too late now. If you take that card back, I'll know exactly what your winning hand is."

His words brought laughter from all of them, and Cassie's face burned. "I guess I don't need it anymore."

Matt jostled her shoulder with his. "Better luck next time."

It didn't get better the next time. She lost miserably with each round, but her cousins and their friends made her laugh so hard she didn't even care. She was sad when the night ended, and even sadder when they packed up the next day to go home.

"See you in a few years," Carla said, giving her a hug.

"We won't forget each other this time," Cassie said.

The drive only took eight hours.

"Everyone just wash up and go to bed," Mrs. Jones said when they pulled into the garage at their house in Arkansas. "We'll worry about unpacking tomorrow."

No argument from Cassie. She dragged her things to her room, then went back to grab a drink of water. She held the cup under the water spigot on the fridge and pressed the lever, but nothing happened.

Odd. Maybe the fridge wasn't working? She turned to the sink and lifted the handle of the faucet. Again, nothing.

"Mom!" Scott came out of the hall bathroom. "The toilet won't flush and nothing's coming out of the sink!"

"Can't be," Mrs. Jones said. She walked through the house, trying sinks and flushing the toilet. "Jim!" she shouted.

Mr. Jones came in, his eyes red and ringed with exhaustion. "What?"

"We don't have any water!"

He scrubbed a hand over his face, then went outside with a flashlight. While he was out, Mrs. Jones went through the mail. She examined one envelope, then ripped it open. "JIM!"

He came back in, and she waved the paper at him. "We didn't pay the water bill and they shut off our water! I thought you did that before we left?"

"I thought I did!" He took the paper from her hand and scanned it.

Cassie removed herself from the room and texted Amity. *Home. No water. See you Monday.*

She scrolled through her phone numbers until she landed on Ben's. Something squeezed in her chest. It had been weeks now since she'd talked to him. No letters, no messages, nothing. Something was definitely wrong.

❧

Cassie woke up earlier than usual on Monday so she could fix her hair and look nice. Mr. Jones drove her to the pick up spot, and Cassie and Riley rode with Mr. Isabel to church.

"I got my new contacts," Cassie told Riley proudly.

"Let me see!"

Cassie leaned closer to her in the car.

"It's too dark," Riley said. "I can't see them."

"Oh, well, when we get to church."

As soon as they stepped into the light inside the building, Riley turned to Cassie.

"Oh, I see! They're a really dark blue."

"Yeah, I love them. They're so cool."

They walked in together, and Cassie grinned at Jason and Tyler, wondering if they would notice.

Tyler did. "Whoa, your eyes are funky."

"Thanks, I think," Cassie said.

"They're blue," Jason said, paying more attention.

"They're my new contacts." Cassie sat and pulled out her Bible.

"I like your natural eyes better," Tyler said. "Brown suits you more."

Ugh! Why was he such a jerk? "Well, that's your opinion." She turned around and faced front, trying not to stew over Tyler's words.

As soon as Mr. Isabel dropped them off at school, Cassie went looking for her friends. She found Amity and Andrea talking to a group of boys, and Cassie inserted herself in the middle of them, clutching her books to her chest and smiling broadly.

"Cassie!" Amity gave her a big side hug, then turned her to face her. "Let's see."

"What are we looking at?"

That was Miles' voice, and Cassie swiveled her head that direction, wondering how she had missed him in the group of boys. Then she gaped.

"You dyed your hair!" Instead of his normal soft brown, the hair was now blond—or trying to be. It had a rather yellow tint to it.

"Yeah. It didn't turn out so well, but my mom said it will grow out soon." He squinted at her. "Your eyes are blue."

"Yes!" A smile broke across her face. "I got colored contacts!"

"I love them," Amity said. "They're so pretty."

"Let me see." Miles' friend Matt leaned in closer. His eyes were also blue, but a much lighter shade. He tossed his blond hair out of his face. "Yeah, that's cool."

"They're kind of dark," Andrea said. "You have to look closely to see they're not brown."

"I couldn't get the light blue. I was allergic."

"They look good," Miles said.

"Oh, guess what?" Amity grabbed Cassie's arm and pulled her to the school. "Cara permed her hair but she hates it! Wait till you see it!"

❦

"Did you have a fun time at Disney World?" Andrea asked Cassie in Spanish class.

"Yes. But I had this stupid canker sore and everyone thought I was from another country."

"Oh? Did you talk like you were British?" Andrea faked an accent, and Cassie burst out laughing

"According to some people, yes." Then she quieted, that dull worry entering her heart again. "I haven't talked to Ben in a month," she said softly. "We haven't seen each other. I'm not sure we're together anymore."

Andrea grew somber, her expression serious. "Have you called him?"

"All the time. He doesn't return my calls."

Andrea mulled over that. "Let's call him tonight. We can three-way in. I'll talk to him first, ask a few questions while you listen."

"If you can get him to answer," Cassie said. "He's never home."

"Maybe he's just not home for you."

Cassie hadn't considered that. Then she shook her head. "His mom wouldn't lie for him like that." Would she? Surely not.

They walked together to lunch after Spanish class, where Cassie got her first look at Cara's perm.

Her hair looked like she'd stuck her finger in an electric outlet.

"I hate it," she said at lunch, confirming Amity's words.

"It's not so bad," Cassie said loyally, but she agreed with Cara.

"Your eyes are fun. Maybe I'll get colored lenses." Cara also had brown eyes, though hers were a light brown.

"You don't even wear glasses," Janice said.

"So?"

"I don't like them," Maureen said. "It makes Cassie look unnatural. Don't do it, Cara."

"Well, it's not supposed to look natural," Cassie said, annoyed. "It's exotic."

"We just like your brown eyes, Cassie," Janice said. "They're pretty."

"You're pretty no matter what," Cara said, and Cassie smiled at her.

⁘

Andrea called Cassie after dinner.

"You ready to do this?" she asked.

Cassie hadn't forgotten about her and Andrea's plan, though she'd tried not to think about it. Her heart hammered in her throat, making it hard to breathe. "Yes."

"You just be quiet. Don't say a word."

"Okay."

Cassie listened to the dialing as Andrea called Ben's number. Then there was the familiar, "Hello?" as his mom answered.

"Hi, is Ben there?" Andrea asked in a sweet voice.

"Yes, he is. Hold on just a second."

Cassie's mouth fell open. No way! Ben was there?

"Hello?" Ben said, his voice coming over the line.

Cassie closed her eyes, remembering how happy his voice made her. How he made her laugh and feel special.

"Hi!" Andrea said, her tone all bubbly. "You don't know me, I go to a different school. But I have a friend who likes you a whole lot and thinks you're the greatest guy in the world. So, do you have a girlfriend?"

Cassie held her breath, and then Ben said, "Yes, I do."

She relaxed, careful not to breathe into the phone. So maybe they hadn't talked to each other in awhile. That didn't mean they weren't together.

"Oh, that's a bummer, she'll be so sad. Who is it?"

"Her name is Angela."

CHAPTER FORTY-TWO

Rivalries

Wait, what?

What did Ben say?

Cassie put her hand to her mouth as shock rippled through her, followed by the burn of tears as they stung her eyes.

"Okay, give me just one second, and I'll be right back," Andrea said. The tone of the line changed, and then Andrea said, "Cassie? He's on mute and can't hear us."

"I can't believe it," Cassie gasped.

"Do you want to talk to him?"

Cassie shook her head, sending the tears cascading down her cheeks. "No." She hung up the phone without saying another word, not even goodbye. Her stomach hurt, and she doubled over. Crying as quietly as she could, she called Amity.

"Amity," she said, her voice cracking.

"Cassie? What's wrong?"

"It's Ben. He's got a different girlfriend."

"What? I can't believe it!"

Cassie couldn't either. He'd been so nice, so kind and considerate.

The line beeped, and she checked to see Andrea calling her. "I better go. Andrea's calling me."

"I want his number. I'm calling him."

"Okay." Cassie fed her the numbers without thinking, then clicked over to talk to Andrea.

"Well, I chewed him out," Andrea said, all fire and brimstone. "I told him I had you on the line and he's a crummy guy to do that to you. I told you you're the sweetest person ever and no one should ever treat you that way. I made him feel pretty bad."

"Thanks," Cassie said, but it didn't make her feel better.

"Guys are jerks, Cassie. They only think about themselves. He should have broken up with you first."

Cassie nodded numbly. Her phone dinged again, and this time it was Amity. "Amity's calling."

"Okay. I'm sorry, sweetie. Give me a call later."

"Okay." Cassie switched over. "Amity?"

"I tried to call him," Amity blustered, fury in her voice. "But his mom answered and wouldn't let me talk to him. I was going to give him a piece of my mind."

"That's okay." Cassie wiped at her eyes, still hurt by Ben's thoughtlessness. "Andrea already did."

"He's a jerk, Cassie. They all are."

Why did they both say that? Ben wasn't a jerk.

Her phone dinged again, and this time her heart tumbled when she saw Ben's name. Was it his mom calling to yell at her? "It's Ben. He's calling me."

"You tell him what you really think of him! Good luck, girl."

Amity hung up, and Cassie took a deep breath before switching over.

"Hello?" she said, pleased at how cool and collected she sounded.

"Cassie?" Ben's voice sounded unsure and timid, something she'd never heard before.

"Yes." She sank down into the chair at her computer desk. She had nothing to say. He could do all the talking.

He cleared his throat. "It's Ben."

"I know."

"Hey, I just wanted to say—well, I'm really sorry. I messed up really bad. I should have been honest with you."

"Honest about what?" she said, finally finding a few words. "That you like another girl? That you don't like me anymore?"

He sighed. "I liked you, Cassie, I liked you a lot. But the long-distance thing was really hard, you know? We never saw each other. We hardly ever talked. It just got to be too much."

Annoyance rode over the top of her hurt like a bucking bronco. He'd stopped liking her but didn't have the nerve to admit it.

"I still want to be friends," Ben continued. "I still think you're amazing. I wish you were closer. Things would have been different."

"Yeah," she said, her words biting. "Friends. We can be friends."

"You're super mad at me, aren't you?"

She picked at a piece of flaking wood on the side of the desk. "There was a better way to end this."

"Cassie, I'm sorry. It's really hard to explain. I didn't want to break up with you, but we weren't really together so—well, I'm just sorry. I didn't want you to get hurt."

"But I did."

There was silence for a moment, and then Ben said softy, "I don't know what else to say."

Cassie blinked, and the last of her tears rolled down her cheeks. But no more came. She took a deep, cleansing breath and let it out. "It's okay. I'll be okay. I'm sorry it ended also. But we'll be okay."

"If you see me next summer, will you talk to me?"

She'd forgotten he'd be at camp again. She didn't want to see him, didn't want to face the humiliation of being the rejected girlfriend. "Yes." She would just have to do her best not to see him. Or maybe not go.

"Okay. Thanks for talking to me, Cassie. And I am sorry."

"I know." She also knew it had taken a lot of courage to call her after the way her friend yelled at him, and knowing she'd been on the phone and overheard what he said. It lent some truth to his words, that he really did care about her. "Thanks for telling me how you felt."

They hung up, and even though Cassie had closure, even though she knew everything would be fine, she still lay back on her bed and cried.

⟢ ⟡ ⟣

Cassie's friends tried to cheer her up at lunch.

"I know," Cara said. "Let's plan this year's Christmas party."

"Great idea!" Maureen said.

"We can do it at my house this year," Janice said. "We have a big living room now."

"How fun!" Cara pulled out a notebook and wrote everyone's names down. "Anyone have a cup or something?"

"I finished my fries." Amity held out an empty fry box.

"That works." Cara took it from her and gave her an evil eye. "You're not going to expect us to invite Melanie, are you?"

"Who's Melanie?" Janice asked.

"Amity's new best friend," Cara said.

"She's not my best friend," Amity protested. "You know her, Janice. She's in choir with us. She's helping me with cheerleading moves so I can make the squad next year."

"I could help you with that," Cara said, clearly miffed.

Amity looked guilty. "You live so far away . . . And Melanie lives near me."

"Maybe we should all get to know her," Janice said. "We can all be her friend."

"She's a snob," Cara said, sounding harsher than her usual self.

Interesting. Cassie filed the information away for future reference.

Cassie watched with only mild interest while her friends put their names in the box. At least she wasn't forgotten this year. But she felt empty. She was single, for the first time in months. Ben didn't want her anymore.

"I got Cassie's name," Amity said, sending her a big smile. She handed the box to Cassie.

Only two slips of paper remained, and Cassie pulled one out. "Maureen," she said, trying to sound excited.

Nothing excited her at the moment.

❦

Amity didn't sit with Maureen and Cassie in choir on Tuesday. Instead, she sat with Melanie. Cassie didn't think much of it, thought Maureen grumbled about it.

On Wednesday, Amity came to school with her hair cut into a layered look with choppy bangs in front. The same haircut Melanie wore.

"What are you doing?" Maureen asked her at lunch. "Trying to copy Melanie?"

"Of course not," Amity said. "I just like her hair."

In choir Amity pulled her chair over to Melanie again. Maureen cleared her throat and said loudly, "Amity, that's the second soprano section. Don't you want to be with us?"

"I will when we sing," Amity replied.

"I don't like this at all," Maureen said darkly. "She's spending too much time with her." She turned to Cassie. "What are you doing Friday? Can I spend the night?"

"Yeah, sure," Cassie said. "I'll ask my mom, but I'm sure she'll say yes."

Maureen brought her new smart phone when she came over Friday night.

"Let's put on a concert and record it," she said, "then send it to everyone except Amity."

"She won't spend all her time with Melanie forever," Cassie said. "She's our best friend."

"I think she's forgotten that." Maureen pushed a button. "Stand up and sing something for us, Cassie!"

Cassie couldn't think of a single song on the spot like that. Except the song she was practicing for Christmas. "Oh, holy night—" she began.

"Nope, cut!" Maureen stopped recording. "It has to be a pop song! Something from the radio!"

Except Cassie didn't know any of those. She hardly ever listened to the radio. "Why don't you go first?" Cassie's phone rang, and she picked it up. "Oh, it's Andrea."

"Don't tell her I'm here!" Maureen said, ducking by the bed as if hiding.

"Why? She won't care."

"Yes, she will. She was supposed to spend the night with me but I told her I couldn't. I didn't tell her I was coming to your house."

Crapola. Cassie hated it when her friends did that. She'd been on the receiving end multiple times, and she hated lying for them. "Okay. I won't say anything about you." She answered the phone. "Hey, Andrea."

"Hey. What are you doing tonight? Want to come over?"

"I can't tonight," she said, and then realized she should have hesitated before being so quick about it. "We're doing a family thing."

"Can I be involved? I'm so bored. I'll stay out of the way, I promise."

Cassie's eyes darted to Maureen, still hovering by the bed. "It's kind of a private family thing."

"Okay." Andrea gave in with a sigh. "Do you know where Maureen is? I was supposed to spend the night with her, but then she told me I couldn't because she would be at her dad's house. But I just went there and she's not there, so I know she lied to me."

Crapola, crapola. Andrea would be on to Cassie any moment now. "No, I don't know. Maybe Cara's house?"

"I'll try there."

Andrea hung up, and Cassie glared at Maureen. "You should have told her the truth!"

"That what, I'd rather be at your house than have her over? That wouldn't go over so well." Maureen rolled her eyes.

"Did you tell anyone you were coming over here?"

"Yes."

"Then she's going to find out! And when she does, she'll be mad at me for lying!"

"Chill out, Cassie. She'll get over it. Everyone does it."

Yes, they did. Cassie included.

"Come on." Maureen handed the phone to Cassie. "Record me."

Cassie tried to put the incident with Andrea out of her head. She pointed the camera at Maureen and pushed the record button. "You're live, Maureen!"

Maureen took a deep breath and began belting out a pop song while she floated around the room, waving her hands and looking love-stricken. She wandered close to the closet, and Cassie jumped up as an idea hit her. She pushed Maureen into the closet and closed the door.

Maureen didn't stop singing, just got louder. She banged on the door, all the while singing her song. Giggling so hard Cassie could hardly hold the phone still, she opened the door, and the shoe rack on top of the door tumbled down onto Maureen.

"Oh no!" Cassie cried, but Maureen didn't stop singing. She climbed out over the top of the shoes and finished her song in the middle of the room. She took a bow and grinned at the camera.

Cassie turned it off, laughing so hard she thought she'd pee her pants. "That was awesome."

"Let's call Amity and tell her."

Cassie scooted over on the bed while Maureen sat down beside her. "I thought Amity was the one person you didn't want to tell?"

"Well, I changed my mind." She dialed the number, and a moment later Amity picked up. Maureen hit a button, and it went on speaker.

"Maureen, hi!" Amity said, and then she laughed loudly. "No, not that color, it looks awful on you."

"What color?" Maureen asked.

"Not you," Amity said. "I was talking to Melanie. I'm spending the night at her house."

Cassie saw the way Maureen's hackles went up. Her eyes narrowed and her lips compressed. "You are?"

"Yes. Where are you? Andrea's calling everyone looking for you."

"I'm at Cassie's. But don't tell Andrea."

"Okay, I won't."

"Why don't you come over too?" Maureen said.

"Oh, I can't. Didn't I just tell you I'm staying at Melanie's?"

"Yeah. Have fun." Maureen hung up the phone.

"You didn't tell her about the video," Cassie said.

"I didn't feel like it." Maureen pressed a few other buttons. "I'll send it to Cara. It will make her laugh."

Cassie sighed. "Amity doesn't talk to me like she used to. I'm not sure we're still best friends."

Maureen looked at her. "I'm not sure any of us are her best friend. I'm not sure I even have a best friend."

"You have me," Cassie said. "Hey, I know! Want to come to a weekend retreat with me after Christmas? There will be a New Year's dance!"

"That sounds fun." Maureen nodded. "How many days?"

"Three, I think."

"Cool. At least I've got you. And I've got Cara. She's the best thing that ever happened to me." Maureen finished sending the video. "She's the only one I know who will always be there for me."

"I will," Cassie said. "I promise. I'll always be your friend."

"Of course you will be. You're friends with everyone."

Somehow Maureen didn't make it sound like a compliment.

CHAPTER FORTY-THREE

The One Left Out

Andrea greeted Cassie Monday morning, then said, "I heard Maureen spent the night with you on Friday."

Cassie sighed. "I'm sorry I didn't tell you. She told me not to."

"It's fine. For some reason she likes to keep secrets. But she's not very good at them. She spent the night with me Saturday and told me all about it."

"She did?" All that guilt over lying for no reason? "I'm glad."

"Yeah. She showed me the video you guys made. We should make one sometime."

"I'd love to," Cassie said. "The next time you spend the night."

"Maybe I can spend the night Thursday. School's out for Christmas break that day."

"I have my recital. How about Friday?"

"Yeah, sure. I'll ask my mom."

Cassie nodded, relieved there were no bad feelings between them.

Maureen and Amity seemed to have patched things up, also. At lunch they sat together, and then in choir, Amity put an extra chair beside her and Melanie, and Maureen sat there, leaving Cassie on the outskirts.

The gesture stung Cassie. Why were they suddenly all friendly without her? Had she said something wrong to Maureen when she spent the night on Friday?

Cassie tried to ignore it, but she felt snubbed. She did her best to sing while swallowing a constant lump in her throat. When class ended, she walked with Riley to the bus instead of Maureen.

The next day in math, Amity moved to the back with Andrea and didn't talk to Cassie the whole time. Cassie snagged her as they left the classroom.

"Amity, are you mad at me?"

"No, of course not," Amity said.

Why are you ignoring me? Cassie wanted to ask. But she just smiled. "Okay, good. Will you sit by me in choir today?"

"Sure. Can Melanie sit with us?"

"Yeah, that's fine," Cassie said, though she wasn't thrilled with it.

Amity didn't notice her response. She'd spotted Melanie walking the other way down the hall and took off after her. "Melanie!"

Cassie uttered a sigh.

She reached the choir room before her friends and sat down, waiting on pins and needles to see if Amity would keep her word and sit with her. Sure enough, she came in and pulled another chair over, then beckoned to Melanie.

"We're going to sit with Cassie today," Amity said.

"Oh," Melanie said, and she looked at Cassie as if she were a strange creature in the choir room. "Okay."

Maureen came in next, and she frowned at them. She sat on the other side of Amity and whispered, "Why are we sitting by Cassie? She's not trying out for cheerleading."

Cassie pretended like she hadn't heard, but the words were a punch to her chest. Did that mean she couldn't be in their group of friends? Why was she suddenly the one being ostracized?

Amity shushed her and gave Cassie a smile, as if suspecting she'd overheard.

Ms. Berry warmed them up with a Christmas song. Cassie sang, but out of the corner of her eye she saw Maureen writing a note to Amity. She caught her name in the slanted bubble writing and tried not to lean her head over to read it. Then Maureen folded it up and placed it in Amity's hands.

Sing, Cassie told herself. She positioned herself so she could see Amity's hands while still looking directly at the board. She didn't make eye contact with Maureen in case she was watching her, and she pretended not to notice what was going on. Then she slid her eyes sideways really fast, scanning the note for her name.

She found it in one sentence. *Cassie still thinks she's our best friend.*

That was all she needed. The words percolated in and around her head, and she found herself leaning away slightly. She wanted to cry. Her voice didn't work anymore. But she couldn't get up and leave, or they would know she'd seen the note. She had to pretend to be normal.

What did they really think of her? That she was some weird tag along, like an annoying little sister they had to be nice to? Why pretend to be her friend?

Amity folded the note up and put it in her purse, then leaned close to Maureen. Whether they were whispering or singing, Cassie didn't know, and she found it really didn't matter. She knew however much she had thought she fit in with her friends, she was wrong.

"Let's stand and sing, girls!" Ms. Berry said, and Cassie dutifully stood, feeling wooden and hollow inside.

Amity stood up a little too quickly, and her elbow jostled Cassie's chest.

"Oh, sorry," Amity said. "Didn't mean to poke your boob."

"You mean her mosquito bites?" Maureen leaned toward them. "Cassie doesn't even need a bra. She could cover them up with band aids."

Amity and Melanie laughed so hard Cassie though Ms. Berry would send them out of class.

Cassie couldn't laugh. She was embarrassed and mortified. Her friends knew she wore a padded bra. They knew her small breasts bothered her. Her face grew hot, and Cassie realized she did know her place. At the butt of every joke.

⁜

Cassie distanced herself from her friends for the rest of the week. She didn't talk much, didn't call them. She almost didn't sit with them at lunch, but she didn't want anyone to wonder what was wrong.

It was the last week of school before Christmas break, and several clubs were having Christmas parties. Miles found her before lunch on Thursday.

"Cassie, don't forget the NJHS Christmas party today!"

Did he want her there, or was he waiting for an opportunity to laugh at her? Cassie nodded. "Yeah. Thanks. I'll be there."

He slowed down and matched her step as she headed for the cafeteria. "You should be happy. It's a party. And we're giving gifts to homeless kids."

Gifts. Oh no. Cassie stopped walking completely. "I forgot."

"Forgot?"

"My gift!" She waved a hand impatiently. "I don't have one for the kids!"

"You can come without one. We're supposed to bring one, but no one's going to tell you you can't come in."

Cassie shook her head. "I'll have to skip it. I'm not going empty handed."

"Don't skip it." Miles put his hand on her arm. "I'll call my mom and have her bring something for you."

She looked at him, really looked at him then. "You will?"

"Yeah. Cheer up, okay? You look sad."

She tried to smile. "Thanks, Miles."

"I'll see you at the party."

He turned and jogged away, and Cassie continued on alone to the cafeteria. At least she had one friend.

"Are you feeling well, Cassie?" Janice asked in science. "You've been quiet lately."

Cassie's emotions felt raw and tender, and the words nearly brought her to tears. Janice was a friend, but for how long? Could Cassie really trust her? She shook her head. "Maybe I'm getting sick."

"Did somebody hurt your feelings?"

Now the tears did come. "I'm fine." She brushed them aside.

Janice leaned over and hugged her, then she raised her hand. "Mr. Adams, can I take Cassie to the bathroom?"

Mr. Adams looked at them. He must've seen Cassie's tear-streaked face, because all he said was, "Sure."

Cassie sensed her classmates looking at her, but she ignored them, just followed Janice to the bathroom.

"So what's going on?" Janice asked as soon as they were alone.

The tears seemed to think now that they had permission to fall, they had to keep coming. They poured down her face, and Janice handed her a wad of paper towels.

"It's just me," she sobbed. "Making friends with the wrong people, I guess. Trusting the wrong people. I thought Andrea was my best friend —and she's not. And then I thought it was Amity—but I was wrong. Then I thought Maureen and I were really close—but she just thinks I'm the group jester."

"No, she thinks she's the jester. She just wants people to laugh at her."

"By making fun of me?" Cassie exploded. Her hand trembled as she wiped her eyes. "I don't need friends like that!"

"I'm sorry, Cassie," Janice said quietly. "Maybe it's time to think really hard who you want to be friends with."

Maybe it was. Maybe she'd been trying for too long and too hard to fit in with the wrong people.

"But don't forget me." Janice squeezed her hand. "I'm your friend."

"And Miles. He's my friend."

Janice cocked her head. "Is he more than that?"

"No." Cassie sighed. "I wanted him to be more than that for so long that I think it finally just wore off. But he's a good friend."

"Yay for good friends. Here." Janice wet the paper towel and wiped Cassie's face. "There. Now let's go back to class."

Janice's words buoyed her up enough that she stopped worrying about Amity and Maureen for an hour. Instead Cassie went to the alto section in choir and sat with Riley and Janice. It was the last day of classes before Christmas break, and Ms. Berry didn't even try to make them sing.

"I got you a Christmas present," Riley said. "When are you coming over?"

"Sometime before Christmas," Cassie said. "Or you can give it to me in church."

"Just call me. We'll get together. Are you doing better about Ben?"

Cassie shrugged. "He's right. We never saw each other. But I miss knowing he cared."

"You'll find someone else."

"I hope so. And soon."

Cassie chatted with Riley while keeping one eye on Amity and Maureen and Melanie. They kept laughing, and she wondered what they were talking about. Couldn't just be making fun of Cassie. Even that would get old. She sighed. They'd like her if she were prettier and funnier. But that wasn't who she was. She was quiet, and smart, and serious.

Riley liked her the way she was.

The intercom turned on, and the voice called for all NJHS members to meet in the cafeteria for the Christmas party.

"See you later," Cassie said, and she joined Janice with several other kids, leaving the choir room and making the walk to the cafeteria.

"Are you feeling better?" Janice asked her.

"Yes. I'm figuring out who my real friends are."

Miles saw Cassie the moment she entered. "Cassie!" He ran over and handed her an adorable little Teddy bear with a Christmas bow around its neck. "Here's your gift for the children's shelter."

"Miles, you're awesome," she said, accepting the bear. "Tell your mom thank you. I owe you."

"Glad you're smiling again."

"Hey, Miss Cassie." Cara joined them, slipping an arm through Cassie's. "There's a slice of pizza over here with your name on it."

Cara was always nice to her, Cassie thought. Cara could be on the list of real friends.

CHAPTER FORTY-FOUR

Christmas Star

"How are you doing your hair for the recital tonight?" Mrs. Jones asked the moment Cassie walked in from the bus. There was no chance to celebrate that school was out for two weeks; right now she had to think about the song she would perform in two hours. "Hot rollers. Curled."

"And dress?"

"The white and black one. With the velvet skirt."

"Get ready quickly." Mrs. Jones dismissed Cassie with a nod and turned her attention to Emily, who would be playing the piano.

Cassie hummed the melody to herself as she rolled her hair around the hot rods, then mouthed the words to each verse. She knew the song inside and out. Tonight had to go perfect. She pulled on the Christmas dress and admired how it looked on her.

"Time to go!" Mrs. Jones called.

"Oh, holy night, the stars were brightly shining," Cassie sang softly. She hair-sprayed the soft curls around her face and then hurried to the car. It was just chilly enough to need a jacket.

Ms. Malcolm took all the jackets and dumped them backstage, then lined up her performers.

"This is your night to shine. I'm putting you in order of when you go onstage."

Cassie waited, her nerves bunching up in her stomach, getting louder and more demanding with each passing second. She needed to sing and get it over with before she forgot the words or the notes or something.

"Cassie." Ms. Malcolm motioned for her. "You're last. We'll end the recital with your song."

"Last?" she gasped out.

"Yes." Ms. Malcolm favored her with a smile. "The grand finale. Bring it in for us."

Oh, no. Her nerves had just grown hands and were clawing up her insides.

The recital stretched on forever. Piano, voice, piano, voice. She heard Emily's stirring rendition of "Carol of the Bells," and then the heart-warming words to "I heard the Bells" by another singer.

And finally, finally, they were clapping, and Cassie knew it was her turn. She walked on stage, and the clapping died away. Ms. Malcolm sat behind the black grand piano, and she gave a nod. Cassie faced the audience and took the microphone in her hand, heart galloping wildly in her chest. The bright lights blinded her, and she couldn't see the audience.

Except the front row. Her dad sat there, face beaming up at her.

This was for him. He wanted her to sing this song.

The intro started, and Cassie counted the measures before coming in. Her voice trembled for a moment as the nerves tried to sweep her away, but then the music caught up to her. It carried her over, took her from the stage and the fright and the pounding heartbeat. Each verse had a message, its own heart, a life. She let her voice float up above the lights on the high notes, let love and hope and joy settle into the notes as she reached the climax of the song.

"Ever-more proclaim." She finished the third verse, her voice carrying off and then ending, leaving nothing but silence in its wake.

The clapping came, followed by cheers, and Ms. Malcolm stood up and extended a hand to Cassie, who bowed. She looked up and met her father's eye. He cried, not even trying to hide the tears that flowed down his face.

Cassie spun and walked off the stage, pride and exuberance rushing through her body.

Ms. Malcolm thanked everyone, wished them a merry Christmas, and then excused the recital. Cassie hurried away to find her parents, but she was stopped with every step.

"Cassandra, that was beautiful."

"What a lovely voice you've got."

"You've really come into yourself. Every year you sing better."

"You're going to be a star someday, Cassie."

"How beautiful you sang!"

She thanked everyone and finally got to her parents. "How was it, Daddy?"

He wrapped her up in a hug, squeezing her tightly. "The most beautiful I ever heard. It was perfect." He held her out at arm's length.

"How would you feel about singing it again in church for Christmas?"

Her chest warmed, and she nodded, flattered. "I can do that."

"Let's plan on it, then."

⸻

Andrea called Cassie after the recital. Cassie had already put on her pajamas and was about to fall into bed. She answered the phone, maintaining the same distance in her heart that she had for the past few days.

"What's up, Andrea?"

"I know we talked about me spending the night tomorrow, but that's the night of our Christmas party at Janice's house."

"Oh, yeah." How could she have forgotten? "I knew that. I just didn't put it together."

"So your recital's over, right?"

"Yes," Cassie said. "It ended two hours ago."

"Can you come over now?"

Cassie looked at her clock in surprise. "It's ten o'clock, Andrea."

"My mom said she can come get you. Please?"

"I'll ask my mom," Cassie said, quite certain she'd say no.

She didn't. Mrs. Jones said, "That's fine, if her mom's going to come get you."

Cassie quickly packed a bag, more than a little surprised by this turn of events.

Andrea's mom picked Cassie up at ten till eleven. Andrea sat in the back, and she hugged Cassie tight when she got in.

"I feel like I've hardly seen you lately. I'm so glad you could come over."

"Me too," Cassie said, though she didn't let down the guards around her heart.

"Now girls, don't be too noisy," Mrs. Wall said as they entered the house. "It's almost midnight, and I'm going to bed."

"Of course." Andrea turned to Cassie as soon as her mom left. She sat down at the kitchen table and stretched her arms out. "What do you want to do?"

"I don't know," Cassie said. She felt like she should have some idea, something to entertain Andrea. But Andrea asked her over, not the other way around.

"Let's make Christmas presents for everyone. Something simple, like bags of candy popcorn."

"Sure," Cassie said.

Andrea pulled out the ingredients. "So Amity and Melanie," she said. "They seem to be getting awfully close."

"Yeah," Cassie said. "Maureen didn't like her at first, but now she seems to." Cassie held back the fact that Maureen had started snubbing Cassie.

"Cara doesn't like Melanie. She thinks she's bringing out Amity's bad side."

"Amity's still being nice, at least," Cassie said. "Maureen is being mean."

"Really?" Andrea glanced at Cassie as they poured the popped corn into a bowl. "What's she doing?"

Cassie didn't want to tell her about Maureen's joke. "Sometimes I don't feel like I'm friends with them anymore."

"We all feel that way. Sometimes I'm not sure if you're my friend."

"Sometimes I'm not sure either," Cassie said.

Andrea turned to her, putting both hands on Cassie's forearms. "You know I'm like your BFF forever and ever and ever."

"Sure," Cassie said, but she didn't know that. People said things they didn't mean all the time. And she'd seen how quickly her friends could change personalities.

"Well, I'm sure we'll all have a blast at the Christmas party tomorrow," Andrea said, mixing the corn syrup with green food coloring. "No fighting."

"Yeah. It will be nice." Cassie hoped so. But she couldn't help feeling like she'd gone back to being the unwanted member of the group. "Hey, we're having a youth retreat at church for New Years. It's just a few days and there will be at least one dance. Want to come?"

"I'd love to. I'll be bored to tears here by myself."

"Great." Cassie smiled, feeling more genuine. At least if Maureen acted weird, Cassie would have Andrea.

⁂

Cassie and Andrea stayed up making popcorn balls and putting them in pretty cellophane until Mrs. Wall got up at two in the morning and made them go to bed. They slept until noon, Cassie only waking because her mom called her cell phone.

"Shane called in sick," Mrs. Jones said, referencing the man they'd hired to work the soccer store while her dad did his real job. "I'm picking you up in ten minutes and I need you to work the store."

"Oh no," Cassie groaned, her head pounding. "I'm so tired."

"I let you go over to a friend's house late last night. Don't make me regret it."

"Okay. I'm up." Cassie hung up and nudged Andrea. "I have to go. My dad needs me to work the store."

Andrea sat up, her brown hair poofing around her face like a distorted halo. "Thanks for coming over." She offered a limp hug. "I'll see you tonight at Janice's house."

"Don't forget the popcorn." Cassie gathered her things together and went outside to wait for her mom.

The radio inside the soccer store played Christmas music, festive songs that lifted Cassie's heart and had her humming as she moved around the store. Shane hadn't done inventory for the week, so she began the arduous task of checking what was listed in the store with what was actually on the shelves.

The door opened, and a woman came in.

"Hi, can I help you?" Cassie asked, putting her customer-service smile in place.

"I want to get my daughter a nice warm-up for Christmas. Matching jacket and pants, you know."

"I know just the thing." Cassie moved to the rack and selected the same warm-up she owned. Even though she didn't play soccer, when she had helped her dad with the paper route a few months ago, she'd always worn her soccer warm-up. "It's the perfect combination of warm but not heavy. She'll love it."

"Hmm." The woman took it from Cassie, feeling the fabric and running her hands over the arms. "She's about your size. Can you try the jacket on for me?"

"Sure." Cassie took it off the hanger and slipped her arms into it. "What school does she go to?"

"Oh, she's only eleven, you wouldn't know her."

Eleven! Cassie forced herself not to react as she zipped up the jacket.

"That looks perfect," the woman said. "I'll buy it."

Cassie took it off, still trying to decide if it was good or bad that she had the body shape of an eleven-year-old. She rang up the warm-up for one hundred and thirty dollars.

"Have a merry Christmas. I hope your daughter loves it!"

"I'm sure she will!" The woman waved.

Cassie walked around the counter and into the bathroom. She stood in front of the mirror on her tiptoes, trying to make herself taller. The truth was, she hadn't grown at all since seventh grade when she went on her big diet to lose weight. Her mom said that was why her breasts never developed, because she didn't have enough fat on her body to grow them.

Cassie studied her face and chewed on her lower lip. Had she accidentally stunted the growth of the rest of her body, also? Would she be the size of an eleven-year-old, prepubescent girl for her whole life?

Andrea called Cassie an hour later while Cassie sat on the floor beside the shoe rack.

"Cassie!" she cried, clearly upset. "The party's been canceled!"

"Canceled!" Cassie lifted up to standing, forgetting how many shoes she had counted. "But it can't be!" The Christmas party was the most important event of the year, the one thing that pulled them all together. It couldn't be canceled!

Cassie's call-waiting buzzed, and she checked it to see Janice calling. "I'll call you back. It's Janice."

"Cassie," Janice said, and she sounded close to tears. "I can't have the party at my house tonight. We've had to cancel it."

"Oh no!" Cassie said, forcing herself to think about Janice's feelings and not her own. "What happened? Are you okay?"

"My mom said no people over. She won't let me go anywhere, either."

"Oh, that's terrible, Janice!"

Cassie's phone buzzed again, and this time it was Cara. "It's Cara, Janice. I'll call you later, okay?" She switched lines. "Cara, I just heard about the party."

"Yeah, so we've changed the location. We're still a go."

Cassie exhaled, a measure of relief filling her chest. "Oh, thank goodness. I knew we'd think of something."

"Of course! We're going to do it at Pizza Hut at four o'clock. It will just be for two hours, though, no slumber party."

"Four?" Cassie glanced at the sign on the door of the soccer shop, even though she knew without looking that the store didn't close until six. "I can't make it then. I'm working."

"Oh, um. Well, I don't know. I'll have to talk to everyone, see if we can change the time."

"That's okay," Cassie said, trying to be brave. "I don't want everyone to change things again. Have a good time, okay?" She hung up the phone before she started crying, and then she called Mrs. Jones.

"Mom," she sobbed, "the Christmas party for tonight was canceled! Janice can't have it at her house, so it got moved to Pizza Hut. But I'll still be working!"

"Oh, honey," Mrs. Jones said, "I'm so sorry to hear that. Maybe they'll still be there when you finish."

Cassie wiped her eyes. "I doubt it." Then she got an idea. "What if we have it at our house?" That was the perfect solution. The Joneses had a large home, and they could easily fit several girls. She held her breath, praying her mom would say yes but not daring to hope either.

Mrs. Jones paused for what seemed a very long time. "Okay," she said. "But everyone has to be quiet and bring their own food. We don't have any party things."

Cassie squealed and jumped up and down, glad the store was empty at the moment. "Oh, thank you, thank you! I've got to go." She called Cara back, excited to share the news. "Guess what? My mom said we can have the party at my house!"

"Oh, that's nice of her," Cara said. "I think everyone's planning on Pizza Hut, though."

"But I can't come," Cassie said, deflating. Did that even matter to anyone?

"I'll ask everyone what they want to do."

Cassie called Andrea next, but she wasn't as excited this time. "My mom said we can have the party at my house."

"That's perfect!" Andrea exclaimed. "There's plenty of space for us there!"

"Yeah, but Cara said everyone still wants to do it at Pizza Hut. So I don't think we're going to my house."

"Oh. Hmm. If everyone's going to Pizza Hut, we should just do it there."

Who would choose pizza over a slumber party? All of Cassie's friends, apparently.

"I'm not going," Cassie said, her eyes stinging. "I'll just give Maureen her present later."

Cassie hung up, and nobody called her to console her.

CHAPTER FORTY-FIVE

Double Meanings

Not even the cheerful Christmas music raised Cassie's spirits as she finished her shift at the store. She glanced at the clock constantly. 4:36. Her Friends were all at Pizza Hut, exchanging presents and having a good time without her. 5:11. What were they doing now? Eating pizza? Telling stories?

At six o'clock Mrs. Jones arrived to take her home. They locked up the store, but Cassie kept quiet on the drive.

"I thought you'd be more excited," Mrs. Jones said.

Cassie shrugged. "My friends aren't coming. They decided they'd rather do Pizza Hut without me." She couldn't keep the bitterness from her voice.

"Hmm," was all Mrs. Jones said.

Cassie wrote poetry at her desk when she got home, pouring out her hurt feelings in words. She waited until a little after seven, and then she called Andrea.

"Hello?" an adult voice said.

"Oh, I was looking for Andrea."

"Yes, this is her mom. She left her phone here. I heard it ringing and answered it."

"She left her phone? Is she back from the pizza party yet?"

"She came home and left again. She's going to a friend's house and won't be home until tomorrow."

"Oh?" Andrea had found another friend's house to go?

Or was it possible she was coming to Cassie's? She crossed her mental fingers.

"Who is this?" Mrs. Wall asked.

"It's Cassie."

"Cassie!" Mrs. Wall laughed. "She has you listed on the phone as Little Heart."

Cassie smiled, remembering the sixth grade joke.

"She just left for your house with a bunch of people!"

"Really?" Cassie gasped out.

"You're expecting her, aren't you? For a slumber party?"

Cassie realized how ridiculous she must sound. She gripped the phone and said, "Yes, of course! I just wasn't sure what time she was coming! Thank you!" She hung up the phone and ran back into the kitchen. "Mom! Andrea's coming over with a few other people!"

"How many?" Mrs. Jones asked as she put dishes into the dishwasher.

"I don't know."

"Here's the deal." Mrs. Jones stepped over to Cassie. "You can have your friends over, but no messes. And you guys have to be quiet. And—" she glanced around the kitchen, her eyes landing on the stove. "You have to clean the stove."

Cassie nodded eagerly. "Okay." She would do whatever her mother wanted. She ran back to her room, wishing she could call Andrea and find out who was coming. But Andrea didn't have her phone. So she called Cara again.

Before Cara even said hello, Cassie said, "You're not coming, are you."

"Oh, yes, I am!" Cara said, her voice bright and cheerful. "I'm right here at my house with everyone else. We just stopped to grab a few things, then we're coming over."

"You're coming?" Cassie couldn't believe it. "Who else is coming?"

"Everyone except Janice. She couldn't come this year, poor thing."

"Oh, I'm so glad!" Cassie wanted to laugh and cry at the same time. Her friends hadn't forgotten her, after all.

⁘

It was nearly an hour later when the girls finally arrived. Mrs. Jones excused herself to her room and warned the other children to leave Cassie and her friends alone.

"We can't make too much noise," Cassie said. "I promised my mom."

"Movie," Andrea said. "Let's make a movie."

"Great idea!" Cassie said. "I don't have a smart phone, though."

"And I forgot mine." Andrea turned to Maureen. "Let's use yours."

"What movie should we make?" Amity asked, relaxing on the couch.

"A soap opera," Maureen said with a giggle. "You can be the desperate housewife."

"Ha ha." Amity stuck her tongue out at her. "You can be the fat old maid."

Maureen shrieked and tackled Amity, who squealed and whacked at her as she slid off the couch. Andrea fumbled to get the camera going, while Cassie said, "Quiet down! My mom said quiet!"

They stilled, giggling, and Cara gathered them all into a circle.

"Before we make a video," she said, "we need to remember why we're here."

Cassie tilted her head at Cara. Speeches weren't her style. She must have something on her mind.

"We're supposed to be each other's best friends. Nobody comes before us." She looked directly at Amity. "Nobody. This Christmas party is the one event of the year where we give gifts to each other. It's a symbol of our friendship, of how we look out for each other. We don't let anyone talk bad about our best friends."

"And we don't talk bad about our best friends," Cassie couldn't help adding.

Cara nodded. "I don't care if you shun the rest of the school, but we include each other. Can we promise?"

She put her hand in the middle, and the other girls added theirs on top of hers. What were they going to do, a soccer cheer? Then someone's finger pinched Cassie's, and she wiggled her hand around to pinch back. Amity's shoulders shook with silent laughter, and Andrea said, "Hey!," and suddenly all ten hands were in the middle, grappling, pinching, poking. Cara was laughing also.

"You guys can't be serious for anything. Let's open presents."

"Presents?" Cassie said. "You didn't already do that at Pizza Hut?"

"No, silly," Cara said. "You weren't there. Why would we do that?"

Because Cassie wasn't that important. Because everyone was happy without her. Because no one needed Cassie.

She shrugged, feeling foolish. "I just thought you would. I'm glad you didn't." She jumped up and ran to her room to get her present for Maureen, a lightness and giddiness replacing the heavy sorrow in her chest. She took things too seriously. Her friends really did care about her.

❦

The Jones threw their own little party before Christmas and invited a few church friends.

I'm coming, Riley texted Cassie. *I've got your gift.*

Cassie had one for Riley, also, thanks to Riley's heads-up. Maureen had really liked the journal Cassie gave her over the summer, so Cassie decided to get one for Riley, also.

Mrs. Jones prepared the family's favorite snacks: salsa, cheese balls, crackers, salami, and punch. One by one people from church began to arrive. Cassie was in charge of taking the jackets as people walked in the door.

"You guys must be new," she said to two young men who arrived early. Judging from their white shirts and conservative haircuts, they were the missionaries, volunteer ministers who spent several months traveling around the world and helping where needed in whatever way they could. Their faces changed monthly as a set of ministers would leave and a new one would arrive.

"Yes, just came in two days ago," the tall one with blond hair said. A pair of shocking green eyes appraised her.

"We met your dad yesterday," the shorter one said. He had darker hair and dark eyes. "He told us all about you. Said you're singing in church tomorrow."

"Yes." Cassie pleated her fingers together and tried not to look nervous. Singing in front of people she knew was so much harder than singing for strangers. "Go on inside, my mom's already set out the food." She turned to the next people and smiled when she saw Riley and her mom.

"Riley!"

"Cassie!"

The two girls hugged, and Cassie took her jacket. "I'm so glad you're here."

"Come on." Riley took her hand, pulling Cassie away from her post. "I've got your present."

"And I've got yours!"

They made their way past the crowds of people into Cassie's room, and Cassie handed Riley the small bag with the journal in it. Riley opened it up and laughed. "Yay! Now I can be a writer like you!" She gave Cassie a wrapped box. "Go on, open it!"

Cassie dug into the paper and ripped it off, then gave a little cry when she saw the perfume box. "Oh my goodness, no way!"

Riley smiled as Cassie threw her arms around her neck. "I know how much you like that one. You always wear it at my house."

"Thank you! And merry Christmas!"

They went back out to join the rest of the party, holding on to each other's arms.

"We got new missionaries," Riley said, nodding at the traveling ministers. The two boys crowded around the cheese ball, pretty much blocking everyone else from getting close. "That one's cute." She indicated the blond with the green eyes.

"Riley," Cassie admonished. "We're not supposed to look at them that way." Though she had to admit Riley was right.

He looked up at that moment, catching their gaze. He held out a cracker lathered with cheese to Cassie. "Want one?"

She shook her head. "I wouldn't want to take away from your

enjoyment."

"I don't think you could." He ate the cracker, not taking his eyes from her.

Cassie's face burned, and she spun Riley around, wheeling out of the kitchen.

"Did he just flirt with you?" Riley asked.

"No way. Missionaries don't flirt. He was just offering a cracker." She couldn't help stealing a glance behind her. The dark-haired minister was laughing and elbowing the blond, who had his head bowed, a grin on his face.

"Maybe sometimes they do," Riley said.

Maybe they did. Cassie would have to pay attention. "Besides, he has to be at least eighteen. Maybe as old as twenty."

"So?"

"So." Cassie laughed. "I'm fourteen, Riley. Nobody that old would notice me."

Christmas morning dawned bright and clear, with blue skies and not a cloud in sight. Definitely no chance for a white Christmas.

Cassie put on the same black and white dress she'd worn to her recital. She smoothed it down and pinned up her hair. At least Ms. Malcolm had agreed to come and play for her.

She spotted Riley right away when she got to church. Riley leaned over, sniffed her, and smiled.

"You're wearing your perfume," she said.

"It's my new favorite."

The new ministers were at the door, handing out programs to the congregation. Cassie normally paid them no mind, but the blond with green eyes spoke to her as she came in.

"Cassie," he said, "good luck. I'm sure someone as beautiful as you must have a beautiful voice."

"Thanks," Cassie said. She shot a wide-eyed look to Riley before separating at the pew.

"Cassie," Mrs. Jones breathed, sliding in beside her, "I think that missionary is flirting with you."

"He can't be. Can he?"

Mrs. Jones shrugged. "They're not allowed to date, but I guess sometimes they can't help noticing a pretty girl."

"Ha ha," Cassie said, not buying it.

The Reeves brothers walked by, and Tyler said, "Singing a solo today, huh, Cassie?"

"Yes," Cassie said, looking up at him.

He winked at her. "Can't wait to hear it."

...ssie could. The longer the sermon went, the more nervous she became. Until finally, the preacher smiled at her and announced her to come up.

Cassie's hands shook, and she found she couldn't meet anyone's eyes as she stood behind the microphone and Ms. Malcolm played the introduction. Butterflies the size of bats beat against her stomach, and she worried she'd get sick.

There was her cue! She took a deep breath, but she was too late. She'd missed it.

Wait, she told herself. Ms. Malcolm had told her if she missed her into, she would just repeat the beginning and no one would know. Cassie forced herself to pay attention and count . . . Two, three, four, now!

This time she was ready for it. She sang the first verse with no problems, and her shoulders slowly relaxed. She managed to put a smile on her face and dared to meet the faces of the congregation. Her dad beamed at her. Riley grinned so hard it looked like her cheeks would burst. Tyler made faces at her. Cassie finished the second and third verses with no further mistakes, bolstered by the encouragement and acceptance of her peers.

This was church, so no one clapped when she finished. But the reverent silence as she returned to her seat spoke volumes.

The preacher closed the meeting, and then Cassie's friends descended upon her. Even Sue, Jessica, and Michelle, girls who normally ignored her, came over to tell her how wonderful she'd done. Riley looped her arm, and they started toward Sunday School.

"Cassie," a male voice said.

She turned to see the traveling minister there. He smiled at her, his eyes shining.

"I knew you would do well, but that was the most lovely song I've ever heard. Thank you for that, Beauty."

Cassie tripped over her words, automatically starting with "you're welcome" before realizing she should be the one thanking him for the compliment. "Um, thanks. And what should I call you? Beast?"

His smile broadened. "Just Brother Brian will work."

Of course. The ministers always added a "brother" or "sister" to their names, like her youth leader and teachers. Cassie dipped her head in acknowledgment, then she and Riley continued on.

Riley tilted her head closer to Cassie. "Definitely flirting."

Cassie couldn't argue with her.

⁓ꙮ⁓

In Sunday School, Sister Mecham reminded them that the overnight youth retreat was the upcoming weekend.

"We'll be staying at Mt. Sequoya in Fayetteville. Just have your parents drive you there."

"Want to room together?" Riley asked.

"I'll have Maureen and Andrea with me," Cassie said. "As long as that's okay, the four of us can room together."

"Yeah, that's fine," Riley said, though she looked a little put out.

Cassie called Andrea first that night. "Want to come to my house before the youth trip? Or should we just pick you up on the way?"

"Just pick me up!" Andrea said. "I'm all packed. You said there will be a dance, right?"

"Yes. Maybe even two. I'm not sure, it's my first time to go."

"Fantastic!"

Next Cassie called Maureen. "Want to spend the night or want me to pick you up in the morning?"

"What's Andrea doing?" Maureen asked.

"I'm picking her up on the way to Fayetteville."

"I don't know. I'll check with my mom and let you know."

"Let me know by Wednesday, okay?"

"Yeah, sure."

Maureen still hadn't called by Wednesday. She didn't pick up when Cassie called, either.

Thursday Mr. Jones took Cassie to the dentist, and after he poked her mouth all over, it hurt too much to talk. So she just texted Maureen.

Hey! You coming over before the youth trip or should we just pick you up?

No response.

Cassie's mouth was almost back to normal near dinner time, and she tried once again to call Maureen. Still no answer, and Cassie knew this wasn't a coincidence. So she called Andrea.

"Hey there, you!" Andrea said. "Ready for tomorrow?"

Cassie let out a little breath of relief. "Yes. We'll be there at eight to get you." She paused, then said, hesitantly, "I can't reach Maureen. Have you talked to her?"

"Yeah, I've talked to her. I wonder why she's not answering you?"

Cassie wondered too. "Well, she's supposed to come with us. I guess my dad and I will just swing by her house in the morning, then."

"Oh." A very pregnant pause followed Andrea's single word. Then she said, "Maureen's not going."

Cassie's defenses flared. "How do you know? She told you?"

"No. But she invited me to spend the weekend with her and her mom in Tulsa."

No, she hadn't. Cassie wanted to deny it, wanted to laugh and say Andrea must be mistaken. But she knew it was true. A hard rock formed in her stomach. Not only had Maureen ditched her and then not told her, but she'd tried to get Andrea to ditch her also!

"Are you going?" Cassie asked, hearing the hollowness in her voice. She didn't want Andrea to. But she wouldn't beg. If that was what she chose, so be it.

"Of course not, silly! I'm going with you!"

Andrea would never know how much those words meant to Cassie.

Mr. Jones was coughing and sneezing in the morning. Cassie sat in the back on the drive to get Andrea, then bolted from the car and ran up the walkway.

There were no cars in the driveway. The blinds were drawn, and the house felt awfully quiet. Paranoia taunted Cassie's mind. She rang the doorbell, her stomach twisting inside.

Nothing. Was it possible Andrea wasn't here? Had she gone to Tulsa with Maureen after all?

CHAPTER FORTY-SIX

Dancing Queens

C assie rang the bell again, her hands beginning to shake. Still no response. She hesitated just short of going to Andrea's window and peeking in. If Andrea had ditched her, Cassie swore she'd never talk to any of them again.

The door swung open, and Andrea poked her head out. "Sorry! I was in the bathroom!" She stepped onto the patio, carrying a duffel bag in her hand.

Cassie could have kissed her. She settled for taking Andrea's bag from her. "That's no problem!" She put Andrea's bag in the back, and they climbed into the car together.

Mr. Jones coughed and opened the door to spit, then pulled away from the curb.

"Your dad sounds pretty sick," Andrea said, eyeing him.

"Yeah," Cassie said. "I'm keeping my distance." She turned to face Andrea. "I'm so glad you're coming. I hope you don't mind, but Riley will be rooming with us."

"Well, I guess that's fine." Andrea looked as annoyed as Riley had. "Guess what. Amity has a boyfriend."

"She does?" Cassie reared back in surprise. "When did that happen?"

"They saw each other before Christmas, and now they're going out. Some guy named Landon."

"Oh, I know Landon," Cassie said. "He was on my soccer team. He's nice." Better than some of the other guys on her soccer team.

"Well, now he's all she wants to talk about. It's really boring."

"Guess it's a good thing we don't have boyfriends," Cassie said. "We won't talk about them."

"Right?"

Mr. Jones drove up the winding road to the top of Mt. Sequoya, then dropped the girls off at the dorms. They followed the directions to their room on the second floor. Riley looked up when they walked in. She already sat on one of the three beds, listening to music.

"Riley, you got a haircut!" Cassie said. She stepped over and cupped the bottom of Riley's short blond hair, now closer to a pixie cut than a bob. "It's so cute!"

"Thanks," Riley said. Her eyes flicked to Andrea, and she put on a big smile. "Hi, Andrea."

"Hi, Riley. Cute hair."

Cassie watched them interact and let out a slow breath. They were being civil to each other. That was a good sign.

⟡

The youth retreat started with a devotional and a welcome, and Cassie took the time to casually glance around the room at all the kids present. They'd come from Oklahoma, all over Arkansas, and Missouri, and there were many faces she didn't recognize. Then she spotted one she did, and she froze.

Her ex-boyfriend Josh.

There was no hiding. Cassie slid closer to Andrea and whispered, "Josh is here."

"No way!" Andrea whispered. "Where?"

"Don't stare! You can find him later."

"I didn't know he was coming!"

"Do you still talk to him?"

She shook her head. "No, we kind of lost touch. It will be good to see him."

"You can see him," Cassie muttered. "I don't want to talk to him."

Andrea gave her own scan of the room. "There's lots of cute guys here."

Yay, Cassie thought. As long as they didn't have to spend time with Josh. Maybe he wouldn't notice her.

She had to give up on that idea when Brother Abrams spotted her after the welcome.

"Well, if it isn't Cassandra Jones!" he said in a booming voice. He came over and gripped her hand. "Looking well and healthy!"

Cassie sensed eyes turning her direction and felt the heat creeping up her face. The last time she'd seen Brother Abrams, it had been on a service trip where she got an ovarian cyst and ended up in the hospital. The whole bus full of kids had to wait for her to be released before they could go home. "I'm all well this time," she said, wishing she could melt into the ground.

"Did this girl cause you trouble?" A man with an accented voice and twinkling brown eyes walked over to them.

"Brother Moda!" Cassie said. Known primarily for his guitar music at summer camp, Brother Moda was a favorite with the girls. But Cassie mostly wanted to see his daughter. She swiveled around, looking through the crowd. "Is Ana Julia here?"

"She couldn't come, I'm sorry to say." He looked at Brother Abrams. "What did Cassie do to you? She fainted on the hike we took a few summers ago."

"I didn't faint," Cassie said, feeling as if she might right now. "I got overheated."

Brother Abrams let out a loud laugh. "She made us take a side trip to the hospital!"

Now she knew she was going to die. Kids had gathered around to listen, chuckling and smiling, curious about the commotion. Cassie spotted Andrea and sent her a pleading look, but Andrea only shrugged. Cassie's eyes met Riley's, and Riley took pity on her.

"Cassie!" she called. "We need to grab a table for lunch or all the seats will be gone."

Thank you, Riley. "So good to see you guys!" Cassie waved and hurried after Riley, who grabbed her arm and giggled so hard Cassie had to pinch her.

Tyler and Jason took the opportunity at lunch to tease Cassie about what Brother Moda and Brother Abrams had said.

"We had no idea you are so fragile," Tyler said. "We'll have to be more careful around you."

"You guys are jerks," Cassie said, though she meant it nicely.

"There's Josh," Andrea said. "Should we invite him over?"

Both boys swiveled to look at him.

"Oh, it's your ex-boyfriend," Tyler said.

Cassie shook her head furiously. "He's with his friends."

"They're pretty cute, too," Andrea said.

Tyler eyed her. "We've met, right? At church dances?"

Andrea spared him a glance before turning her gaze back to Josh's table. "Yeah."

"What's your name?" Tyler asked, pursuing the conversation even though Andrea didn't act interested.

"Andrea." She stood up. "I'll be back." With that, she marched over to Josh's table.

"I don't think she likes me," Tyler said, looking forlorn. Cassie felt a bit sorry for him, something she hadn't expected.

"Don't worry about it." Jason picked up their trash. "We'll see you guys in the next class."

Riley watched them go and let out a heavy sigh. "I like you, Tyler," she said.

"Maybe you should tell him," Cassie said.

Riley shook her head. "If he were interested in me, he would show it."

❧ ⚜ ❧

The next two classes crawled by, as everyone became anxious for the upcoming New Year's Eve dance. Finally the class dismissed, and Cassie, Riley, and Andrea hurried back to their room to get changed.

"This dress is hideous," Andrea said, pulling out the red dress she'd brought.

Cassie glanced over at it. "I think it's lovely."

"What did you bring?"

Riley took a short green dress off a hanger. "This is mine."

Cassie had brought a flowery blue dress. Normally she loved the dress, but she'd worn it so many times before that today it looked boring. She offered it to Andrea. "Trade you."

Andrea looked it over. "It's pretty, but do you think it will fit me?"

"Try it on."

It fit Andrea better than it ever did Cassie, showing off all of Andrea's curves and flattering her figure. Andrea smoothed down the long skirt and smiled at herself. "Thanks, Cassie!"

Cassie got Andrea's dress on, but after that she had trouble. It was too big in the shoulder area and kept sliding to one side, exposing her bra strap. That wouldn't do. "I need safety pins."

"I'll find some for you," Riley said.

Andrea put makeup on Cassie while they waited, and moments later Riley returned, brandishing the pins.

"Let's fix you up." Andrea pinned the shoulders up and drew back, frowning. "Well, it will have to do."

Cassie examined her reflection. Pinned up, the shoulders dwarfed her, almost like shoulder pads. Her head looked even smaller than normal, and she wanted her blue dress back. Too late for that. "Yeah. I guess so."

They took a few selfies, then hurried through the dorm down to the activity room, where the dance would be held. One of the youth leaders stood at the door handing out headbands that flashed "Happy New Year!" every few seconds. Music already blasted through the room, and the girls stepped onto the dance floor.

Cassie wiggled her shoulders, giddy with excitement. Who would ask her to dance? Would she meet someone amazing?

Jason, the older of the Reeves brothers, stepped her way, bowing to her. "May I have this dance?"

"Yes." Cassie glanced back to see Tyler asking Andrea. Cassie held her breath, worried Andrea would turn him down, but she accepted.

"That guy over there keeps looking at you," Jason said, redirecting Cassie's attention.

She followed his gaze. "That's Josh."

"Ah, yes. Your ex-boyfriend."

"Spin me," Cassie instructed, and Jason did. Now Josh couldn't stare at her. "He didn't take our break up well."

Jason gave her a stern look. "That's why my mom says we shouldn't date before we're sixteen." Then he winked at her. "But I understand."

Cassie smiled, glad he didn't judge her. "I guess Tyler likes Andrea?"

"Eh." Jason lifted a shoulder. "He likes a lot of girls."

Riley would be relieved to hear that. Maybe she'd make the list, after all.

The song finished and Jason thanked her for the dance. Cassie barely made it to the wall before a boy with familiar glasses and blue eyes stepped up to her.

"Cassie," Josh said, a big smile on his face. "Want to dance?"

No, she did not! Her hands trembled. All she could think when she saw him was how much she'd disliked kissing him, and then how she'd lied to everyone about when and how she and Ben started going out. It made her feel bad inside every time.

But she didn't want to be rude. One dance. She could give him one dance. "Sure." She extended her hand, and he whisked her onto the dance floor.

"We haven't talked in a while," he said.

Not since they'd broken up. "Yeah. How's life?"

"It's great. I talk with your friends sometimes, but never you. How's your new boyfriend?"

Did he ask her to dance so they could rehash this? "I don't have a boyfriend."

"Oh, you don't? But you did, right? Right after we broke up?"

She met his eyes, as bold as she dared. "I went out with one guy, but it wasn't serious. We're not together anymore." *And it's none of your business!* She kept that sentiment to herself.

"Oh, well, I'm sorry." He didn't sound sorry.

Cassie lifted one of her well-padded shoulders. "I'm not. It's like I told you. I'm too young for a relationship."

They drifted into a silence, one that felt thick and awkward rather than jovial and friendly. Would the song never end?

It finally did, and Josh released her hand with a smile. "You're pretty as ever."

"Thank you," she said, trying to keep a polite expression on her face. She returned to the wall just as Riley did. "Ugh!"

"Bad dance?" Riley said.

"Just Josh. You dance with him next time."

"I don't want your leftovers."

Cassie glanced around for Andrea and saw her laughing and talking with Josh's friends. Riley sucked in a breath, and Cassie looked up to see Tyler approaching them. Cassie could practically hear Riley's prayers as Tyler pointed his finger—at Cassie. Then he took her hand and led her to the floor.

Behind her, she heard Riley hiss, "Of course you, Cassie!"

"Hi, Cassie," Tyler said formally, as if they hadn't spoken to each other before.

"Hello, Tyler," Cassie said, allowing him to spin her in a circle. "How are you?"

"I'm great." He sighed. "I can't figure out why Andrea doesn't like me, though."

Cassie couldn't figure it out, either. If Tyler liked Cassie . . . But she banished those thoughts. Riley already had a crush on him. Just because he had such deep blue eyes . . . "Yeah, I don't know. She's kind of weird sometimes."

"Aren't all friends?"

"I suppose."

He spun her around again, and then he said, "I mean, it's not like I'm creepy or something, am I?"

Now she laughed. "No."

"Is my deodorant not working? My breath bad?"

She only laughed harder. "You're fine. She's just different." Cassie spared a glance back at Riley and saw her just standing there, arms over her chest, an annoyed expression on her face. "Do me a favor and ask Riley to dance."

"Why?"

Why did he have to ask that? "Because she hasn't danced that much."

"I don't want to."

She stomped a foot in exasperation. "Tyler!"

"What? She's not my friend like you are."

Like she was. The sentiment warmed her heart. She remembered just a few years prior when Tyler rudely antagonized her and made her life miserable. "Just ask her."

He gave her a knowing look. "Does she have a crush on me?"

She couldn't answer that honestly, so she evaded it. "Just ask her."

The song ended and he gave her one last spin, then said, "All right." He let her go and started to walk away.

"Tyler," Cassie called after him.

He paused and looked at her.

"Andrea doesn't know how lucky she is," she said.

Tyler's face broke into a gorgeous smile, one that left her slightly breathless. She shook it off and rejoined Riley.

CHAPTER FORTY-SEVEN

Special Attention

Cassie stepped back against the wall and pondered the confusing emotions broiling inside her. Riley had a crush on Tyler, and he had a crush on Andrea. Why would Cassie suddenly find herself drawn to him?

A boy Cassie didn't know came over and asked her to dance. She worried about leaving Riley, but just as she thought it, Tyler stepped up to Riley.

"Want to dance, Riley?"

Her whole face flushed red, and she took his hand. As Tyler led her away, he caught Cassie's eye and nodded.

"Thank you," Cassie mouthed. Then she let herself be whisked away to dance.

"Well?" Cassie said when the dance finished and she met back up with Riley. "Was it everything you hoped it would be?"

"Oh, he's so dreamy," Riley sighed. "We didn't talk much, but I could stare into his eyes all day and not get tired."

Cassie giggled. "Glad it was such a nice experience for you."

"Hey, you guys." Andrea came over, dragging a boy behind her. "This is James."

Tall with dark curly hair, James nodded at them.

"He lives in Tahlequah like Josh." Andrea smiled at him like he was a fatted lamb.

"You dated Josh, right?" James asked Cassie, a deep bass voice erupting from his throat.

She nodded, face growing warm. "For a little bit."

"Speaking of Josh," he said, "here he comes."

Josh sauntered over, looking very confident and sure of himself. "Cassie, want to dance?"

She couldn't believe it. "We've already danced."

"We have too," Andrea said, tugging on James' arm. "But we're going to dance again."

Cassie suspected Andrea was taking pleasure from her discomfort. She looked around, wishing someone would save her, but saw no one. "Um, well." She didn't want to dance with him again. She shouldn't have to do something she didn't want to. "I'm not going to dance right now." She hooked an arm through Riley's. "We're going to walk around a bit."

"Yeah, I'm tired of dancing anyway. Let's walk around."

Cassie shot Riley an expression of annoyance. She tipped her head closer, intentionally keeping Josh out of the conversation. "Bathroom break."

They walked through the halls for a few minutes with Josh on their tail when Riley pointed at the restroom sign.

"Oh, I need to step inside real quick."

"Sure, no problem." Cassie shot Josh an apologetic smile before following her inside. Then she looked at Riley, and they both had to cover their mouths to muffle their giggles.

"How long do you think we have to hide in here?" Riley asked.

"Just to the end of this song, I think. He won't follow me forever, will he?"

"You and your boys." They collapsed into giggles again.

The song ended, and the noised quieted down in the hallway. "Let's go," Cassie said. She opened the bathroom door and stepped out, then drew to a halt. Riley crashed in behind her and let out a little squeal.

Josh was still waiting for them.

"We're going back to the dance floor now," Cassie said. Her mind raced. How could she get rid of him?

They traveled back to the dance as a silent trio. They stepped into the room, the floor shaking with the beat of the music, and Cassie smacked right into a boy.

"Hi," he said, grabbing her shoulder to keep her from falling. "Want to dance?"

She had never seen him before in her life. A few inches taller than her with short blond hair and blue eyes, he had a friendly, inviting smile.

"Yes!" Cassie said. "I was just about to ask you!"

"Oh, well, great." He smiled again, and Cassie only felt a little guilty leaving Riley behind with Josh.

"You saved me," Cassie said, heaving a huge sigh of relief. "I was trying to get away from Josh."

The boy peered around Cassie. "That boy who was with you?"

"Yes, him."

"That's weird that he would follow you around. How do you know him?"

For some reason Cassie felt reluctant to tell him they had dated. "He has a crush on me."

"Ah." A twinkle lit his eye. "That could be problematic."

"Yes, it can be!" She laughed. "I'm Cassie, by the way. I live in Springdale. You are. . . ?"

"Oh, right. I'm Zack Amos. I live in Fayetteville."

"My grandma lives there!" Cassie found herself chattering more than usual. Perhaps out of relief from escaping Josh. "Do you know her? Her last name is Jones, Gretta Jones."

"Sure, I know her. She's friends with my mom. We see her at church sometimes."

He kept smiling. It was like he couldn't stop. Cassie found it sweet, endearing.

"What do you like to do, Zack?"

"I love soccer. And I just got my license—"

"My dad has a soccer store!" Cassie said, interrupting him. Then the second half of his sentence caught up to her. "Wait, you can drive? Are you sixteen?"

He nodded. "Yes, just turned it."

The song ended, and then the D.J.'s voice boomed, "All right, ladies and gents! It's time for the count down! Grab your noisemakers and your streamers, and join me in the count down to the new year!"

Cassie looked at Zack and shouted with everyone else, "Ten!"

Riley ran to her side and handed her a noisemaker. "Nine!"

The dance floor filled up as everyone crowded to the middle. "Eight! Seven! Six! Five!"

Cassie bounced on the balls of her feet, excitement rolling through her. "Four! Three! Two! One!"

She pressed the noisemaker to her lips and blew, and confetti fell on them from all directions. Andrea sandwiched herself between Riley and Cassie and snapped a photo of the three of them. Cassie cheered and clapped, euphoric.

The crowd splintered off into little groups, everyone heading back to their rooms. Zack caught Cassie's eye and gave her a wave and a big smile before he left the room also.

One year down. The best was yet to come.

☙ ❧

"Look who's speaking today," Riley said, drawing Cassie into the chapel the Sunday after the youth retreat.

Cassie's eyes went up to the podium, and she wasn't surprised to see the missionaries. As traveling ministers, one of their assignments was to speak in church every so often.

"That's nice," Cassie said.

Riley lifted her eyebrows. "So nice."

Cassie elbowed her friend and ignored her, then settled into the pew with the rest of her family. They sang the hymn and a prayer was offered. The preacher said a few words before inviting the dark-haired missionary to come up and speak.

"Hello," the young man said into the microphone, giving his throat a good clearing. "I'm Brother Fitsu. My mother's side of the family hails from Japan, but the only thing I know from my heritage is a little origami." He went on to tell a bit more about himself, then he asked the congregation to be watchful of their neighbors and each other and let the missionaries know if they knew anyone who needed help with anything.

He seemed like a nice guy, but Cassie only half paid attention to him. She really wanted to see what Brother Brian would say.

Brother Brian got up next. He shuffled some papers at the microphone and cleared his throat several times before lifting his face to the congregation. "I'm Brother Brian," he said. "And I'm really nervous to speak to all of you." His eyes flicked to Cassie, and she gave him a reassuring smile. He sort of smiled and faced forward again. "I'm a new Christian. My family didn't go to any church growing up, so the gospel of Christ is new to me. I felt the call to serve the Lord but put it off because of feelings of inadequacy and fear. So I'm a bit older than the other missionaries. At twenty-five, I sometimes feel like the old man in the group."

Cassie's mouth fell open in a silent gasp, and she quickly shut it. Brother Brian wasn't just a little older than her—he was eleven years older than her! She looked at her mother, who shared a wide-eyed look of surprise.

I was imagining it, Cassie thought, sitting back to listen to the rest of his sermon. *No way was he flirting with me.*

He concluded his sermon and the preacher closed the meeting, then everyone dismissed for Sunday School. Cassie waited at her pew for Riley to make her way down the aisle. The missionaries had already moved to the back of the chapel where they could greet every member as they walked out.

"Good sermons," Cassie said to Brother Fitsu and Brother Brian.

"You were my inspiration," Brother Brian said. "I saw you sitting there and thought, 'if she can sing a song in front of the entire congregation, I can give a sermon.' I draw my strength from you, Beauty."

"Thanks," Cassie said, because she once again had no idea what to say. "Don't say a word," she murmured to Riley as they walked into the hallway.

People were already walking through the foyer, entering the chapel for the next sermon, and Cassie spotted a familiar face.

Zack walked in beside two other boys and two people who had to be his parents. He spotted her, then waved.

"Who's that?" Riley asked.

"That's Zack." Cassie returned the gesture. She tilted her head, considering him as he went into the chapel. "He's kind of cute."

Riley elbowed her. "You think they're all cute!"

"Not all of them!" Cassie protested. Though she had to admit, the boys around her were getting better looking.

"Everyone has to get to bed at a decent hour!" Mrs. Jones ordered after church. "It's back to school tomorrow!"

"All ready? Cassie groaned. It felt like they'd barely gotten out, even though they'd been out two weeks already.

"And girls, I want you to clean this room," she added, eyeing the mess that littered the girls' floor.

"Did you see the blond boy at church?" Cassie asked Emily as soon as their mom left. "The one who waved at me?"

"I think so. He had two brothers who looked a lot like him?"

"Yeah, that's him!"

"I saw him," Emily said. "Why?"

"That's Zack. He's the one I danced with on the youth trip who saved me from Josh."

"Oh, Zack!" Emily said his name slowly, breaking it into two syllables. "Do you like him now?"

"I think I might." Cassie lowered her voice. She hadn't told anyone, not even Riley, and it terrified her to say the words out loud. It was like the feelings became more real when spoken, when told to the universe. Her heart had been closed solid since Ben, and the soft flutterings of a crush, that initial interest, left her expectant and restless.

CHAPTER FORTY-EIGHT

Stealing the Show

"**W**hat are you going to do?"

"I don't know. He goes to church with Grandma. Maybe I'll start spending more time with her."

Emily rolled her eyes. "She's so weird."

"I think she's gotten a little bit better," Cassie said, hoping it wasn't wishful thinking. Grandma had always belittled her and made her feel bad when Cassie was younger. But as Cassie aged, her grandmother seemed to think of her more as a peer, even a friend. It wasn't really Grandma's fault she acted that way; she'd had a stroke when she was younger and had the mental capacity of a teenager.

Not that that made it any easier.

"I'll see Zack at dances, too," Cassie added. "He lives in Fayetteville. That's not so far away. But he's sixteen. He can date. Like, really date. Why would he ever even look at me?"

Cassie fell into a sad silence, and then Emily said, "Cheer up! You'll be sixteen in a year and a half!"

The two of them stayed up late cleaning their room, finally turning out the light after midnight. Cassie snuggled into the warm blankets and listened to the wind howling outside, knowing morning would come way too soon. She closed her eyes and drifted off.

Her alarm woke her at five, just like always. Cassie got up and slapped it silent, then shivered in the cold of the room. She ran to the bathroom and turned on the heating vent, changing her clothes so quickly the room didn't even have a chance to warm up. When she came out, her dad was in her room, sitting on her bed.

"Daddy," she said, surprised. She dabbed toothpaste on her brush and set to work cleaning her teeth. "What are you doing here?" she asked around the brush handle.

"Have you looked outside?" he asked.

"No." She spit into the sink and looked back at him. "Why?"

"You should."

Curious, she moved to the sliding glass door closest to Emily's bed and peeked outside.

Pristine, white snow covered every inch of the deck. Lots of it.

"It snowed!" she cried.

"Three feet of snow."

She turned to see her dad smiling. "There's no school today. Which means no religion class. You can go back to bed."

Cassie dove back into her bed, burrowing under the covers. "You can turn out the light when you leave!"

He laughed as he walked out the door and turned out the light.

⚬∽✹∽⚬

The snow didn't melt the next day, or the next. And the city had no snow plows to clear the roads.

The first two days were fun. Cassie got her book ready to submit to the publisher, wrote in her journal, watched movies, and read.

By the third day she was dying of boredom.

She called every one of her friends one by one, but they were just as bored as she was, and the conversations languished. She needed something else. Something exciting.

And then she thought of Zack. She could call him.

The thought immediately filled her with excitement and dread. She tried to cast it away, but now that it had been planted, it wouldn't leave. Would he be happy to hear from her? What would they even talk about?

Mrs. Jones sent the kids on a mission to clean the bathrooms in an attempt to cure their boredom, But it just gave Cassie the opportunity to role play in her brain scenarios of calling him and what they would say. By the time she put away the toilet scrubber, her mind was made up.

Finding a phone number of someone from church was fairly easy. They kept a directory of all the names and numbers of people from the neighboring congregations. All she had to do was remember his last name, which she hadn't forgotten from the moment she met him. She looked it up in the directory and ran her finger underneath the family number. His whole family would know she'd called.

She couldn't turn back now, or she would always wonder. Cassie dug out her phone and dialed the number.

"Hello?" A woman's voice answered on the second ring.

Cassie cleared her throat, fighting the suddenly violent beating of her heart in her throat that made it difficult to speak. "Hi, is Zack there?"

"No, he's not. Can I take a message?" The woman's voice sounded friendly and curious.

The hammering in Cassie's neck lessened slightly. She didn't get to speak to him. "Sure. Tell him Cassie Jones called. We met at the youth retreat last weekend. He can call me back." Cassie rattled off her number, hoping she didn't sound too forward.

"I'll let him know, Cassie."

Cassie hung up, feeling let down from the adrenaline rush to call and then not reaching him. Now she felt stupid for calling.

⊙〜⚙〜⊙

By Saturday the snow had melted enough to get on the roads again, and Riley came over.

"I've been bored out of my mind for days," Cassie said. "For once I actually hope we go back to school on Monday."

"I'm sure we will." Riley sat down at Cassie's desk and began looking through her music. "Do you know all of these songs?"

Cassie joined her. "Mostly. Some are songs Miss Malcolm has given me to memorize."

"So what have you done for the past few days?"

"Well . . . yesterday I called Zack."

Riley's expression brightened as if she sensed juicy information. "Who's Zack?"

"He's the guy I showed you on Sunday. The one that I thought was cute."

"Oh yeah, the one that saved you at the dance."

"Yep, him."

"And?"

Cassie pouted. "He never called me back. What does that mean? That he doesn't like me?"

Riley shrugged. "Maybe all it means is he never got your message."

"I don't think so."

"I have an idea." Riley grabbed her hand. "Let's call Tyler."

"Because you like him?" Cassie couldn't help teasing.

"And then you can call Zack again. Maybe this time he'll answer."

Cassie shook her head. "I can't call two days in a row when he didn't call me back. It makes me look desperate."

"Okay, so you don't have to call him. But call Tyler. He's your friend."

"Me?" Cassie said. "You're the one who likes him."

"I don't want to talk to him, I just want to hear him talk! So you call!"

"Fine." Cassie sat down on the bed and pulled her phone out. She found Tyler's number and pressed the button.

It rang once before Tyler answered.

"Tyler?" Cassie said, just to make sure he was the one to answer his phone.

"Hi, Cassie," his deep voice said on the line, and for some reason it pleased her to know he had her number saved in his phone. "What's up?"

"Is he there?" Riley asked.

Cassie nodded, and Riley moved from the desk to the bed to sit next to her. "Oh, not much. I've just been really bored the past couple of days."

"Yeah, me too," Tyler said. "I'm actually looking forward to school on Monday."

Cassie laughed and settled into the pillows on her bed. "Same."

"Tell him I'm here," Riley said. "Maybe he'll want to talk to me."

"Riley is here with me," Cassie said obediently.

"That's cool. I had some friends over yesterday."

"Did you want to talk to her?"

"No. Hey, who do you like right now?"

Cassie looked at Riley and shrugged, not wanting to admit what Tyler had said. "I'm not telling you. But I know who you like."

Tyler gave a self-deprecating laugh. "Yeah, I kind of made a fool of myself for her. She obviously doesn't like me."

Cassie clicked her tongue, sympathy squeezing her heart. She remembered the depth of Tyler's eyes when they had danced and he told her how he felt about Andrea. "Riley likes guys with blue eyes," she said spontaneously.

"Hey, I have blue eyes," Tyler said.

"I know," Cassie said, her voice coming out low and sultry.

Riley burst out laughing, and Cassie clapped her hand over her mouth, face burning. Hopefully Tyler hadn't—

"Well. I'm glad to know you feel that way, Cassie." His tone was teasing, but Cassie handed the phone to Riley and buried her face in her pillow.

Still laughing, Riley said, "Hey, Tyler. It's Riley."

Cassie heard his voice speaking on the other end, but she couldn't tell what he said. Riley glanced at her.

"Yeah, she's right here. She can't talk at the moment. Oh? Yeah, that's cool. See you in church tomorrow." Riley closed the phone.

Cassie lifted her face from the pillow. "He hung up?"

Riley shrugged one shoulder. "Said his mom wanted him to go to the store with her so he had to go." She handed the phone back to Cassie. "Ready to call Zack?"

Cassie shook her head and put the phone on the blankets. "I think I've had enough self-embarrassment for today."

☙❧

By Sunday the roads had cleared completely, other than a knee-high pile of dirty white slush built up along the sides. Mr. Jones drove the family to church, and he had no sooner parked the car before Cassie saw Riley running out of the building toward them.

She bounced beside the car door until Cassie got out, then she grabbed Cassie's arm and hauled her away.

"Zack is here! I saw his family!"

Cassie inclined her head toward her friend. "What's he doing here so early?"

"I don't know! Come on! Let's go say hi!"

Cassie's heart immediately started its war beat up in her throat, and she wasn't sure she could face him after he hadn't bothered to return her call. "I don't know."

Riley shook her. "Come on! He's looking awfully cute!"

That was tempting. Cassie pictured Zack with his church-boy haircut and blue eyes, just like Tyler's. "Maybe we can just take a peek."

Riley giggled and pulled Cassie into the building.

They walked down the hall together, and Cassie tried not to look from side to side.

"There," Riley whispered. She jerked her chin in front of them. "He sitting on the chair."

Cassie saw him, dressed in khaki pants and a button-up shirt. Before Cassie could turn and run the other direction, his eyes slid down the hall and met hers.

"Hi," Cassie said, face burning, wishing she'd run while she had the chance.

His face creased into a warm smile. "Hi."

And that was that. Cassie turned around and went down the hallway as quickly as she could, not wanting to ask him if he got her message and why he hadn't called her back. Instead she dashed straight to the bathroom, Riley on her heels. The door closed behind them, and Cassie turned around to grip Riley's hands.

"He said hi to me!" she gasped out.

"I'm sure he likes you," Riley said, and the two of them giggled like maniacs.

"There will be another youth dance after Valentine's Day," their Sunday school teacher said right before church ended. "Be sure to invite your friends. This will be a fun event."

Cassie's heart warmed at the thought of another opportunity to dance with Zack.

"I can't wait!" Riley said. "Maybe this time Tyler will dance with me two times."

"Oh, I'm sure he will," Cassie said, though she wasn't sure of that at all. Tyler wasn't always nice, and lately he seemed to think he didn't have to be nice to Riley.

Cassie went to the bathroom before school on Monday to seek out her friends, since the colder weather had forced them indoors for their morning gossip.

"Cassie!" She was immediately greeted with hugs and exclamations as Cara and Andrea saw her.

"It's been forever!" Andrea said.

Cassie laughed, appreciating her friends' eagerness. "It's only been a week. I just saw you at the New Year's dance." Cassie brightened. "Speaking of! There's another dance next month!"

"A dance?" Amity walked in, clutching her books to her chest. "Did you say there's another dance?"

Cassie nodded, pleased to be the center of attention again. "Yes! It's going to be so fun!"

Amity turned around as Maureen walked in. "There's a dance in February!"

"Great!" Maureen said. "Let's invite Melanie!"

Cassie frowned. Since when did they get to invite other people? The dances were Cassie's thing, and she got to say who could and couldn't go.

"We can ask her to come, right?" Amity said, turning large, hopeful eyes on Cassie.

Cassie swallowed. How was she supposed to say no?

CHAPTER FORTY-NINE

Friendly Girls

"Yeah, of course," Cassie said, the words digging into her throat.

Amity and Maureen squealed and jumped up and down as if Cassie had just told them Christmas was coming again. Cassie rolled her eyes and met Andrea's gaze. Andrea also rolled her eyes, and Cassie was glad she wasn't the only one unhappy with this turn of events.

"Look at this." Janice handed Cassie and Andrea a sheet of paper in first hour. "Today the yearbook is voting on the ninth grade Hall of Fame."

"Oh, that sounds fun," Andrea said.

"I always look at that page in last year's yearbook," Cassie said. "I like to imagine what I would be famous for."

"Best hair, most likely to get a date, smartest, friendliest." Andrea read down the list and lifted her face. "You could get it for the smartest, Cassie."

Cassie frowned. "But I'm not the smartest." And that wasn't what she wanted to be known for, anyway. She'd rather be known as the prettiest girl, the one most likely to get a date. Not that she was, but it would be nice if everyone else thought so.

"I think you could be the friendliest, Cassie," Janice said. "You're nice to everybody, not just your group of friends."

"Well, I try to be," Cassie said, feeling a little guilty for not doing a better job.

"So how does it work?" Andrea asked.

"It's fill-in-the-blank. Everyone gets to do it their science class."

"You think I have a chance of being the friendliest?" Cassie asked.

"Sure. I'll write you in."

"Me too," Andrea said. "I'll tell everybody also."

Cassie turned around and faced forward as Coach Benson called the class to order, but she felt a twinge of anxious excitement. Maybe she would actually get to be in the yearbook as someone cool.

True to her word, Andrea told everyone in the classroom and in the hallways to write Cassie's name in for the friendliest. Cassie grabbed her friends at lunch to make sure they knew.

"I already put you down," Amity said. "I knew you'd hit me if I didn't."

"I would not!" Cassie protested, though she was pleased Amity had put her name in.

"I asked Melanie in third hour if she wants to come to the dance, and she said yes!" Amity told them all in math.

"I was thinking about coming this time," Cara said to Cassie as they left the classroom. "But if she's coming, I'm not."

"I think we're all tired of feeling like we're not good enough for Amity," Janice said.

⟨⟩~❦~⟨⟩

Finally sixth hour arrived. Mr. Adams handed out the green sheets of paper that were the yearbook ballots, and a little buzz filled the classroom as the students whispered and shared names.

"Put Cassandra Jones for the friendliest!" Janice said.

Several kids shot glances her way, and Cassie's face warmed, but she beamed appreciatively at Janice.

They finished filling out their sheets, and Mr. Adams started class. Cassie took notes without paying much attention, her mind on the voting and what she hoped would be good results for her.

"And don't forget," Mr. Adams said as the bell rang, "Science Fair projects are due in two weeks."

Science Fair? In two weeks? Cassie's eyes went wide with alarm as she put her binder away. She'd known it was coming, but that soon? She hadn't even started it yet! This, on top of her life map project for English, which was due Monday! There went her weekend.

Judging from the murmurs of dismay in the classroom, she wasn't the only one stressing.

"Guess I know what I'm doing for the rest of the week," Jaclyn said.

"Me too," Cassie agreed.

She waited for Janice after class so they could walk together toward the choir room.

"When do we find out the answers?" Cassie asked, clutching her binder to her chest.

"Sometime tomorrow," Janice said. "After everyone has had the chance to vote."

"Good luck, Cassie!" Jaclyn called in the hallway.

"Yes, I voted for you!" Luke said as he came out of another classroom.

Cassie put a smile on her face that she hoped was super friendly.

※

The intercom clicked on during third hour the next day for morning announcements. Cassie was in English class, and she didn't pay any attention until the girly voice said, "And now for the ninth grade Hall of Fame. First, the girls."

Cassie's friends Nicole and Leigh Ann both turned around and smiled at her. Cassie wished they wouldn't; it just made her more nervous.

"For the best hair: Jaclyn White."

That made sense. Jaclyn had super curly hair and big dimples when she smiled.

"Most likely to get a date—" She read off the name of a girl Cassie didn't know.

"Most likely to succeed—"

Cassie held her breath. She did not want this one.

"Nicole Bass!"

Nicole's face flushed pink, and the kids around her clapped. Cassie found herself squeezing her pen as she waited for the next one.

"The friendliest ninth grader: Cassandra Jones!"

Cassie closed her eyes and bit hard on her lip to keep from squealing, but Nicole and Leigh Ann squealed for her.

"Yay, Cassie!"

"Good job!"

Cassie opened her eyes and smiled and didn't pay any attention as the boys' names were read.

"We need the students to come to the yearbook room during lunch tomorrow so we can get their pictures. Thank you for your time."

The intercom clicked off, and Ms. Talo congratulated them before continuing with class. Cassie stared at her paper, feeling the grin slide across her face. She had finally gotten voted as someone cool.

※

Andrea planned a big party at her house on Friday night, and she made it no secret Melanie wasn't invited.

"But I want her to be a part of our group," Amity said at the lunch table.

"No way. She's not one of us. We don't want her."

Amity looked around the table for support, but even Maureen sat close-lipped.

"It's bad enough you've invited her to our dances," Andrea said. "She can't come to my party."

"Well, maybe I won't come either, then," Amity said.

"Then don't!" Andrea said snippishly. "Go be with your new best friend. You still have each other."

The fighting made Cassie uncomfortable, but she agreed with Andrea.

Either Melanie didn't want to come over or Amity's loyalty to her old friends was still stronger, because Friday night when Cassie got to Andrea's house, Amity was already there.

"Decided to join us after all?" Cassie asked.

"What are you talking about?" Amity said as if no weirdness had ever happened. "I always planned on coming."

Cassie caught Andrea's eye, and Andrea gave her a roll.

The doorbell rang again, and then Janice came in, followed by Maureen.

"Hey guys!" Maureen said. "Look when I brought!" She brandished a DVD in her hand.

"Oh, what is it?" Andrea grabbed the movie from her hands. Then she gave a shriek. "Oh my goodness, I heard all about this one! It's supposed to be even bloodier than the first one!"

Amity joined her, looking over Andrea's shoulder. "Oh, I don't know if I can watch it! Horror movies give me nightmares!"

Cassie slipped the movie from Maureen's hands and looked at it. "No way am I watching that." Cassie didn't watch horror movies. Not only did they give her nightmares, but they took away her sense of peace and well-being.

Maureen gave an aggravated sigh. "I knew you would say that."

"Well, if Cassie wants to watch something else, I'm sure Andrea's got something," Janice said. "A good romance, maybe. You would like that, Amity."

"I am not watching a romance," Maureen said.

"And I'm not watching a horror movie," Cassie said.

The doorbell rang again, and this time Cara came in, all smiles and hugs. Maureen immediately launched her into the discussion.

"Horror movie or romance?" she said.

Cara put her sleeping gear down in the living room. "We always watch romances. Let's do a horror movie."

"Cassie doesn't want to watch a horror movie," Janice said.

"Then Cassie can put on a romance in the other room," Maureen said.

The words stung, and Cassie swallowed against a lump in her throat.

"Oh, that doesn't sound like much fun," Cara said. "We can watch a romance."

"No, you guys go ahead," Cassie said. She didn't want their pity. She didn't want them to do something to make her feel better. "I've got things I can do."

"Well, that's decided," Maureen said, and she walked to the other room to put the movie in.

Janice gave Cassie a sympathetic look. "I'll watch a romance or a comedy with you if you want."

Cassie waved her off. "No, it's totally fine. I'll be just fine here in Andrea's room. I have my book." She pasted a smile on her face and watched as each one of them left the room, then she collapsed backward onto Andrea's bed and sighed. Would it always feel like she was still trying to fit in with these girls? Would she always be the odd one out?

She pulled out a book she'd brought and settled in for the duration. If she wanted to, she could call her mom and go home. But that would take her one step further away from her friends.

She heard them screaming and shrieking and then laughing in the other room, probably as somebody got hacked to death in the horror movie. She tried to concentrate on her book and not give in to the desire to join them. She wasn't kidding when she said it would give her nightmares. But she felt so left out.

The movie finally ended, and the girls filed into Andrea's room, still rehashing scenes and shrieking at the memories. Amity settled onto the bed next to Cassie, accidentally elbowing her as the bed jostled.

"Oh, sorry," Amity said. "I didn't mean to get you in the boob." Then her lip twisted as if she could barely contain herself, and she giggled. "Oh, I forgot you don't have any boobs. Hope I didn't hurt your bra."

The other girls didn't try to contain their laughter, and Cassie's injured pride refused to stay quiet. "Sure I do. They're just small."

"And under-developed!" Maureen said. "My dad's got bigger boobs than you do."

Andrea and Amity shrieked with mirth, and even Janice and Cara giggled.

The words tore at Cassie's ego, and she took slow, shallow breaths, willing herself not to cry. She tried to smile like it was a joke, but her lips trembled. "It's just because I didn't eat enough food last year."

"Well, that's your fault," Andrea said. "We might not be as skinny as you, but at least we don't have to put our boobs on every morning."

Everyone laughed except Janice, who had her eyes on Cassie with what looked like sympathy. But Cassie laughed also, refusing to show them how much they hurt her.

The conversation moved past her. Cassie didn't hear what else they said. She sat and fumed in silence. What she couldn't figure out was why she continued to consider them friends. She gave and gave and they only took.

Cassie didn't call her mom and ask her to come get her, though it was close. Instead she remained aloof from the other girls the rest of the slumber party and barely said goodbye when it was time to leave.

"Did you have fun?" Mrs. Jones asked Cassie when she picked her up.

"Yeah." She didn't say anything else. Too many details, and her mom would start to smell out the truth.

"Well, great. Because when we get home, I need help cleaning. The missionaries are coming over for dinner."

The missionaries. Cassie perked up at that. Brother Brian always made her feel special.

With all of the homework Cassie had piling up, including advanced English and her science fair project, Cassie asked Mrs. Jones to drop her off at the library first. She spent most of the day brainstorming what would be a good project and finally decided to do one on the power of the sun's rays. That decided, she found a few books that indicated how to make solar water heaters.

Brother Brian and Brother Fitsu came over for dinner that night. They sat together, but Brother Brian made sure to tell Cassie how lovely she looked. And then he complimented Mrs. Jones on the food and said how much he was enjoying his time in Springdale.

"You've only been here a few weeks," Cassie said. "Do you think you'll be here longer?"

He smiled at her. "I'm quite sure of it. We haven't finished doing our work here. There is still lots to do."

Cassie smiled back at him, glad he'd be around a little bit longer. "I'm sure you're having lots of success. You genuinely care about the people."

"I definitely try," he said, and something about his expression made her face grow warm.

CHAPTER FIFTY

Killer Hearts

"**W**hat are you doing for your project?" Cassie asked Riley in church on Sunday. They weren't in the same science class, but every ninth grader was required to do a project.

"I'm doing mine on seeds. Something about shelf life and how long it takes for them to grow."

"Oh, that sounds cool," Cassie said, impressed. She didn't like to garden or dig her fingers into the dirt, but it was something Riley was good at.

Tyler stepped out of the classroom in front of them and walked down the hall.

"There's Tyler," Riley said, and her face took on a slightly panicked, slightly hopeful look.

"Tyler!" Cassie shouted.

He slowed his gate, glancing behind him. He came to a stop and waited for them to catch up.

"What's up?" he drawled, bumping Cassie's shoulder with his own. He was big enough that the force of it made her take a step backward.

"Not much. Just saying hi."

Tyler raised an eyebrow. "I hear you've been calling Zack Morris."

Cassie's face flushed hot. "Where did you hear that?" she sputtered.

Tyler's eyes grazed over the top of Cassie's head and landed on Riley. "A little bird told me."

Cassie shot Riley a murderous glare. "Well, he's just a friend. We met at the New Year's dance."

"Are you sure that's all he is?" Tyler wiggled his eyebrows like caterpillars over his forehead. "From what I understood, it sounded like more than that."

Cassie glowered. "You were misinformed."

"Whoa, misinformed. Such a big word."

"Sorry if I'm testing the limits of your vocabulary," Cassie said, a smile pulling up at her lips.

"The limits of my vocabulary? Dream on. You don't even know how far my limits are."

Riley cleared her throat, and Cassie gave a little jump, suddenly remembering her. She looped her arm through Riley's. "Well, we're going to sit in the chapel now. See you later, Tyler."

"Can you try not to flirt with Tyler when I'm standing right there?" Riley said as they walked away.

"I wasn't flirting!" Cassie said. "We were just having a friendly conversation. And besides, you told him about Zack."

"Only because he wanted to know who you like. And you were definitely flirting."

"Good morning, beauty," Brother Brian said, interrupting their discussion.

Now Cassie knew her face was blushing as heat brushed her cheeks. "Good morning, Brother Brian," she said. She felt like she should head to her seat without saying another word, but when he extended his hand, she took it. He gave her a squeeze, his fingers warm, and a smile lit his eyes.

"Seeing you is one of my favorite parts of Sunday."

"Thank you," Cassie said. The flattery went to her heart, but she came to her senses and pulled her hand away. He was a missionary and eleven years older than her. She and Riley stepped around him and continued to the benches.

"Speaking of flirting," Riley said.

"He is definitely not flirting," Cassie said.

"He doesn't talk to me that way," Riley said.

To that, Cassie had no argument.

❦

After church Cassie spotted her grandma on the other side of the chapel. Grandma went to church with the Fayetteville congregation, and usually Cassie didn't see her, but now Grandma was standing in the foyer as if waiting for something.

"Grandma," Cassie said, rather cautiously. Grandma had had a stroke when she was in her twenties, and she wasn't always nice.

Grandma spun around, all four-foot-five of her on her six-inch heels. "Cassandra! You're just the person I was looking for!"

"Yes?" Cassie said.

"Zack's mom told me you've been calling him. I was mortified! Nice girls don't call boys! You need to stop right away!"

Cassie's face burned with indignation. "Did his mom tell you I need to stop calling?"

"Yes! She said my granddaughter won't stop calling her son!"

The shame heated her face. She had only called twice! Or was it three times? Was that why he never called back? "Okay! I won't call him anymore!" Cassie turned around and made a beeline for the bathroom, afraid she would cry and Grandma would see. How utterly mortifying!

⟨ೲ❁ೲ⟩

Cassie stayed up late working on her life map project for English. She couldn't rouse herself when her alarm went off and missed the bus. Mrs. Jones had to drive her to school, and Cassie got an earful about it the whole way there. But it was worth it, because at least she had her project done when she stepped into English class.

She took it to Ms. Talo's desk. "Here's my life map. Where would you like it?"

Ms. Talo looked up from her grade book. "Look at you, miss efficient. You can put it by the cubbies in the back." Ms. Talo pointed, and Cassie followed her instructions.

"Show off," Jimmy said when Cassie walked past his desk.

Cassie paused and examined her poster board on the back wall, black with a yellow brick road highlighting her life so far. It didn't look that amazing. "What's yours look like?" She peered around him but didn't see anything.

Jimmy shrugged. "I'll let you know tomorrow. I haven't done it yet. I don't believe in getting things done early." He winked.

"Early?" His words confused her. Cassie looked toward the door as her other classmates came in, and she noticed none of them had posters with them. She moved away from Jimmy and sat down in her desk next to Nicole.

"Where is your life map?" she asked.

"I'm almost done with it." Nicole glanced at Jimmy and then looked away, her face turning pink.

Cassie didn't miss the interaction between the two of them, but she was more focused on the life maps. "Isn't it due today?"

"No, tomorrow." Nicole opened a notebook, her eyes glossy.

Cassie couldn't ignore the signs of her friend's distress any longer. "What's going on?"

"Jimmy and I broke up." Nicole whispered the words so quietly it was more of a breath than a sentence.

"Oh, I'm so sorry." That explained why Cassie hadn't seen them walking together lately and why Nicole looked upset. But Cassie had something else to puzzle out, and that was her staying up late to work on a project that wasn't due today.

Ms. Talo clapped her hands, getting the class's attention. "I've got a surprise for you today, guys! We're going to watch a movie!"

"Can't wait," Jimmy said, yawning loudly.

"What movie?" Leigh Ann asked, ignoring Jimmy.

"It's a Shakespeare play," Ms. Talo said, beaming. "Called *Much Ado About Nothing*. And the best part about it is, we're going to put this play on as a class!"

That led to more groaning and head rolls, but Cassie straightened up in excitement. She hadn't done any acting in years, but she loved to sing, and that was like acting. This was her chance to be a starlet.

Ms. Talo put the movie on, and Cassie immediately fell in love with the character of Hero, the wronged, innocent lover.

"We'll finish watching it tomorrow," Ms. Talo said as the bell rang. "But you can already think about the cast and what part you'd like to play!"

Cassie already knew she wanted to be Hero.

She put her books away in her locker before going to lunch, irritated she had lost sleep over the stupid project. She walked into the cafeteria and spotted her friends at their table. But as she got closer, she saw there was no space for her.

"Hello, guys?" she said, and their faces lifted up to hers. "Where am I supposed to sit?"

"Oh, Cassie!" Cara said. "This other kid sat at our table, so sorry, we forgot . . ."

She didn't have to finish the sentence. They forgot to save a seat for Cassie.

"It's fine. I'll sit somewhere else." Cassie turned away quickly before they could see the sting of tears in her eyes.

"Sit here, Cassie, we can make room," Janice said, scooting down the bench.

But Cassie didn't want to. "I'm good. I've got other friends." She walked away and searched out Nicole. Nicole didn't even bat an eye when Cassie sat next to her, just smiled at Cassie and continued talking to Leigh Anne as though having Cassie there were the most natural thing ever.

Cassie opened her lunch bag and removed the crackers and cheese, wondering at how easily her friends could forget her as if she wasn't even one of them.

Was she one of them?

⚬⚬⚬

Science fair projects were due soon, and Mr. Adams let the students draft out their ideas during class. Cassie knew what she was going to do, so instead of working on her science project, she spent the hour talking with Janice and writing a note to Cara.

"Sometimes I think you and Cara are the only people who actually like me," Cassie said. She drew a long, tall-stemmed flower on the paper with large petals around the center.

"I think we all feel that way. All of us wonder where we fit in."

Cassie gave a grunt and wrote her name on one of the petals, then Janice's name on another, followed by Andrea's. "What does that say about us if our friends aren't always nice?"

"I don't know. Maybe we need new friends."

"Maybe." Cassie wrote Amity on the last petal and then folded up the note for Cara. "I just feel like it takes so much work to be friends. Nobody really understands me and I don't feel accepted. I have to try so hard. I don't think friendship is supposed to be this way."

"That makes me so sad," Janice said. "I think you're right. Friendships should feel natural, and we should feel loved and supported."

"Not judged and self-conscious," Cassie said.

The bell rang, signifying the end of class, and Mr. Adams said, "Don't forget projects are due on Friday!"

Cassie and Janice walked through the hall together, heading to choir. Cassie spotted Cara at the lockers and stepped over to give her the note.

"Oo, a flower!" Cara said, opening the note.

"I was trying to be artistic like you."

Cara's eyes roved over the paper, and she frowned. "My name is not on the flower petals."

"What?" Cassie pulled it back. "How can it not be?" She'd drawn the right number of petals for all her friends.

Cara leaned over her shoulder. "Janice is on two of them." She started laughing and then put a pout on her face. "You don't like me after all."

"Of course I do!" Cassie said, her face burning. She fished a pen out of her bag and crossed out one of Janice's names, quickly replacing it with Cara's. Then she handed the note back. "Here!"

Care batted it away. "I don't want it anymore!" Then she snatched it back. "Give me that."

Everyone was laughing, Cara included, though Cassie felt bad. "It's just because I was talking to Janice the whole time in science, I got confused."

"Don't worry about it. I'll always remember your true feelings." Cara pretended to wipe the tears from her eyes.

❦

Amity and Maureen sat next to Melanie in choir again. The three of them chatted excitedly. Melanie had all kinds of questions about the upcoming dance.

No one even glanced at Cassie. Nobody mentioned that it was her dance they were going to. Nobody told Melanie that if it weren't for Cassie, there would be no dance to go to.

Cassie stewed in silence and wished she hadn't told Amity and Maureen about the dance. She should've just taken Andrea and Cara and let Amity find out when it was over. Then she could feel bad that Cassie hadn't invited her.

The more Cassie thought about it, the more she wanted to get back at Amity and Maureen.

Cassie escaped the choir room ahead of the other girls and went to her locker to switch out books before going to the bus. Andrea joined her.

"I'm so mad about them inviting Melanie to the dance. It's supposed to be our thing."

Cassie slammed her locker and straightened up, energized with anger. "Me too. They totally ignored me in choir and just talked to her like she's their new best friend."

"Urgh."

Amity stepped into the hall then, and her eyes scanned over them until they landed on Cara. "Cara!" she called out. "Can you come over tonight and help me study? I just realized we have a math test tomorrow and I'm so not prepared."

"No," Cara said without any hesitation. "I have to go home today. I bet you can find someone else to help you, though."

The annoyance was so evident in her voice that Cassie and Andrea couldn't help exchanging looks. But Amity did not pick up on it. Instead she turned to Cassie and gave her a wide-eyed smile. "Can you come over and help me? You're really good at math."

Cassie wanted to be like Cara and give a flippant reply, but she craved Amity's friendship even more. Was this the only way she could get Amity to notice her? By being her study buddy? "Let me call my mom and ask her, but I'm sure she'll let me." She would have to, because by now Cassie had missed her bus. She stepped around the corner to make the call, and Cara joined her.

"She's using you. Don't let her walk all over you," Cara hissed.

Cassie nodded even as her mom answered the phone and Cassie requested her permission to stay. Mrs. Jones gave it.

"Great!" Amity said when Cassie told her. She grabbed Cassie's arm and hooked her elbow through, pulling her outside. "I have to ace this test. I know I will if you help me."

Cassie wanted to remain aloof, to hold on to her anger and give Amity a taste of her own medicine, but she lacked the will power. Instead she gave in to Amity's magnetic pull and let herself be dragged to the car.

Now that it was just the two of them, Amity was sweet as pie. She brought up the dance every other question, and it took hours to get through the algebra assignments.

"Do you think Josh will be there?" she asked.

"I'm sure he will be," Cassie said. "He was at the New Year's dance Andrea and I went to."

She liked the spark of jealousy she spotted in Amity's eyes.

"Did Andrea dance with him? I wish I could've gone."

"We all danced with him. Andrea liked some other guys there, though."

"And you? Did you dance with him?"

"A few times."

Amity fiddled with her pencil and squinted her eyes at Cassie. "But you're sure you don't like him anymore?"

Cassie lifted an eyebrow. "So sure. I actually like this other guy now."

Amity put her pencil down, interest piqued. "You like a guy? Who?"

"You don't know him. He lives in Fayetteville."

"Will he be at the dance?"

Cassie allowed a small smile. "I hope so. I think so."

Amity squealed. "I can't wait to meet him!" She paused, the smile falling from her face, and she said, "I've been really worried about you and food. Are you still making yourself throw up?"

A shot of cold ran down Cassie's spine. "No! I don't make myself throw up."

"But you did last year."

Cassie shook her head. "Only once. Maybe twice. It's not something I ever did like a habit."

Amity studied her carefully. "And you don't do it anymore?"

"I even eat." Cassie picked up one of the carrot sticks from the veggie tray in front of them and bit into it loudly. "See?" The truth was, since becoming a vegetarian over the summer, Cassie felt healthy. She could focus on food in a good way now.

Amity looked slightly mollified. "I'm still watching you."

Not that closely, Cassie thought. Or Amity would have noticed that Cassie ate just fine, as long as it wasn't meat.

⟡

Valentine's Day was quickly approaching, and there was only one boy on Cassie's mind. But now she wasn't allowed to call him. So instead she drafted out a letter, hoping it didn't sound too sappy. She talked about how much she had enjoyed getting to know him and hoped they would have the opportunity to talk soon, maybe at the next dance. Then she closed it in an envelope and mailed it.

It usually only took a day for mail to get from Springdale to Fayetteville. If Zack got the letter, read it, and wrote her back right away, she could have a response within three days.

She crossed her fingers and hoped to hear from him soon.

"Spend the night Friday for the dance," Andrea said to Cassie on Tuesday. "We can go up together, since Amity and Maureen are going with Melanie."

That sounded like a plan to Cassie. Despite how friendly Amity had been when they studied together on Monday, she had barely spoken to Cassie once they were back in school. And it wasn't just Cassie. She had taken to sitting at Melanie's table at lunch, and Cara and Andrea were just as mad as Cassie. Even Maureen got her feelings hurt when Amity told her not to sit with her and Melanie.

"Yeah," Cassie said. "I'd love to spend the night." At least she wouldn't have to feel left out.

"I know it's only January," Ms. Berry said in choir, "but it's time to start thinking about if you would like to sing at the end-of-the-year assembly for your schoolmates. This is a special year as you move from junior high to high school, and I would like a good representation of my choir students."

Cassie remembered the students who had sung at the ceremony last year. She was a singer; she sang solos all the time for recitals. She turned in her seat, excited by the prospect but not wanting to do it alone.

"Amity—" she began, but Amity had already turned to Melanie and said, "Hey, let's do something together."

Cassie's heart sank. She stared at Amity, feeling as if she'd been betrayed. How had she lost another best friend?

"Oh, that would be a blast!" Melanie said.

A burning, painful lump rose in Cassie's chest. She pasted on a smile and turned her head. "Maureen, want to do a duet with me at the end of the school year?"

Maureen gave a rapid shake of her head. "No way. I could never sing in front of people."

"Okay," Cassie said, still wearing the forced smile.

So that was that. Either she sang by herself, or she didn't sing at all. Funny how she didn't feel like singing anymore.

⊙〜❀〜⊙

Only a few days later, the holiday itself arrived.

Valentine's Day.

The most depressing day of the year.

Once again, Cassie was single.

Her friends chittered happily around the table, all of them talking about the boys who liked them and had given them a valentine. Even

Janice, who had never had a boyfriend, had gotten a valentine, and Maureen had gotten three.

Cassie sighed and picked up her carrot sticks. Why did nobody love her? Zack had never even written her back.

Andrea noticed her and bumped her shoulder. "Cheer up, Cassie. You'll get a boyfriend again."

"When? I just want someone to think I'm special."

"Aw, poor Cassie," Amity said. "We should call Zack for you."

"I'm sure he's thinking of you, too," Cara said. Her boyfriend went to a different school, but he had still had a valentine gram delivered to her.

"He's not thinking about me at all," Cassie said glumly. "He's probably glad I haven't called him lately."

"He probably thinks you don't like him anymore," Amity said.

"Well, what am I supposed to do?" Cassie snapped. "His mom told my grandma to tell me I need to stop calling, so I wrote him a letter, and he never responded. I have a valentine for him. I'm going to take it to church tonight."

Her friends gave her sympathetic looks.

"I'll call him right now," Andrea said, pulling out her phone.

"No, don't call him." Cassie pushed Andrea's hand away. "I'm sick of begging for somebody to like me. So tired of this. What's wrong with me?"

"It's because you don't have any boobs," Maureen said, which brought laughter from the others and a scowl from Cassie.

"That's so not true," Janice said.

"Besides, no one can tell," Cassie said. "I wear a padded bra." When were her boobs going to grow? She'd been eating real food for at least six months now.

"A padded bra's not the same thing," Amity said. "Guys can tell the difference."

Could they? "Well, that's a stupid reason anyway," Cassie said. "I don't want a guy that's only interested in that."

"And that's why you don't have a guy right now," Janice said. "Because that's all ninth grade boys are interested in."

For some reason, it didn't make Cassie feel any better.

CHAPTER FIFTY-ONE

Conflicts and Love

Cassie tried not to let her depression linger, but each Valentine-less class just made it worse. Was she so unlovable? She ignored the office runners every time they came into the classroom delivering Valentines. And then in sixth hour, the runner stepped up to Cassie's desk.

"Cassie Jones?" the girl said.

Cassie looked at her in surprise. "Yes?" Had she actually received a Valentine?

"I've got some Valentines for you!" The girl proceeded to drop five Valentines on Cassie's desk.

Cassie gave a little gasp of surprise. "Who are they from?"

The girl smiled and shrugged. "Happy Valentine's Day!"

As soon as she left, Cassie flipped open the Valentines, one by one. One from Nicole, one from Riley, one from Janice, one from Luke, and one from Emmett.

Cassie's heart warmed, and the gloom from earlier dispelled itself immediately. Not only did she have friends, she had friends who actually cared about her.

Even though Cassie didn't have church that night, she asked her mom to drive her past the chapel after voice lessons anyway.

"Why?" Mrs. Jones asked. "What's going on at church?"

Cassie checked her purse to make sure the envelope with Zack's Valentine was still inside. "Nothing. I mean, the Fayetteville unit is there."

"Oh." Mrs. Jones threw out the word and arched an eyebrow. "And does that mean there's a certain someone you're hoping to see?"

"Yes. Just want to give him this Valentine."

"All right." Mrs. Jones smiled. "I'll park in front of the door for you."

They didn't speak anymore on the drive, which was good because Cassie was so nervous that she almost threw up. She tried to imagine where in the chapel Zack might be.

Mrs. Jones stopped in front and Cassie flew out, clutching her purse to her side. She stepped into the building and spotted a girl walking the other way.

"Excuse me," Cassie said, and the girl paused.

"Are you in the Fayetteville unit?" Cassie asked.

"Yes," the girl said.

"Do you know Zack Amos?"

"Sure. I know the whole family."

Cassie exhaled, her heart pounding in her chest. "Is he here tonight?"

"Yeah, I saw him and his brothers earlier."

Cassie lost her nerve. She couldn't wander through the church looking for him. She pulled the envelope from her purse and thrust it into the girl's hand. "Will you give this to him?"

Now the girl gave her a strange look. "I can tell you where he is and you can give it to him."

"No, that's okay. I've got to go." Cassie turned around and ran out the doors.

She could only hope the girl would do what Cassie had asked and deliver the note.

❧

Cassie worked on her science project until Mrs. Jones told her it was time to get ready for bed. Just as she put on her pajamas, her phone rang.

It was a little after nine. Cassie walked over to her desk, wondering who would be calling. She'd already talked to most of her friends, helping Amity and Andrea with homework and thanking Janice and Riley for the Valentines.

Her heart give a little pitter patter when she recognized the number. Zack.

She flipped the phone open and tried to sound calm. "Hello?"

"Hey, is this Cassie?" The tenor voice that came through the line was definitely Zack's.

"It is," Cassie said, gripping the phone tightly.

"Hi, it's Zack. I got your Valentine."

Cassie closed her eyes and hoped this was a good thing. "Yeah, well, happy Valentine's Day."

"To you too. Sorry, I would've stepped outside to see you if I'd known you were coming to church."

"You would have?" Cassie squeaked. "But I thought . . ." She'd thought he wasn't interested. "My grandma told me I wasn't supposed to call you anymore."

Zack laughed. "Your letter was really nice. I'm just not very good at writing back. And I don't have a phone, so I don't always think about calling people either. But you can call me. My mom was just joking. She didn't think your grandma would take it seriously."

Cassie's face warmed, and she was both elated and embarrassed. "That sounds like my grandma. She's always confused."

"Anyway, I'll write you. I've got some pictures from the New Year's dance, I'll send you some."

"Oh, that would be fantastic!" Cassie said, practically floating inside.

"I'd like some pictures of you, too," Zack said.

"Sure. I'll write you another letter and send some."

"Perfect. Will you be at the dance?"

"Yes," Cassie sang out. "Will you?"

"Yes. Save a dance for me, okay?"

All of them, Cassie thought. But what she said was, "Absolutely. Happy Valentine's Day!"

"To you too, Cassie."

Cassie closed her phone and fell backward onto her bed, a big smile spreading across her face. Valentine's Day wasn't such a flop after all.

☙ ❧

Cassie could hardly wait to tell her friends the next day at school that Zack had called her. She gathered with Andrea and Cara in the bathroom and told them all about the phone call.

"Do you think he likes you?" Andrea asked, her eyes trained on her reflection as she applied makeup.

"Oh, no," Cassie said. "He's just being nice. He's so sweet."

Amity and Melanie fluttered into the bathroom, giggling about something. Cassie hesitated to speak in front of Melanie, but she wanted to tell Amity. "Guess what? Zack called me yesterday."

"That's nice," Amity said, then she turned slightly so her back was to Cassie.

Melanie looked more interested. "Who is that?"

Cassie's face warmed. "No one."

"Just a guy she has a crush on," Amity said.

Such a jerk! Cassie vowed never to tell Amity anything again.

By the time she went to choir and Maureen also ignored Cassie, sitting with Amity and giggling with Melanie, Cassie decided it was definitely time for new friends.

☙ ❧

Riley called after dinner. After the way her so-called friends were treating her, Cassie wanted to spend some time with Riley, who sometimes felt like the only person who really knew her and accepted her the way she was.

"Give me an hour and I'll take you to her house," Mrs. Jones said.

"How late can you stay?" Riley asked when Cassie showed up.

"A couple of hours. My mom wants me home so I can get a good night's rest." Cassie settled down on Riley's bed with a huff. "Oh! I'm so mad at my friends."

"Why? What did they do?" Riley said down next to her.

Cassie crossed her arms over her chest, feeling self-conscious. "Amity and Maureen ignore me in choir. And Andrea and Amity and Maureen were all making fun of my chest size."

"Why would they do that?"

"Because they're not my friends."

"I'm your friend," Riley said, and Cassie favored her with a smile.

"I know. That's why I am telling you. You never make fun of my body."

Riley shrugged. "I know it's one of the things you have issues with. They should know that too."

"There was a time when you weren't always such a great friend, but I'm really glad I've got you now." Cassie spoke her heart sincerely. In fifth grade Riley had ditched Cassie to go to another girl's birthday party. But that was a long time ago, and both girls had grown and matured.

"I'm just glad you don't hold my mistakes against me."

The girls settled down to watch a movie. Cassie must've fallen asleep, because then her phone was ringing. She lifted her head from the couch and felt around on the ground until her hand closed around the small device.

"Hello?" she said.

Mrs. Isabelle entered the room and started talking to Riley, but Cassie couldn't hear their conversation because of her dad's voice.

"I'm on my way to get you."

"Okay. We're just watching a movie."

Riley had finished talking to her mom and was staring at Cassie with an expectant expression on her face.

"Be there in ten," Mr. Jones said.

"Great." Cassie hung up and looked at Riley. "What?"

"Who was that?"

"My dad." Cassie lifted an eyebrow. "Why?"

"What did he say?"

"That he's coming to get me. Why?"

Riley narrowed her eyes. "Did you hear what my mom said?"

"No . . ." Cassie was starting to worry. "What's going on?"

Riley knitted her brow together. "Brother Brian is leaving. We just found out. He'll be gone by tomorrow."

A knot formed in Cassie's stomach. "No way. He just ate dinner at my house. He said there was lots more work to do here and he wouldn't be leaving for a while."

"I guess he was needed elsewhere. They have a new missionary coming."

Cassie stood up and opened her phone, but she didn't know who to call. She didn't have the missionaries' number, and what could she do? Her eyes burned at the thought of him leaving when they had just barely started get to know each other. "I'll ask my dad when he gets here."

Mr. Jones didn't know what was going on either. "Are you sure?" he said when she told him. "This is the first I've heard of it."

"That's what Riley said. I don't know. He didn't say anything at dinner."

"It must've just happened, then."

"Call them," Cassie begged. "You have to find out what's happening."

"I will," he promised. But he didn't take his cell phone out of his pocket, and Cassie knew she'd have to wait till they got home.

Mrs. Jones sensed the drama as soon as they walked in. "What's going on?" she asked, ushering Mr. Jones and Cassie into the master bedroom.

"Brother Brian has been transferred to another location," Mr. Jones said. "At least, that's what Cassie heard. We're going to find out if it's true."

Mrs. Jones' eyebrows shot up in surprise. "But they don't have transfers until Thursday. Isn't this a bit unusual?"

"It would be, yes. So I'm going to call and find out."

Cassie hovered nearby as her father called, trying not to be too anxious.

"Yes, hello, this is Mr. Jones. I was calling to speak with Brother Brian. Is this Brother Fitsu? Thank you, please put him on the line."

Cassie leaned in closer, straining her ears but unable to pick up the words on the other end.

"Yes, wonderful to speak with you again. We heard a rumor and just wanted to see if you could either confirm or deny it for us. Are you being transferred?" Mr. Jones fell silent for a long moment, then he said, "I see. Well, that's too bad. I know we will be sad to lose you."

"It's true?" Cassie cried. Now she couldn't stop the stinging in her eyes as tears rushed upward. Once a missionary was transferred, they never came back. Cassie would never see him again.

"Why don't you tell her yourself? She's right here." Mr. Jones handed the phone to Cassie and gave her a sad smile. "Say your goodbyes."

Cassie took the phone and went down the hall to the bathroom, where she locked herself in. "Hello? Brother Brian?"

"Hello, beauty," his voice said on the line, warm and friendly. "I guess this is goodbye. I won't see you again."

"It's so sudden," Cassie said. "Why do you have to leave so quickly?"

He cleared his throat. "I don't really understand everything. But some people just feel it's best if I go." He gave a sigh. "I wish I were ten years younger. I'd come back and see you."

"Come back anyway. You're my friend."

He chuckled. "You're sweet. I don't think anyone else would see it that way, though. It's best if this is goodbye."

Why did his leaving make her feel so sad? "Goodbye, then."

"If I get the chance, I'll write you. I want you to remember, Cassie, that I love you. You are a very special person, and you gave me a lot of strength and courage while I was here in Springdale."

Somehow when Brother Brian said those words to her, it was like hearing them from a teacher or a cousin. "Good luck wherever you go. I know you'll have the same success there that you did here."

"Thank you, Cassie. Can I talk to your dad again?"

Cassie took the phone back to her dad, and then her mom held her while she cried.

"Why does he have to go? He's the best missionary we ever had."

"He's certainly the one you formed the closest bond with. And I think, Cassie, that might be why he has to go." Her mom gave her a squeeze. "Remember while they're being traveling ministers, they're not supposed to have a relationship with someone of the opposite sex."

Just because a bond had developed between them, he had to go? Was this her fault? Cassie swore from then on she would keep her distance from the traveling ministers.

CHAPTER FIFTY-TWO
Full of Doubts

On Friday morning, Andrea announced to everyone that Cassie was spending the night with her.

"And we'll go to the dance together," she said as she put on her mascara.

"Well, I'm spending the night at Melanie's house," Amity said. "We're going together."

"You are?" Maureen sputtered, dropping her lip gloss on the scuffed linoleum floor. "I thought you were coming to my house."

"Change of plan," Amity said airily. "We'll pick you up before the dance."

"Cassie and I are going to call all the boys and let them know we're coming," Andrea said loudly.

"Can I come?" Maureen asked.

"No," Andrea said, her voice quite bossy. "This is a private party." She linked her arm through Cassie's and pulled her out of the bathroom.

Cassie caught a glimpse of Maureen's face as they marched past, and she couldn't help the twinge of guilt in her gut. She had wanted Maureen to get a taste of her treatment toward Cassie, but now she felt bad for being a part of it.

Andrea was all happiness when they got to her house. She rummaged through her drawers and pulled out swimsuits. "Let's go swimming!" She tossed one of the suits at Cassie.

"Swimming? Are you crazy?" Cassie picked up the suit with her index finger and thumb, wrinkling her nose at it. "It's February!"

Andrea smirked at her. "In the hot tub on the patio, silly. Come on, we can even use the bubble bath."

Cassie follow Andrea's example, and ten minutes later they were both stretched out in the jacuzzi tub, bubbles billowing around their armpits.

"I am so mad that Amity is bringing Melanie to the dance," Andrea said. "She's going to hit on every guy there."

"It won't matter," Cassie said. "The guys already like us. They're not suddenly going to go crazy for her."

Andrea shot Cassie a look like she was daft. "You don't know guys and cheerleaders. You'll see. They'll take one look at her and forget us."

"That makes no sense," Cassie said. "It's not like she's going to be wearing a badge that says 'cheerleader' across it. They won't even know."

"Cheerleaders act different. They throw themselves at the guys. Kind of like Amity does."

Cassie filed that information away for future use. "So if you're a cheerleader you automatically get the guys?"

Andrea gave an exaggerated nod. "Yep. That's why everyone wants to be one."

Except Cassie, who hadn't known being a cheerleader was the secret to having a boyfriend. Was it too late? Could she still get on that boat?

Andrea reached out of the tub and picked up Cassie's phone. "Call Tyler and ask him if he's going to be there."

Cassie didn't even reach for her phone. "Of course he's going to be there. Tyler and Jason always go to the dances."

Andrea rattled the phone at Cassie. "Call him anyway!"

Cassie sighed and pressed Tyler's number. "Why? You don't even like him."

"Hello?" Tyler's voice said.

Cassie's annoyance melted away when he spoke. "Hi, Tyler. It's me, Cassie."

"Well hello, you Cassie. And I know it's you, your number's in my phone."

Cassie smiled. "Well, good, because yours is in mine."

"What's going on, Cassie with the phone?"

His playful mannerisms warmed her heart, and she settled back into the bubbly water. "Just hanging out with a friend."

"Riley?"

"Not this time. I'm at Andrea's house."

"Andrea?" His tone changed, going from friendly to excited. "Let me talk to her."

"What's he saying?" Andrea asked.

Cassie covered the phone with her hand and said, "He wants to talk to you."

Andrea took the phone from Cassie's hand without another word.

Cassie crossed her arms over her chest, trying not to scowl. That was very different from when Riley had been with her. Why did he like Andrea, anyway? She wasn't interested in him.

Although from the way Andrea giggled and flirted on the phone, Cassie began to think she was wrong. Then she reminded herself that Andrea did this with every guy. It was like a game for her, to see how many of them she could get to like her. She collected them like charms on a bracelet.

Cassie would collect them too if they would only notice her.

"I guess Riley likes you?" Andrea said into the phone, bringing Cassie's attention back the conversation.

"Andrea!" Cassie said. "Don't tell him that!" She hadn't meant to let that slip to Andrea. Riley would kill Cassie for telling!

Andrea moved her shoulder away from Cassie when Cassie tried to hit her. "Do you think she's pretty?" Andrea laughed at whatever Tylor said on the other end. "What about Cassie? Do you think she's pretty?"

Cassie frozen in her second attempt to hit Andrea. She couldn't help leaning closer, anxious to catch Tyler's answer. But she couldn't hear anything on the other side, just a tiny little whisper of his voice.

"Yeah, that happens to everyone," Andrea said. She winked at Cassie. "I'm gonna go now, but we'll see you at the dance tomorrow, right?" Her voice had become suddenly seductive, and Cassie squirmed at how uncomfortable it made her.

"Don't tease him that way," she said.

"Until tomorrow, then!"Andrea snapped the phone closed and put it on the table next to the tub, her eyes sparkling, a big grin spreading across her face. "Don't you want to know what he said?"

"Of course I do." Cassie climbed out of the tub, grabbing a towel and wrapping it around her body as steam rose into the frosty air. "But he likes you, and you're mean to tease him."

"How do you know I don't like him too? I might. I'm just not sure."

Cassie glared at her, and Andrea climbed out beside her, putting the hot tub lid in place.

"He doesn't think Riley is pretty," Andrea said.

"Well, I do," Cassie said, not about to be appeased. She couldn't help adding, "And what about me?"

Andrea lifted an eyebrow, dangling that information in front of Cassie. "Let's go inside and I'll tell you."

Cassie followed Andrea back to her bedroom, and Andrea found two robes for them to snuggle into. They crowded on her white bed, lounging against the pillows.

"Well?" Cassie said, unable to stand it anymore. "What did he say?"

"He said of course he thinks you're pretty. He used to like you, but you never showed any interest."

Cassie gaped at her, stunned. How did she miss that moment? If she had ever known Tyler had a crush on her, she would have gladly crushed on him back.

"Not that any of that matters now," Andrea continued cheerfully, "because you like somebody else." She lifted her gaze and studied Cassie carefully. "Or do you like Tyler?"

The burn crept up Cassie's face, and she stuttered for a moment. "No. No, I don't."

"Not at all?"

"I don't know," Cassie admitted. "I could like him, maybe. Someday. When I'm older. He's like the marrying type, you know? You can like him for now." And her face grew so hot she wanted to dive into the freezer.

Andrea had Cassie's phone out again and was scrolling through it. "Fair enough. You concentrate on Zack and I'll concentrate on Tyler. Here it is. Zack's number."

Panic raced through Cassie, and she reached for the phone. 'Don't call him."

"But you like him." Andrea kept the phone out of reach and pressed the call button.

"But we just talked on Wednesday!" Cassie stood up and tried to get the phone, but Andrea stood as well and turned her back on Cassie.

"Hello, is Zack there? Oh, hi, Zack!"

Cassie backed away, not wanting to make a scene with Zack on the phone. "I swear, Andrea Wall, if you embarrassed me . . ." Cassie's threat trailed off because she had nothing sufficient to say.

"No, you don't know me. I'm a friend of Cassie's. Cassie Jones? Anyway I just wanted to know if you think she's pretty. You do?" Andrea flashed a grin at Cassie. "Do you like her? As in, more than just a friend? Ha ha. Yeah. Would you ever go out with her?"

Cassie groaned and buried her face in her hands. Now she would never be able to face Zack again.

"You would?" Andrea tugged on Cassie's leg. "That's awesome. Are you going to be at the dance tomorrow? Yes, I'll be there with Cassie. Can't wait to meet you!"

Cassie lifted her face and glared at Andrea. "He probably likes you now too!"

"Cassie, he said he thinks you're pretty and that he likes you as more than a friend. He even said he would go out with you!"

"He did?" Cassie blinked in surprise.

"Yes. He likes you!"

A warm, euphoric feeling settled into Cassie's chest, and she leaned back against the bed. "Why does this have to be so hard to figure out?"

Andrea patted her arm. "Let's wait and see how things are at the dance."

The dance. Tomorrow night. Prickles of anticipation, excitement, and dread danced across Cassie's chest. In just a few hours, she would have the chance to be near Zack again, maybe even be in his arms. And she would find out once and for all if he liked her the way she liked him.

Episode 5: Super Star

CHAPTER FIFTY-THREE
Mother May I

Saturday night of the dance finally arrived.

Cassie had spent the day with her friend Andrea, but then her mom wanted her to come home and help with the cleaning before she left for the dance.

Her friends followed, gathering at Cassie's house so they could ride together. Amity brought Melanie, and Janice came for the first time ever. Even Cara decided to come, in spite of Melanie's presence. And of course Maureen and Andrea came.

Cassie did her hair in curlers and then fluffed up the curls as she did a quick head count of her friends. Six. She was bringing six people to the dance.

Mrs. Jones piled everyone into the van and they made the half-hour journey to Rogers, a neighboring city. Cassie sat up front but kept her head turned back to watch everyone. Melanie was being super sweet, and everyone was engaged in conversation except Cara, who just rolled her eyes and remained quiet. Cassie knew it was an expression of irritation that Melanie had come along.

The closer they got to the chapel, the more Cassie thought about Zack. She hadn't danced with him since the New Year's dance. He had promised to be here tonight. That meant something, right? Like he would be there for her? She kept picturing his smile, and something trembled in her chest every time she did.

Mrs. Jones dropped the giggling gaggle of girls off at the chapel, and Cassie was suddenly so nervous she didn't want to step inside.

Andrea looped her arm into hers and said, "Your knight in shining armor awaits. Let's go in."

Cassie forced a smile and bit down so hard on her tongue she tasted blood.

"Ow!" She pressed a finger to the tip of her tongue and examined the bloody mark on her skin. "My tongue is bleeding!"

Andrea clicked like a nervous hen. "How did you do that? Come on, let's go to the bathroom!"

As the other girls made their way into the dance, Cassie and Andrea made a beeline for the bathroom in the back. Cassie used toilet paper to dab at the blood, but all it did was stick to her tongue. She kept her hand under the sink and washed her mouth out with water.

"I'm okay," she said, meeting Andrea's eyes in the mirror. "Let's go in."

"Well, at least you're not nervous anymore," Andrea said

Just like that, Cassie was nervous again.

The dance had already started when they walked in, and Cassie's eyes quickly swept over the crowd. There was Tyler, Riley, Tyler's brother Jason, all of her friends from school, and several other boys, including her neighbor Beckham and his friends. Josh was there, too, and Cassie hoped he wouldn't spend the whole night trying to dance with her.

And then Cassie saw Zack, and her heart skipped a beat. *Leave him alone*, she told herself. *Don't go and harass him*. But she couldn't pull her eyes from his profile.

He turned his face slightly and met her gaze, his mouth instantly turning up in that smile she knew so well. His eyes crinkled, and he waved.

Her face hot, Cassie waved back. Then she turned and intentionally paid closer attention to what her friends were saying so she wouldn't be tempted to stare at him anymore.

The next song came on, and boys congregated around the girls. Cassie glanced around but didn't see Zack. Beckham asked her to dance and she said yes. She buried her thoughts of Zack and focused on Beckham, who was a year younger than she was. After a few minutes of mindless chatter, the conversation went dry, and Cassie waited for the song to be over.

A fast song came on next, and the girls formed a huddle, jumping and throwing their arms in the air together. Cassie laughed and jumped until her legs hurt and she was sweating. She grabbed a drink of punch and downed it just as another song came on.

A slow song. The perfect dancing song. She put the cup down and didn't dare look around. This would be the moment, the perfect moment for Zack to ask her to dance.

Someone was making his way toward her. She saw the approaching figure and told herself not to look, but she wasn't strong enough. Cassie turned her head and met the gaze of Zack as he approached. A radiant smile crossed his face, and she smiled back.

"Cassie," he said, extending a hand. "Would you like to dance?"

"Yes," Cassie breathed.

He took her hand and guided her onto the dance floor. His other hand went to her waist, resting itself just above her hip, and Cassie had never been so aware of the warmth of another person's body. She couldn't tear her eyes away from his. She doubted he felt anything for her—he was just kind and considerate and knew she liked him.

"So what have you been doing these days, Cassie?"

"Nothing interesting," Cassie said, hoping she wouldn't bore him. "I'm finishing a science fair project."

"Are you good at school?"

Her face warmed. "I like school. I try to do well."

"Me too. Grades and my future are important to me."

"What about sports? How's soccer going?"

"I sprained my ankle last fall, so I haven't been playing as much. I have to be careful not to hurt it again."

"That's no good! We love soccer."

Zack's face lit up. "Yeah, you said your dad owns a soccer store. The soccer store? That's your dad's store?"

Cassie nodded. "It's the only one in Springdale and Fayetteville. Even people from Missouri shop there."

"We go there all the time."

"I work there a lot," Cassie said. "I've never seen you."

"Well, I guess it's really my dad that goes. I've been in it before, though. I'll have to look for you next time."

Cassie wondered if she should increase her working hours just in case Zack came in.

"What else do you like to do?" she asked. What she really wanted to ask was how he felt about her. Just thinking about asking made her heart pound fiercely in her chest. They'd been talking to each other on the phone for more than a month now, and she had sent several letters. It was enough time for him to develop feelings for her, wasn't it?

But she could not ask, in spite of Andrea asking him. She didn't trust Andrea, and if he said he only liked her as a friend, she would be devastated.

So she didn't ask.

The song drew to a close, and Zack gave her a big smile. "Thanks for dancing with me." He squeezed her hand before letting go.

"Thank you," Cassie whispered, hating that she had to let go. Already she missed the feel of his hand on hers.

Andrea waved at Cassie, and Cassie started toward her, just as Josh intercepted.

"Cassie—" he began.

"Josh!" Andrea hurried over, squealing. "So good to see you! Have you met Melanie?" Andrea pointed, holding Josh's attention as she indicated the pretty blond next to Amity. "She's new! You should go dance with her!"

"Yeah," Josh said, his eyes focused on her. "I'll go ask her."

"You're welcome," Andrea said as Josh spoke to Melanie and then they took to the dance floor. "Now he likes her instead of you."

For some inexplicable reason, Cassie felt a little jealous not to have all of Josh's attention.

I don't want it, she reminded herself.

She didn't dance with Zack again, and Cassie sighed with disappointment when the dance ended and the lights came on.

"Please help clean up!" a woman with graying brown hair said, rolling a giant trashcan into the room.

Riley popped over to Cassie's side at the table as she cleared cups.

"Tyler didn't even dance with me."

That was because he had spent most of the dance with Andrea, but Cassie kept the thought to herself. "Did you have fun anyway?"

"Sort of. I saw who you were dancing with." She gave Cassie a sly grin.

"Yeah." Cassie smiled at the tablecloth as she pulled it up. She couldn't help the glowing happiness she felt inside. "What do you think of him?" She spun around to face Riley but found somebody else behind her—Zack.

"Think of who?" he asked, blinking at her innocently.

"Oh. I thought you were Riley." Where had she gone? Face hot, Cassie did a quick scan for her friend before spotting her several feet away at the trashcan. "That's Riley," she said lamely, as if that could cover her faux pas.

"But that's not who you were talking about," Zack said, the corner of his lip twirking upward.

She wasn't going to say it, not out loud. "I was talking about some guy she has a crush on."

"Who?"

"Tyler," Cassie blurted before she could think better of it. "But don't tell him!" Even though Andrea already had.

"I won't. Tyler is my friend. His brother Jason and I are the same age."

Cassie should have thought of that! She wondered how she had missed meeting Zack until now. She just hadn't noticed him.

Zack started for the door, and Cassie trailed along behind, still holding a pile of trash. She dumped it in the can.

A woman stood in the doorway watching them. She smiled at Cassie and said, "Hi."

"Hi," Cassie said.

Zack stopped in the hallway in front of Cassie and waited for her to catch up. "Do you know her?"

"No. Do you?"

His eyes crinkled as if at an inside joke. "Yes. She's my mom."

His mom! Cassie whipped around, but she was gone. The same woman who told her grandma to tell Cassie to stop calling him! What did she think of Cassie walking along next to him now? Cassie wanted to kick herself. If only she had known! She turned back to Zack. "Does she know me?"

"Yes."

He left it at that. He didn't tell Cassie how his mom knew her, and Cassie didn't dare ask. She could only hope it was a good thing to be known.

⁂

Cassie stayed after school on Thursday so she could try out for "Much Ado About Nothing." Nicole was there also.

"What part do you want?" Nicole asked.

Cassie glanced around at the few other students lingering in the classroom. "I want the part of Hero," she said. She recognized the other girls and hoped they weren't very good actresses.

"You would be a great Hero. I want Beatrice!"

"Is Jimmy trying out?" Cassie asked, not seeing him in the room.

Nicole shook her head. "I wouldn't try out if he were. We don't really talk to each other anymore."

"That's so sad," Cassie said. She'd had the same experience herself. After you broke up with a boy, you weren't friends anymore.

It only made her really glad she had never gone out with Miles. He was one of her best friends now.

A few boys shuffled into the room, Emmett and Luke and Andrew and Matt. She waved, and they came over to talk to them.

"What part are you trying out for?" Andrew asked her.

"Hero. You?" Cassie liked Andrew, but only as a friend. She crossed her mental fingers he wasn't trying out for the part of Claudio, Hero's love interest. It would be much more exciting to have a cute boy to play against.

"Benedick."

"I'm trying out for Beatrice," Nicole said. "If I get the part, we'll be lovers." Her face reddened, but everyone else burst out laughing.

Ms. Talo clapped her hands and got everyone's attention. "Okay, I'm going to have you read the part you're trying out for with your classmates. We'll start with anyone trying out for Beatrice. Come stand over here."

Nicole and several other girls, including Cassie's friend Jaclyn, stepped forward. They all read the same monologue. Cassie thought Nicole acted the part the best and put the most emotion into her words.

"Wonderful. Now everyone who's trying out for Benedick."

Several boys stepped forward. "I'm trying out for both parts. Is that okay?" Luke asked.

"That's fine. You'll just be up here again in a little bit."

They ran through their monologues, and Cassie chewed on the sides of her finger as she realized she would be up next.

"All right, then!" Ms. Talo said, her eyes sweeping the remaining girls. "Who is trying out for the part of Hero?"

Cassie didn't raise her hand. She looked around at the three other ninth-grade girls and did a quick comparison. Taller, prettier, smarter. Were they dynamic? Slowly she raised her hand, adding herself to the mix.

Ms. Talo smiled. "Let's get started."

Since Cassie had raised her hand last, she got to go last. This only made her more nervous as she analyzed the other girls' performances. But it also gave her an advantage. *I should say that line differently*, she thought. And then, *there wasn't nearly enough emotion in her voice when she said that*.

When it was her turn, she took a deep breath, smoothed her hands on her jeans, and walked to the front of the classroom. She wished she had memorized the monologue given to them, but she hadn't. She looked at the words and said them with as much emotion as she could. "'Now, Ursula, when Beatrice doth come, as we do trace this alley up and down, our talk must only be of Benedick. When I do name him, let it be thy part to praise him more than ever man did merit.'"

Cassandra pressed her hand to her chest as she spoke and batted her eyelashes, feigning passion. She looked around the room and spoke to her classmates as she read the last line: "'Now begin, for look where Beatrice like a lapwing runs close by the ground to hear our conference.'"

Ms. Talo clapped enthusiastically. "Fantastic job. Now, who is trying out for Claudio?"

Cassie took a careful breath as she rejoined Nicole in the back of the room. Nicole reached over and gave her elbow a pinch.

"You were the best. I'm sure you'll get the part."

"You were too," Cassie said loyally, although she couldn't recall Nicole's performance much anymore. Her heartbeat still thumped in her ears, adrenaline slowly receding. She studied the boys trying out for Claudio, trying to decide which one she would rather play against. Emmett was her friend and had been for years. She didn't know Matt very well. He was in second hour computer class with her and Jaclyn, but mostly she remembered him because whenever he passed their table at lunch, he took the time to flirt with Amity. At least he was cute, with blond hair parted on the side and an elfish face.

Stop analyzing them, she told herself. *You haven't gotten that far yet.* But she hoped she would.

CHAPTER FIFTY-FOUR
Blue Weather

There was a big argument going on in the bathroom when Cassie got to school the next day.

"It was the stupidest thing," Janice was saying to Andrea. "You should not have done that."

"It was just one time," Andrea said, sounding totally put out. "Everybody does it."

"Not me," Cara said. "My parents would ground me for life."

"What?" Cassie asked. "Everybody does what?"

Andrea rolled her eyes and pressed her lips together.

"Andrea smoked pot yesterday," Janice said, chastisement heavy in her voice.

"And my parents overreacted," Andrea said. "Total overkill."

Cassie's mouth dropped open. "Andrea! How could you do that?"

"I knew I couldn't tell you. You always overreact. You're like my mom."

The comment hurt, and Cassie closed her mouth before saying anything else.

"Maybe if you listened to your mother, your friends wouldn't have to mother you," Janice said.

"What's going on?" Amity come into the bathroom.

Cassie turned. "Andrea smoked pot yesterday."

Amity gave a gasp. "Andrea, what happened to just say no?"

"Seriously?" Andrea said. "All I did was try it."

Amity looked wounded, and Cassie was glad to see someone else on her side.

All through first hour, Janice upbraided Andrea, though Andrea just rolled her eyes.

By the time the girls met up for lunch, though, the sensitive issue seemed to have been forgotten. Cara bumped her hips against Andrea's, and they sat next to each other at the table. Amity kept flashing a mirror at Andrea and giggling like crazy at Andrea's silly faces.

None of them spoke to Cassie. They giggled and laughed together through lunch and fourth hour without even glancing Cassie's way. By the time fourth hour ended, she found herself fighting tears. Here she was surrounded by friends and yet feeling so alone. She slipped into the bathroom before fifth hour and called her mom.

"Cassie? What's wrong?" Mrs. Jones said, surprise in her voice.

"Nothing, nothing," Cassie said, not wanting to admit the way she felt. "My science fair project is due tomorrow and I have a lot left. Can you pick me up? I'm really anxious about getting it done."

Silence was the only response, and Cassie worried her mom would say no. But then Mrs. Jones said, "Okay. I'll be there in half an hour."

"Thank you," Cassie breathed out, immediately grateful she wouldn't have to put on a happy face for seventh hour.

She checked out during fifth hour. Her mom pried at her in the car, trying to discover if there was something wrong. Cassie disclosed how terrible her friends were making her feel and left it at that. Then she buried herself in her science fair project, writing up reports on how well the solar energy warmed the objects left inside her plastic containers.

Sixth hour went by, and then seventh hour, and then school was out. Cassie checked her phone every few minutes, but nobody texted her. Nobody called to make sure she was okay or to see what had happened to her.

The wound that was her feelings grew larger.

⊙⌒◈⌒⊙

Cassie stayed up late printing her essays for her science fair project. She designed beautiful color graphs on the computer, and then hit the print button. When they came out of the printer, however they were outlines with no color at all.

"Daddy?" she called. "Why isn't this printing right?"

Her dad came into the computer room and examined the printer. "Looks like we're out of color ink. Try printing it in black-and-white."

Cassie looked at the full-color graphs she had designed. "That won't look nearly as good. "

"I don't know what your options are."

Walmart was open 24/7. Cassie opened her mouth to suggest it, but her dad quickly said, "I'm not going to the store right now. It's ten o'clock at night."

Cassie looked back at her computer with desperation. "I guess I'll try and print it in black-and-white."

The graphs looked terrible without color. The shadowing differences between the shades was so slight that no strong conclusion could be drawn from looking at the graph.

"This is not going to work," she said, getting anxious. She spotted a box of markers tucked away on the shelf and got an idea. "I'll just have to draw them."

Her dad came into the office half an hour later as Cassie sat on the floor with a ruler and a pencil, carefully stenciling the bars for her graph.

"You're going all out, aren't you?" he said.

Cassie didn't look at him as she slowly colored in the first bar. "This has to be perfect."

It was after midnight before she finished. She put the entire trifold project by the front door so she wouldn't forget it and then fell into bed and closed her eyes.

❦

Cassie struggled to wake up in the morning, but when she remembered her science fair project was due, a jolt of adrenaline rocked her from her bed. She brushed her teeth and pulled on the skin around her eyes, trying to look more awake.

Cassie didn't say anything to her friends the next day about her feelings, and nobody asked her where she'd gone.

She didn't breathe easy until she turned her project in to Mr. Adams' classroom before first hour. She hoped she had done a good enough job explaining solar energy and the power of the sun. Mr. Adams glanced at her posterboard long enough to check her off in the gradebook, but he didn't say anything else.

In first hour Cassie said good morning to Janice and Andrea and then sat down, blurry-eyed, and tried to focus on her work. Coach Benson drew on the board something about the legislature, and Cassie's eyelids shuddered over her eyes. She forced them open, but her head and her chest pulled on her like ten pounds of gravity. She let her head fall forward to the desk, her hair cascading around her like a curtain and closing out the light of the classroom.

Coach Benson's voice jarred her awake. "I know I must be really interesting you, since half of you are snoring or sleeping."

Cassie sat up, feeling guilty, but the rest of the classroom laughed, and she felt some relief that she wasn't the only one.

"Late night?" Janice asked.

"Yes." Cassie sighed. "Just trying to get my science fair project done."

"I'll be posting the cast list for 'Much Ado About Nothing' when school is out today," Ms. Talo said in third hour.

Crapola. Cassie had been so anxious about science fair and her friends she had almost forgotten about the play. Now she had something else to be nervous about.

Amity was so proud of her project that she didn't stop talking about it all through lunch. "I tested ten different shampoos so I could prove once and for all what they do for hair. And now I know which one I'll be using because it makes my hair the softest."

Miles stopped by the lunch table as the girls were putting away their trash. "I saw your project, Cassie. The one on solar energy?"

Cassie's face warmed. "Yeah, that one was mine."

"It looks really neat."

"Thanks. What did you do yours on?"

"Product insulation. I practiced on an egg. All the projects are up in the gym. You should go see them."

"I will."

⁂

Mr. Adams congratulated everyone on their projects in sixth hour, telling them what a great job they had done and how they had exceeded expectations.

"The science fair projects are in the gym, and I encourage all of you to look at them. Your science teachers will be judging them and deciding who continues on to the high school science fair."

Cassie barely heard what he said. She tapped the eraser of her mechanical pencil on the desk, wondering if Ms. Talo had already posted the cast results. Was it worth checking her English class before going to choir? *No*, she told herself. Ms. Talo said after school. She could wait one more period

Cassie sat on the edge of the soprano section in choir, as close as she could get to Riley and Janice in the alto section. Amity and Maureen didn't talk to her, as usual. She felt lonely, sad, and rejected, and even her anticipation over the cast list diminished. Cassie scooted closer to Riley, put her head on her shoulder, and let her emotions get the best of her. Riley patted her arm but didn't say anything.

Amity noticed, just as Cassie had known she would. If there was drama or gossip, Amity was always quick to get in the middle of it.

"Cassie, what's wrong?" she said, moving over to Cassie and pulling on her shirt.

Cassie brushed her off, and Riley said, "You're not who she wants to talk to right now."

Amity disregarded Riley's words. "I am closer to her than you are."

Riley's eyes narrowed. "Looks like she prefers me to you."

"Cassie?" Amity said. "Want to sit by me and Melanie?"

Cassie shook her head.

Amity waited a moment as if she thought Cassie might change her mind, then she patted Cassie's arm and said, "I'll call you tonight."

Cassie managed to dry her tears and finish up the day in choir, and she and Riley walked out together.

"So what's wrong?" Riley asked.

"Nothing's wrong, really. I just feel so lonely."

"You have me," Riley said.

"I know it," Cassie said. After all she and Riley has been through in the past five years, Riley was more like a sister that a friend.

She said bye to Riley and then ran down the hallway toward her English class. She had to hurry or she would miss the bus, but she had to know the results.

A sheet of paper was taped to the door. Cassie held her breath and put her finger to the top name. *Hero*, it said. *Cassandra Jones.*

"Yes!" she cried so loudly that several students around her turned to look. A few other kids were also looking at the audition list.

"Did you make it?" Nicole ran over.

"I did!" Cassie turned back to the list, anxious to see who else had made it before she had to run to the bus. "So did you! You're Beatrice!"

Nicole squealed and the two girls hugged and jumped up and down.

"Who are we playing opposite?"

Cassie hadn't even checked to see who got the part of Claudio. She turned back to the list. "Matt."

"I'm playing against Andrew."

"He's a good choice. He's nice." They'd done a choir program together a few years ago, and he had always been friendly to Cassie. "I better get out of here now, or I'll miss my bus!"

"Well, congratulations, Cassie! See you later!"

Cassie sprinted for her bus, feeling happier than she could recall feeling in several days.

❦

"Church is different this weekend," Mrs. Jones said at dinner. "It's a regional conference."

"How is that different from the usual conferences we have?" Cassie asked, putting a little bit of ranch on her plate to dip her broccoli in.

"Usually conferences are just those cities around us, like Rogers and Bentonville. But this one will have all of those cities, plus most of the cities in southern Missouri and even a few from Kansas and Tennessee."

"That's a lot of people!"

"Exactly my point. So we have to leave early because the conference is being held in Joplin."

Cassie had known there was a conference coming, but she had assumed it would be the normal kind. "I'll never find Zack," she sighed.

One of the best parts about conferences was seeing her friends from other units, and she'd look forward to seeing him. She'd written him a letter but hadn't mailed it yet, and so far she hadn't received anything from him.

It's no big deal, she reassured herself. *I'll get the chance to talk to him later.*

She went to bed feeling more at peace with herself and how the day had gone.

Amity never did call.

⚬⟶⟶※⟵⟵⚬

Sunday morning they left early for church because Joplin was an hour away and they still had to pick up Grandma in Fayetteville. Grandma asked about Zack the whole way, and Cassie regretted every telling her about him.

They finally arrived at a giant basketball stadium where the conference was being held. It was already so crowded, and an usher guided Cassie's family upstairs to the balcony. As they walked past the rows of people already seated, Cassie spotted her friend Elise.

"Elise!" Cassie said, waving. The last time she she'd seen Elise was at church camp over the summer, when Elise still sported black hair and a partially shaved head. Cassie was relieved to see the natural blond growing in, and when Elise turned her face toward Cassie, she looked healthier than before, less melancholy.

"Cassie!" Elise said, her eyes lighting up. She stood up and pushed past her family to reach Cassie in the aisle. She flung her arms around her neck, and Cassie laughed.

"You look great!" Cassie said. "How have you been?"

"I think I'm good." Elise nodded. "Yeah, I'm doing well."

Cassie opened her mouth to say something more, but Mrs. Jones called out, "Cassie! Let's go!"

Cassie gave Elise an apologetic smile. "I'll catch up with you later, okay?"

Elise nodded. "I'm sure I'll see you soon!"

The two girls waved, and then Cassie followed her parents up the stairs leading to the balcony.

Cassie's little sister Emily nudged her. "Cassie, isn't that Zack?"

Cassie turned around to look before she thought better of it.

Sure enough, she spotted Zack and his family coming up the balcony steps behind them.

What were the chances? Cassie couldn't believe it. Zack saw her staring and a smile crossed his face. Cassie couldn't help returning it, then she turned around and hurried up the steps ahead of him.

Her family filed into their seat, and Cassie saw her grandma's eyes latch onto the Amos family as they sat in the row in front of them. Grandma let out a little chuckle.

"Cassie, Zack is here. You don't even have to call him to talk to him," she said, quite loudly.

Cassie wanted to disappear into her chair or sink it to the ground in embarrassment. Both Zack and his mother turned around. Zack's eyes found hers, and he gave her a reassuring wink, but that in no way lessened the shame burning her cheeks. Why couldn't she have a normal, happy, kind grandma like everyone else?

In spite of Grandma's antics, Cassie was able to focus on the speakers during the conference, all while sending surreptitious glances in Zack's direction. He smiled a lot at his brothers, but he also spent a good amount of time listening and taking notes.

Cassie decided she had the best seat. She could sit and study him in profile without him knowing. And she really liked his smile.

As soon as conference ended, the two families stood up to leave. Before Cassie could react, her grandma grabbed Zack's arm.

"Talk to my granddaughter," she said. "She really likes you."

CHAPTER FIFTY-FIVE

Super Early

Now Cassie knew she was going to die. But Zack just said, "Okay," and then stepped away from his family to talk to her. Except Cassie had no idea what to say now. "Hi," she said, feeling like idiot.

"Hi," Zack said. "Pretty nice conference."

"Yes," Cassie said. She would've agreed with anything he said.

The conversation stalled. Zack looked down, shuffling his feet, then looked up again. "Well—" he began.

Before Cassie had to try to think of something more to say, Annette ran up the stairs and grabbed her arm.

"Cassie! We are all in the car waiting!"

Cassie said a mental prayer of gratitude and told Zack, "I'll see you later, then."

"Yeah. I'll see you."

Cassie allowed Annette to pull her down the stairs, wishing she had the ability to talk with boys as easily as Amity and Andrea did.

❦

"Cassie," Mr. Adams boomed at the beginning of sixth hour, "please see me after class."

Cassie never could tell if her teachers were angry with her or not. Certainly she hadn't done anything wrong. She nodded meekly and tried to ignore the curious stares her classmates were giving her.

Mr. Adams handed out test scores, and even though she'd gotten a 96% on it, Cassie worried.

"You'll be okay," Janice said. "I'm sure it's nothing."

Cassie smiled and nodded, trying to feel reassured. Even Jaclyn gave her a "good luck" smile as she walked out of the room.

Cassie put away her pens and pencils and closed her binder, then moved to the front of the classroom. "Yes, Mr. Adams?"

He looked at her over his white mustache, his blue eyes very serious. And then he gave a little smile, and the corners of his eyes crinkled up. "Congratulations. Your science fair project was selected to move on to the high school round."

"Really?" Cassie said, hardly believing it. Sure, she spent the past week working hard on that project, but she hadn't given it much thought before then. She thought of Jaclyn, who'd spent the past month researching the possibilities of light speed and warp drive. "What about Jaclyn?"

Mr. Adams shook his head. "I was only able to select one student per classroom, and yours is the one I picked."

So if Jaclyn had been in a different classroom, maybe hers would've been picked? That didn't seem fair, but Cassie pushed aside the guilt and allowed herself to feel pleased with his selection. "Well, thank you! What do I have to do now?"

"This Friday instead of coming to school, go straight to the high school. I'll be setting up science fair in the gym. Take your whole project."

Cassie nodded enthusiastically. "Okay. Great!" She held her binder to her chest and hurried from the classroom before she was late to seventh hour.

"What did he want?"

Cassie pulled up short, startled to see Jaclyn waiting in the hallway. "Oh." How could she tell her? "He said my project gets to move on to the high school judging."

Jaclyn must've suspected it, because she didn't look surprised at the news. But disappointment glittered in her eyes. "He didn't say anything to me about mine."

Cassie didn't know what to say to that.

Jaclyn blinked, and a solitary tear trekked down her face. "You only worked on yours for a week. It wasn't even that important to you." There was no masking the bitterness in her voice.

Cassie swallowed. "I'm sorry."

Jaclyn blinked again and then shrugged. "It's not your fault. I'll be fine. Good luck." She turned and continue down the hall, but that didn't stop Cassie from feeling bad.

❦

Cassie's first drama practice was after school on Monday.

She stepped into the classroom with Nicole, more nervous than when they had the auditions. Jaclyn was there also, playing one of the extras.

The boys had already come in, Andrew and Matt and Kevin. Matt didn't glance at Cassie but joked with Andrew and Kevin. Matt's blond hair fell in his face, and his big grin made him look more impish than usual.

"Has everyone been studying their lines?" asked Ms. Talo.

Cassie nodded, as did everyone else.

"Great. Then let's run through the scene where Beatrice and Benedick are arguing in the chapel."

Nicole and Andrew ran through their lines splendidly, until the part where Andrew said, "I will stop your mouth."

He put his hands out to grab Nicole's face, and Cassie caught her breath. This was the moment where he was supposed to kiss her.

But Nicole pulled away and began to giggle. She put her hands up to her face and wouldn't stop laughing.

Ms. Talo put her hands on her hips. "Oh, don't be such ninnies. Give her a good kiss, Andrew."

Andrew's face flushed red. He leaned toward Nicole again, but she shied back, laughing so hard her whole body shook. Finally Andrew grabbed her hand and kissed the back of it.

Cassie thought she would cry from laughing. Ms. Talo did not look pleased.

"You're going to have to practice that kiss. That wasn't good."

Nicole only laughed harder.

Ms. Talo turned toward Cassie and Matt. "Your turn. Let's hope you do better. Let's run through the scene where Claudio believes he is marrying someone else and then he discovers it is actually Hero."

Cassie stepped forward, running through the lines in her head. This was the wedding scene. After the horrible act of betrayal, Claudio believed Hero had died of heartbreak. Realizing the error of his ways, he agreed to marry someone else of her father's choosing. When the veil lifted and he realized it was actually his beloved, a happy reconciliation occurred.

Matt stepped up as well, all joviality gone from his face.

"Look her in the eye, but remember she has a veil over her face, so you don't know who she is," Ms. Talo said.

"'Give me your hand before this holy friar. I am your husband if you like of me,'" Matt said, looking her in the face and extending his hand.

The seriousness in his expression made Cassie catch her breath. He was a very good actor.

She reached up her hands and pulled up an imaginary veil. "'And when I lived I was your other wife—'" she began, just as Matt gasped and fell to his knees.

"'And when you loved—'" Cassie tried to continue.

"Hug her! Hug her!" Ms. Talo said.

Matt thrust his arms around Cassie's waist, his hair pressing into her belly.

"Not like that!" Ms. Talo shrieked as the other kids in the room busted up into laughter.

"I can hear it kicking!" Kevin said.

Cassie lost her focus and began laughing as well.

"Did you get a heartbeat?" Andrew teased.

Face turning pink, Matt jumped to his feet.

"Now hug her!" Ms. Talo said.

Matt crushed Cassie to him in a hug, but she was no longer into the scene. She kept picturing his head against her stomach listening for a baby and laughed so hard she was afraid she'd pee her pants.

Ms. Talo gave a great sigh. "We'll call that a day. Go home and practice those lines so we can get them correct, and I'll see you guys tomorrow."

Cassie joined Nicole and Jaclyn in the back, both of them holding their bags and laughing.

"That was way more fun than I expected it to be," Cassie said.

"That was the best after-school activity I've ever gone to," Nicole said.

⟋⟍⟋⟍

Cassie could not remember the last time she was excited about going to Wednesday night activities, but tonight was the Fayetteville/Springdale dance. Zack would be there. He had to be there.

Riley waited in the foyer for Cassie, and when Cassie arrived, the two girls went in together. The first person they saw was Tyler. Cassie waved and went over to talk to him while Riley fidgeted behind her.

"Hey," Tyler greeted. "Zack is not here."

Cassie's face flushed. "Zack?"

"He is who you're here to see, right?" Tyler raised an eyebrow.

Cassie sputtered slightly. "I'm here to see a lot of people."

"But then Zack especially." Tyler wiggled his eyebrows up-and-down.

Cassie had never told Tyler she liked Zack. How did he know?

One of the adult leaders stood up and silenced everyone so they could say a quick prayer, and then the upbeat music began for the dance. Tyler's eyes focused somewhere past Cassie's head.

"Never mind. Looks like he's here."

Cassie spun around and saw Zack and his brother walking in. He caught her eye and flashed that smile she found so endearing. Behind her, Tyler chuckled.

"Looks like you can relax now."

Cassie didn't know if she wanted to smack him or hug him. But Tyler walked away before she could do either.

It was a much smaller dance since it was in Fayetteville instead of

Rogers, with only the two units there. After half an hour Cassie had already danced with most of the boys there, but Zack so far had not asked her. She took a water break and then went over to the chairs to reapply her lipstick. Riley collapsed next to her with a sigh.

"I don't think Tyler is going to ask me today," she said sadly.

Tyler had already asked Cassie twice. "I'm sure he will." He couldn't avoid Riley all night. "Zack hasn't asked me either."

Riley clicked her tongue. "I think that's about to change."

Cassie lifted her head to see Zack approaching. She smiled at him, her heart starting its crazy pitter-patter, and then Zack said, "Will you dance with me?"

"Yes," Cassie said, somehow more nervous now than she had been last time. Her hand trembled when she took his, and when he led her onto the dance floor, her heart pounded in her throat.

"You look really nice," he said.

"Thanks. You too." Then her face flushed hot. Was that weird? It was okay for guys to say things like that, but what about girls?

"My mom said you seem nice," he added.

Oh groan. If only Cassie had known that was his mom. She would've talked to her a little more.

Zack asked about her siblings and they talked about his brothers, who he called "annoying."

"Do you drive?" Cassie asked.

"I have my license, but I don't have my own car. So I use my mom's van sometimes."

Cassie remembered Josh's beaten up car. She decided driving a van would be better. "What kind of car do you want?"

Zack shrugged. "I haven't thought about it. I'm saving my money up to be a traveling minister. I want to serve people."

Of course he did. Could he be any more perfect?

The dance ended, and Zack squeezed her hand. "Thanks for the dance, Cassie."

"Anytime," she breathed. She watched him walk away, a giddy happiness flooding up inside of her. She turned around and spotted Tyler talking to his brother Jason. She bounced over to them and grab Tyler's arm, then pumped it up and down.

"He danced with me! He danced with me!"

Tyler laughed with her. "See? Aren't you glad you came?"

Cassie danced with a few more people, and then Riley came over and pulled her to the corner.

"Cassie, you're not going to believe this," she said.

"What?" Cassie was still floating on cloud nine, but something in Riley's expression told her it was serious.

"I overheard Tyler talking to Zack. He was telling him that you're obsessed about him and won't stop talking about him and really like him."

Cassie froze, absolutely stunned. Tyler wouldn't do that to her. He was her friend. "Are you sure?"

"I heard it myself."

"Hey, Cassie!" Tyler came over then, grinning at them. "You won't believe—"

Something inside Cassie snapped. Before she even knew what she was doing, her hand came out and slapped Tyler across the face.

A gasp rippled out from all of the kids standing around them, including Sue and Michelle and Jason. It seemed like everyone had witnessed it. Tyler's mouth dropped open, and then his face turned a funny color, and he turned around and stomped away.

"You hit him!" Riley said.

Shame broiled through Cassie. She hurried after Tyler. "Tyler, I'm so sorry—"

Michelle grabbed Cassie's arm. "Leave him alone. It's going to take a while to cool off." Then she flounced over to Tyler and put her arm around him.

All of Cassie's earlier elation vanished. Somehow she had managed to ruin this night.

CHAPTER FIFTY-SIX
High School Day

Friday morning Cassie caught a ride with Jason and Tyler to their house after the early church class so Jason could take her to the high school for her science fair project. Amity and Miles had also been selected to move on, and she was relieved she'd spend the day with friends.

Tyler didn't say a word to her in the car. As soon as they were in his house, he went to his room and closed the door.

Cassie looked at Jason and gave a wobbly smile. "He won't be mad at me forever, will he?"

Jason looked at her kindly. "I would say to give him a month. He's quite upset."

A month! Wasn't he being a bit overdramatic? "Why is he so angry?"

Jason lowered his voice conspiratorially. "My dad said slapping a guy is one of the worst things you can do to him. I think you wounded his pride quite a bit."

"But we'll be okay, right? We'll go back to being friends again?"

Jason brushed her off. "Of course you will. He won't stay mad forever. How can he? We're like family."

Cassie hoped Jason was right.

She rode around with Jason while he took Tyler to school, though Tyler said not a word. Then Jason drove them both to the high school. Cassie gaped as she saw the sprawling campus in front of them. This was where she would go to school next year. It was a bit overwhelming to think about.

"Do you know where you're supposed to go?" Jason asked.

Cassie looked at the science fair project behind her and back at the massive campus. "I haven't a clue."

Jason parked the car. "Well, I guess we better start looking."

She picked up her project and held it under arm. "We're just going to walk through the school?" Good thing she didn't know anyone. Everyone was sure to stare.

"Unless you figure out where you're supposed to go."

Cassie racked her brain for a clue, but she couldn't remember a thing.

They started at the front entrance and went through a long hallway. Jason poked his head in several classrooms and shook his head each time. "Nobody here."

He stopped and asked a teacher walking by. "Do you know where the science fair projects are being displayed?"

"I'm not sure. Let me get with one of the science teachers."

"Jason, you don't have to stay and help me," Cassie said, mortified this was taking so long.

"It's no problem. I want to make sure you get where you're supposed to be."

The teacher came back. "All the science fair projects are in the old gym across the courtyard."

"Thanks," Jason said. He turned to Cassie. "Do you want me to walk you there?"

Cassie absolutely did. This mammoth of a school building intimidated her. But she shook her head. "I can make it. Thank you so much for your help."

"Anytime. Good luck." Jason waved and went down a different hallway.

Cassie watched him go, trepidation rising in her chest. Where was the old gym?

She walked back outside and went past a large auditorium. Students entered it in long lines. Was this it? It didn't look like a gym.

And then she spotted Miles walking into a building on the other side of the grass. Cassie waved her arm. "Miles!" she called.

He turned around, project under his arm, and smiled. "Hi, Cassie." He waited for her to join him.

"Is this where we're supposed to be?" she asked, peering around him.

"This is the gym." He led the way inside, and Cassie followed.

Tables had been set up and students were already opening their projects on top. Miles found an open table.

"There's a space next to me," he said. "If you want to set up here."

"Thanks." Cassie opened her display. "I'm saving a spot for Amity also." She put her purse down next to her trifold. "What's going on in the big auditorium?"

"I don't know. Let's check it out." Miles went back to the doors and surveyed the groups of kids. "Must be a field trip. I saw a Fayetteville bus parking behind it when we drove by."

Fayetteville! That meant Zack might be there! "Let's go closer."

Miles followed her across the courtyard over to the auditorium.

They looked like younger kids, seventh or eighth graders. Still Cassie lingered and watched the buses arrive, just in case any from the high school came.

"We better go back," Miles said. "We don't want to miss the judging."

"Amity should be here by now." Cassie looked at her phone. Amity hadn't texted yet. Hopefully she hadn't forgotten.

The judges had arrived by the time Cassie and Miles went back in, and they were putting name tags in front of each project.

There was still no sign of Amity, and Cassie was beginning to panic. Amity would forfeit her place if she didn't show.

And then, just as the judge walked past Cassie's spot, Amity burst in.

"I'm here, I'm here!" she said, sliding to a halt next to Cassie's table.

"You're late," the judge said, eyeing her distastefully.

"I know, I know. Sorry." She set up her trifold poster and flashed a brilliant smile. "I'm ready!"

"Name?"

"Amity Stafford."

The official wrote her name on a sign and taped it to the front of the table. "We'll have judges out until lunchtime, after which you're free to go back to school."

Both girls nodded, but as soon as the official walked away, Amity shook her head. "I'm not going back to school."

"No way," Cassie agreed.

They spent the morning with Miles, walking around and looking at the different projects. Matt was there too, and Cassie waved at him. He gave a small wave in return, then continued messing with his project.

Cassie turned to Amity. "Amity, tell me about the time you slapped that guy last year."

Miles turned around, his eyes bulging. He looked at Amity. "You slept with a guy last year?"

"What?" Amity exclaimed. "I did not."

"No, no, no!" Cassie waved her hands back and forth. "That's not what I said! I wanted to know about when she *slapped* a guy."

Miles burst out laughing. "I thought that was odd! First that Amity would sleep with a guy, and second that you would actually just talk about it, Cassie!"

Amity laughed also. "What did you want to know?"

"How long was he mad at you? Did he ever get over it?"

"He didn't, I guess. We weren't friends after that, but I didn't care.

There are other guys."

Yes, there were. But losing Tyler's friendship didn't seem like an option. Cassie looked at Miles, the boy she had crushed on for years and was now one of her really good friends. She wouldn't want to lose his friendship either. "Would you forgive me, Miles, if I slapped you?"

He gave her an odd look. "Why would you do that?"

"Just say I did. Would you forgive me?"

"Yeah, probably. You're Cassie. You're my friend."

Such a genuine answer. Cassie hoped Tyler would come to the same conclusion.

"Oh, there's a judge at my table!" Amity said. She rushed off. Cassie looked over and spotted an old woman examining Amity's project.

"Guess I'll get back to mine also," Miles said.

"Same."

A man was reading Cassie's poster when she got there.

"Hi," Cassie said. "I'm Cassandra Jones."

"Hello, Cassandra. This looks like quite an experiment you've done."

Cassie smiled. "It was challenging but fun."

He nodded. "I can tell you're a very thorough student."

She didn't say anything, but remained silent while he read through every item on her poster.

"Great job, Cassandra. So tell me, why do you think there was a difference between heating something in a plastic bottle and heating something in a glass bottle?"

Crapola. He expected her to actually know that? She drew upon what research she could remember. "I can't be sure, but the plastic bottle was thinner and allowed the sun rays to enter at a different angle. Possibly it filtered less of them also. That might be why the contents of the plastic bottle got warmer faster."

"Very good. You spent a lot of time on this. It's nice to see such dedication." He wrote a few things on his clipboard and walked away.

Cassie let out an exhale. And she giggled. Worked hard on this? She should have worked hard on this.

Amity ran over as soon as he left. "What did he say? Your guy seemed so nice. Mine was an old hag!" She crossed her eyes and stuck out her tongue.

"But there are only three people in your division. You know you'll place. There are like seven in mine."

"You'll make it." Amity grabbed her hand. "Come on. Let's find my mom and go to lunch."

⟡

"Congratulations, Cassie," Mr. Adams said when she walked into sixth hour on Monday.

Cassie drew up short, suspecting what he meant but not wanting to jump to conclusions. "On what?" She glanced around and was relieved to see Jaclyn hadn't come in yet.

"On your science fair project." A smile sprouted behind his mustache. "You got first place. You get to go on to regionals."

Cassie clutched her book to her chest and let out an excited squeak. "Regionals! I can't believe it!" She'd worried that Mr. Adams picked her because she was one of his favorites, but the judge didn't know her. If he picked her, that must mean the project actually was good.

She looked for Miles in the hallway between classes but didn't see him. Was he going on also?

Normally in choir Cassie sat next to Janice and Riley, but after the fun she and Amity had together on Friday, she took the chance to sit close to her. "Guess what!" she said.

"No, you guess what!" Amity said, collapsing into the seat next to her.

"You've got news too?" Cassie suspected it was the same news.

"I got second place in the science fair!" Amity squealed. "I'm going on to regionals!"

"No way! That's fantastic! I got first place in my division! So I'm going on also!"

Amity rolled her eyes. "Of course you got first place. You're always one step ahead of me."

The sentiment surprised Cassie. She hadn't thought Amity even cared about school. "Well, congratulations. At least we'll be there together."

"Yeah. I'll have someone to talk to when I'm with all the nerdy smart people."

Melanie came in then, and Amity turned her attention away from Cassie. Cassie tried not to let the words sting. That was how Amity saw her, wasn't it? The nerdy smart girl.

At least Amity wants to be my friend, she thought to herself.

But sometimes she wasn't sure if that was true.

⚬⟆⚬⟅⚬

Cassie had to stay almost every day after school to practice for the play, since the performance was on Friday.

Ms. Talo freaked out on Tuesday when Matt slung his arm around Cassie's shoulders for the fourth time.

"She was your fiance, not your soccer buddy! And now she's your wife! You thought she was dead because of you! Show some passion!"

Cassie had to bite her tongue to keep from giggling, and she couldn't help feeling sorry for Matt.

He heaved a sigh and gave her a look of absolute frustration, and then he grabbed her around the waist and crushed her against him. Cassie jolted in surprise, especially when something bubbly erupted in her stomach.

"Yes!" Connor crowed. "That's it! You love her!"

"But not too much love. No babies." Kevin gave them a mockingly stern look.

Matt got it right the next time they ran through the scene. When Cassie lifted her veil, he jumped to his feet and threw his arms around her body, pulling her so hard against him that she struggled for breath as she tried to get her lines out.

"Not so much passion," Ms. Talo said, but she was smiling. "Let her finish speaking before you ravage her."

Cassie's face warmed.

There was something pleasant about the way Matt kept his hand on her waist throughout the rest of the scene. It startled her, and she kept glancing back at him.

"Here's the list of items you'll need for the play performance," Ms. Talo said after rehearsal. She handed the papers out to each student. "Our performance is Thursday next week, so that gives you some time to get it together."

Cassie looked over what she needed. A simple dress for the opening scenes and then a white one for the wedding scene.

"Where are we supposed to get these?" Nicole asked.

"If you don't have something suitable at home, you can rent something at the shop in Fayetteville," Ms. Talo said.

Cassie folded the paper and slipped it into her pocket. Rent a dress? Her mom would not be happy about that.

She followed Nicole out and told her what she'd felt when Matt hugged her.

"Why would he have that effect on me?" she asked as they walked out the front of the school to wait for their parents.

Nicole shrugged. "Maybe you're just getting into character. Hero loved him. You're just a fantastic actress."

Cassie clung to those words. That had to be true. It couldn't be that she was actually starting to like Matt. She was still head over heels for Zack, even though he never returned her calls and hadn't written her.

"Do you think the play's going all right?" Nicole and Andrew had their lines down.

Nicole pressed her lips together, smirking. "I don't know. But practices have sure been fun."

CHAPTER FIFTY-SEVEN

I Do

Mrs. Jones looked over the costume requirements after dinner. "I have a nice green dress in my closet that would work well as your dress in the first few scenes. It looks kind of medieval or renaissance."

Cassie chewed on her lower lip. "And the other dress? Should we look at the rental company?" A few years ago they had rented costumes for Halloween, so she knew they would have something.

Mrs. Jones narrowed her eyes, considering the question. "I don't want to spend the money if we don't have to. I might be able to find something in my closet."

Cassie pictured her mom's adult dresses and couldn't think of anything that was white or would look appropriate. She and her mother were two very different sizes. "I don't think we'll find anything," she said tactfully, not wanting to be rude.

Mrs. Jones gave a small smile. "I still have my wedding dress."

Cassie's eyes went wide. An actual wedding dress? And her mother's, at that? "Can I see it?"

"Let's take a look."

Cassie followed behind her mother to the master bedroom.

"It wasn't my favorite wedding dress," Mrs. Jones said. "It never fit me right under the arms."

Cassie exhaled as her mother unzipped the dress bag and removed the white gown from within it. It was long-sleeved with lace around the neckline and a train that extended behind the gown. "It's beautiful."

"Try it on, let's see if it works."

Cassie slid out of her jeans and T-shirt and pulled the dress over her shoulders. It draped over her frame, flaring out around her hips. "It fits perfectly." Cassie gave her mom a suspicious look. "Am I the same size you were?"

"Not even close. I was probably ten or fifteen pounds heavier than you. It's much looser on you. But it sure looks lovely." Mrs. Jones came behind Cassie and pulled the train up, then attached it to something at Cassie's back. "There's a button for the train so it doesn't drag." She stood in front of Cassie and surveyed her, her eyes soft. "It's beautiful."

"Can I use it, then?"

Mrs. Jones nodded. "Just remember, this is my wedding dress. Be very careful with it."

"Oh, I will!" Cassie said.

More than a week and a half had passed since Cassie slapped Tyler. Her eyes turned his direction when she walked into church class Friday morning, but he looked away from her and immediately began talking to Sue. It was a very deliberate slam.

Cassie followed along with the lesson plan. She wasn't even sure when they had become good friends, but she was certain she relied on his friendship now. She didn't want to face the day alone.

"Do you think your mom would let you spend the night tonight?" she asked Riley.

"I can ask her."

Cassie nodded. "Call her."

Riley called her mom while Mr. Jones drove them to school. "Hey, Mom. Cassie wants to know if I can spend the night tonight."

Cassie looked at Riley with big eyes and stuck out her lower lip, then pressed her hands together in a begging gesture.

"Please?" Riley added, taking the cue from Cassie. "She really wants me to."

"I need you," Cassie said, feeling the tears shimmer in her eyes.

"She needs me, Mom. Okay." Riley disconnected the call with a sigh. "She said no."

"Why?"

"I don't know." Riley looked disappointed also. "Sorry."

"That's all right." Cassie sighed. "I'll get through this."

Cassie lingered after church on Sunday, hoping to catch a glimpse of Zack. It had been so long since they'd spoken. Yet every time she pictured his smile in her head, she wanted to see him in real life. He was the kind of person she knew she could spend years talking to and never run out of things to say.

"Waiting for Zack?" Riley asked, coming over with a mischievous glint in her eyes.

"Have you seen his family come in?"

Riley shook her head. "Maybe they're out of town this week."

Tyler walked down the hall, his eyes straight ahead, and Cassie focused her attention on Riley so she could pretend not to see him. Then he drew to a stop next to them.

"Cassie," he said.

Cassie swiveled to face him, astonishment widening her eyes.

"I'm not mad anymore. Just wanted to tell you that."

Relief lit inside her, and she wanted to throw her arms around his neck and tell him how sorry she was for hitting him. But when she opened her mouth, what came out was, "It's about time!"

She knew instantly it was the wrong thing to say. Tyler's shoulders stiffened, and he looked affronted. "Well. Anyway."

"No, no, I didn't mean that the way it sounded!" She put a hand out to keep him from walking away. "I mean, I'm just so glad. I hated not talking to you."

He looked mildly pacified. "It took me a while. I had to think things over. I get that you were mad, but you never even heard what I had to say. You really don't know what happened." His eyes slid toward Riley as he spoke, though he didn't outright accuse her.

Cassie nodded in acknowledgment, face burning with humiliation. "I'm sorry."

"Yeah, well." He gave her a small grin. "Don't do it again."

Cassie had to laugh. She waited till he was out of earshot before grabbing Riley's arm and squeezing it. "He's not mad at me anymore!"

"I heard," Riley said. "But he didn't say a word to me the entire time."

⁂

"Don't forget today we have dress rehearsal," Cassie said Wednesday morning, coming into her mom's room.

Mrs. Jones was asleep, or at least laying in bed. She lifted her head at Cassie. "I remember. I'll meet you at the auditorium with the dresses in an hour."

"Don't forget," Cassie said again.

"I won't, honey."

Cassie nodded, then shouldered her backpack and hurried the rest of the children out to the bus.

She bypassed the bathroom, not wanting to talk to Amity or Andrea, and instead found Nicole by her locker.

"Are you ready for the dress rehearsal?" she asked.

Nicole nodded, though she looked uncertain. "The dress I got for the wedding is too tight."

Cassie gave Nicole a quick once over. She was taller than Cassie and of a medium build, but she was perfectly proportioned. "I'm sure it looks fantastic on you. Quit worrying about it."

She found Matt and Kevin and a few of the other actors, and they made their way to the English room.

Nicole looked around. "Where's Andrew?"

"I haven't seen him," Matt said.

Cassie grabbed Nicole's arm. "Maybe he forgot!"

"We better find him!"

"He's in my first hour class. This way." Cassie led the way to her civics class.

Sure enough, Andrew was sitting inside. Cassie poked her head in and hissed, "Andrew!"

He looked up and arched both brows at the sight of the two of them standing there beckoning him. He put his pen down and walked over to the door.

"What is it?"

Nicole whacked him on the forearm. "Today is the dress rehearsal! You're supposed to be in Ms. Talo's room!"

Panic raced across his features. "I completely forgot!"

"Well, it's a good thing we found you! Come on, get your stuff." Nicole looked ready to haul him away.

Andrew returned to his desk and gathered his things, then followed them out the door.

"You have your permission slip, right?" Cassie asked.

Andrew stopped dead. "Permission slip."

Nicole gave him an exasperated look. "We are going on a field trip. You need a permission slip."

"But I didn't get it signed." Andrew was clearly panicking now.

Cassie gave a long-suffering sigh. "Give it to me."

Andrew focused on her. "What?"

She wiggled her fingers. "The permission slip. Give it to me."

Both of them watched her as Andrew handed over the form.

"Pen?"

One landed in her hand. "What's your mom's name?"

"Lora."

Cassie sat down on the floor just long enough to carefully sign Andrew's mother's name across the bottom of the permission slip. Then she handed it back to him. "Now your permission slip is signed."

"You just forged her signature!" Nicole said.

"Did you want him to come to the dress rehearsal or not?" Cassie continue down the hall, leaving them to follow her.

"Doesn't look like my mom's signature," Andrew said.

"But it looks like an adult's, and that's all anyone is going to look at,"

Cassie said. Her friends might make fun of her for having adult handwriting, but it definitely came in handy.

The tardy bell had rung by the time they got there, and Ms. Talo was fit to be tied.

"Where have you guys been?" she demanded. "Never mind. The bus is here and waiting. It's our turn for the stage at nine-twenty, so we had better go. Permission slips?"

Cassie gave her friends a satisfied smile as she handed over her form.

Most of the kids had brought their costume changes with them, but since Mrs. Jones didn't want the wedding dress at school, she preferred to meet them there. Cassie's insides hopped around as the bus parked behind the art center auditorium, nervous her mother would have forgotten. Even if she remembered, she couldn't be late.

She breathed out a sigh of relief which she spotted the familiar van.

Mrs. Jones already waited in the foyer, and she handed Cassie the two costumes when they walked in. "Good luck. I can't wait to see you up there."

"Thanks." Cassie gave a brief smile and felt how clammy her hands were as she accepted the dresses. Hopefully she would get all these jitters out today.

Nicole and Jaclyn were already in the dressing room. Nicole had on a long lavender dress and kept messing with the top.

"It's way too tight! My boobs are falling out!"

It did leave Nicole a bit busty, with more cleavage than usual. Cassie knew she wouldn't have that problem. "Just leave it alone. It doesn't look as bad as you think." Cassie adjusted her own dress, glad for the padded bra that gave her at least the appearance of something up top where normally there would be nothing.

"You look darling," Nicole said, staring at Cassie as she slipped on the green dress.

Cassie smoothed down the skirt. "Thanks."

Ms. Talo rapped on the bathroom door. "Let's get started! Our time is going to run out!"

Shooting Nicole and Jaclyn a last desperate look, Cassie pushed open the door and walked out.

The first scene was when Claudio and Hero met, and Cassie played the part of a sweet girl smitten by the attentions of this handsome boy. And Matt did look handsome, wearing a billowy white shirt with a black vest and black pants. His blond hair kept falling in his face, a perpetual grin lifting the corners of his mouth.

It was Nicole and Andrew who stole this first scene, antagonizing each other with cutting remarks. Which made the next scene, when Andrew/Benedick confessed his feelings for Nicole/Beatrice, that much more hilarious.

Then there was Don John, Claudio's illegitimate brother. Sick with jealousy, he framed Hero and made it look as if she had cheated on Claudio. Grief-stricken and full of rage, Claudio verbally attacked Hero, publicly slandering her character. Cassie/Hero drew up her emotions and sobbed, hysterically defending herself before screaming and throwing herself on the ground in a dead faint.

The next scene was all Nicole and Andrew, as Nicole sobbed out Beatrice's agony over the accusations against her cousin Hero, and Andrew/Benedick confessed his love for her with a kiss that left the make-shift audience cheering. Then Nicole joined Cassie in the dressing room for a quick costume change.

"It's going great," Cassie said breathlessly as she slipped into her mom's wedding dress. "Everyone is remembering their lines and the audience is laughing when they're supposed to!"

"I know!" Nicole switched into her wedding gown also for the last scene. "And Andrew looks cuter than I've ever seen him."

Cassie cast a sideways glance at Nicole. "I was just thinking the same thing about Matt."

Nicole wiggled her eyebrows up and down. "I guess we're just a couple of boy-crazy girls."

"I suppose that's true," Cassie laughed.

The two girls pulled the veils in front of their faces like they were supposed to.

The closing scene started without a hitch. Matt/Claudio stepped forward and took Cassie/Hero's hand. Then he spoke his lines, looking into Cassie's eyes through the veil. And then Cassie lifted the veil from her face. "'And when I lived—'"

Immediately Matt brought his hands to his mouth in what should've been a gesture of shock and relief. He let out a wail, long and high-pitched, that echoed through the auditorium.

Cassie stopped talking. She looked at Matt, who had finally stopped wailing, and she started giggling. She fought to wipe the smile off her face and deliver her last lines. But all she could picture was his expression as he shrieked in delight at seeing her.

The audience was starting to giggle also, which wasn't supposed to happen right now. This wasn't one of the funny scenes. Cassie delivered her lines in a hurry, and Matt grabbed her up for the perfunctory kiss. As his mouth airbrushed the sides of her lip in a fake kiss that the audience would think was real, Cassie found herself wishing he really would kiss her.

And the scene ended with Ms. Talo shooing them off the stage, where she gave them all very serious looks.

"I don't know whether to applaud or cry. It was all perfect until the end. What are you doing, Matt? This isn't a funeral! It's a wedding! And the woman you love, the one you thought you killed, is alive! No more howling!"

Cassie couldn't keep a straight face. She glanced at Nicole to see her also fighting laughter. Cassie worked hard to look serious lest she bring Ms. Talo's wrath down upon her.

"Go, change your clothes. Good thing this was the dress rehearsal. We have to get it right tomorrow!"

Cassie and Nicole hurried away, exchanging smiles.

Mrs. Jones was waiting when Cassie came out. She took the dresses from Cassie and said, "You did fantastic. You and Matt look like a real couple up there."

"Did we?" Cassie tried not to show how much this pleased her. "He kind of messed up there at the end."

"Even if he messed up, you guys did amazing. I can't wait to see the real thing."

CHAPTER FIFTY-EIGHT

Clearing the Air

T he date for the play finally arrived. Cassie was a bundle of nerves all day in school, though her friends hardly seemed to notice. Cassie sat with Nicole and Andrew and a few others she felt closer to these days than her usual friends.

She rehearsed her lines on the bus. She wanted to do perfect.

"Let me help you with your hair," Mrs. Jones said, entering Cassie's bedroom after she had put on the first dress.

Cassie hesitated where she stood in the middle of the room, running a brush through her long dark hair. "How will you do it?"

"It was common to wear hair up back then. Or partially up, often with braids."

"I don't want to look like I'm ten," Cassie said.

Mrs. Jones shook her head. "You won't."

"Okay, then." Cassie still felt a little trepidation, not sure of her mother's hair-styling skills. But she followed her mom back to the master bathroom and stood still while her mom brushed and played with her hair.

Mrs. Jones French-braided several pieces of Cassie's hair, so it ended up like three French braids, and then she twisted them together into a bun. Cassie spun her head from side to side and admired the braids.

"They look beautiful."

"Do you need help with your makeup?"

"No. I can do it."

"Good luck, then. We'll leave in twenty minutes."

The whole family piled into the car to watch Cassie's play. They arrived at the auditorium forty minutes before Cassie's class would be presenting.

"Oh my goodness, your hair looks fantastic!" Nicole said. "Can you do mine?"

Nicole's thick blond hair lay in soft waves against her shoulders. "I didn't do my hair," Cassie said. "My mom did."

"You can just braid mine and pull it over to the side."

"Okay," Cassie said. She did as Nicole asked, and Nicole did the same thing Cassie had, turning her head from side to side to admire the braid.

"Thank you! Looks great!" Nicole patted down her dress, her eyes widening. "I forgot the knife!"

"The one you threaten to kill Claudio with?" At Nicole's nod, Cassie said, "It will be okay. Just shake your finger hard."

"And I forgot the note!"

Cassie laughed. "Well, you better hurry and write one, because the note you give to Claudio for the dead Hero is pretty important."

"Okay." Nicole took several deep breaths. "I can do this."

"You can do this," Cassie said, feeling a bit braver.

Until they were actually on the set, and suddenly she forgot her words. She stuttered over her lines when she met Claudio for the first time and was supposed to be smitten by him and him by her.

"'I will do any modest office,'" Matt whispered to her, barely moving his mouth.

When had his eyes become so blue? Cassie shook off the thought and spouted off the line.

That was the only mishap. When Andrew did the scene where he spoke to himself, the audience laughed at all the right places. When Nicole shook her finger in Andrew's face and sobbed for the injustice done to her cousin, the audience didn't breathe. And when Andrew grabbed her hand and kissed it, they gave a collective sigh.

Cassie's stomach twisted with anticipation. Would Matt kiss her also?

The final scene arrived, the wedding scene, and Cassie and Nicole and a few extras stepped onstage in their white gowns with veils over their faces. Cassie had a bouquet of flowers in her hands. She stood silently listening as Matt gave his speech of repentance and sorrow for the loss of his love. He reached for her hands, and she handed the bouquet to Nicole.

Or she thought she did. Nicole's hand reached out for the flowers, but Cassie let go too soon, and the whole bouquet landed on the stage. Nicole hesitated, as if unsure if she should pick them up or let them go.

Then the worst thing happened. A little giggle escaped Cassie's lips.

She knew the audience couldn't hear it, but Matt did. He paused in his speech and looked at her.

"Stop laughing!" he breathed.

She had to stop. It was her time to speak. Gathering her wits, she lifted the veil from her face and began her own monologue. Matt let out a gasp and drew back before falling to his knees and clasping her hands.

Scenes that had gone wrong rushed through Cassie's mind, from yesterday when Matt let out the loud wail to their first practice, when he pressed his head to her belly as if listening for a baby. Her voice trembled as she fought to keep the humor under control, but hopefully it came across as fighting tears.

Then she finish speaking and Matt got to his feet, clasping her to him before turning her head sideways and giving her the fake kiss.

No real kiss. Cassie's heart gave a tumble of disappointment.

The audience rose to their feet, clapping and cheering, and the cast gave a bow before starting the wedding dance. Now Cassie could laugh and smile and release the nervous tension. Matt's knees rose high in the air with each leap of the dance as if he were one of the ten lords a leaping from the "Twelve Days of Christmas." Which only made Cassie laugh harder.

Something tugged on the back of her dress. She turned her head in time to see Matt stepping on the train.

"Matt! Get off the dress!" she said, taking it away from him.

Too late. The button that held the train popped off, rolling across stage as the train fell away from the back.

The curtain fell before anyone could notice, and Cassie scurried across the stage to get the button. She couldn't lose that.

"What are you doing?" Nicole asked, following. "Is everything okay?"

"Just lost a button." Cassie had no pockets, and the audience was calling for another curtain call. She stuck the button in her mouth, where she was sure not to lose it. Then they hurry to the front of the stage to bow one more time.

She smiled broadly and gripped Matt's hand tightly in her own, wondering when she would have another chance to touch him like this. Then they turned around and hurried off stage.

"Door to get off, door to get off," Nicole said. She tried the first door she came to and opened a closet.

"Oh yes, if we're looking for brooms," Matt said, and for some reason Cassie thought it was hilarious, and her fit of giggles started up again. And then she gasped.

"I swallowed the button!" she cried.

Matt looked at her strangely. "What button?"

"The one to my mom's wedding dress!" What would she tell her mom?

Matt lifted an eyebrow. "I think that's one button she's not gonna want back." He opened another door. "And here is the way off."

Cassie followed him. "I didn't do that bad, did I? Even though I was giggling?"

He shook his head. "Nah, it was fine. You did choose the wrong time to laugh."

"I was picturing the time you put your head to my stomach as if you were listening for a baby."

Now Matt laughed also. "Yeah, that was funny." He turned left and went to the men's dressing room without another word.

Cassie turned around and nearly bumped into Andrew. "Hey, good job. Everyone laughed. You did awesome."

"You too." He undid his fluffy bowtie from around the ruffled shirt. "It was fun."

"And you don't have to kiss Nicole anymore." Cassie smiled.

Andrew glanced around, then leaned closer and said, "Says who?"

Cassie arched an eyebrow. "Oh!" she said, delight filling her voice. She wondered if Nicole knew about this new development.

Cassie was still floating high when she went to school on Friday. She spotted Nicole and Andrew talking to each other in the locker hall and flashed them a big smile. She glanced around for Matt, wanting to get together and relive the adventure from the previous night.

"You look happy today," Janice said when Cassie walked into civics.

"The play last night was amazing." Cassie put her books down, unable to keep the smile off her face. "You should've seen it."

"How fun," Andrea said, though she didn't look that interested.

Janice looked a little guilty. "I would have liked to see you."

Cassie shrugged like she didn't care. She didn't expect anything from them these days. "I had friends there. And my family." She left it at that, letting them interpret it the way they wanted.

The morning announcements came on, and Cassie pulled out a notebook paper, reviewing her vocabulary words for the science quiz that afternoon.

"In the way of birthdays, we'd like to celebrate..."

Cassie paused to listen for her friends' names so she would know if she needed to tell them happy birthday today.

"Cassandra Jones . . ."

She lifted her head.

"What? It's your birthday?" Andrea said.

"Cassie! Why didn't you tell us?"

Cassie shook her head. "It's not my birthday." But it was on Monday, something she felt her friends should know without her telling them.

"Happy birthday, Cassie!" Coach Benson said.

"It's not my birthday," Cassie said. Nobody seemed to hear her, though, and she realized it was futile. She could either spend the rest of the day correcting people or she could just say thanks.

❦

When Cassie walked into her computer class second hour, first thing she noticed was Matt. He was talking to another boy, sitting in the teacher's rolling chair and skidding across the floor. He looked at Cassie when she walked in, and she tried to think of something flirty to say.

"Hey," was all she managed. Never mind that just last week she'd been practicing air kisses with this boy.

"Hi," he said, then he turned back to talking with Kevin.

Cassie sat down at her desk, feeling an odd mixture of elation for saying hi and disappointment because he didn't talk to her more.

This was no good.

She couldn't keep her feelings to herself. She had to tell someone. Not Amity, who Matt already flirted with and who seemed to always set her eyes on the boys Cassie liked.

❦

Nicole smacked her before she walked into third hour. "I can't believe you didn't mention it was your birthday!"

Cassie opted for the truth on this one. "It's actually not. My birthday is on Monday."

"Same difference!" Nicole said. Her eyes glittered, and she hugged her books to her chest. "Guess what?"

Cassie was pretty sure she could guess, but she decided to let Nicole say it. "What?"

"I heard Andrew might ask me out!" Nicole bit down hard on her lower lip. "What should I do?"

"Do you like him?"

"I think so. We sure had a lot of fun doing the play together."

Cassie felt a stab jealousy. Just like she had with Matt. "Then I would say yes. I had a lot of fun with Matt too."

Nicole gave her a sideways look. "Are you thinking of him as more than just a costar?"

Cassie shook her head, not wanting to reveal her hand to anyone yet. "No. He was nice though."

"Good, because I almost forgot. My brother wanted to know if you're single."

"If I'm single?" Cassie wrinkled her nose. "Like, I'm not married."

Nicole laughed. "He means like if you have a boyfriend." The warning bell rang, and Nicole grabbed her arm. "Let's go in. We'll talk at lunch."

Cara called out to Cassie as she walked into the lunch room. "Cassie! We didn't know it was your birthday! Come sit with us!"

Cassie was tempted, but her friends hadn't really talked to her all

353

week, and she wanted to know what Nicole was going to say. "It's not my birthday. I'll talk to you guys later, okay?" Then she sat with Nicole.

"What were you saying about your brother?"

"Okay." Nicole swiveled on her seat at the table to face Cassie. "So my family came to the play last night and my brother thought you were hot. He wanted to know if you have a boyfriend."

"Who's your brother?" Cassie couldn't recall ever seeing him.

"Well, he's a junior at the high school, so you wouldn't have met him."

Cassie had just opened up her water bottle to take a drink, and now she sputtered. "Oh! He's at the high school?" It wasn't the first time someone older than her had been interested in her, but it still caught her off guard.

"Yes. If you're interested, I thought we could go on a double date. Maybe go to the movies, go skating."

Cassie couldn't see her parents going for that. "I'm not allowed to date."

"So we can all just have a get-together as a group."

That sounded like fun. Maybe it was a possibility. "Okay. Yeah."

"Great." Nicole beamed. "I'll call you later and we'll set something up."

⟡

"Hey, what's going on with you?" Cara popped into the seat next to Cassie in math class. "First it's your birthday and you don't tell any of us, and now you won't sit with us?"

Cassie looked at her in mild surprise. "I didn't think anyone cared," she said before she could rethink it.

Cara scowled at her. "We're your best friends!"

And lousy friends they were. Cassie felt much closer to Riley and Nicole. Still, Cara made her feel bad. "It's not my birthday. My birthday is Monday."

"What are you doing for it? Who are you having over?"

Cassie hadn't thought about it, really, with all the concentration on the play. "Do you want to come over?"

Cara's face brightened. "Sure!"

"Okay. Come over tonight." Now, though, Cassie would have to invite other people. She didn't really want to invite Amity or Andrea. Maybe Janice.

⟡

Cassie walked into science in sixth hour and spotted Jaclyn and Janice. Cassie sat down between the two of them and said breathlessly, "I have something to tell you guys."

Janice turned to face her. "What is it? You've been awfully reclusive lately. You haven't sat with us at lunch in a week."

Cassie waved that off. "I think I like someone." She pressed her knuckles to her mouth and gave a little squeak.

"You do?" Jaclyn said, arching an eyebrow. "Who?"

Cassie only shook her head, not trusting herself to speak.

"Not Zack?" Janice looked surprised.

Cassie pressed her finger to her lips. "Don't tell anyone."

Jaclyn gave a gasp. "I know who it is!"

Cassie looked at her, her face burning. "Don't say—" she began, but Jaclyn was already talking.

"Matt! You like Matt!"

Cassie couldn't even deny it. She knew the truth burned on her face.

"Matt?" Janice wrinkled her nose. "How do you even know him?"

Jaclyn spoke right over Janice. "Oh, Cassie, that kind of thing happens all the time. People can't help it, when they've been working close together. And since you got to pretend like he was your fiancé, it's only normal that the feelings would become real."

"Oh." Janice nodded. "I'd forgotten you guys were in that play together. Does he like you?"

Cassie shook her head. "I don't think so. Only as a friend. Don't tell anyone, okay?"

"My lips are sealed," Janice said, and Cassie gave a relieved smile. She did not want Andrea or Amity finding out.

CHAPTER FIFTY-NINE

Two Birthdays

B y seventh hour, Amity and Maureen had heard about the birthday party.

"You invited Cara but not me?" Amity said, clearly miffed.

Well, it's my birthday . . . Cassie thought. She didn't say that. "You can come too."

"Gee, thanks for the consolation prize," Amity sniffed.

"What about me?" Maureen asked.

"Sure." She spotted Melanie listening again, and Cassie moved to the outer section to sit by Janice and Riley before Melanie could invite herself as well.

Of course, that meant Riley and Janice heard all about it.

"You haven't invited me to one of your parties since, like, sixth grade," Riley said as they walked out to the bus. "And I'm one of your best friends."

Cassie sighed. "I'll have to have a separate party with you. Do you want to be there with Amity and Maureen? They're not nice."

"So why did you invite them?"

"I didn't. They invited themselves."

"So say no."

"I'm not so good at that."

⁓⁎⁓

Cassie's mom picked her up after school, and Amity ran over to the van to talk to Mrs. Jones for a moment.

"My dad will bring me by around six, if that's okay," Amity said.

Luckily Cassie had already told her mom about the sudden birthday party, so she didn't bat an eye. "That sounds perfect. We'll see you then."

They pulled away from the school, and Mrs. Jones said, "Where did you want to go for dinner?"

"There's that new catfish place down the street." Cassie was a vegetarian and ate mostly vegetables. If she did eat meat, it was fish.

"That sounds perfect. I don't think it opens until four-thirty, so let's go shoe shopping."

Shoe shopping might be something her friends enjoyed, but all Cassie could do was look at the rows and rows of shoes and wonder why someone would need all of these. She wore the same tennis shoes every single day. Other than having a pair for church, she didn't see the need for more.

She and her mom managed to kill time until the restaurant opened. They walked inside, and the first thing Cassie saw was Luke setting out utensils.

"Hey!" she said. "You work here?"

"Hey, Cassie!" he said, giving her a hug. "Happy birthday."

Her face warmed. "Thanks."

"Yeah, I got a job here when I turned fifteen. I can't wait tables but they let me clear them!"

"How much do they pay?" Cassie asked, intrigued. Her dad didn't pay hardly anything at the soccer store.

"Eight bucks an hour. I just live a few blocks away, so it's convenient."

"Nice," she said.

She and her mom had to wait a few minutes for the buffet to officially open, and then they attacked with vigor. Normally Cassie was a bit careful with her food, trying to maintain her small frame, but today she ate everything she wanted to.

"I'm so full," she groaned, and she picked up another hush puppy and then put it back down.

"Look how quickly your friend busses the tables," Mrs. Jones murmured, nodding toward where Luke cleared tables into a big plastic bin.

His movements were very efficient. Cassie couldn't help staring, as it looked like she was watching a movie in fast forward. Luke quickly cleared off the plates, stacked them, loaded the used forks on top and put them in the bin, followed by all the cups. Table after table he did in the same manner.

Cassie kicked her mom's foot under the table. "Stop staring!"

"I can't believe how quickly he works!"

Cassie laughed, somewhat embarrassed, but she also couldn't pull her eyes away from watching his hands sweep up the articles of food and the used plates. "I think he deserves a pay raise."

"So how are things with Zack?" Mrs. Jones asked, taking a sip of her soda and leaning back in her chair.

"I don't know. He hasn't talked to me in weeks. I don't know what I feel for him." Her thoughts shifted back to Matt and his impish smile and blue eyes.

"Is there someone else you like?"

Of course there was Matt, and for some reason Tyler's face flashed into Cassie's mind. She shook her head. "Maybe. I'm not sure."

A twinkle entered her mother's eyes. "What about that boy who was in the play with you?"

Now Cassie's face burned. "Yeah, he's cute. And nice. But I'm pretty sure he likes Amity."

Mrs. Jones wrinkled up her nose at that statement. "Why would he like Amity over you?"

Cassie rolled her eyes. Parents never saw reality. "Oh, I don't know. Because she's beautiful and she's got big boobs and she's really good at flirting with the boys."

"You're beautiful," Mrs. Jones said, but that was all she could add.

Cassie laughed. "Yep. And I've got a lovely padded bra and I don't know how to talk to boys without getting nervous."

Mrs. Jones patted her hand. "It will happen, sweetie. Soon all of these boys will open their eyes and see what they've been missing."

That was so not happening anytime soon. But Cassie kept the sentiment to herself.

⚬⚬❀⚬⚬

Cassie and Mrs. Jones got home from dinner to find the family waiting for Cassie in the entryway.

"Happy birthday!" her younger siblings chorused.

"Thanks," Cassie said, grinning at them.

"Is it ready?" Mrs. Jones asked.

"It's in the living room." Mr. Jones said.

"What is?" Cassie asked, curious.

"Your birthday present."

Cassie raised an eyebrow. She thought going out to dinner was her birthday present.

"Close your eyes," Emily said. "I'll lead you."

It was a bit disconcerting letting her sister guide her, but Cassie followed blindly into the living room.

"Okay, you can open your eyes!" Mrs. Jones said.

Cassie did so. In front of her was a large, beautiful wooden box, big enough for her to crawl inside. Heart designs had been carved on the outside. "What is this?"

"This is called a hope chest. It's made of cedar. This is where you put special things that you collect and want to keep forever."

"Wow, it's beautiful," Cassie said. She wondered what she would put in it. Her journals, maybe?

"We'll put it in your bedroom tonight," Mr. Jones said.

She watched Mr. Jones put the hope chest at the foot of her bed.

"I'm not going to remember it's there tomorrow," Cassie said. She always walked around the left side of her bed to get to the light and turn it on.

"Sure you will."

Maureen and Cara arrived shortly after.

"Happy birthday, Cassie!" Cara said, giving her an envelope and an air kiss.

"Thank you!" Cassie opened the envelope and found a gift card from both of them. She smiled, hiding her disappointment. She would have loved to see what kind of present they got her. "Thanks."

"Did you have a nice day?" Maureen asked, joining her on the bed.

"Yeah, it was fine." Cassie settled in beside them, hugging a pillow and feeling more comfortable than she expected. "I saw Amity write 'best friends' on a note to Melanie. I guess they're pretty close now."

She expected Maureen to shrug it off like it was no big deal, but instead, she said, "Amity wishes. They're not best friends."

"I hate that she acts that way," Cara said. "Like we're not good enough for her and she needs someone else."

Mrs. Jones poked her head into the bedroom. "Amity's here!" she said cheerfully, almost as if in warning.

Amity bounced in, a big smile on her face. "Hi, guys!" She dropped onto the bed beside Cassie.

Cara turned away from her, obviously still miffed from their earlier conversation. But Maureen brightened.

"Hey, I know! Let's make another video!"

"Oo, I love it!" Amity said, and she smoothed her hair back from her face. "You take it, Maureen."

"But I want to be in it," Maureen protested.

"I'll take it," Cara said, pulling out her phone. "Go ahead."

"I want you in it, Cara," Amity said, to which Maureen said, "And not me?"

"No, no, it's fine," Amity said, but she looked annoyed.

"Go ahead," Cara said, pointing the phone at her. "I'm recording. Start your video."

"Well, we didn't even talk about what we're going to do," Amity said, just as Maureen picked up a pillow and lobbed it at Amity's head.

Amity shrieked and threw it back at Maureen, then grabbed another and smacked Cassie's face with it. Cassie blinked, a little dumbfounded by the change of events, then she remembered the pillow in her arms. She lifted it and thumped Maureen on the head. Maureen took the pillow from her, and Cassie reached around for the crocheted blanket she kept on her bed. She snatched it up and lifted it over her head, ready to wallop Amity in the face with it. But when she pulled, it wouldn't come. She turned around and saw the cloth had gotten stuck on a spoke of the headboard!

Cara burst out laughing and pulled the phone down. "You guys! Cassie trying to free her blanket from the bed was the funniest thing I ever saw! Come watch!"

The girls put the pillows down and gathered around Cara. The moment Cassie jerked on the blanket, they all shrieked with laughter, and Cassie held her side and gasped for breath.

"So who do you like now, Cassie?" Amity asked.

No way was Cassie telling her. "Still Zack, I guess. Though not as strong as before."

"Do you think he likes you back?" Maureen asked.

"I don't know. He's always nice at dances. But he doesn't call me or anything."

"It's because you're too serious," Amity said, and Cara elbowed her.

Cassie frowned. "What do you mean, I'm too serious?"

"Nothing," Amity said, but Maureen answered for her.

"You just use lots of big words and are really intense. Guys like girls that are fun to be around."

"And I'm not fun?" Cassie said, already feeling the sting from their words.

"Of course you are," Cara said.

"But you're not like, you know, always playing around," Amity said.

"You don't flirt," Maureen clarified.

"Right," Cassie said slowly. She understood now. She wasn't goofy and giggly around guys, and that made her unattractive.

She wanted to defend herself and tell her friends they were wrong, but she wasn't so sure they were.

⁘

They slept in Saturday morning, and then Cassie invited them to go with her to a sports activity in Rogers.

"Sports?" Amity said, wrinkling her nose. "I don't like to get sweaty."

"Me either," Cassie said in total agreement. "I hated PE last year. But all the same boys will be there that are at the dances! It should be fun!" And Cassie knew she'd have a lot more fun if her friends were there also.

"I can't," Cara said. "I have cheer practice today."

"And I'm going to watch," Maureen said.

Cassie suspected she'd made that up just now.

"And you, Amity?" Cassie asked. "We don't have to sweat much. I promise. We'll just hang out and talk to the boys. Zack will probably be there." Cassie brightened at the thought. While she wasn't sure exactly how she felt for Zack, she still liked him enough that she wanted to see him. "And Ryan," she added as an after thought, remembering the boy Amity had liked at the last dance.

"I don't think my mom will let me," she said. "We always have so much else going on Saturdays."

Cassie knew Amity didn't have anything today. She felt a rush of frustration for these girls who only occasionally wanted to hang out with her. She should have invited Riley. Or even Andrea. Andrea usually enjoyed the church activities, even if it didn't include just a dance.

"Okay," Cassie said. "Thanks for coming over."

The girls left shortly after, and Cassie and her sister Emily got ready for the sports day. Mrs. Jones drove Cassie and Emily to the chapel in Rogers where the activity was being held. Cassie looked around for Riley but didn't see her. She did, however, spot Zack almost right away. He smiled when he saw her, and the smile reminded Cassie of why she been drawn to him in the first place.

"All right, kids!" a youth leader that Cassie didn't recognize said. "We'll start with a prayer, and then we'll have different stations set up. Here in the middle of the gym is the volleyball station. Outside we'll have the running station. In the primary room, we've set up some hula hoops. Also outside, I have a softball station. And in the women's Sunday school classroom, we have bowling. The other half of the gym will have the basketball hoops down. All day long, you can wander to the stations you want. This is your chance to explore and participate in the sports that make you happy and maybe try some new ones."

No sports made Cassie happy. The closest one was soccer, which was not one of the options he had listed.

Somebody said a prayer to get the day started, and then everyone separated and spread out.

"Where are you going?" Emily asked.

"I have no idea. Maybe bowling." Cassie was relieved now that her friends hadn't come. This did not look like a fun day.

Emily followed her to bowling, where they joined a long line of kids rolling a plastic ball toward plastic pins. Lame. As if bowling weren't bad enough with real pins. Cassie took her ball and rolled it toward the pins. The ball rolled sideways and missed the pins completely, which brought laughter from the watching teams.

"Stupid," Cassie muttered, retrieving the ball to try again. She got two rolls before the next person got a turn.

The next roll only went slightly better, managing to hit the pins on the periphery. She turned away, discouraged and already hating this activity, and nearly bumped into Zack. "Oh!" she said in surprise. "I didn't know you had come in here!"

"Yeah, I thought I would try my hand at bowling."

Cassie rolled her eyes. "Turns out I'm terrible at it."

"Well, you can't be good at everything."

"If I could just figure out one thing I'm good at."

"I'm not very good at sports either. Only soccer."

"I remember. Too bad we're not playing soccer here."

Zack glanced over his shoulder, looking out the window. "It's beautiful outside. Are you going to go run?"

Cassie wrinkled her nose. "The truth is, I hate any kind of physical activity. I'd much rather sit down and read a book."

Zack laughed. "So reading is something you're good at."

Cassie's face warmed. "Yes. If reading were a talent, it would be my best."

Zack inclined his head toward the door. "Maybe running isn't so bad if you're with a friend."

Was Zack a friend? Could he be more than that? "I'm willing to give it a try."

He turned around and walked out of the room, staying nearly at her side as she paced him. His fingers were so close to hers, but not quite touching. Sometimes she thought he liked her. Why didn't he take her hand? Because she was too young for him? "I turn fifteen on Monday."

"You do?" Zack turned and looked at her. "Happy birthday."

"Just one year away from being able to date," Cassie said, and then she blushed at her boldness. Zack was already old enough. He wasn't going to wait around for her.

But Zack just smiled. "That's fun. I'm sure you'll have lots of dates."

Cassie's face burned and she didn't comment. That was not what she had meant to imply.

It turned out Cassie did not enjoy running even when she had a friend with her. Zack was quite good at it, but he never showed any annoyance or impatience with her for stopping every ten feet to catch her breath and rub her side.

"I'm just not good at this," she said. "I'm not athletic."

He shrugged. "You don't have to be."

They went back inside and grabbed a drink. Some kids called Zack over to play basketball with them, and Cassie sank down onto the steps leading to the stage. She spotted Tyler and Jason playing basketball, and they waved to her.

"Come play with us!" Tyler said.

Cassie lifted her cup of water. "I'm taking a break."

"She ran really hard," Zack said. "Is it all right if I play with them?" he asked her.

Why did he think he needed her permission? "Sure. Go head."

The rest of the day followed in a similar manner. The activities were boring and strenuous for Cassie, and Zack hung out with her for most of the day. When it finally ended, she and Emily went outside to wait for Mrs. Jones.

"It was good to see you," Zack said, waving as he and his brothers climbed into his mom's van. "I'm sure I'll see you next month sometime."

Cassie waved, and then she and Emily climbed into the blue van when it appeared.

"How was it?" Mrs. Jones asked.

"Horrible," Cassie said. "Next time I'm not coming."

"You hung out with Zack the whole time," Emily said.

"Zack?" Mrs. Jones looked at Cassie in the mirror. "Is there something going on between you?"

Cassie lifted her shoulders in frustration. "I don't know. He's really nice to me. But he doesn't say anything. I can't tell if he likes me."

"I bet he does," Mrs. Jones said. "I bet if you were sixteen he would ask you on a date."

The thought warmed Cassie's heart, but it wasn't enough. She couldn't ride on expectations for a year.

CHAPTER SIXTY

Brainiacs

Cassie's alarm went off at five o'clock on Monday, just like every school day, waking her for her early morning church class. She groaned to herself and dropped an arm over her eyes, wanting nothing more than to stay in bed a little longer.

But today was her birthday. She threw her legs off the side of the bed and stumbled around in the dark.

She collided hard with something at the edge of the bed, crashing both legs into jagged corners. Pain shot all the way down her calves, and she gasped loudly, hands shooting outward.

The hope chest! Her hands landed on the unforgiving cedar lid.

"I knew it," she moaned, righting herself and making it to the light switch without injury this time. "I knew I would hurt myself."

She turned on the light and winced as she examined her legs. Already a deep purple welt went from the top of her inner thigh all the way down to her calf. On both legs.

Those were going to be ugly bruises.

They once again announced Cassie's birthday, and Cassie had to endure the unending amount of teasing.

Somehow admitting to her friends that she liked Matt was like opening up Pandora's box. The feelings that Cassie had barely entertained became a roaring fire, and now all she could think about was Matt.

Cassie looked up to watch him walk by when he entered computers. He had gotten a haircut, and his blond hair was no longer long in the front, but cut short with a bit of a spiky look to it.

"I like your haircut," she blurted, then felt like an idiot.

"Thanks," he said, giving her an odd look.

He didn't say another word to her the rest of class.

"So since you had two birthdays this week, are you sixteen now?" Leigh Ann asked an English class.

Sixteen. Driving. Dating. "Hey, I'm good with that!" Cassie said.

She spotted Andrew walking out to the buses after choir, and she put a skip in her step, feeling closer to him since the play.

"Hello, Andrew!" Cassie said, slipping her arm in his and walking with him to the bus.

He gave her an amused smile. "Hi, Cassie. Why are you so happy?"

Cassie pressed her finger to her lips, not willing to reveal her secret but unable to keep it entirely. "Oh, no reason. I just maybe like someone."

He lifted an eyebrow knowingly. "Might this be someone I know?"

She changed the subject. "And you? How are your crushes?"

"I only have one. And I'm pretty sure you know who it is."

Cassie lowered her voice to conspiratorial whisper. "Nicole?"

He didn't give her an answer before stepping onto the bus. Cassie followed him and dropped into the seat in front of him.

"So?" she said, flipping around. "Nicole?"

Andrew smiled reluctantly. "Yeah. I've liked her for a long time, really. But after working with her in the play, now I can't help it. She's such a fun, awesome person."

"She's a great person," Cassie agreed. "I think you should go for it."

He looked thoughtful. "Maybe I will."

On Wednesday she spotted Matt outside of her algebra class after lunch. Cassie clutched her book to her chest and leaned against the wall, waiting for the classroom door to open. Cara and Janice were involved in a conversation, as were Andrea and Amity, and none of them noticed her staring at Matt.

He did. He turned his head slightly and caught her eye, then gave her a smile. Cassie's insides melted, and she smiled back.

The math teacher opened the door and ushered them in. Cassie stole one last glance over her shoulder. Matt had already disappeared.

❧

Cassie went home with Amity on Thursday night, since both of them had to go to the university for the regional science fair. Even though the girls weren't super friendly in school these days, Amity was very sweet when it was just the two of them.

"You hardly talk with us anymore," Amity said with a pout, as if she actually cared. "You're always sitting with your new friends."

The friends who never made Cassie feel like she didn't fit in. But she kept that sentiment herself. "We have classes together. Anytime you want to talk, just come over."

"Are there any dances coming up?"

Cassie shrugged. "I'm sure there are. I'll let you know as soon as I know something."

An impish glint entered Amity's eyes. "How's Zack?"

"He's fine, I guess. I don't really see him much."

Amity gave her a surprised look. "You don't seem too upset about that."

"Why should I be? There are lots of guys out there."

Now Amity's eyes went wide as if she smelled gossip. "Who do you like now?"

"Who do you like?" Cassie returned.

"Jared," Amity said without hesitation. "He's in my math class."

"Oh, Jared!" Cassie said. "He's so nice." He was in her civics class too. "Isn't he going to the science fair thing tomorrow?"

"Yes. He got an honorable mention." Amity narrowed her eyes, clearly not letting go of the earlier conversation trail. "And you? Who do you like?"

Cassie couldn't keep it to herself anymore. "Matt," she blurted. "He's in my computer class. We were in the play together."

Amity's eyes went wide. "Matt! He's so cute! You guys would be such a sweet couple."

"He's in your science class, isn't he?"

Amity nodded. "He got second place in his division, didn't you know? He'll be there tomorrow too."

"What?" Cassie said. How had she not known this? She leaned back against the wall on Amity's bed, digesting this information. "Looks like tomorrow is going to be a lot of fun."

Amity flashed a bright smile. "The best school day ever."

Amity's mother woke them early the next morning. "Come on, girls. We don't want to get stuck in the morning traffic."

Amity groaned and buried her head beneath her pillow, but this felt like sleeping in for Cassie. She was used to getting up for her early morning religion class. She couldn't help the tingling excitement she felt at the thought of spending all day outside of the classroom with Matt. Maybe this would be the day when he finally noticed her.

Amity turned on the radio in the car and sang loudly to every song that came on. "Sing along, Cassie."

Cassie rarely listen to the radio and didn't recognize any of the songs. When the radio was on in the car, her mom picked the station, and it was always some oldies station. So she just smiled and bobbed her head and tried to come in on the melody.

Mrs. Stafford parked behind an auditorium at the University of

Arkansas, and the girls removed their projects from the truck of the car. They followed Mrs. Stafford into a room inside filled with kids their age setting up their projects. Right away Cassie spotted Jared, and she was about to nudge Amity and point him out when Amity's face lit up.

"Matt!" she said, lifting her hand and waving wildly.

Where? Cassie spun and then saw him standing with his project at a table. He tossed his head when he saw the girls and smiled.

Amity used her hips to maneuver through the crowd and make her way to his table, leaving Cassie behind. "Excuse me. Sorry. Coming through," Cassie mumbled apologetically, following Amity's footsteps. By the time she got to Matt's table, Amity was laughing at something he'd said and setting up her own poster beside his.

Something hard tightened in Cassie's stomach. Wasn't Amity supposed to be interested in Jared?

Amity turned around and saw her. "There's an empty table over there, Cassie," she said, pointing two rows over.

"Thanks," Cassie said, burning with indignation. She'd been a fool to tell Amity who she liked. She was certain the only reason Amity was flirting with Matt now was because she knew Cassie liked him.

Cassie got her poster set up, and when she turned around, Jared had joined Amity and Matt. Suspecting that this day would not go as she wanted it to, Cassie wandered over to join them.

Amity latched onto her, giggling, and Matt kept right on talking, never once glancing in Cassie's direction.

"Hello, gang!" Mr. Adams' voice boomed out, and he smiled as he joined them. "Looks like you're all set up! The judging won't take place for another hour, and then the award ceremony isn't until after lunch."

"What do we do with the kids until then?" Mrs. Stafford asked.

"There's a museum here on campus. You could take them there. There's also a bookstore."

Bookstore. Cassie perked up at that.

"Then we'll come back for the judging and take them to lunch after."

"Who would like to do the museum and who would like to do the bookstore?" Mrs. Stafford asked.

"Bookstore," Cassie said.

"Oh, you would say that!" Amity gave her a little shove. "You're so predictable!"

"Yeah," Matt said, chiming in. "We don't have to read today. We're not in school."

"Who wants to do something as boring as reading anyway?" Amity followed up her insulting statement with a giggle. Cassie wanted to punch her in the face.

"I like books," Jared said. "I'll go with Cassie to the bookstore."

Mrs. Stafford shook her head and looked at the other mothers present. "I don't like the idea of splitting up."

"Let's do the museum first," Jared's mom said. "And then if there's still time, we can do the bookstore."

Amity's mom looked relieved. "That sounds like a plan. Cassie? Does that sound okay?"

What did she expect Cassie to do, cry because they weren't going to the bookstore? "Of course. That's totally fine with me." The question irritated her. She never said she didn't want to go to the museum; she said she preferred the bookstore.

It was raining outside, and Cassie huddled close to Amity to try to stay warm. "I've got an umbrella in the car!" Mrs. Stafford said, and she ran down the steps to the parking lot.

"Oh yeah, I forgot my mom sent me with one." Matt dug around in his backpack and pulled out a little blue one. "I rode with Jared, but I've got it here. Amity, you can share with me."

Amity immediately released Cassie's arm and jumped under the umbrella with Matt. "We'll see you guys there!" she said with a wave.

Mrs. Stafford returned with an umbrella that she shared with Cassie, and Jared walked with his mom under one as well. Cassie glared ahead at Amity walking with Matt, her hand tucked into the crook of his elbow.

They arrived at the museum shortly thereafter, and they folded up their umbrellas and leaned them against the wall. It was a museum on the history of music, and Cassie wandered through the displays with little interest. She enjoyed singing, but the rest of this did not engage her.

Jared stepped to her side as she thumbed through a case of old record labels. "Amity sure is following Matt around."

"Yep." The knowledge filled her with cold fury.

"I guess she likes him, huh?"

Cassie glanced at him, wondering if he felt a little bit hurt. Maybe betrayed. Had Amity spent time flirting with him in class? In a sudden impulse, Cassie said, "No, actually. She likes you."

Jared looked at Cassie and blinked in clear surprise. "Me? But she's not even talking to me."

Cassie shrugged and shoved away the nagging guilt. "Sometimes she gets a little shy around guys she really likes. She told me last night. You're the one she likes." Which was true, or at least that's what Amity said.

Jared straightened up, his eyes looking a little brighter. "That's great to know. Thanks, Cassie. If only all girls were as easy to talk to as you are."

Cassie ground her teeth together as he walked away. Easy to talk to. A good friend. She wanted a guy see her as more than that.

She had to giggle as she watched Jared come up on Amity's other side and engage her in conversation. She wouldn't be able to spend the whole day flirting with Matt now.

They spent over an hour killing time at the museum while Cassie wished they had gone to a bookstore. Then they returned to the auditorium to be present as the judges came through. Cassie's booth was separate from her schoolmates, and she watched them joke with each other enviously. The kids on either side of her were from other schools, and she knew she should make friends and get a conversation going while she waited for the judges, but she didn't want to. Wallowing in her own misery at the moment was more validating.

The judges came by her booth all at once, and two of them start taking notes while the third asked her questions. Cassie answered all of them competently and pointed out the experiment she had done using solar power, as well as the results. Their faces looked suitably impressed, but only the first judge asked questions. Then they continued on.

It was almost lunchtime when the judging was concluded.

"The award ceremony will be in two hours," Mr. Adams said, gathering the four of them together. "That gives us time to grab a quick lunch. Anyone hungry?"

The boys responded enthusiastically, but Cassie just gave a little smile. She was still a vegetarian, and she got tired of defending that choice to people when everyone asked where she wanted to eat. She said she'd go wherever the majority wanted. Which ended up being Mexican.

They walked down Dixon Street, the Main Street near the university, and went to Jose's. For being lunch on a weekday, the Mexican restaurant was quite crowded.

"It'll be an hour wait to get your food," a waitress told their group. "I can get you seated right away though."

"I don't know. Should we do it?" Mrs. Stafford asked.

"We don't have anything else to do with the kids," Jared's mom said. "At least here we can sit and relax."

That decided it.

Cassie looked over the menu and picked a quesadilla, and then because it seemed to be calling her name, she ordered a fried ice cream. She'd never had one before, but Amity swore they were the best.

"Did you see the bruises on Cassie's legs?" Amity asked Mr. Adams and her mom.

"No. What bruises?" Mrs. Stafford asked.

"It's nothing," Cassie said in embarrassment. "I hit my legs getting out of bed the other day."

"The bruises are awful," Amity said, seeming to enjoy the attention much more than Cassie. "Show them, Cassie."

She was wearing a skirt today that barely hit her knees, so all she had to do was turn her legs outward to show the bruises running from her thigh down to her calves.

Mr. Adams winced and Mrs. Stafford gave a gasp.

"Oh, those look terrible!"

"Those are really ugly bruises, Cassie," Mr. Adams said. "I think maybe you're not getting enough protein."

"She's a vegetarian," Amity said.

Mr. Adams nodded. "Definitely need to eat more protein."

"I got beans in my quesadilla," Cassie said. At least she was eating. That was more than she'd been doing a year ago.

She ate the rest of the meal without talking to Amity, who was too busy stealing Matt's nachos to notice. Jared spent lunch vying for Amity's attention also, apparently determined to make her feel at ease.

Cassie felt nothing but frustration.

The fried ice cream arrived for dessert, looking like a circular rice crispy treat with whipped cream and a cherry on top. As soon as the waitress put it in front of Cassie, Amity snatched the cherry and ate it.

"Hey!" Cassie said.

"Sorry," Amity said, grinning with the cherry stem hanging out of her mouth. "That's my favorite part."

"And that was my ice cream!" Cassie said.

Not that Amity was paying attention anymore.

By the time they returned to the auditorium, the beans and cheese and ice cream were doing a number on Cassie's stomach. She grabbed Amity's arm. "I have to go to the bathroom. Save a spot for me?"

"Of course."

Cassie hurried to the bathroom, not wanting to walk into the awards ceremony after it started. What if she won and wasn't present? She finished up and washed her hands, then rushed back to the auditorium.

The lights were off, and a man stood on the stage speaking into a microphone. Cassie crept down the dark aisle, searching for Amity. Finally she spotted her.

"Amity!" she hissed, causing everyone in the row to turn and look at her.

Amity waved, then looked around. There were no empty seats. On one side of Amity sat Matt and on the other sat Jared.

Seriously? She couldn't even save Cassie a seat?

Cassie turned to look for another seat, but Amity said, "We'll scoot down! There's one at the end!"

Cassie waited awkwardly while Amity asked everyone in the row to scoot down one. The man on the stage kept talking, and the rows around them shot them dirty looks. Finally she breathed a sigh of relief as she moved down the row and sat next to Amity.

"Thanks for saving me a spot," she said.

"No problem," Amity said.

Apparently sarcasm was lost on her.

But then the man began calling out the awards, and Cassie forgot to be frustrated. "We had three different categories this year: biology, earth science, and physics. In biology, the honorable mention goes to Amity Stafford."

Amity squealed and everyone clapped as she made her way to the front to receive a certificate. Cassie clapped politely and then tuned out the rest until they got to her category.

"In earth science, honorable mention goes to Keisha Smith."

Cassie clapped again, her heart starting to beat faster. She didn't want honorable mention; there was no prize money with that. But it was better than not placing at all.

"In third place, Cassandra Jones."

Again everyone clapped, and Cassie exhaled in a mixture of relief and disappointment. At least third place got ten dollars. But it would've been nice to place higher.

"First place goes to Matt Spivot."

Matt! Matt got first place! That was worth fifty dollars! Cassie expected to feel jealous, but instead a surge of pride filled her that he had done so well. Beside him, Amity cheered like she was at a football game. He grinned widely and went on stage to get his prize.

The ceremony finally ended, and Cassie went to her isolated table to pick up her science fair project. A strange melancholy burned at the back of her eyes. She had thought today would be so amazing. But all it did was make her feel second best. Again.

CHAPTER SIXTY-ONE

Lost in Love

A ndrea called Cassie as soon as school was out on Friday.
"You weren't in school today and Cara said you spent the night with Amity. Where were you guys?"

"We had a science fair thing at the university," Cassie said. She lay back on her bed and stared at the ceiling.

"Was it fun? Amity said you kept flirting with Matt."

Cassie bolted upright. "What? I hardly talked to him! Amity sat by him and kept touching him and giggling!"

"Okay, okay." Andrea laughed. "That sounds like what she would do. What are you doing? Come over for a bit."

Cassie's soul sighed. What she really needed was to branch out into new friends. But she felt stuck in an endless cycle of being angry at them while still clinging to the comfort their social circle offered. "Yeah, sure. I'll ask my mom to bring me over."

She half expected Mrs. Jones to argue about Cassie being gone again, but she didn't. She drove her the twenty minutes into town, and Cassie hopped out of the car.

"I'm meeting your dad in Fayetteville for a date," Mrs. Jones said. "I'll pick you up on the way home. Probably in four hours."

"Okay." Cassie headed up the front walk.

"Hi!" Andrea said, greeting her with a tight hug. "My mom's taking us to the mall." She pulled Cassie into her room and looked over her clothes. "You can't wear that, though."

Cassie knew without looking at her jeans and T-shirt that it didn't meet Andrea's fashion standards. "I didn't bring anything else."

"Put my clothes on." Andrea winked at her and hauled a pair of cut-off shorts from the closet. "These will look fantastic on you! Your legs are so skinny and tan." She added a button-up, sleeveless plaid shirt. "Go on, try them on."

Cassie slipped out of her jeans and into the shorts, and she couldn't help admiring how toned and sexy her legs looked in the mirror. "They make me look taller."

"You look so hot. Now the shirt."

"Wait." Cassie turned around and examined her rear. The shorts didn't cover much; if they were any shorter, she'd risk showing off her underwear. "I can't wear these."

"Of course you can. I do it all the time."

Cassie wavered as she looked again at her reflection. For once she looked older than her age of fifteen. Then she thought of what her mom would say if she saw the shorts, and Cassie shook her head. "Give me a different pair. One that's a bit longer."

Andrea rolled her eyes, but she found a pair of cut-offs that didn't leave Cassie feeling exposed.

"You good now?" Andrea asked, clearly annoyed.

"Yes," Cassie said, a bit sheepishly. "Sorry." But why should she apologize? Why should she feel pressured to wear something that wasn't comfortable to her?

"It's fine. Let's go."

Mrs. Wall drove them to the mall and then let them walk around on their own. They ate dinner at the cafe overlooking the parking lot, giggling and pointing to people who walked by, oblivious to being watched.

"Look at those two guys," Andrea said, pointing to the tall boys as they walked by. "They are such hotties."

One of them turned and elbowed his friend, and both of them looked at Andrea.

"Andrea!" Cassie grabbed her friend's finger and shoved it under the table.

"Let's go," Andrea said. "They've seen us!"

The girls put their napkins on the table and hurried out of the restaurant, only to bump into the two boys as they walked in the front entrance to the mall.

"Hey, there you are," one of the boys said in accented English. He smiled, wavy brown hair falling across his forehead. "My friend here thinks you're cute."

The other one nodded at them, his straight dark hair partially hidden under a baseball cap. "Holá," he said.

"He doesn't speak English really well," the boy said, still looking straight at Andrea. "But he wanted to know if he could get your number. He can text."

"Yeah, sure!" Andrea said, and she fed him the digits.

"Thanks," the first one said. "Do you mind if I use it also? I might call sometime. You know. Maybe we can get together."

"I'd love that," Andrea giggled.

They waved and walked away, never once glancing at Cassie.

"What am I, invisible?" Cassie sputtered, hurt and embarrassed.

"It's because you didn't wear those shorts." Andrea hooked her arm through Cassie's, and Cassie examined Andrea's clothes closer. She wore the short shorts, and a bit of her stomach showed when she walked.

"Why should I have to show skin to get a guy to notice me?" Cassie said.

"That's how it works, Cass." Andrea gave her a sympathetic look. "Balloons! Come on, this will cheer you up!" She hauled Cassie over to a man handing out floating pink orbs to children as they left the mall.

"How is that supposed to cheer me up?" Cassie said, but Andrea ignored her.

"Can we get one?" she asked the man.

He looked at them and laughed. "Sure."

They tied the balloons around their wrists, and then Andrea grabbed Cassie and ran outside. Laughing, she ran around the parking lot chasing her balloon. Cassie couldn't help it. She laughed also.

Andrea's phone rang, and she stopped to check it. "Oh, it's Tyler!"

"Tyler?" Cassie followed Andrea to a bench on the sidewalk. "Does he call you a lot?"

"Hello?" Andrea said into the phone. "Hi! I'm great. Just hanging out at the mall with Cassie. Yeah, she's right here." She pulled the phone away and said, "He says hi."

"Hi," Cassie mumbled.

"Oh, it was so funny, we were watching these cute guys and they saw us! Then they came over, but they only wanted to talk to me! They didn't even look at Cassie!"

"Andrea!" Cassie slapped her arm, hot tears stinging her eyes in humiliation. How could Andrea tell that to Tyler? Was she trying to make Cassie look bad?

"Yeah," Andrea laughed. "They both got my phone number, and it was like Cassie wasn't even there!" Pulling the phone away again, she said, "Don't feel bad, Cassie. Some day they'll be interested in you."

Cassie stood up and walked away before Andrea could see the tears rolling down her cheeks. This was friendship? *I hate her*, she thought. *I hate them all.*

❧

Both Maureen and Andrea called Saturday afternoon, but Cassie ignored them. She didn't want to talk to either of them. She did, however, call Riley and vent to her.

"I can't believe Amity hung all over Matt after I told her I liked him. And then Andrea made fun of me in front of Tyler!"

"I never did like them," Riley said.

"I always thought it was because you were jealous," Cassie admitted.

"It's because they're fake."

Were they? Cassie hated to believe it.

She avoided looking at Tyler in church on Sunday. He didn't say anything to her, either, so it wasn't difficult. Then on her way out of the chapel, she spotted Zack and his family stepping inside.

"Hi, Cassie," Zack said, giving her his friendly smile.

Cassie stopped and smiled back. "Hi."

And that was it. Nothing melted inside of her. His smile didn't reduce her to goo. She turned away, disappointed to realize her crush had moved from Zack to Matt.

⚬∾≈∻≈∾⚬

"It's this Saturday," Amity blubbered at lunch on Monday. "Cheerleading tryouts are this Saturday. I'm going to Melanie's house every day this week. She's helping me with my routine, and I just know I'll make it this year."

Cassie didn't say a word. This was the first time she'd sat at their lunch table in over a week, and she'd missed all the cheerleading hype. Just like last year, she secretly hoped Amity wouldn't make it. Since becoming friends with Melanie, Amity had changed. She was meaner and more secretive, and Cassie could just imagine what would happen if she were on the team.

Cara glanced at her phone and then back at Amity. "That's four days away."

"I know." Amity squeezed her hands together. "This is it. It's my last chance."

Janice looked down the table at Andrea and Maureen. "Aren't you guys trying out?"

Maureen shook her head. "Not this year. I don't really care anymore."

"Yeah," Andrea agreed. "I'm over that scene."

Amity rolled her eyes. "You guys are just afraid you won't make it since you didn't in junior high. But you're trying out, right, Cara?"

Cara shrugged and took a sip of her chocolate milk. "I don't think so. One year was enough for me." She stood up and threw her milk carton in the trash.

"She's not trying out because she knows she's not good enough," Amity hissed, leaning across the table to make sure everyone heard. "She never should have made cheerleading to begin with. She's the worst one out there."

"Hush your mouth," Janice said, slapping a hand at her. "She's coming back."

The table fell silent and Amity went back to her fries, sneaking peeks at Cara as the other girl sat down.

⚬───✦───⚬

"Cassie, someone called for you today," Mrs. Jones said when Cassie got home from school.

Cassie pulled her phone out of her purse and checked to make sure it was on. "I didn't see any calls come through."

"This one came on my phone."

Cassie frowned at her mother. "Why would they call you to talk to me?"

Mrs. Jones shrugged and handed her the phone number. "They called on the landline. You can call them back that way or use your own phone."

Cassie didn't recognize the number. Deciding she would rather continue to keep her phone number a secret, she wandred into the kitchen and picked up the cordless phone, then dialed the number.

"Raspberry Publications, how can I direct your call?" a woman's voice said.

Cassie nearly dropped the phone in surprise. She stole a glance at her mother in the living room and saw a smile creeping up Mrs. Jones' lips. Apparently her mom had known who called but hadn't told her. "I, um, hi. This is Cassandra Jones. I missed a call from you guys earlier."

"Yes, hi, Cassandra! We've been reviewing your manuscript and are interested in pursuing it. We're a boutique publisher, and we like to get the author's input for the cover design. Did you have anything in mind of what you might want?"

Cassie tried to imagine what cover she would put on her book. Four girls walking through a forest? Maybe doing some kind of best friend handshake with a lake in the background? "I don't really have anything. I could maybe brainstorm something."

"Why don't you think about it? We're going to send you some forms, if you don't mind, and if you decide to continue with the process, we'd be happy to discuss this in more detail."

Cassie's head spun. The woman hadn't come out and said it, but . . . "Does this mean you're going to publish my book?"

"It means we would like to. Take a look at the contract we'll send you and then get back with us, all right? And since you're a minor, your parents will have to sign as well."

"Okay. Okay. Thanks." Cassie hung up the phone, placed it on the counter, and then squealed and jumped up and down.

"What is it?" Mrs. Jones asked, appearing in the doorway. "What's going on?"

"They want to publish my book!" Cassie jumped up and down some more. "It's going to get published!"

"Cassie, that's fantastic!" Mrs. Jones hugged her. "I'm so happy for you."

Cassie couldn't stop grinning. "They're mailing me a contract for us to look over and sign. And I need to go brainstorm cover designs!" Cassie ran to her room and pulled out a notepad, ready to start drawing.

☙❖❧

Cassie waited after school on Tuesday for her mom to join her for class conferences. Since next year was high school, the teachers wouldn't stop stressing how important it was to pick the right classes. Cassie spotted Amity in another classroom, and they waved at each other.

High school would be a whole new ballgame, and it terrified Cassie. What if her classes were too hard and this was the year they discovered she was dumb?

"Sorry I'm late," Mrs. Jones said, letting out a breath as she dropped into a chair beside Cassie.

"Hello, Mrs. Jones," Coach Benson said. Cassie's civics teacher was her academic adviser. "Cassie's such a fantastic student. I'm excited to see what classes she chooses."

"What should she pick?" Mrs. Jones pushed her hair back and focused on the sheet of options in front of her.

"Here are the core classes she has to pick, but based on her grades and aptitude, I'd recommend she take all advanced classes."

"All advanced?" Cassie uttered. "What if it's too much for me?"

He winked at her. "It won't be."

Twenty minutes later they had her classes picked out. She'd continue with Spanish, starting Spanish 2, and advanced English, choir, Biology 2, geometry, history, and P.E. P.E. again! She couldn't believe kids were still forced to take that in high school.

"This looks like a fun schedule," Mrs. Jones said as they walked out of the classroom. "A few hard classes, but it's good for you to be challenged."

Amity and her mother walked out of the classroom in front of Cassie, and Cassie called out, "Amity. What classes did you get?"

Amity paused and consulted her schedule. "English, biology, choir, history, geometry, and cheerleading."

Cassie brightened. "We might have a few classes together!"

Amity looked over Cassie's paper. "Choir, for sure."

"Of course." Cassie was confident they would both make the select sophomore choir.

"Maybe history and geometry. But with our luck, we won't have any of the same classes." Amity rolled her eyes.

Cassie tried not to panic at those words. Making new friends had never been easy for her. Not when they'd moved to Arkansas, and not when she started over in seventh grade. She felt confident about entering high school because she wasn't going in alone.

"I'm sure you'll have at least a few classes together," Mrs. Stafford said, smiling at them.

"You definitely will," Mrs. Jones said. "You'll see. High school is a blast."

CHAPTER SIXTY-TWO
Clinical Studies

Mrs. Jones drove Cassie to the mall after the conference so they could buy a dress for her spring music recital.

"Maybe something flowery," Mrs. Jones said, fingering a few dresses in the Dillard's department store. "You know, for spring time."

Flower prints sounded so elementary school, and Cassie was getting ready for high school. "I want something more sophisticated." She found another rack and thumbed through. "Oo, this is lovely." She pulled off a cream-colored dress with a short, flowing skirt and embroidered flowers around the waistline. The soft fabric glided over her fingers.

"It sure is pretty. Want to try it on?"

"Can I?"

"Sure!"

They went into a dressing room, and just as Cassie had suspected, the dress slid over her shoulders and drifted around her body, hugging her chest before dropping in an Empire waistline. "Oh, it's beautiful!" she gasped out. Her heart leapt, and she loved the dress. Even though she worried she hadn't prepared well enough for the recital, now she looked forward to it.

But when she looked at her mother, Mrs. Jones was frowning. Her eyes were on the hem. "I think it's too short."

Cassie looked back at her reflection. The skirt stopped four inches above her knee. "Oh, that's definitely not too short."

"Your dad won't like it."

"So?" Cassie laughed and twirled. "I love it."

"We can't do it, Cassie. It's too short."

Cassie stopped and stared at her mom. "Seriously?"

"Yes, Cassie. Find a different dress."

She shook her head. "No. It's got to be this one."

"I won't debate this with you. We're not getting this dress."

"Mom!" Anger shivered through Cassie, and she clenched a fist. "I don't wear things that are too short! All my friends know I won't! I don't ask for clothes, I never complain about not having the cool styles. I want this dress. It's what I'm asking for."

But Mrs. Jones didn't back down. "I've raised you better than this. If I tell you it's too short, it's too short. You'll be sending boys the wrong message about what kind of person you are."

Boys. Wrong message. Cassie's mind flashed back to the words Andrea had said over the weekend. *You'll never get a boy without showing some skin*, or something like that. Cassie exhaled slowly. She wanted this dress. She really did. But she wouldn't be able to convince her mom. "Let me try on a bigger size. Maybe it's longer."

"Fine."

Cassie tried on every size they had, all the way to the biggest. And only when she reached the largest size did the length hit her knees, which was what Mrs. Jones wanted. But by that point, the dress had become so large and billowy that it slid off both shoulders.

"I think this dress is a no, Cassie."

Cassie put it back on the hanger, wanting to cry. "You pick one, then. No flowers."

Mrs. Jones returned to the dressing room with a cute summer dress, a white bodice and a black skirt. The top dipped low in a V in the back, and Mrs. Jones smiled.

"This is lovely. It's still sexy without showing too much skin."

Cassie tried it on. The V-line in the back went low enough that Cassie wouldn't be able to wear a normal bra. Why was this better than the other dress? It was pretty, but it didn't give the same innocent, girly, flirtatious feel that the other one had. "Fine."

⚬﹏⚬

Cassie set her alarm to get up early so she could curl her hair before her church class Thursday morning. The ninth graders had a field trip to the high school, and Nicole said her brother was in the musical and they would see him. Cassie wanted to look nice if she was going to meet him. Her feelings were all mixed up about him. She just wanted some boy to notice her and like her.

But when she finally heard the alarm going off, she realized she had slept through it. She scrambled out of bed and quickly threw on her clothes, having only ten minutes to get ready.

But her hair! It hung plain and boring past her shoulder blades. Long, dark, and straight. Not what she planned for looking glamorous today.

On impulse, she grabbed the cold curling iron from the bathroom counter and shoved it into her purse. She had plenty of time at school. She could do her hair there.

She kept herself awake in her religion class by putting on makeup and studiously avoiding looking at Tyler. They hadn't spoken since Andrea mentioned Cassie to him on the phone.

As soon as she got to school, she plugged the iron into the outlet in the bathroom and began curling her hair.

"Good morning!" Cara said, coming in and giving Cassie a hug.

"Morning," Cassie said. She wished she were better friends with Cara because she seemed to be the only person besides Janice who actually liked her.

Amity came in next, talking excitedly about some cheerleading videos she found online that she was sure would give her the best skills ever. She stopped and looked at Cassie.

"What are you doing?"

What did it look like she was doing? "I'm curling my hair."

Andrea and Maureen joined them at the mirror. Maureen frowned at Cassie. "What are you doing?"

"I'm curling my hair," Cassie said, feeling irritated.

The conversation moved past her. Amity kept bringing it back to cheerleading tryouts on Saturday, especially when Melanie walked into the bathroom. Amity squealed and grabbed her hands like she was a celebrity.

Melanie's eyes glanced at Cassie in the mirror, and then she said, "What are you doing?"

Seriously? Cassie finished curling the last piece of hair and unplugged the curling iron. "It's a curling iron. It was plugged in and hot. What do you think I was doing?" Not caring if she sounded rude, Cassie wrapped a cloth around the hot rod and stuck it in her backpack. Then she tossed her hair and walked out of the bathroom.

In the middle of second hour, the intercom turned on and excused all the ninth graders for the field trip. Cassie walked next to Jaclyn, keeping Matt in her line of sigh. He was walking with his friends, Kevin and Jerry, and didn't spare Cassie a second glance.

She exhaled. He just wasn't interested.

Nicole was standing in the parking lot scanning the crowd. She waved when she spotted Cassie. "You have to sit with me. I told my brother we'd be together so he could look for me and you." Nicole wrapped her finger around one of Cassie's curls, which was already starting to relax. "Your hair looks so pretty."

"Thanks."

Cassie sat with Nicole and motioned Riley over when she got on the bus. Riley and Jaclyn sat down in front of Cassie. Cassie did a quick search for Amity or Cara, but they must've gotten onto a different bus, and Cassie found she really didn't care that much.

The girls were quite goofy on the drive, singing songs about flying. But the closer they got to the high school, the more nervous Cassie became.

"What's your brother's name?" she asked Nicole.

"Sean. He's so nice. Too bad we won't be able to talk to him."

"Yeah," Cassie said, though secretly she was glad for one less thing to be nervous about.

The buses parked behind the high school auditorium, and the students filed en mass to the seats facing the stage. Nicole pulled Cassie right over to the middle and sat down with her.

"He'll be able to see us here," she said.

"What did he say about me, again?" Cassie wove her fingers together and pulled on the joints.

"Well, after he saw you at the Shakespeare Festival, he told me he though you were cute. And I said, 'she's only fifteen,' and he said, 'she's your age?' It was really funny."

"Sounds funny," Cassie said.

The lights dimmed in the auditorium and a hush fell over the students. Then orchestra music filtered through the air, the curtain lifted, and a man walked on stage. He began to sing in a strong operatic voice, telling a story in song.

"That's not him," Nicole said.

"I figured," Cassie replied.

The man stepped back and new scenery rolled on, complete with a girl hanging out a window. She immediately launched into song, waving her handkerchief, and another cast member ran out, skidding to a halt under her window. He pressed his hands to his chest, and then began a rousing choral response to her words.

"That's my brother," Nicole said, grinning.

All Cassie could see was the back of him. He had a nice voice and was definitely tall. The stage lights made his hair look almost white, though she suspected it was the same golden blond as Nicole's. "He's cute," Cassie said, for lack of anything better to say.

"He'll see you when he looks for me."

That moment didn't come until midway through the musical, during the intermission. Right when the curtain was about to close, the boy and girl joined hands and flitted off stage. As they did, Sean's head turned and scanned the audience. Nicole lifted her hand in a little wave, and he smiled.

"He saw me," Nicole said as the curtain fell. "So I'm sure he saw you. Let's hang around after and see if we can talk to him."

The play continued, a little on the boring side, but at least they weren't in school. When it ended, Nicole tried to elbow her way through the crowd to get to the cast members, but a teacher stood in their way.

"Go out the same way we came in," he said. "The buses are waiting."

"My brother was in the musical," Nicole said. "I just wanted to say hi."

"You'll see him after school, right?"

"Yes, but—"

"Then continue to the buses."

Nicole pouted, but Cassie was relieved. She wouldn't have to be friendly and flirt just yet.

※

All Amity could talk about the rest of the day Thursday and all day Friday was cheerleading tryouts. She brought it up at lunch, in math class, and in choir she and Melanie talked loud enough about it to make sure everyone knew they were trying out.

"I cannot wait for this to be over," Janice said, rolling her eyes.

"No. Kidding."

"Just a few more days."

"Yeah." Cassie laughed, but then her thoughts turned elsewhere. She had her own competition to worry about on Saturday, and that was whether she would make the Festival recital or not.

Cassie distracted herself at home by working on her cover designs in her bedroom.

"I am not a very good artist," Cassie said.

Her sister Emily leaned across the desk to look at the sketches Cassie had made. "The faces are a little distorted."

"No kidding." Cassie crumpled up the piece of paper, her fifth attempt at designing a cover. "I think I'm just going to have to tell them I can't do this."

"I could do one for you," Emily said.

"Yeah, maybe." Frustrated with the effort's, she shoved aside her notepad and pencils. "I'll worry about it later." She glanced at the clock on her phone. Somehow it had gotten late, and she had to sleep so she'd be ready to get up early and sing tomorrow. "I'll brainstorm and tackle this tomorrow."

※

"Wake up, Cassie!"

Cassie couldn't get her eyes to obey. She was aware of her mother in her room, opening the blinds and shaking the blankets. But Cassie had stayed up late working on book stuff and just wanted to sleep.

"Cassie, come on. You've got clinic this morning. You have to get a superior to be in the recital tonight."

Cassie's eyes shot open as adrenaline took a nose-dive through her system. The recital! She remembered the black and white dress they'd bought, the song she'd been practicing. "That's today!"

"Yes! We leave in an hour! Get ready!"

Cassie hummed her song in her head as she pulled half her hair up. She had wanted to curl it but didn't have time now. Her hands trembled. Making the recital required her to have a superior score. Only the very best got to move on.

She paused as the words to her song slipped away from her. Now was no time to be nervous! She shook her head and started the verse over, concentrating. This time she didn't forget. She pulled her dress on over her head and had to admit it looked nice. She looked sophisticated. Not flirty and girly like the other dress, but still good.

Ms. Malcolm was waiting in the tiled entryway of the art center when Cassie walked in.

"Hurry up," she hissed, marching Cassie down the hall. "You're almost late. You could have missed it."

"Sorry," Cassie mumbled, trying to ignore the way her heart suddenly started leaping about in her chest.

The judge smiled at her when she walked in, but it didn't put Cassie at ease. She handed her music to the judge so she could follow along, and then stepped back and waited. *One, two, three . . .* She counted the measures until she entered, took a preparatory breath, and came in on time. The words danced in front of her mind's eye, one step ahead of her. She fought back a wince when the third stanza of the second verse sounded more staccato than legato, but she managed to smooth it out by the end.

"Thank you. That was very nice," the judge said, smiling at her.

The look Ms. Malcolm gave from behind the piano wasn't so courteous, and Cassie sighed. She should have prepared more.

"Was it that bad?" she asked her teacher as they returned to the entry way.

Ms. Malcolm flipped through the music. "You tripped up at measure seven, went too fast on measure thirty-two, and forgot to slow down at the end. We'll see what the judge says."

Not too promising. Cassie gave her mom a weak smile and tried to act like it didn't matter.

"I guess I won't make the recital."

Mrs. Jones looked disappointed also. "That's all right. There's always next year."

Cassie swallowed hard and climbed into the car. It would be the first year she didn't get a superior rating at clinic. And of course it would happen on the year she was finally old enough to go to the recital.

They had barely pulled into the driveway at home when Mrs. Jones' phone rang. She slid it out of her purse and parked the car. "Hello?" Her eyes shot toward Cassie, who immediately sat up straighter and leaned closer. "She did? Well, that's fantastic! Yes, we'll be there, she'll be excited!"

"What is it?" Cassie asked, afraid to hope.

Mrs. Jones put her phone back and beamed at her. "You got a superior rating! You made the recital!"

CHAPTER SIXTY-THREE

Final Straw

Cassie tried to pretend she didn't care if Amity made cheerleading or not, but as the day rolled by, she couldn't help glancing at the clock and thinking, *Amity is trying out now,* and then, *Tryouts are over.* Her heart gave a thud in her chest. Had Amity made it? In spite of their differences the past few months, the thought of losing Amity as a friend completely saddened Cassie. They hadn't lost Cara when she made cheerleading, but Cara had decided she didn't fit in with that crowd. Somehow Cassie doubted Amity would be the same way.

Nobody called Cassie to tell her the news, and finally when she could resist no longer, she called Amity.

"Hi, Cassie," Amity said, answering on the first ring. "I bet you're calling to tell me not to feel bad."

Cassie opened her mouth to respond, but Amity continued without preamble.

"I really don't care anymore," Amity said. "Cheerleading was super important to me last year, but this year, I don't care. I've got my friends. So it doesn't matter."

So Amity hadn't made it. "I'm so glad you're okay with it, Amity. And you're right. You have your friends, and we don't care if you're a cheerleader." *In fact, we like you more if you're not.*

"I know. Thanks for calling, Cassie. I appreciate it."

The girls hung up, and Cassie sighed, feeling unresolved. Amity had not made cheerleading, but Cassie had a feeling their friendship was dissolving anyway.

Two more hours before the recital.

This time she was not in a rush. Cassandra took the time to curl her hair before putting half of it up. She brushed blush over her cheekbones and mascara over her lashes. Then she drew back and smiled at her reflection.

Combined with the new dress her mom had bought her, the one with the sophisticated white top and black skirt, she looked stunning.

They arrived at the art center almost an hour before the recital started. Cassie looked around for familiar faces and spotted a girl she knew from choir. They waved at each other, but that was the extent of it. They weren't really friends.

"Cassie." Ms. Malcolm bustled over in a glittery gold dress, dressed to the nines as if about to accept an Oscar. "Congratulations. You're lucky you got a superior rating after all the mistakes you made."

Thanks for the reminder, she thought. But she smiled gracefully and said, "I'll definitely be on my guard this time. I won't make those mistakes again." She was certain she wouldn't. She had practiced her song at least five times since the audition to make sure she didn't mess up again.

Miss Malcolm gave her a dubious look but hurried away to talk to another student.

Cassie took a step across the entryway toward the auditorium doors, but a man hurried to her side and stopped her.

"Excuse me," he said, "are you performing tonight?"

"Yes." Cassie noticed the microphone in his hand and looked past him to see a very large camera sitting on the shoulders of his companion.

"Do you mind if we interview you for the news tonight? It will be really quick."

It took two seconds for his words to settle into Cassie's mind. "I would be on TV?"

He nodded and waited for her response.

Cassie straightened her shoulders and imagined she must look really beautiful for them to ask her. "Sure!"

"Great." He pulled out a tiny microphone on a string and pinned it to the top of her dress, then opened a notepad. "Can I get your name and age?"

"Cassandra Jones. I'm fifteen."

"Okay, I'm gonna have the camera start rolling, and then I'll just ask a few questions. I'll edit our interview to just a few minutes."

Cassie nodded, unwelcome butterflies surging up in her chest.

The cameraman held up a hand and counted down from five to one finger, and then the man in front of Cassie spoke.

"I'm here right now with Cassandra Jones from Springdale, Arkansas, as she gets ready to perform at tonight's annual recital of the arts. What are you performing for us tonight, Cassandra?"

"I'll be singing 'Kitty of Coleraine.'"

"I understand there's something of a rigorous selection process to be in this recital. What did you have to do?"

"We had a clinic this morning. In order to sing in the recital, you have to get a superior rating. It's the highest rating awarded."

"And you got that rating, I'm assuming?"

Cassie laughed. "Yes, but I was really surprised. I thought I did horrible on my performance."

He smiled back at her. "You must not have done as bad as you thought. How do you feel now that you've made it here?"

"Well, it's a great honor. I get to perform with other artists who have worked really hard for this. It's a privilege to be here, and I am really grateful to my teacher Ms. Malcolm for helping me get this far."

The man nodded at her. "Thank you, Cassandra. I think we can expect great things from you in the future." He put the microphone down and unpinned the one on her dress. "You were a natural. I wouldn't be surprise to see you on television someday."

Cassie could not wipe the smile from her face as she walked into the auditorium.

She hadn't even sung yet when the text messages started rolling in as her friends saw her on the evening news.

You were on TV! Amity said.

You looked so beautiful! Andrea texted.

I hope to be as good of a singer as you someday! Janice said.

Cassie sighed, relishing the feeling. It felt nice to be adored.

And to top it off, her performance went so well that even Ms. Malcolm was pleased with her.

⟡

Maureen called Cassie as Mrs. Jones drove her home from the recital.

"Hey, I saw you on TV tonight."

"Yeah, that was a total surprise." Cassie flipped open the mirror on the visor and examined her reflection in the yellow light. Makeup made her eyes pop, and she hoped she could find a copy of her interview later.

"Well, you looked great. I'm sure you did fantastic."

"Thanks," Cassie said, mildly surprised. Maureen didn't usually call to pump her full of compliments.

"So who is this guy Tyler that Andrea likes?"

"Oh, Tyler." Cassie snapped the mirror shut. "He's a friend of mine from church. Andrea's had a crush on him for a while."

"Do you have a crush on him too?"

Cassie frowned. She didn't want to delve into her conflicting feelings for Tyler. "No. We're just really good friends."

"I hope he knows that."

Cassie pressed the phone closer to her ear. "What do you mean?" Had Tyler said something to Andrea? Was it possible he liked Cassie as more than a friend?

"Oh, Andrea told him that you said she can have him right now because you'll get him when you're older. You said he's the person you want to marry so you don't want to date him yet."

An icy cold feeling rolled from Cassie's face to her shoulders. She had expressed a sentiment similar to that to Andrea, but she'd never in her life dreamed Andrea would tell Maureen. She tried to laugh it off. "That was years ago. Andrea has a good memory."

"Well, she told Tyler."

A knot formed in Cassie's throat. *No*, she told herself, *Maureen is just creating drama*. "No, she didn't."

"Yes, she did. I was there."

Cassie saw her mom looking at her from the driver's side, but she focused on staring at the road. "It's really no big deal. None of it's true. Hey, I gotta go." She hung up, not caring if Maureen thought the ending was abrupt.

"What's wrong?" Mrs. Jones asked.

Cassie didn't answer. Her hands shook as she called Andrea.

"Cassie, hey! I saw you on—"

"Did you tell Tyler that I'm waiting to date him until I'm older because he's the guy I want to marry?" Cassie interrupted, her fury making the words spit out quicker than she wanted.

There was a moment of silence, and then Andrea said, "Yes."

Cassie trembled with fury. "Thanks a lot! Some friend you are!" She slammed the phone shut, wishing she could somehow show Andrea how angry she was.

"Cassie, honey, what happened?"

"Nothing!" Cassie turned away from her mom and wiped at the hot tears escaping her eyes.

Her phone rang. When she saw it was Andrea, she sent it to voicemail. A text message came through. Cassie told herself not to open it, but she did anyway.

I'm so sorry. I was jealous of your friendship with him and wanted to make sure he didn't like you. I'm a horrible friend.

Fingers flying over the keyboard, Cassie texted back out a quick reply. *Yes, you are.*

Episode 6:

Crushing It

CHAPTER SIXTY-FOUR

Catching the Eye

C assie sat in silence as Mrs. Jones drove her home from her recital. All her excitement over her superior rating and performance was dashed to pieces in light of Andrea's betrayal. Her hand trembled in her lap, and she swore she'd never forgive her friend.

Cassie's phone rang again as Mrs. Jones pulled into the driveway. She glanced at it and saw Nicole's name. She sniffed and wiped the tears and remained sitting in the car after her mom turned it off.

"Hello?" she said, trying to sound like she had her emotions under control.

"Cassie!" Nicole squealed. "Sean saw you on TV, and now he's absolutely determined to go on a date with you. Are you available next Friday? We could go to the drive-in movie."

Cassie stuttered, so caught off guard by the change in mental directions. Nicole had been trying to set Cassie up with her brother for several weeks now. "I'm—I'm not allowed to date."

Nicole laughed. "Of course not. He didn't think you would be. So we thought we'd invite a few other people and make it a friend outing. Like Janice and Miles. What do you think?"

"Did you already talk to them?"

"No, but I can. We're all friends."

Cassie sniffed, some of the hurt from Andrea's betrayal dissipating in the fluttering excitement of an almost-date. "I'll talk to my mom, see what she says."

"Probably shouldn't tell her my brother's eighteen, but I'll be there too. We'll all just be hanging out."

Eighteen! Even Cassie hadn't realized how old he was. She gave a little laugh. Why were the older boys always the ones interested in her? "Okay. I'll let you know as soon as I know."

◌∽᎗᎗

Cassie thought church would be awkward on Sunday after Andrea told Tyler Cassie wanted to marry him, but since she was already in the habit of avoiding him, it wasn't that different. He didn't say anything to her, but every time she saw him in her peripheral vision, her face burned with embarrassment.

She told Riley everything Andrea had said, and Riley looked angry enough to punch something.

"I would never tell her another secret again," she said.

"I won't! It wasn't even a secret, I didn't even say that! She totally twisted my words."

Riley nodded sympathetically. "Don't tell her anything."

Cassie didn't intend to. She carried the anger with her to school on Monday, avoiding the bathroom where she knew her friends would be.

"Cassie!" Cara stepped up to Cassie at her locker, her hair half up and half down, clutching her books to her chest. "I looked for you in the bathroom but you weren't there."

"I'm mad at Andrea." She switched out her books and glowered at the locker.

"Not too mad to come to my birthday party, I hope."

Cassie stopped glowering and looked at Cara. "You're inviting me to your birthday party?"

Cara nodded. "We're going to Tulsa." Her eyes sparkled. "My mom said we could get a hotel room and stay overnight. I'm inviting everyone except Amity."

Cassie checked herself to make sure her mouth hadn't dropped open in astonishment. "Why not Amity?"

"I'm only inviting people I feel close to, and she's putting on so many airs lately I don't even like her."

Those were harsh words from Cara, who never said anything mean about anyone. "When did you say it is?"

"Not this Friday, but next."

"I don't think I have anything. I'm pretty sure I can come."

"Great." Cara smiled and gave her arm a squeeze. "It will be so nice to have you there. I feel like I haven't gotten to talk to you in forever."

Cassie nodded, feeling a bit guilty. She had intentionally pulled away from her friends, feeling like no one would notice or care. She hadn't meant to hurt anyone's feelings.

"Did you hear about Cara's birthday party?" Maureen asked Cassie in choir. She moved over to a chair near where Cassie sat next to Janice and Riley.

"Yes," Cassie said, glad Maureen couldn't hold this one over her. "Cara already invited me. I told her I would come."

Maureen lifted one eyebrow. "Oh, good, I was afraid you wouldn't be able to."

Cassie held back a sigh. Maureen just wanted to create drama. "Why would you think that?"

"Because Cara is having the party from Saturday to Sunday, and you can't come on Sundays. Right?"

Cassie held very still. She tried to replay Cara's words in her mind. Cara had said Friday. Hadn't she? Cassie was ninety percent certain, though becoming less sure by the moment. "She said it was on Friday."

Maureen hummed. "You might want to double check. So nice of her to include you." She stood as if to leave, and then added, "Oh, did you hear about Andrea's date with Tyler on Friday? That's when she told him all about your secret feelings for him."

Maureen smiled, and Cassie swore she saw the malice in her eyes.

"Cassie doesn't even care," Riley said. "She's not interested in Tyler."

"She told you about it?" Maureen looked mildly interested.

"Yes," Riley fired back. "And she doesn't think Andrea is a very good friend."

"I'll be sure to tell her you said that," Maureen said.

"Already did," Cassie said. *So take that, Maureen!* she thought. But she didn't say anything else. She recognized the shark look on Maureen's face. Anything she said would be used against her.

༼ ༽

Cassie's parents gave her a definitive answer on the Friday night outing that evening.

"You're not allowed to date yet," Mrs. Jones said. "But we're fine with you going with your friends to a movie. So you can go."

"Yes!" Cassie said, pumping her fist. Things were working out better than she expected. This weekend a date, and next weekend Tulsa! Who cared about Maureen or Andrea or Amity?

She called Nicole as soon as dinner was over. "My parents said yes! I can go!"

"Oh, this is fantastic news. Sean will be so excited."

"Yeah, I can't wait to talk to him in person."

"He's home right now. Do you want to?"

Cassie's stomach suddenly clenched, and her heart leapt into her throat. "Oh, no. I don't need to do that."

"He's really easy to talk to. Like me."

"I'm no good on the phone. Who all is coming to the movie?"

Nicole followed right along with the subject change. "You and Sean, of course, Janice and Miles already said they can come, plus me and Andrew."

"Oh, Andrew is coming?" Cassie smiled, glad her friend and Andrew were getting along so well. "He's so nice."

"And you're okay that Matt's not coming?" Nicole teased.

"Of course! One guy at a time."

❧

Andrea spent every day that week being super nice to Cassie, but Cassie would not be swayed. She remained frosty and kept her distance, sitting by Cara or Janice whenever the girls were together.

By Thursday, Amity had figured out everyone was invited to a party except her.

"I wouldn't have been able to make it anyway," she said airily. "I'm spending the night with Melanie that weekend."

"That's good," Cara said. "She's your best friend, isn't she?"

For some reason, Amity didn't have an answer for that.

Cassie's dad's soccer store employee was sick, and Cassie had to work the store that evening. She was at home studying for a science test when an unfamiliar number popped up on her phone. Cassie tilted her head and studied it a moment before answering. "Hello?"

"Is this Cassie?" a female adult voice asked.

"Yes," Cassie said.

"Hi, Cassie. This is Cara's mom."

"Oh! Hi." Cassie closed her science book, intrigued. Her friends' moms didn't usually call her.

"There's been a change in plans for the Tulsa trip, so I wanted to call you directly and let you know."

Oh. Cassie felt it in the pit of her stomach. She was being uninvited. "What's going on?"

"We've had to change the dates to tomorrow. Can you still make it?"

Tomorrow! But tomorrow was her date with Sean! Cassie waffled for a moment, torn. She wanted to go to Tulsa with Cara. She wanted to strengthen that relationship. But she also really wanted to go on a date with Sean.

"I don't know. I have some other plans tomorrow. I can try and get them changed."

"I understand. Just call and let me know what you decide. Cara really wants you to be able to come."

"I'll call you back." Cassie hung up the phone and then ran out to the kitchen where her mom was. "Mom! Cara changed the weekend for her birthday party!" Cassie quickly filled her in on the details and the dilemma.

Mrs. Jones looked sympathetic.

"You'll just have to call Nicole and see if you guys can change your outing. Or not go to Tulsa. Which one is more important to you?"

Cassie debated for half a second. Tulsa. This opportunity would not come around again. Having a date might.

She ran back in her room and called Nicole. "My friend Cara was having a birthday party next Friday, and she switched it to this Friday. I don't know what to do. I want to go to her birthday party, but I really want to go out with you guys."

"Go with Cara," Nicole said immediately. "We can reschedule. Sean is actually a little nervous because the weather looks cold for tomorrow, and it's not much fun at a drive-through movie if it's cold."

Immense relief rushed over Cassie, and she wilted against the chair at her desk. "Are you sure?"

"Absolutely. We'll find another time."

"I really want to go," Cassie said. "I'm not trying to bail on him."

Nicole laughed. "I know. I'll tell him."

They finished their conversation, and Cassie called Cara.

"Cassie? Are you going to make it?" Cara said as soon as she answered.

"Yes! I'm coming!"

CHAPTER SIXTY-FIVE
Big City Girls

F riday after school, Andrea, Janice, Cassie, and Maureen piled into Cara's mom's suburban.

"All Amity could talk about in choir today was how much she wished she was coming with us," Maureen said with an eye roll.

"Did you change the weekend to this weekend so Amity couldn't come?" Janice asked Cara.

Cassie look at Cara, intrigued.

Cara shrugged. "She said something happened with Melanie and they were switching their sleepover for next weekend to this weekend. She thought that meant now she could come to Tulsa. I guess she didn't realize I wasn't inviting her. So we had to switch our dates also."

Cassie had never seen Cara so angry at someone.

"You guys are the ones that really matter," Cara said. "Amity has already replaced us."

"Friends forever," Maureen said, putting her hand in the middle of the car.

"Forever," Janice said, placing her hand on top.

"Friends forever," Cassie, Andrea, and Cara chorused, joining the hand huddle.

Right now it felt real. It felt like forever. Cassie's heart warmed with friendship and acceptance. She worried about what would happen to them when they went to high school. She always felt like the one who didn't quite fit in. Could this weekend be a new start for her?

They filled the two-hour drive to Tulsa with songs and gossip. Then they stopped for a quick dinner before going to the ice-skating rink.

"I've never been ice-skating," Janice said.

"Oh, I have," Maureen said. "It's so easy. Just follow my lead."

Cassie had been ice-skating before too. Once, when she lived in Texas. She remembered going with her best friend Tammy. She didn't remember anything else about it.

They got to the rink and switched their shoes out for ice skates. Then they giggled and grabbed each other and the walls as they tried to get the skates on their feet.

"These are so tight!" Andrea said.

Cassie didn't comment, just laced hers up. She was still angry at Andrea but didn't find it worth her time to bring up.

"I'm ready," Cara said. Her arms flew out slightly as she caught her balance. "Who wants to go on the rink with me?"

Everyone looked at Maureen, who had just managed to get her other skate on.

"Not me!" Maureen said. "I don't want to face plant right now!"

That brought laughter from them, and Cassie exchanged an eye roll with Janice. So much for being the expert.

"I'll go." Cassie walked stiffly all the way to the rink, then slowly eased herself onto the ice. The sensation of standing on something solid but not dependable had her clinging to the walls.

"Bend your knees."

She looked over her shoulder as a boy skated over. He looked a little younger than her, but he had a friendly face.

"What?" she asked.

He gestured at her. "Bend your knees. It will change the way you distribute your weight, and you'll keep your balance better."

Cassie did as he suggested. Her ankles wobbled a bit, and she worried they wouldn't support her. But the boy stayed with her, encouraging her, giving her tips and pointers. After a few rounds across the rink, Cassie felt like she'd figured it out.

"Thank you."

"No problem. I'm Brad. What's your name?"

"Cassie." She spotted her friends gingerly easing themselves onto the ice. "We're here for my friend's birthday."

"Cool. Where are you guys from?"

"Springdale. Arkansas."

"That's too bad, kind of far away."

"I guess." She waved at Janice, who pulled up beside them and skated next to Cassie. "This is Janice. Janice, this is Brad."

"Hi, Brad. How are you doing this, Cassie? You make it look so easy!"

"Brad helped me."

"Can you help me?" Janice looked at Brad around Cassie.

"Sure."

Cassie dropped back and started to skate off to let the two of them work together, and Brad said, "You're not leaving, are you?"

"Oh." Cassie lifted an eyebrow. "I thought you would want me to."

He shrugged. "You can stick around, keep practicing your moves." He flashed a smile. "How old are you, anyway?"

"Fifteen," Cassie said.

"Fifteen!" There was no mistaking his surprise.

"And you?" Janice asked.

He looked a little embarrassed. "I'm thirteen."

Just a kid! Too bad. He was cute.

Janice shrugged. "It's not that big of an age difference."

"I'm in eighth grade," Cassie said. And she had a date next weekend with an eighteen-year-old. It was enough to make her giggle. Where were the boys her age and why weren't they interested in her?

"I'm just going to see if any of my other friends need help on the ice," Cassie said.

"Who's the guy?" Maureen asked when Cassie got to her side.

"Just a nice boy who is helping me skate."

"He is more than that," Janice said, skating over to them. She looked put out. "All he did was talk about you the whole time he was helping me."

"Talk about me?" Cassie looked at her in confusion. "Why?"

"Because he thought you were cute and he liked you. Never mind that you're not interested in the least because you're going on a date with Nicole's brother next weekend." She skated off, nearly tripping and falling before catching her balance in time.

Maureen laughed. "Looks like you made someone jealous."

"I didn't mean to," Cassie said. It was true, she wasn't interested in him. He was cute, but he was too young.

Cara skated beside them.

"Janice is mad at Cassie," Maureen said to her.

Cara rolled her eyes. "I had hoped that by not inviting Amity, we wouldn't have any fighting. I should have known better."

Now Cassie felt horrible. "I didn't mean to make her mad."

"Of course not." Cara skated off, leaving Cassie unsure if Cara was also mad or not.

❧

They left the skating rink half an hour later for the Doubletree Hotel where they were staying.

"The breakfast buffet is included with your stay," the receptionist said as Mrs. Barnes checked them in. "You've got two rooms connected by a door. And the pool is right around the corner in the solarium."

Maureen tugged on Andrea's arm. "Let's go check out the pool." The two of them ran off and returned a moment later, bouncing with excitement.

"The pool is huge!" Maureen said.

"And there's a hot tub!" Andrea said.

"Let's go change into our swimsuits!" Janice said.

Mrs. Barnes chuckled and handed Cara a room key. "Go ahead. Your dad and I are in the room next to yours."

A hotel room all to themselves! The girls raced to the elevator and giggled goofily when they got to the room. They fought over who would sleep in which bed before Cara made assignments, putting Andrea and Cassie and Maureen together and herself with Janice.

"We'll be squished," Maureen said, making a face.

"Cassie doesn't take up hardly any room," Cara said.

"But Andrea snores!" Maureen said.

"I do not!" Andrea said.

"Oh hush." Cara had already stripped and was pulling a bikini over her chest. "You guys will still be here squabbling while I'm sitting in the hot tub."

That stopped their arguing. Andrea put on her own bikini, and Cassie worried she'd feel out of place in her one piece until she saw Janice also had one. In high spirits again, their arguments forgotten, the girls crowded into the elevator and went down to the bottom floor.

The solarium was empty. Maureen examined the rest of the room while the other four dipped into the hot tub.

"There's a sauna here," she said.

"Come into the hot tub with us," Cara said.

Cassie shivered delightfully as the hot water crept up her toes and past her hips. She slid lower into the hot water until it reached her shoulders. Maureen climbed in across from her.

"So, Cassie," she said. "How's it going with Matt?"

Cassie's face warmed with annoyance. Why did Maureen bring that up? How did she even know? Cassie supposed she shouldn't have expected Amity to keep it a secret. "He's just a friend. That's not changing." Even though every time she saw him in computer class, she wanted to run her fingers through his hair and touch his hand. It had been so long since she had kissed anyone, and a sigh of longing escaped her.

"She's pining for him," Andrea said, and they laughed when Cassie blushed.

"No, I'm not," she said.

The clatter of footsteps on the ramp followed by the chatter of male voices silenced them. The girls swiveled their heads and watched several pairs of legs—muscular, hairy legs—make their way around the corner and down the ramp. Cassie caught her breath as five strong, sculpted abs attached to teenage boys, wearing nothing but their swimming trunks, came into view.

They were elbowing each other and laughing, completely unaware of their audience. And then as they rounded the hot tub and approached the pool, their eyes landed on the girls. Almost as one unit, they switched directions from the pool toward the hot tub.

"Hi," one of them said, smiling at them as he reached the hot tub. "Mind if we join you?"

"If you think you can handle the heat," Cara said.

Cassie's attention had been captivated by the boys, two of whom had to be twins because they looked exactly alike. But now her eyes swiveled to Cara, surprised by the flirty response. Cara had had the same boyfriend for three years, and Cassie had never seen her flirt with anyone.

The boys hooted at her response, and the one who had spoken smiled.

"I think we can handle it."

The boys added themselves to the hot tub, settling in all the spaces where the girls weren't sitting. Cassie scooted closer to Andrea, feeling suddenly self-conscious as her shoulder bumped the arm of one of the nearly naked boys.

"What are you guys doing here?" Cara asked.

"You first," the boy said.

"Fine," Cara said, though she didn't actually look like she minded. "We're here for my birthday. I just turned fifteen."

The boy clapped, and his friends did with him. "Nice. Happy birthday."

Cara smiled gracefully. "Thank you. Your turn."

"Well. I'm Mike, that's my brother Mark, that's Anthony, and that's Tobie and Silas. We're here for a wrestling competition tomorrow. We're on the wrestling team from Ponca City."

As he spoke, a muscle in his chest began to bounce. Cassie couldn't tear her eyes from it. It spasmed and contracted while he didn't seem to be aware of it.

"Where is Ponca City? Sounds like a redneck town." Maureen giggled.

Mike laughed also. "I guess you could say it is. It's about two hours from here."

"We're from Springdale," Cara said. "That's Maureen, she's by Janice, Andrea, and Cassie."

They all murmured hellos, and the boy next to Cassie turned his head to look at her.

"You must be the young one in the group. Must be fun to hang out with the older kids."

"Young one?" Cassie was the oldest. The insult burned her cheeks, and she pushed out of the hot tub. "I'm going to go sit in the sauna." She wrapped her arms around her thin, undeveloped body, wishing she could hide behind a towel. Tears stung behind her eyes, but she blinked them back. She had no padded bra to make her body look more girly in a swimsuit, and there was no hiding her stunted growth.

She let herself into the sauna and laid back on one of the benches, wishing she'd brought a book.

The sauna door opened with a squeak, and Cassie bolted upright. One of the twin boys walked in, and Cassie blinked at him.

"Mind if I come in?" he asked.

She shook her head.

He sat next to her and pulled his feet up onto the bench. "Feet are weird-looking, aren't they?"

Cassie pulled up her own feet and examined them. At one point, both of her feet had weird angles poking out by the big toe, but when she was eleven years old, she had been bit by a poisonous snake. The left foot swelled up like a bowling ball, and when the swelling went down, the sharp angle had also vanished. Now only the right foot had a weird angle, and it looked even stranger without its match.

"Yes," she said, not revealing any of these thoughts. "They're weird."

They drifted into silence, and just as Cassie was wondering why he'd come in here, he said, "Sorry for what I said in the hot tub. I didn't mean to offend you."

Cassie shifted her head to rest on her knee and looked at him. This must've been the twin who was sitting next to her. Mark. "It's fine. Everyone thinks I look younger than I am."

"Which will be really great for you someday! You'll be like, thirty, and everyone will think you're twenty."

She gave a half hearted smile.

He cleared his throat. "Your friends told me you're really nice. They also said you don't think you're very pretty. They said you used to not eat, and I—well—I didn't want you to feel bad."

Cassie turned her gaze away and stared at the door, an embarrassed heat rushing to her face. Bad enough that her friends had told a stranger about her insecurities, even worse that he now thought he had to reassure her.

"Well, thanks for coming in here." That was all she said. She wasn't going to thank him for talking to her like she was some lonely girl desperate for friendship.

Mark leaned back on the palms of his hands. "Do you want to go back out there?"

She waved him off. "I'm not quite ready, but you're welcome to. I really came in here to be by myself for a little bit."

He hesitated for a moment, as if wavering between honoring her wishes and not wanting to leave her alone. Then he stood up. "Don't stay in here too long. It's not healthy."

She bobbed her head and watched him leave, then wished she could disappear into the floor. She didn't want to go back out there. What must all of those boys think of her?

She stayed in the sauna as long as she dared, and then Janice poked her head in.

"Cassie? The boys are gone."

As if she'd known that was the reason Cassie was still hiding in there. "Oh? I was about to come out anyway."

Cassie rejoined her friends in the hot tub. Maureen opened her mouth to say something, but Cara shot her a look, and she very quickly closed it.

☙ ❦ ❧

The boys were all the girls wanted to talk about for the rest of the evening. Andrea called Amity and told her about them.

"They were wrestlers, and they were so hot! You could see their muscles rippling underneath their skin! And they were so nice. Each one of them liked one of us."

"That's not true," Maureen grumbled. "All five of them liked Cara."

"Who has a boyfriend," Janice said, tossing a pillow at Cara.

"Hmm?" Cara said, not taking her eyes off the television. But Cassie thought she saw a little smile on her face.

Cassie's friends had coordinated with the boys what time to meet for breakfast, so by eight in the morning, they rose from their beds.

"I don't know why we bother," Maureen said. "They're not interested in us. Only Cara." But that did not prevent her from braiding her hair and putting on makeup.

Sure enough, the boys were already at the breakfast buffet when they got there. They hopped up, pulling chairs out and offering them seats at a nearby table. Cassie did a quick headcount and then mentioned to Andrea, who sat next to her, "One of the twins isn't here."

Andrea's eyes scanned them as well, and she said to the other twin, "Where's your brother?"

"Mark? He said he'd come down later. He's still up in the room."

"He didn't want to come and say bye to us?" Maureen said.

Mike shrugged. "He's like that sometimes."

Andrea got a glint in her eye that Cassie recognized. "Can I see your room key?"

"Sure." Mike pulled the key out of his back pocket and handed it to

402

her.

"What's your room number?"

"Four-oh-seven."

"Thanks!" Andrea grabbed Cassie's arm, turned around, and ran out of the cafeteria. She didn't stop until they reached the elevators. She pressed the button, then she hauled Cassie inside and burst out laughing.

"What's going on?" Cassie asked, laughing even though she didn't know why.

Andrea pressed floor four. "If Mark doesn't want to come to us to say goodbye, fine. We'll go to him."

Cassie's mouth fell open. "Andrea!"

Andrea's only response was to giggle, and then the elevator doors opened and she raced down the hall. Cassie ran after.

Andrea knocked on the hotel door, and when no one answered, she inserted the key and opened it a crack. "Hello?"

"Don't you dare walk in there," Cassie said. "What if he's changing?"

Andrea pushed the door open. "He would've said something. He's probably just sleeping."

Cassie sure hope Mark didn't sleep naked. Even if every inch of skin she'd seen yesterday was mighty fine.

"Hello?" Andrea said as she stepped inside, Cassie on her heels.

No one answered, but Cassie heard the shower going in the bathroom. "He's taking a shower!" She gestured at the closed door.

Andrea walked right up to it and knocked. "Mark?"

The shower kept going, and Andrea knocked again. "Mark?" she said, louder this time.

The water turned off. "Hello?" a male voice called from inside.

"Mark, it's Andrea and Cassie. We're out here."

As if that weren't obvious.

"What are you doing?" Mark said, sounding a mixture of incredulous and curious.

"We wanted to talk to you and say goodbye!" Andrea said.

Cassie bit her lower lip and giggled.

"Well, I'm in the shower!"

"You got clothes in there, right?" Andrea said.

"Yeah, but—"

"So we'll wait right here for you!"

"But—"

"Hurry up!" Andrea sang. She grabbed Cassie's arm and wandered over to one of the double beds.

They heard the shower turn back on.

"He didn't sound too excited that we're up here," Cassie said.

Andrea waved her off. "It's just because we surprised him. He's excited."

The shower water turned off, but Mark did not emerge right away. Finally the bathroom door cracked open.

"Are you girls still in here?"

"We're right here!" Andrea said.

"I'm only wearing my boxers."

He sounded nervous about that, though Cassie couldn't figure out why. Weren't boxers just little exercise shorts boys wore?

"That's no problem! We just came up to say bye!" Andrea said.

"Well, okay, if you don't think it's weird." He stepped out of the bathroom, wearing only a pair of little shorts, his sculpted abs and chest in full view. Cassie knew Andrea was admiring him as much as she was.

Andrea hopped over and wrapped her arms around him in a hug. "How come you're not downstairs admiring Cara like the rest of your team?"

He shrugged. "I mean, she was pretty, but she wasn't top of the world stuff."

Cassie liked him more and more. "Let's take a selfie."

"Yes!" Andrea whipped out her cell phone.

Mark obliged, and they all smiled for the camera.

"Bye! It was so nice to meet you!" Andrea said.

"Yes. Thanks for being so nice." Cassie wanted to say more, but not here.

"Thanks. Have fun this weekend."

The two girls fluttered out of the room, faces flushed and giddy with what they had just done.

"What till we show his picture to the others! They'll be so jealous!" Andrea said, grabbing Cassie's arm and leading her to the elevator.

CHAPTER SIXTY-SIX

Rain Check

C ara brought pictures of her birthday party to school on
Monday.
"I had them printed at Walgreens yesterday," she said as
everyone giggled over the boys in the bathroom before school. "Those
wrestlers were so hot."

"You're not allowed to say things like that," Andrea said. "You have a
boyfriend."

Cara shrugged and gave a little smile. "I'm not married to him, am I?"

Cassie giggled along with the rest of her friends as they perused the
photos of Mark and his brother. There was even one photo of Cassie
skating with Brad.

"Hi, guys!" Amity came in, followed by Melanie. "Did you guys have
fun in Tulsa? We had such a great weekend!"

"We had a blast." Cara held her hand out to Cassie. "I'll show you the
pictures again in math. I've got to go."

"Pictures of what?" Amity stopped in front of the mirror and preened
her hair, which she had put in kinky curls.

"All the hot guys who stayed at the hotel with us." Cara winked at
Cassie and Andrea. "See you guys."

"You've got pictures of the hot guys?" Amity took a few steps after
Cara.

"Oh, they were so fine," Andrea said, a smug expression on her face.
"Five boys and five girls. It was perfect." She hooked her arm through
Cassie's and pulled her out of the bathroom. Leaning her head close to
Cassie, she whispered, "Did you see her face? She is so jealous."

Cassie had seen. She felt a little bad at how vindicated it made her feel.

Cara clearly wasn't the only one who was miffed by Amity's behavior.

⟲〜⁂〜⟳

"Everything's a go for the drive-in movie this Friday," Nicole said in English class on Wednesday.

"That sounds perfect," Cassie said. She was doing her best to get over Matt, who hardly ever even looked at her in computer's class and certainly didn't give her the time of day. If she could only fall for Nicole's brother, it would make things easier on her heart. "You have people to come with us?"

Nicole nodded. "My friend Kristin is going to come. She's over at my house all the time, and Sean knows her. It should be really comfortable."

"I can't wait," Cassie said, and she meant it.

Nicole called Cassie Friday around five o'clock.

"Hi," Cassie said, a little breathlessly. Her family was about to eat dinner, but she was still trying to figure out what to wear. "Should I wear a sweater? Is it going to get cold?"

"Um," Nicole said, and in that one syllable, Cassie heard the problem.

"What's wrong?" she asked.

"Well, it does get a little chilly at the drive-in. But Kristin just called, and she's sick. She's really sorry, but she can't come. Are you still okay to go?"

Cassie put down the sweater she'd been holding up to herself, her heart sinking. She debated asking her mom, but she already knew the answer. "I won't be able to go if there's not another person coming. Let me call my friends. Maybe someone can go with us."

"Okay. I'll call around also. Call me a soon as you get someone."

"Okay," Cassie echoed.

She tried Andrea first.

"Hi, Cassie," Andrea said, her voice soft. Behind her it sounded like someone on a microphone droned in the background.

"I'm supposed to go on a date tonight," Cassie said without preamble. "But my mom says somebody has to go with me. Can you come?"

"You want me to be your chaperone?" Andrea sounded amused. "I can't. I'm at a banquet with Maureen and Cara for Maureen's uncle."

"Oh. Okay. I'll try a few other people."

"Good luck! I hope you get to go on your date."

"Thanks," Cassie said.

She tried Janice next.

"I can't tonight," Janice said, her tone regretful. "I'm behind on a couple of assignments, and my mom is making me stay home until they're done."

"Just for a few hours," Cassie begged. "My mom won't let me go without someone else."

"I'm sorry, Cassie."

"Cassie! Come for dinner!" Mrs. Jones' voice called from the kitchen.

Cassie squeezed the phone in her hands, not wanting to stop calling until she had secured someone to go with her and Nicole. "Coming!"

She tried Riley next, even though she had her doubts about taking Riley along on a date. Riley didn't have a cell phone, and Mrs. Isabel picked up.

"She's not in right now, Cassie. Can I have her call you back?"

A lump formed in Cassie's throat, and she started to worry she wouldn't find someone. "Yes, please."

She hung up the phone and wracked her brain. Who else could she try?

There was Amity. Cassie and her friends were still giving Amity the cold shoulder, not that Amity seemed to have noticed. She was so busy with her new best friend that she hadn't reacted, except with a little bit of jealousy that she hadn't been at the birthday party with all the cute guys.

Cassie hated to admit that she missed her friendship, but she'd gotten so tired of being made fun of and ignored. Maybe doing an activity together was just the thing they needed to rekindle their friendship.

Cassie called Amity's number. "Amity," she said as soon as the phone answered, "I'm going on a date to the drive-in tonight. Want to come with me?"

"Hi Cassie," a mature female voice said. "This is Mrs. Stafford."

"Oh," Cassie said, her face warming with embarrassment. "Sorry. I meant to call Amity's phone."

"You did, sweetie. Amity forgot her phone. She's at Melanie's house. You can call her there."

No way. "Thanks." Cassie hung up the phone and buried her face in her hands. She had tried everyone.

"Cassie!" her mom called, all patience gone from her voice.

"Coming!" Cassie snapped back. She was too anxious to eat, and not at all prepared to tell her mom what was going on.

What if she just didn't tell her mom that nobody else could come? It wasn't really that big of a deal, was it?

"You're not eating much," Mrs. Jones remarked.

"I'm just excited for tonight," Cassie said. Lying didn't sit well with her, and she hoped everything would work out for it to become a true statement.

Her phone rang on the counter. Cassie jumped up.

"No phones at dinner," Mrs. Jones reminded her.

"It might be Nicole. We're still trying to make plans for tonight."

"Well, okay."

Cassie hurried into her bedroom and closed the door. "Did you find someone?" she asked breathlessly. "I didn't have any luck."

"I did find someone!" Nicole said.

"That's great!" Cassie breathed a sigh of relief. "Who is it?"

"Miles Hansen."

Miles Hansen. Cassie closed her eyes.

"You're friends with him, right?" Nicole continued. "It'll be so much fun!"

Cassie nodded and cleared her throat. "Yeah, Miles is a great friend. I don't know if it'll be okay with my mom, though."

"Oh?" Nicole sounded unsure. "Why not?"

"Because he's a boy. And my mom will think it looks like a double date." A surge of frustration rolled through Cassie's chest. Why couldn't it be enough that she had Nicole with her? Why did she have to find one more person?

"Do you want to ask? Or are you sure she'll say no?"

"Let me ask."

Feeling as if she walked to the gallows, Cassie made her way back to the kitchen.

"Mom, there's been a complication. Nicole's friend Kristin can't go to the drive-in." Her mom opened her mouth to speak, but Cassie hurried on. "So Nicole found someone else to go with us. Miles."

Mrs. Jones' brow furrowed. "Miles? As in, the boy you've had a crush on for years?"

"Had," Cassie said. "Now he's just a super good friend, I swear."

Mrs. Jones shook her head. "That's not gonna work."

Cassie had suspected as much, but that didn't stop the tears of frustration from rising behind her eyes. "Come on, Mom! That's not fair! Nicole will be there. I'm not gonna be alone with him!"

Mrs. Jones set her jaw. "You're only fifteen. You're lucky I let you go at all."

Cassie turned around and stomped back to her room. She wanted to point out that her mom let her go out with Josh when she was only fourteen and her chaperone was little Annette. But somehow she doubted throwing that in her mom's face would win her any points right now.

Instead she called Nicole back. "My mom said no," she said, working hard to keep her voice from trembling.

Nicole made a sad noise in her throat. "That's okay. Let me talk with

Sean, we can reschedule for a different weekend."

Again. Cassie blinked hard. "Sure."

"Well . . . are you okay with that?"

"I mean, we don't have any other option, do we?"

"Hang on."

Nicole abandoned the phone. Cassie could hear her speaking somewhere nearby but not close enough for the mic to pick up the words. And then Nicole returned.

"How about this? We go roller skating. There's lots of people at the rink. Your mom won't have to feel like we're isolated."

Hope returned to Cassie's heart. This just might work. "Let me ask."

She returned to the kitchen. "Mom? What if we went rollerskating? Me, Nicole, Miles, and Sean. But lots of other people will be there."

Mrs. Jones looked thoughtful. "You can go rollerskating with them if you take Annette and Scott along."

"Okay!" Cassie put the phone back to her ear. "My mom said yes! As long as I bring along my little brother and sister."

Nicole laughed. "Sounds like we'll have to ride in my mom's van. It's a plan! Pick you up in an hour!"

⊙ シ シ ⊙

Sean was ten minutes late picking Cassie up, and she was just starting to worry he wasn't coming when an unfamiliar van pulled into the circle drive in front of the house.

"Bye, Mom!" Cassie said, pushing her siblings out the door before her mom could have a chance to follow her.

Nicole had been sitting up front, but she climbed into the back now, leaving the passenger side for Cassie. Cassie slid into the seat and glanced at Sean, inexplicably shy. He looked like she remembered, tall with blond hair the same color as Nicole's, and bright blue eyes. But he looked so much older than she expected.

"Hi," he said.

"Hi," Cassie returned.

And that was it, the extent of her vocabulary for the moment. She racked her brain, trying to think of something more to say.

"You have so many potholes coming up to your house!" Nicole leaned forward between their two seats. "I thought we were going to knock a tire off the van!"

"Yeah, everyone says that." Cassie attempted to smile.

"I just told Nicole to get ready to deploy the lifeboats and to make sure she put her oxygen mask on before she put Miles' on," Sean said.

Nicole and Miles burst out laughing, and Cassie couldn't help joining them.

"No, he really did," Nicole said.

"And I told Nicole if she secured her oxygen mask before mine, I'd have to steal it away from her," Miles said. He met Cassie's eye and winked.

Cassie smiled and relaxed a bit. These were her friends. She might not know Sean, but she knew everyone else. She didn't need to be shy around these people.

❦

"I'm a terrible skater," Nicole said.

Cassie sat beside her and helped Annette and Scott get their rollerskates on before she tackled her own. "It's not like anybody's actually good at it."

"Yeah, but some people are actually bad at it." Still, Nicole didn't hesitate to head out to the rink, cartwheeling her arms as she fought for balance.

"So do you fit in the 'not actually good' or the 'actually bad' category?" Sean asked.

Cassie directed her attention to where he sat across from her, lacing up his own skates. "Definitely in the 'not actually good' category. You?"

He smirked. "I'm in the 'actually good' category."

Cassie couldn't help laughing. "Let's see your skills."

Still smirking, he stood up and rollerskated onto the rink—backwards.

"Okay, I'm impressed," Cassie said, following him. She skated just behind him, going slow enough to keep her balance.

Sean pivoted and skated beside her. Across the rink a squeal echoed, and Sean laughed. "That's Nicole."

They both turned to see her hugging the wall while Miles skated along beside her.

"She hasn't fallen yet," Sean said. "That's impressive."

"Setting the bar high," Cassie said. "Now I know what to aim for."

"Attention, skaters!" The DJ's voice boomed from the balcony overlooking the rink. "Let's everyone clear the rink for the couples' skate!"

Cassie made her way off the rink before it occurred to her that maybe she and Sean should skate. She sat down on one of the benches and glanced at him as he sat beside her. *Take his hand and go skate,* she told herself. But she couldn't bring herself to move. Her heart thumped a little harder in her chest. *Do it, do it now. Before you lose this opportunity.*

But no matter how much she told herself, she couldn't find the courage to say anything. She finally cleared her throat just as the announcer said, "And all skaters are invited back to the rink! The couples' skate is over!"

"Well, let's go back on, then," Sean said.

Cassie followed him, the bitter disappointment of cowardice in her throat. She had missed their opportunity.

Nicole joined them, and they skated together for a bit. Then Miles skated by and touched Nicole's arm.

"Tag, you're it." Then he was off.

"No," Nicole groaned. "I'm so bad at this."

She lunged for Cassie's arm, but Cassie slid out of the way, and Nicole's arms spun to regain her balance.

Sean laughed at her. "You probably have better luck chasing Miles down."

Nicole narrowed her eyes at them. "I'll be back." She slowed down and drifted behind them.

Sean turned around and skated backwards, and a moment later Nicole's squeal reached them from her position.

Sean shook his head. "She got the wall. Not Miles."

Cassie smiled, though she felt like she'd gotten to the most exciting part of the book only to have it be a let-down. She and Sean skated side-by-side, laughing at Nicole's antics.

"And it's time for another couples' skate!" the announcer boomed. "Let's have everyone else clear the rink!"

She had another chance. Cassie's heart immediately leapt into her throat. She couldn't let this one go. She turned to Sean as he started to make his way off the rink and held out her hand.

Sean didn't hesitate. He took her hand, but he gripped it wrong, and the two of them wobbled for a moment as he rearranged his hold. Cassie tried to laugh, but she felt awkward and embarrassed, her heart still pounding too hard in her chest.

Sean grinned at her, and then the two of them skated hand-in-hand around the rink. Cassie didn't feel butterflies or fireworks or anything that melted her, but there was a nice, warm feeling just knowing she was next to someone who enjoyed her company, or at least wanted to get to know her.

"You can't skate backwards now," Cassie said.

"Oh yeah?" Sean spun in front of her, then took her hand in his other hand, continuing to skate backwards while pulling her forward.

"You're very talented," Cassie said.

"This is what a couples' skate is supposed to be like. But not that many people know how to skate backwards."

"I'm so lucky to be with one of the talented few," Cassie said, and Sean's laugh echoed off the wall next to them.

The skate ended and they went back to avoiding being tagged by Nicole. But when another couples' skate came on before the night was over, Cassie and Sean didn't hesitate to take to the rink.

Mrs. Jones wanted Cassandra home by ten-thirty, and Sean pulled the van into the Jones's driveway at 10:27.

"I didn't get you home late!" he said with a grin.

Cassie laughed, absolutely delighted with the friendship they had sparked this evening. Sean was funny and cute and respectful. Plus she knew his sister, and that meant he had to be a good egg.

Mrs. Jones invited them all in, and she put out chips and salsa for them to eat while they re-counted the outing. Annette told how she'd seen Cassie and Sean doing the couples' skate, and Sean's cheeks turned pink. They teased Nicole for squealing all evening, even though she only fell once.

Half an hour later Miles mentioned he needed to get home, so Sean and Nicole said goodbye to Cassie and headed out to the car.

Nicole lingered. "So, do you like him?" she whispered to Cassie.

Cassie did like him. Not the way she liked Matt or Zack or other boys she had crushes on. "I think he's great. I think if I spent more time with him, my feelings for him could become really strong."

Nicole gave a little squeal, a sound Cassie had become very familiar with. She squeezed Cassie's hand. "Sean is such a great guy. We'll have to hang out again."

Cassie followed her out, and she gave Sean and Miles both a hug good night before going back into the house.

"Well?" Mrs. Jones said, pouncing on her right away. "How was it?"

Cassie heaved a sigh and collapsed into a chair at the table. "It was so much fun. I had a really great time with him. But—" She shook her head. "Where could it possibly go for me from here? Next year Sean goes to college. College! I'll be a sophomore in high school."

"You're not even sixteen," Mrs. Jones added. "If he wanted you to go to his senior prom, you wouldn't be able to."

Cassie pushed the chair in front of her with her toe. That sounded so unfair. "But what if I really like him?"

Mrs. Jones gave a sympathetic smile. "I would suggest not letting yourself. He's a nice guy, but he's too old for you. You're in different stages of life. Just have fun for now."

Cassie recognized the wisdom in her mom's words. Just have fun. Tonight had been fun. Way more fun than the angst she had felt since developing a crush on Matt. She stood up. "From now on, I'm just going to have fun."

CHAPTER SIXTY-SEVEN

BBQ Surprise

I t was one thing to say Cassie was done having crushes; it was quite another thing to put it to action. She walked into second hour on Monday and noticed Matt hanging out with Kevin. His hair had grown a little bit longer, and he kept tossing his head to get it out of his face.

Something swelled in Cassie's heart. She wanted to step over to him and run her fingers through that hair.

No! she yelled at herself. *Get over him!*

Nicole sat next to Cassie in third hour. "So Sean said he likes you too," she said. "He's not sure what to do, though, since you're so young."

Cassie nodded. "I've had the same worries."

"He wrote you a note. Here." Nicole fished through her binder and then frowned. "I must've forgotten it! I'll bring it tomorrow."

Maybe it would be best if Cassie developed a crush on Sean. He was interested in her, at least.

The next day the ninth graders had a field trip to the Jones Center for their tenth grade prep convention. The students were all abuzz as they gathered in the cafeteria to load the buses.

"The other junior highs will be there too," Jaiden said. "Since we're the ones who will be making up the sophomore class next year."

"We really should be touring the high school, not the Jones Center," Esther said. "That's where we'll be going to school.

Cassie agreed. Every time she went to the library and saw the massive high school across the street, her throat got a little bit dry and her stomach a little bit crazy. It was huge. It looked more like a college than a high school. It didn't matter that they got an additional three minutes of passing time between classes. Cassie just knew she'd be running through the halls trying not to be late.

The students boarded the buses.

"Cassie," Andrea called. "Come sit with me."

Cassie obliged, dropping into the bus seat beside Andrea.

"You look really nice today," Andrea said. "Your hair is pretty."

"Thanks." Cassie wore her hair parted down the middle and hanging straight from either side of her face. She had put in some large hoop earrings and wore a sleeveless shirt that tied in a knot at her belly button. Andrea's compliment made her feel more confident.

"Tyler will be there," Andrea said.

"You still like him?" Cassie said, keeping her tone light. She and Tyler had not really spoken since Andrea told him all those stories about Cassie.

"Well, yeah, he's still pretty cute." Andrea laughed.

The buses pulled into the Jones Center ten minutes later. As the students gathered in the chapel for the opening announcements, Cassie spotted Tyler.

"Tyler," she said, catching his eye and waving. He gave a brief bob of his head before turning his back on her.

Ouch. The dismissal wounded Cassie, but she faced forward, refusing to let him see his affect.

"Oh, there's Tyler!" Andrea said, seeing him also. She pushed past Cassie to sit on the bench behind him. Cassie couldn't hear what they said, but Tyler turned around to talk to her, and they laughed and joked until the teachers silenced them.

Cassie glared at them.

Whispers attracted her attention, and she turned her eyes to the girls sitting on the bench directly in front of hers. All four of them were casting glances her way and then whispering. What now? Did she have a big milk stain on her pants?

One of the girls turned around and faced Cassie. She had bright pink lipgloss and golden highlights in her brown hair. "Excuse me. Aren't you Tommy Higgins girlfriend?"

Tommy Higgins? "What?"

"Sorry, that question probably came out of nowhere." The girl gave a friendly smile.

"You're fine," Cassie said, face warming as she realized it was identity confusion. "Sorry, I don't know who Tommy is."

"Oh." The girl lifted her eyebrows. "You look just like his girlfriend."

Cassie kept smiling and nodded.

The microphone squealed as a teacher stepped up to it, and the girl said, "Well, I guess we'll see each other next year in school."

She turned back around, leaving Cassie to wonder who Tommy Higgins was and what his girlfriend looked like.

Several teachers got up and introduced themselves and talked about the different electives they offered at the high school. Rooms throughout the Jones Center had been set up for students to walk in and out of and learn about the curriculum.

"We know you've already picked your core classes for next year, but if you find an elective you really want to sign up for, now's the time to do it. Or you can start planning for what you want to do the rest of your years at Springdale High School."

The teacher finished talking, and then one of them said, "Our concluding speaker will be Jack Mellas, Central Junior High's class president."

This announcement was met with cheers from the Central students, but Cassie had heard only the last name. She sat up straighter. Mellas? Like, Elek Mellas? She vaguely recalled that Elek had a younger brother. A boy with clear skin and thick curly dark hair stepped up to the microphone, and she knew it was Elek's brother.

She hadn't heard anything about Elek in months. She had to talk to his brother. She could hardly sit still through his speech, so anxious was she for him to finish it so they could talk.

Everyone clapped again when he finished, and then the students disbursed for the different rooms. But Cassie shot out of her bench and went to the podium to intercept Jack.

Several other kids were talking to him, and Cassie waited until they left before stepping forward.

"Jack?" she said, searching his face.

He smiled but otherwise only looked at her vaguely. "Yes?"

"Do you know who I am?"

He tilted his head. "No?"

"I'm Cassie. Cassie Jones."

His eyes lit up with recognition, and he exclaimed, "Cassie! I didn't recognize you!"

He extended his hand, and she took it, giving it a squeeze. "How are you? Class president! Elek would be so proud."

Jack looked distinctly uncomfortable. "Yeah."

Cassie pressed on. "Have you talked to him lately? How's he doing?"

Jack's smile wobbled. "My mom talks to him more than I do."

"Can I get your phone number? Would you mind if I called you? I've just worried about him all year."

"Yeah, sure, I'd love to talk to you." He pulled out his phone and got Cassie's number as well.

She pushed down her eagerness to know more about Elek. "But how are you? Are you doing okay?"

"I'm doing great. I'm not going to live the same life as my brother." He said it with such finality that it finally dawned on Cassie that he was angry with Elek. She gave his arm a squeeze.

"Great to talk to you. I'll give you a call." She waved, then wandered out to examine the different electives offered at the high school.

Andrea flagged Cassie down as the field trip ended and the kids headed back to the buses.

"I heard you were talking to their class president," Andrea said.

"I know him. Elek is his brother."

Andrea just wrinkled her brow, apparently not recognizing the connection. It suddenly occurred to Cassie that maybe Jack didn't want everybody to know his brother was in jail.

"I know his brother. We just haven't seen each other in a long time."

"Oh. Well, apparently Jack is really popular with the ladies." Andrea wiggled her eyebrows up-and-down. "Could be a good opportunity for you."

"Opportunities. I have plenty of opportunities." Cassie was suddenly annoyed, and the words shot out before she could rethink them. "I went on a date with an eighteen-year-old last weekend, but it's not a relationship that can go anywhere. And then there's Jack, cute, smart, friendly Jack, who I'm not the least bit interested in because the guy I like is on that bus—" Cassie pointed to the bus beside them as Matt walked on— "and he is so not interested in me that he doesn't even look at me when I walk into class."

Andrea looked sympathetic. "Tell you what. Why don't I spend the night tonight? Maybe your mom can take us out for ice cream."

That actually sounded delightfully fun. "I'll ask."

Her mom said yes. Mrs. Jones picked both girls up from school, and then they stopped at Andrea's house so she could grab a few overnight things.

"Can we stop at Braum's and get some ice cream?" Andrea asked, and Cassie couldn't believe it when her mom agreed.

The two girls sat at a separate table and giggled over their ice cream sundaes.

"So what would you say if you had the chance to be alone with Matt?" Andrea asked.

Cassie took a spoonful of ice cream and sucked it from her spoon. "Probably nothing. I'm too chicken to talk to guys."

"No, you're not. I've seen you talk to plenty of guys."

"Yeah, but when I like one, it's a lot harder."

"So you should tell him you like him."

"No way! He would never talk to me again."

Andrea shook her head. "Maybe he doesn't know he's supposed to be looking at you that way. You have to tell him so that he starts thinking, oh, Cassie might be someone I could like."

There was truth to Andrea's words, but the thought of rejection chilled Cassie's heart. "I couldn't."

"You should always tell a guy when you like him. It makes them notice you."

A van swung into a parking spot in front of the ice cream store, the headlights washing over Andrea and Cassie. Then a girl jumped out of the side door and ran into the store.

"Andrea, Cassie!" she said breathlessly, and only then did Cassie realize it was Amity.

"Amity!" Andrea said, recognizing her at the same time. "What are you doing here?"

"We were driving by and I saw you guys in the window," Amity said, beaming. "What are you doing?"

"Andrea's spending the night," Cassie said.

"Oh, that sounds like so much fun!" Amity said. "You guys want to see our new van? My mom just bought one!"

"Sure," Andrea said.

What was special about a van? Cassie's family had had one for as long as she could remember. But she followed Andrea outside so they could admire the Stafford's car.

"Now my mom can fit a lot more people inside. She could pick all of us up from school and we could go somewhere."

"Where is Melanie tonight?"

Amity looked wounded. "I don't hang out with her every weekend. She's not my only friend."

Andrea raised an eyebrow at Cassie, but they both refrained from saying anything.

Mrs. Jones came out of the ice cream shop. "Ready to go, girls?"

"Ready," Cassie said, hooking an arm through Andrea's. For a brief moment, she considered inviting Amity to come along.

But then she remembered how Amity flirted with Matt after Cassie told her she liked him, and how all of her friends suddenly knew as well. No, she didn't want to have to worry about what Amity was going to do or say.

She and Andrea stayed up late talking. Cassie was careful about what she said, knowing it could come back to stab her in the back. Her friends couldn't keep secrets, and Andrea in particular sometimes made things up.

Andrea's mom called in the morning, early enough that it woke them.

"Hello?" Andrea said groggily, sitting up on Cassie's bed. Cassie rolled over and tried to ignore her. She noticed her sister Emily wasn't in bed anymore.

"But it's still so early," Andrea groaned. "What? Really?"

Really what? Cassie fished around under her pillow until she found her own phone, and then she sat upright when she saw the time. Almost ten-thirty!

"Okay. Yeah. See you soon." Andrea put away her phone. "My mom is on her way to get me now. We slept so late."

"I can't even believe it." Cassie widened her eyes, trying to shake off the sleepiness.

A knock came on the door moments before Mrs. Jones poked her head in. "Cassie, we're gonna leave in twenty minutes to go to your sister's soccer barbecue."

"What soccer barbecue?" If this had been mentioned before, Cassie didn't remember it.

"At her soccer coach's house," Mrs. Jones said.

"Do I have to go?"

"No, I suppose not. But I'll give you a list of things to do here at home if you don't come."

"That's fine. Give me the list." She went into the bathroom and brushed her teeth while Andrea gathered her things.

The doorbell rang, and Mrs. Jones said, "Andrea, your mom is here."

Andrea turned around and gave her a hug. "It was great to talk to you. You can spend the night at my house next time."

Andrea left, and Mrs. Jones handed Cassie the list of chores. Cassie's eyes ran over it. Clean all the toilets, empty all the trashes, do the laundry and fold the towels, give the dog a bath . . .

Give the dog a bath? She didn't even remember the last time someone had bathed Pioneer. Was this a joke?

"Mom!" Cassie poked her head out the door of her bedroom. "You really want me to do all this?"

Mrs. Jones shrugged from the kitchen as she put a few things away from the counter. "You're going to be here. You may as well make yourself useful."

Forget this. "I'm coming." Cassie disappeared back to her bedroom and pulled out a pair of jeans. She threw on a T-shirt, stuck her hair in a ponytail, and ran out the door with her family.

❦

Annette's soccer coach lived out in Sonora, a city just east of Springdale but a good half an hour from the Jones's house, so Cassie buried herself in a book during the drive. The sun had risen high in the sky, and even through the car windows, she could feel that the day was going to be warm. She hoped she wouldn't be too hot in her black T-shirt.

She was already regretting coming when the Joneses parked their car with several other vehicles on the side of the road. What was she going to do at a barbecue for a whole bunch of nine-year-olds, anyway?

"Don't bring your book," Mrs. Jones warned as Cassie got out with it in her hands.

"What else am I going to do?" Cassie said.

"Keep an eye on your sister."

"Great," Cassie grumbled. So she'd really come here to be a glorified babysitter.

The gate to the backyard was open, and other families were walking through it. Cassie shoved her hands in her jeans pockets and followed.

"Hi, girls! Hey, Ashley! Rebecca! Annette!"

The soccer coach stood at the gate, grinning and greeting each girl cheerfully as they walked in. Cassie slipped past him to the deck with patio chairs, a barbecue grill, and a stone pathway that led away into the woods. And then she froze.

Standing next to the grill with tongs in his hand and flipping hamburgers was Matt.

CHAPTER SIXTY-EIGHT
Little Kid Games

C assie wanted to disappear. How had she not known Matt's dad was Annette's soccer coach? Had he spotted her? She whirled around, looking for a place to hide, but there was nowhere. She faced forward again and saw Matt looking at her. Their eyes met, and then he returned to turning hot dogs as if he hadn't seen her.

Cassie's heart sank. That was even worse than if he hadn't noticed her at all. Her chest constricted and her eyes burned. "Jerk!" she breathed. She spotted her parents sitting down and joined them.

"Can't I get my book?" she pleaded. Heat beat down on the long sleeves of her black T-shirt and warmed her face, though she wasn't sure if the heat came from Matt standing nearby or from the sun.

"Meat's ready!" Matt's dad called. "We have the whole assortment of sides and hamburgers and hot dogs! Come on up and get them!"

"Just sit here with us," Mrs. Jones said.

Did her mom know whose house this was? Cassie found no sympathy in this corner. She followed her parents into line and loaded her plate with fruit salad and potato salad, since she didn't eat meat.

Cassie returned to her corner on the patio and picked at her food. Her stomach was a mess of knots, and she had a hard time feeling anything but anxious.

"Hey, Cassie."

She froze when the male voice spoke to her. It wasn't possible that Matt was talking to her, and yet when she lifted her face, he stood there smiling down at her. She nearly choked on the fruit in her mouth. Swallowing quickly, she said, "Hey, Matt."

He dropped into the empty seat beside her as if she had invited him. Cassie glanced toward her parents, but they were busy speaking to each other and didn't look her way. Was this really happening?

"Want to go down to the dock when you're done eating?" Matt asked.

Cassie peered through the trees in the direction where she knew the lake was. "How do we get there?"

"There's a path through the trees. I'll show you."

Take a walk with Matt through the woods to the lake? Cassie couldn't even believe it. "Yes, sure. That would be fun." She stopped just short of saying, "I'd love to." She didn't want to sound too eager.

"Great." Matt got a plate of food and returned to sit by her.

Now Cassie really couldn't eat, not with him beside her. She wiped at her brow and said, "It's so hot."

Matt stood up. "You're in a long-sleeve shirt. Come on, let's find something else for you to wear." He led the way into his house, through the sliding glass door and the kitchen, and up another flight of stairs.

She caught her breath when they stepped into a room. His room. Cassie stood by the dresser and picked up several rocks sitting on top while Matt went to the closet.

"You like rocks?"

He came out with a T-shirt in his hands. "Those are geodes. I collect them. Here. Wear this."

She caught the T-shirt he threw at her. "Where do I change?" She certainly wasn't doing it here.

He opened the door beside the closet. "Just use the bathroom. I'll wait for you."

Cassie let herself inside and locked the door, then took several deep breaths as she stared at her reflection. She was at Matt's house. In his bedroom. In his bathroom! And he wanted her to walk to the dock with him, and he got her a T-shirt without her even asking . . . did he like her? He must like her!

A glowing feeling wrapped itself in her chest, and Cassie felt like she must be beaming like a ray of sunlight.

She stepped out of the bathroom to find Matt waiting in his bedroom. He had taken one of the rocks apart and held it in his hands. Cassie looked at it curiously, but Matt just put it back together.

"Ready?" he said.

"Yes."

"Come on, then." He filed out of his room, and Cassie followed.

He slowed down on the stairs and waited for her to catch up. "If it were warmer we could go swimming," he said. "But even though the air is warm, the water will be freezing."

"Oh. That's okay." It wasn't like she'd brought a swimsuit.

He led her behind the patio and down a path that wound over rocks overhangings close to the lake. "Just keep an eye out for snakes. Sometimes they like to chill out here on these rocks."

Cassie slowed down, surveying the terrain around her warily. "Poisonous snakes?"

"I haven't stopped to ask." He turned around and shot her a teasing grin. "Afraid of snakes?"

Cassie started walking a little faster, hurrying to catch up to him. "Let's just say I had an unpleasant run in with a snake a few years ago."

"Oo, sounds like an exciting story."

They had reached a small dock, and Matt stepped onto it.

"Matt!" a little voice squawked.

Cassie turned around to see a girl with golden blond hair coming down the path, Annette in tow.

"Oh boy," Matt said. "Here comes the terror herself."

"I am not a terror!" she said. "Dad says you better not be down by the lake. You have to go home right now."

Cassie turned to look at Matt, afraid he was in trouble.

"Yeah, okay. I'm coming." He folded his arms across his chest and didn't budge. "You might not want to wait for me."

"Now!" the little girl shrieked.

"Come on, Tina," Matt said. "You don't have to wait for us."

"Yep," Cassie said. "Go on back to the barbecue. We'll come along."

Tina narrowed her eyes at Matt and looked at Cassie, and abruptly she seemed to change tactics. "Come on." She grabbed Annette's wrist and turned down the pathway. "We don't want to watch them *kissing* anyway."

Cassie straightened up, heat rushing to her face. "Annette! Don't you say anything to Mom about kissing!"

Matt doubled over, laughing.

Annette gave her a curious, wide-eyed stare. "Are you?"

"No!" Cassie sputtered. "I mean, it's none of your business!" The thought made her heart pound in her neck. If Matt kissed her, would she kiss him back? Her last experiences with kissing made her nervous to try.

The two little girls climbed back up the path, whispering and casting glances over their shoulders.

"Well." Matt pushed off the dock as soon as they were out of sight. "I guess we better go up before my dad does get mad at me." He poked Cassie's shoulder as he passed her. "Oh no! A snake just touched you."

Cassie laughed, her skin thrilling where he touched her. She watched to see if he would take her hand, but he didn't.

The food had been put away, and a hula hoop contest was going on next to the patio. All of the little girls had the wide bands around their waists and were attempting to keep the hoop spinning.

"Yikes. I'm horrible at that," Cassie said.

Matt look to her, a mischievous gleam entering his eyes. "Let's see it."

Cassie shook her head. "No way."

"How hard can it be? You just have to shake your hips." He gave a humorous imitation.

"Let's see you do it first then."

"Tell you what. You do it, and I'll do it too."

Cassie didn't want to. She would make a total fool of herself out there. But she would look even stupider if she backed down. "I'll only do it if you do it also."

In response, he stepped over to the pile of hoops and grabbed one, then another, which he held out to Cassie. Still hesitant, sure she was about to make the biggest fool of herself, Cassie accepted the hoop.

"Ready, go!" Matt began shaking his hips, and the circular band rotated around his waist once, twice, and then it slowed and fell down to his ankles.

He looked ridiculous, and Cassie couldn't stop laughing.

"Oh, come on! Let's see you do better!"

At least he made it impossible for her to take herself seriously. She couldn't wait to tell Andrea about this. Cassie held the hula hoop around her waist and then spun it. Immediately she began rotating her hips, trying to keep the hula hoop up. But just as it had with Matt, it began a gradual descent. She squealed when it got to her thighs and she spread her knees wider, doing everything possible to hold it there. But instead of circling around her knees, the hula hoop dipped one side down toward her feet. Cassie leaned forward to pull it back up and nearly lost her balance. She stumbled back up, her feet doing a quick step. One foot went down on the bottom of the hula hoop while the back of it got stuck around her shoulders. Cassie straightened up, and the hula hoop gave a sharp tug before breaking apart.

Cassie froze, stunned as she held the C-shaped plastic hoop, no longer a circle.

"You broke it!" Matt said, coming over to examine the pieces.

Tina ran over also. "You broke my hula hoop!" she exclaimed.

"I'm so sorry," Cassie said. "I don't know what happened!" Just when things had been going so well.

But Matt, who seemed to think every thing in life was a joke for his amusement, just started laughing. "That I have never seen before. It takes some wicked talent to break one." Even Tina joined in with his laughter, and Cassie wilted with relief that no one was angry at her or thought her an idiot.

Matt's dad got a cooler full of ice and sodas, and Cassie abandoned the hula hoops. She grabbed a chilled lemonade and sat down on a swingset. She kicked off the ground and noted how her family was the only one left.

Matt came over and grabbed her sandals, then spun her swing in a circle before letting go. Cassie gripped the ropes tightly, not wanting to fall out. Then he sank into a swing beside her.

"Are you cooled off now?"

"Yeah, it's pretty nice now."

He was looking right at her, talking to her, and Cassie's heart pounded harder. What had Andrea said? That she should tell him she liked him? "You know, I think this is first time you've ever really talked to me."

Matt laughed. "We had play practice together for weeks."

"Yeah, but when I try to talk to you at school you just kind of ignore me. Do I scare you?"

He laughed again. "Yeah, right. You don't scare anyone. Except maybe the hula hoops."

He hopped off the swing and walked away, and Cassie swallowed back her nerves. Had she said something wrong? She watched him bend over the ice chest and stand upright again. He had something in his hands, but she couldn't tell what. Then he looked at her and gestured for her to come over.

Cassie slowed the swing and jumped off, then joined him. He took her hand and dumped a handful of ice in it.

"Ice war," he whispered. "Come on. Let's get our sisters."

Cassie grinned, putting her lemonade down on the table and grabbing another handful of ice.

Matt let out a war whoop and then descended upon their families, chucking handfuls of ice. Cassie followed his example. Shrieks and yells ensued, but it only took moments before her siblings had also grabbed handfuls of ice and were chucking it back.

"Take cover!" Matt yelled at Cassie, and he opened the sliding glass door to the kitchen and dove inside. Cassie flew in after him and ducked behind the counter. She was laughing so hard she could hardly breathe, and Matt pressed a finger to his lips. She quieted down and studied his profile as he peered around the counter. Her chest warmed. If nothing else, she knew Matt was her friend.

Mrs. Jones came into the kitchen. "Cassie?"

Cassie stood up, melted ice dripping from her fingers.

Her mother smiled at her. "It's time to go."

Cassie couldn't argue the point, since they were the only ones here, but she didn't want to leave. She turned to Matt. "I guess I should give you your shirt back."

"Yeah. Let's go on up to my room again."

"I'll wait right here," Mrs. Jones said, arching an eyebrow.

Cassie did the shirt switch quickly in the bathroom, then came out and handed it back to Matt. "Thanks so much. I had so much fun today."

"Here." Matt took one of his rocks and placed it in her hands. "You can have one of my geodes."

"Really?" She looked at the bumpy rock in her hand. "Thank you!"

"Open it."

Cassie pulled on it, and to her surprise, it came apart easily. It had already been broken open. She gasped when she saw the glittering crystals inside. "It's beautiful!"

"That's what a geode is."

And he was giving it to her. One from his collection. She thought her chest would burst from happiness. She smiled at him. "I'll see you Monday."

She could hardly wait. What would things be like between them at school?

⁓⦿⁓

Cassie was all tingly and giddy when she got up for school Monday morning. She looked at the new geode sitting on her dresser and wondered what Matt would say to her today. Had he secretly had a crush on her this whole time but hadn't gotten the nerve up to do anything until she went to his house?

She picked her clothes carefully, trying to show off her slender waist and minimal curves. She couldn't wait to tell Janice and Andrea what had happened over the weekend.

She told Janice all about it as they walked from first hour civics to Cassie's second hour computer class. Cassie's heart rate picked up as they neared the classroom. She would see Matt here.

"Good luck," Janice said.

Cassie barely heard her, because then she spotted Matt, laughing with Kevin as they approached the classroom from the opposite direction. Cassie waited for the two of them to walk by, and then she purposefully bumped Matt's shoulder with her own. She waited with a smile on her face for him to turn around and tease her, to joke with her like he had on Saturday.

He didn't even glance at her.

Cassie's smile dropped from her face, and she turned to Janice, indignation flashing across her face. "How could he?" she sputtered. "Just ignore me! As if—"

"Yeah, but he smiled," Janice said. "You couldn't see it from where you were, but he smiled when you touched him."

"He did?" Cassie's heart switched gears as euphoria flooded her. "Why didn't he say something?"

Janice shrugged. "I don't know. Maybe he's shy in front of Kevin."

But not in front of his dad or sister? Cassie set her doubts aside and tried to be happy that he'd smiled.

Matt didn't talk to her the rest of the day, and she had to replay every conversation they had together on Saturday to keep from feeling discouraged. She sat by Andrea at lunch and told her everything.

"That sounds like so much fun," Andrea said. "We have to work on our Spanish skit. Why don't you come over after school tomorrow and we can talk some more?"

Cassie nodded. "I'll ask my mom."

❦

Cassie stared at the number she had typed into her phone for a good ten minutes before getting up the nerve to call. It was Matt's number, and his best friend Kevin had given it to her. Even though Matt had not spoken to her at all in school, she was going off of the smile Janice said she'd seen. Maybe, just maybe he was shy.

She finally hit send, and then nearly hung up when his voice answered.

"Hello?" he said, sounding curious.

"Matt? This is Cassie."

"Oh, hi, Cassie."

She tried to analyze his tone of voice. He didn't sound disappointed or annoyed, but he didn't sound overly excited either. Now what was she supposed to say? "How was your day?"

"Okay, I guess. Have a C in computers."

"You do? I thought it was all easy for you!"

"Well, it is. I understand what we're doing. I just don't always do it."

"That blows my mind. You're so smart. I have no clue what we're doing in there."

"I bet you have an A, though."

"Well, yeah. I don't like my grades to fall below that." Did that make her sound like a total dork?

"Do you have an A in algebra also?"

"Yes, but just barely," Cassie said, jumping on an opportunity to not look so nerdy. "Ms. Allred doesn't like me. She's always getting me and Cara in trouble."

"No way," he said, amusement in his voice. "How could any teacher not like you? You're so quiet."

"Apparently not in algebra," Cassie said, giggling.

She relaxed as the conversation flowed naturally, and Matt kept making her laugh. When she finally hung up, they had talked for over an hour, and a happy feeling nestled into her heart.

CHAPTER SIXTY-NINE

Back Stabbers

Mrs. Jones said yes to the Spanish project, so Cassie rode home with Andrea and Mrs. Wall on Tuesday.

"Tell me again everything Matt said on Saturday," Andrea said, sitting close to Cassie on her bed.

Cassie smiled, remembering the way Matt had touched her, teased her. "He was so nice to me. He even gave me one of his geodes."

"One of his geodes! What is that?"

"It's this rock," Cassie said. "It doesn't look like anything special on the outside, it's like round and bumpy. But when you split it open, it's full of crystals. He had lots of them. He gave me one."

"Wow! It sure sounds like he likes you!" Andrea picked up her phone and tapped it in the palm of her hand. "I have an idea. Let's call him."

The idea immediately thrilled and horrified Cassie. She never knew what would come out of Andrea's mouth. She shook her head. "No! We can't call him."

"Cassie, you can't go on like this forever. You need to know. Either he likes you or he doesn't. And if he doesn't, well." She shrugged. "You move on. But if he does!" She smiled broadly. "You'll be able to figure out where to go from here!"

Cassie nodded slowly. "Okay. You call him. But leave me out of it."

"No problem," Andrea purred. She dialed Matt's number, and a few minutes later his voice carried over the phone.

"Hello?" Matt said.

"Hi, Matt!" Andrea said in a very flirty voice. "This is Andrea, from school!"

"Hi, Andrea."

"How are you?" Andrea scooted closer to Cassie so she could overhear the conversation.

"Doing great. Just working on my math."

"Oh, right, because you're one of the smart kids. Hey, do you like anyone right now?"

The pause was loud to Cassie from where she sat, and then Matt said, "Not really. I just like to flirt."

He liked to flirt? But there wasn't anyone he was interested in? Cassie squirmed at the revelation.

"There's not any girl you're interested in?" Andrea pressed.

"I don't usually like a girl until I know for sure she's going to like me. I don't want to be rejected."

And then, from somewhere in the background, a male voice shouted, "Matt! Don't say anything to her! Cassie is over there!"

"Kevin," Cassie and Andrea said at the same time, recognizing his voice.

"I better go," Andrea said. "See you tomorrow." She hung up the phone, and Cassie buried her face in her hands with a groan.

"He so knows I was the one calling. How did Kevin even know I'm here?" Cassie peeked between her fingers, not sure she wanted to know.

"Well, we got some answers, right? He waits until he knows for sure that a girl likes him before he likes her."

"Which means he doesn't like me," Cassie said as the realization sank in. "He knows I like him."

"Maybe he's not sure," Andrea said.

"No," Cassie snapped. "He knows. Saturday meant nothing to him. I mean nothing to him. He just likes to flirt."

"Well, anyway," Andrea said, "we better get to work on the Spanish project."

"Oh, right." Cassie opened her binder, trying to take her mind off Matt and her tumultuous feelings. She pulled out her papers. "I already wrote a script. Now we just have to memorize it."

☙ ❧

Cassie was dreaming. The overly bright colors of her school hallway told her she wasn't awake. Nicole was there in her dream, and she pressed a finger to her lips and said, "Shh. Don't make a sound."

Silence followed Nicole's order, and Cassie remained still as well.

Too quiet. Even for a dream, there should be something more going on. With a start, her eyes snapped open.

Several faces peered down at her, watching her with amused, inquisitive smiles on their faces. Including her English teacher, Ms. Talo.

Cassie pushed her face off her desk and blinked several times.

"What?"

The students burst out laughing.

"We were waiting to see how long it would take you to wake up," Jimmy said.

"We tried to wake you first," Leigh Ann said. "And then we just gave up and watched you."

Cassie's face flamed, and she grabbed get her books when the bell rang. "Thanks, guys. I get up super early."

Nicole walked with her out of the classroom, still laughing. "You definitely need more sleep." She fished around in her backpack and pulled out a piece of paper. "And I finally brought that note from Sean."

"Oh, Sean. He's so sweet." Cassie accepted the note, already knowing that no matter what it said, she wouldn't pursue a relationship with Sean. He was just too old for her, though she wished he weren't.

No matter how she tried, Cassie couldn't make heads or tails of the programming assignment for computers. She sat at her dad's old main frame and kept typing in codes, but it wouldn't spit out the results she expected.

Matt would know the answer. Cassie tapped her fingers on the computer desk, hesitant to call him. His conversation with Andrea left her unsure. But still . . . she picked up her phone and hit his number.

"Hi, Matt, it's Cassie," she said when he answered.

"I know. I have your number saved."

Okay, so no surprises there. Cassie opened her mouth to ask her question, when he continued with, "You don't have to call every day."

That stopped her. A warm, embarrassed flush crept up her neck and into her ears. Every day? She didn't call every day. "I'm sorry. Did you want me to stop calling?" Even she heard the insulted tone in her voice.

He hesitated a little too long to answer, and Cassie wanted to hang up. Then he said, "You can call. Just not every day."

"I needed some help in computers, but I just figured it out. Thanks." Cassie hung up, hot tears in her eyes. He definitely was not interested in her.

Cassie avoided talking to Matt or even looking at him in school on Wednesday. Her friends were excited about the upcoming lock-in at Lokomotion and hardly noticed that she seemed down.

"You're coming this year, right?" Amity asked Cassie as she moped at lunch.

"Sure, if I'm invited."

"Well, of course you are!" Cara said. "We do everything together!"

"There's a school dance right before then," Janice said. "We can all go together."

Amity nodded. "I'm so excited! I can ask my mom to give us a ride."

"Cassie is coming over to my house," Andrea said. "My mom already said she'd give us a ride."

This was the first Cassie was hearing about it, but she gave Andrea a grateful smile, glad somebody wanted her around.

"Well, doesn't Cassie have a church dance on Saturday? Maybe my mom can give us a ride to that."

Oh, yes. The church dance. At least that was something to look forward to.

Janice fell into step beside Cassie as they walked down the hall. "You okay? You seem a little down."

Cassie had avoided talking about this with anyone, but now that Janice asked, the tears of humiliation pricked her eyes. "I talked to Matt last night. He pretty much told me not to call him anymore."

Janice furrowed her brow. "That's rude. Why would he do that?"

Cassie shook her head. "He said I call every day. He doesn't like me. Maybe he even hates me."

"I'm sure that's not it. He must've meant something else. He's in my fifth hour class. I'll talk to him and let you know in science."

Cassie's first reaction was to tell Janice not to, but she swallowed it back. What could it hurt? Things couldn't be worse than they were.

Cassie got to sixth hour first, and she sat by Jaclyn and waited for Janice. As soon as she walked in the door, she collapsed into the seat next to Cassie.

"Well?" Cassie asked, dying to know. "What did he say? Did you talk to him?"

Janice nodded and pulled out her notebook. "He said he doesn't mind talking to you, he just wishes you wouldn't call every day. He said he doesn't hate you, but he gets really tired of you always hitting on him."

Cassie's jaw dropped open, and indignation flashed through her veins. "I don't hit on him all the time! He's the one that hit on me!" She pictured the day they'd spent together on Saturday, only now every happy memory was tainted, a dark hue overlaying the image. "He's so fake." She clenched her fist around her pencil, fighting tears.

Janice gave her a sympathetic hug. "I'm so sorry."

What else was there to say?

Cassie didn't speak to Matt all day Thursday or Friday. She didn't call him. A part of her hoped he would miss her and talk to her, even call her. But he didn't.

Cassie went home with Andrea after school on Friday to get ready for the dance. Andrea's newest boyfriend, a short eighth grader named

Kyle, was there. Cassie had met him a few times and he was always friendly, but since he was a grade younger, Cassie didn't know him too well.

"Do you think Matt will be at the dance?" Andrea asked Cassie as she wrapped her hair around the curling iron.

"I'm trying not to think about it," Cassie said.

"I'll tell him to dance with you," Kyle said.

Cassie met his eyes in the mirror and gave him a grim smile. "That's all right. If he wants to dance with me, nobody will need to tell him to do so."

"Well. We'll make sure somebody wants to dance with you." Andrea helped Cassie pick out a pair of shorts and a loose top to go with them. "There, you look beautiful."

Cassie smiled at her reflection and wished she felt beautiful.

Janice, Maureen, and Cara were already at the dance when Cassie, Andrea, and Kyle arrived. The dance hadn't started yet, and Cara handed them each a roll of streamers and told them they weren't quite done decorating. Andrea and Maureen took one corner of the room, and Kyle followed Cassie to another.

"What am I supposed to do it with this?" he said, tossing the roll back and forth in his hands.

"You just kind of throw it around," Cassie said, who had never understood the purpose of streamers either.

"Really?" Kyle took the roll and chucked it across the room, scattering crinkly paper the whole way.

"Not like that!" Cassie said, and then she burst out giggling. "And I thought I didn't know how to do it!" Still laughing, she showed Kyle how to stretch the streamers in U-shaped patterns across the room. She turned around to look for her friends, and her laughter cut off short.

Matt was here. He stood just inside the door, talking to someone out of sight. Cassie couldn't see who the other person was, but Matt kept reaching his hand out like he wanted to touch her.

The music started and the dance got underway, but Cassie didn't tear her eyes from the doorway. Finally, a casual smile on his face, Matt turned around and walked into the gym.

The girl in the doorway followed.

Amity.

CHAPTER SEVENTY
True Confessions

C assie swallowed hard, feeling her smile drop into the pit of her stomach. She didn't want to be here anymore. She put the streamers down on the ground and went and sat on the bleachers.

"Are you okay?" Kyle asked, following her.

"I'm fine," she said, unable to tear her eyes from Matt and Amity. A moment later, the two of them were dancing. Cassie thought she would throw up.

Kyle followed her gaze. "Oh, it's your friend. Who is she dancing with?"

Cassie didn't say a word.

Andrea came over and stole Kyle away for a dance. A new song came on, but Matt and Amity didn't separate. One time Amity threw back her head and laughed, then she turned slightly and met Cassie's eyes. She froze until Matt said something else, and then she spun back around to him.

"Hey, don't you look pretty." Nicole sat down on the bleacher beside Cassie. "Too bad my brother doesn't attend junior high dances. He would want to dance with you."

"I wish he were here. At least someone would dance with me."

The song ended, and Cassie's eyes started twitching toward the dance floor, hardly daring to look. And then she sucked in a breath when she saw Matt walking toward her. She kept her eyes lowered, her heart rate quickening. It had to mean something to him, all the flirting he had done a week ago.

Matt came to a stop in front of her and extended a hand. "Nicole, want to dance?"

He may as well have stabbed Cassie in the chest.

Nicole shot Cassie an uncertain look, but Cassie waved her onward. As soon as they walked onto the dance floor, Cassie jumped up and escaped to the bathroom. She dropped into one of the stalls, locked the door, and sobbed.

The bathroom door opened, and Andrea's voice called out, "Cassie?"

Cassie cleared her throat. "Here."

There was a pause, then Andrea said, "Are you okay? Kyle and I are ready to go."

Cassie dropped out of the stall and wiped her face with a paper towel.

"What's wrong?" Andrea asked.

"Let's just get out of here."

Andrea gave Cassie a hug and rubbed her back, and they headed for the doors. Kyle waited out front.

"Cassie!" Amity ran out of the building and stopped when she saw them.

Cassie turned around and looked at her, daring her to say something, waiting for some kind of explanation.

But Amity faltered. "I'll see you at Lokomotion."

Cassie climbed into the car without another word. She holed herself up in the corner of Andrea's room and cried some more. Andrea tried to make her feel better, but nothing helped.

"We're gonna watch a movie," Andrea said. "We have an hour before we need to leave for Lokomotion. Want to watch with us?"

Cassie waved them off. "I just need to be by myself right now."

"Okay. Come on, Kyle."

Andrea left the room, but Kyle lingered.

"That boy's an idiot. You're a whole lot prettier than Amity."

Cassie tried to smile, but it didn't work. "If that were true, he would've danced with me."

Kyle shook his head. "He just isn't paying any attention. If I'd met you before I met Andrea, I'd be going out with you." With that he turned around and walked out of the room.

⁓⁓☙⁓⁓

Kyle couldn't go to Lokomotion, so his mom came and got him right before Andrea and Cassie left. Cassie figured she cried every last tear out of her body, and she felt a little bit better as the two girls walked into the family fun center.

Amity, Janice, and Maureen stood by the check-in desk. Amity turned around and saw them. She walked over to Cassie.

"Come with me to the bathroom," she said, taking Cassie's hand.

Cassie's heart gave a little tumble, and suddenly she did not want to go to the bathroom with Amity. She did not want to hear what Amity had to say. But she went along anyway.

As soon as the door close behind them, Amity said, "Are you mad at me?"

In all honesty, Cassie was. Amity knew Cassie's feelings for Matt but had completely disregarded them when she spent the evening dancing with him. How would saying that help anything, though? Amity would become defensive and they would argue. So Cassie shrugged.

"No. It just kind of frustrated me that you and Matt danced with each other the whole time."

"He would have danced with you if you had asked him."

"I didn't want to ask him!" Tears rose in Cassie's eyes again, and she shook them off, irate that she had any left. "I can't even talk to him without him telling people I'm hitting on him! Why didn't he ask me?"

Amity began to cry too. "I want to tell you something, but I can't."

Cassie gave Amity a startled look. Why was she crying? "Tell me what?"

"I can't tell you, I'm afraid I'll lose you!" Amity sobbed harder.

Cassie's own tears dried up in the face of this new development. She shook Amity's arm. "What is it?"

"I didn't mean to! I didn't mean to say it, I didn't think he would believe me!"

"Amity, what?"

Amity only shook her head. She grabbed several paper towels and blotted her eyes. Cassie waited for her to calm down, then she asked again.

"What is it? What did you say?"

"It's nothing." Amity attempted a smile. "That's all, really. As long as you're not mad at me."

"I'm not." Cassie waited for more, but Amity was not forthcoming.

Amity threw the paper towels away. "Come on. Let's go back out there."

Cassie mulled over Amity's words as they played bumper boats in the little pool. What had she meant, that she didn't mean to tell him? Had Amity told Matt Cassie liked him? Was it because of Amity that he said Cassie was always hitting on him? The more she thought about it, the better Cassie felt. Maybe this was all a big misunderstanding.

They did the go carts after the bumper boats, and Cassie laughed and joked with her friends, feeling lighter than she had in a week.

It was after two a.m when they decided to play a round of miniature golf. Cara swiped her club too hard and sent the ball careening off the course. Maureen whooped and played after her. Amity waited behind Cassie. Cassie set her ball on the turf and lifted her club, just as Amity blurted, "I like Matt."

Cassie halted, the blood freezing in her veins. She slowly pivoted her head to look at Amity. "What?"

Amity's face turned bright red, but she repeated, "I like Matt. And I didn't mean to, but I told him. And he said he likes me too."

Cassie sucked in a breath, the information hitting her like a punch to the stomach. "How could you do this?" she whispered.

Amity's face looked stricken. "I wasn't going to tell him."

"Yes, you were!" Cassie exploded. "If you were going to keep it a secret, you wouldn't have danced with him all night!"

Amity burst into tears. She dropped the golf club and ran off the course.

"Amity?" Maureen called, and she ran after her.

Cassie's fists clenched, and she trembled with barely concealed anger. Of course, somehow Amity got the sympathy, as if Cassie were the big bad guy.

"There's something else," Janice said, re-directing Cassie's attention. "But I don't think Amity is going to tell you."

Cassie didn't even want to know. "What?"

"Matt asked her out."

The punches just wouldn't stop coming. "Oh," Cassie said, and the voice didn't even sound like her own.

"Amity said no," Janice said. "You should know that."

The tears began to flow again, big, jagged streaks down her face. She felt like she been played. Matt was the biggest flirt, and the whole time he was interested in someone else.

"I can't stay here," Cassie said.

"Cassie, it's okay," Andrea said, and her friends gathered around her, but Cassie pushed away from them.

"I just need to be alone." She ran back toward the arcade. She had no idea where Amity had gone, but she suspected it was the bathroom. So instead Cassie found a quiet corner by some bushes. She curled up, wrapping her arms around her legs, and sobbed, her heart breaking.

Cassie wasn't sure how long she sat there crying her heart out before Nicole walked by. Nicole did a double take when she saw her sitting there, and then she crouched into the bushes beside Cassie.

"Cassie? What's wrong?"

Cassie only shook her head. She felt even stupider explaining how she had managed to delude herself into thinking Matt might like her.

But Nicole wasn't in Cassie's advanced classes for no reason. She sat down beside Cassie and mimicked her posture, wrapping her arms around her knees. "This has to do with Matt, doesn't it."

Cassie bobbed her head. "He likes Amity. She told him she likes him too. He actually asked her out." Saying the words out loud cut through Cassie, and the tears wouldn't stop.

Nicole put an arm around Cassie's shoulder and held her. "I know how you feel. When Jimmy and I broke up and I found out he liked someone else, it tore me up."

"It's always Amity. I'll never be anything next to her."

Nicole was quiet for a long moment. Then she said, very quietly, "How much can Amity possibly like him when she likes every boy in school?"

Nicole's words were like a healing balm to Cassie's heart. They soothed her. She had thought the same thing but felt guilty for it. Now, even though it didn't change anything, she felt a little better knowing she wasn't the only one who noticed.

"It would all be so much easier if you could only like my brother."

Cassie wiped her eyes and gave a wobbly smile. "Things are never that simple."

<hr>

Cassie was one of the last ones picked up after the lock-in. She stayed with Andrea and Janice in the parking lot, while Maureen, Amity, and Cara stood nearby. They all made small talk together, though every time Cassie looked at Amity, she felt a stab in her heart.

Her friends had been picked up by the time Mr. Jones got to Lokomotion. He took Cassie straight to the soccer store, where she had promised to work for him if he let her go to the lock-in.

Cassie ran the register for clients, but having gone all night with no sleep started to pull on her eyelids. Her head drooped several times between customers. By lunchtime, her head pounded, and she was afraid she'd be sick.

"I'm going to work on inventory in the back," she told her dad. He waved her off, and she slipped into the stockroom. She sat down on the floor and pulled down several shoeboxes, then opened them and checked their contents.

What was she supposed to be checking? Both pairs of shoes were there. The right sizes were in the right boxes. Her vision swam in front of her, and she couldn't remember what else she needed to do. She fell back on the cheap carpet and closed her eyes.

Cassie slept for hours. She only woke when her mother shook her shoulder, laughing.

"Cassie, let's go home. Your dad just called and told me you were sleeping back here."

Cassie blinked groggily and pushed to her feet, too tired to even respond.

"How was the night? Did you have fun with your friends?" Mrs. Jones asked as Cassie pulled her seatbelt on in the car.

"Fine. It was great." Cassie leaned her head back and closed her eyes again. It was easier to sleep than to think.

⟡

Cassie woke up sometime in the afternoon. It took a moment to remember where she was and why her heart hurt so much.

And then it came to her, the memory of her friend's betrayal and Matt's rejection burning her eyes. There was a church dance tonight, and she didn't even want to go. Her friends would be there, and Cassie did not feel like competing with Amity or Andrea right now.

Cassie changed her clothes into something casual and brushed her hair without enthusiasm. Depression hung around her like heavy rain clouds. When they left for the dance, Mrs. Jones could tell something was wrong, but Cassie did not feel like explaining how she had humiliated herself.

Amity and Andrea were already there, and they cheerfully waved Cassie over. Soon the boys began to arrive, and Cassie glared as Amity giggled and flirted with every one of them.

"Would you like to dance?" James said, holding his hand out to Cassie.

James was one of the Tahlequah boys and always ready with a smile and a kind word. But what she really wanted to do was go home and cry into her blankets. Since that wasn't an option, she put a smile on her face and nodded.

They walked out onto the dance floor, and Cassie saw Amity dancing with Zack. Zack! Indignation spiked through her even though she knew she had no right to feel possessive. She looked at James and said, "Is Amity prettier than I am?"

He gave a patronizing smile and said, "All girls are pretty in their own way."

Cassie resisted stomping her foot in annoyance. "That's not what I asked," she said, her tone irritated. The tears were forming behind her eyes again. She blinked several times, willing them to stay away.

James tilted his head at her. "No," he said softly. "In my opinion, Amity is not prettier than you."

Cassie smiled, knowing the glistening in her eyes must be evident. "I think you're the only guy who thinks so."

"Definitely not." The song ended, and he tapped her chin. "Keep your chin up. These are the hard days. People will recognize your value."

"Thanks," Cassie said. She moved off the dance floor and joined Riley, waiting to see who would ask her to dance next.

She wasn't surprised when she saw Zack making his way toward her. He smiled at her, the same charming, endearing smile as always, but this time it did not make her heart skip a beat. Cassie smiled back, but all she felt was friendship for him.

"Hi, Cassie," he said, reaching his hand out. "Would you like to dance?"

"I would love to."

Cassie and Zack moved in their little two-step square around the dance floor.

"Did you enjoy dancing with Amity?" Cassie asked.

"Is that one of your friends?"

"Yes. The girl you just danced with."

"Sure, she's nice."

Cassie wanted to ask more questions but felt it would make her look a little desperate. She glanced around and saw Amity dancing with Josh's friend Elijah. Amity was giggling and touching his arm, then placing her hand on his chest, a flirtatious smile never leaving her face.

Cassie rolled her eyes. Did guys actually like girls who played them? Anyone could see what kind of a person she was, yet every guy here seemed to like her.

She tuned back in when she realized Zack was talking to her and she hadn't been paying attention.

"What do you think? Is it a good idea?"

Cassie had no idea, of course, what Zack was talking about. She didn't want to admit that, though. So she turned the question around. "Do you think it's a good idea?"

Zack gave a shrug. "It could be fun. If you're around this summer, anyway."

Crapola. What had she missed? Had Zack just asked her to do something?

The song ended, and Cassie released his hand. "Sure. I think it sounds great." Whatever it was, surely he would call her first so they could work out the details.

Zack gave his endearing smile again. "Great. I'll talk to you about it later, then."

Cassie returned to the wall to find her friends giggling around Amity. "What is it?" Cassie asked.

Andrea turned to Cassie. "Elijah told Amity she's the most beautiful girl he's ever seen, and he kissed her. Can you believe it? It's so romantic!"

"Are you kidding me?" Cassie exclaimed. "I thought you were head over heels in love with Matt!"

Amity look affronted. "I am. I like both."

Cassie turned away, anger burning in her chest. They deserved each other, Matt and Amity. Two players who only fooled around with other people's hearts.

CHAPTER SEVENTY-ONE

No More Glamour

Amity talked about Elijah for the rest of the night at the dance, but by Monday, she only had swooney eyes for Matt, and Cassie wanted to punch her.

But she refrained.

"I have an announcement," Ms. Berry said in choir. "The elite high school choir, Unity, is having try outs this Friday, if any of you would like to try out."

A warm expectation blossomed in Cassie's chest. She had been singing solos for years and was one of the best singers in her choir. She was born to be in Unity.

School let out early for a pep rally, and Cassie and Janice joined Amity and Maureen as they walked toward the gym. Melanie called out to Amity, who moved ahead with her but didn't ditch them completely.

"I think she's trying to be a better friend," Janice said into Cassie's ear.

Cassie might have agreed if Amity didn't spot Matt the moment he walked into the gym. Her face lit up, and she grabbed Cassie's hand.

"Let's sit behind him."

Cassie had no desire to. Her heart still hurt whenever she thought about the weekend, and she knew the best thing she could do was forget about Matt. "What about Josh's friend? You kissed him on Saturday."

Amity brushed it off and pulled Cassie up the stairs, leaving her no choice but to follow. "He lives in Tahlequah. It's not like he could be my boyfriend. We can just kiss every once in a while."

Well, that sounded totally twisted and wrong. Couldn't Matt see that was what he would be getting? Why would he choose Amity when he could have someone like Cassie, who would love him with all her heart and not share herself?

They climbed into the row behind Matt and Kevin, and Janice gave Cassie a sympathetic smile. Cassie gritted her teeth as Amity poked Matt in the back and played with his hair and flirted with him through the entire pep rally. Apparently it was only Cassie he didn't like hitting on him. He was totally fine with Amity doing it.

ᨶᨠᨶᨠᨶᨠ

Cassie sat by Jaclyn in computers the next morning and struggled to figure out the coding issue.

"I don't know what I'm doing wrong, but every time I hit the button to start the sequence, it freezes."

Jaclyn scooted her chair over to examine Cassie's coding. "I don't know. What's the outcome you're expecting?"

"It's supposed to spell 'hello,' and then the letters break apart in a little dance."

"Hm." Jaclyn turned around and scanned the classroom. "I bet we can find someone here who knows how to do it." Raising her voice, Jaclyn shouted, "Matt!"

"Not him!" Cassie hissed.

Too late. Matt had turned around, and Jaclyn waved him over.

Cassie swiveled to face the computer screen, her cheeks burning. She did not want to talk to him. She did not want him over here.

"What's up?" Matt asked from behind her.

"Can you take a look at Cassie's coding? She can't get it to work."

"Sure." Matt grabbed a chair and sat next to Cassie. "What's going on with it?"

"I didn't ask her to call you over here," Cassie said. "This wasn't my idea. I can figure this out."

He gave her an odd look. "Okay. So you don't want my help?"

"No. I mean." She sighed. He was already here. "Yes, if you can figure out the problem."

"All right, let me take a look." Matt leaned across the keyboard and typed a few things. "It looks like this line of code is incomplete. And I think you're trying to accomplish twenty things with this one." He deleted the line and then hit enter. All of the lines and the coding scrolled down and then vanished.

"Where did they go?" Cassie leaned forward and pressed the Down arrow, trying to move the screen.

"They must've moved to the bottom." Matt tried to get his fingers onto the keyboard, but Cassie pushed him away.

"I'll find it!" She scrolled as far as she could go, but nothing appeared. So she scrolled upward. Still nothing.

"Let me try," Matt said.

Cassie pushed off of the desk and crossed her arms over her chest. Seriously? "You've ruined my project."

Matt didn't respond. He scrolled up and down several times before shaking his head.

"I'm so sorry. Did you save it?"

"No!" Cassie snapped. "I was just now building it!" She shoved Matt off and pressed a few buttons. Still nothing. "Thanks a lot! I have to start over now!"

"I'm sorry." Matt lifted his hands up defensively and backed away.

Cassie whirled away from him, her cheeks flaming. Already she felt bad for yelling at him, but she was so angry at him for rejecting her and leading her on that it felt good to have a reason to lash out. She knew he'd been trying to help, but her entire project was gone.

❧

Miss Malcolm helped Cassie pick a song from a popular movie that she was already familiar with for her Unity try outs, and Cassie practiced and practiced. She sang it for her friends at church and for everyone in choir at school.

"I'm going to try out also," Janice said.

"What about you?" Cassie asked Amity and Maureen.

"No way," Maureen said. "I've never wanted to sing a solo."

"Yeah, I don't think so," Amity said. "I'll leave the singing up to you."

Cassie made all of her friends join her outside during lunch on Friday so she could sing her song to them.

"What do you think?" she asked, wringing her hands.

Maureen shrugged. "Sounds good," she said, sounding disinterested.

"You did a great job," Andrea said. Cara nodded.

"It's perfect," Janice said. "You're going to make it for sure. I just hope I do also."

Janice hadn't even made Unison in eighth grade. Cassie doubted she would make it. But she offered a loyal smile and said, "That would be so fun. To be in there together."

Cassie rode with Janice and Kendra, another girl in choir, to the high school after school for the tryouts. Dozens of students stood around the choir room, waiting their turn. Cassie's nerves jumped into overdrive when she saw all of the older kids.

"Who are we kidding, trying out with them?" she whispered to Janice. "There's no way we can compete with them."

"I know," Janice whispered back. "But we're already here, so we may as well try."

The high school students had formed little clusters inside and outside the building, where they practiced their songs. Cassie, Janice, and

Kendra went into one room and closed the door. They had music for the judges, but alone in the room, they just sang a Capella.

Janice sang a jazz song, and Cassie realized she had a rich, deep alto voice. She clapped when Janice finished.

"Your voice is very pleasant to listen to. It's like chocolate."

Janice giggled. "I like that. I sing like chocolate."

"My turn." Kendra got up and sang a Broadway piece. She imitated the accent of the actress quite well, and her voice was fluid, crystal clear. But it lacked any distinguishing factor, and Cassie thought her rather boring. But she clapped politely when Kendra finished.

"You're up, Cassie," Janice said.

"Okay." Cassie took a deep breath and brushed her clammy palms against her jeans. She hummed a little the way Miss Malcolm had taught her to warm up her throat, and then she launched into the song.

She started too low, and Cassie figured that out two stanzas into it, but she didn't start over. As she carried on, she suddenly felt childish in her jeans shorts and hoodie. Kendra wore a sundress and Janice was in a button-up blouse. Cassie didn't even have her hair down.

Kendra and Janice both clapped when Cassie finished.

"That was good," Kendra said.

"I started too low," Cassie said, brushing off the praise.

"It's okay," Janice said. "When you try out, you'll be singing to the music. You won't have any problems being on the right note."

Cassie refused to be comforted, feeling all kinds of nervous. "I didn't do that great."

"You did better at lunchtime today," Janice agreed. "You've got to quit being nervous and just sing."

Cassie performed all the time. She even had auditions at various times of the year. Why should this make her so nervous?

For some reason it did. Knowing she was being evaluated, judged on her singing abilities, made it much harder to sing.

Hours passed by. Cassie checked her phone; it was a little after five. They had been there since three. It gave her and Janice and Kendra plenty of time to run through their songs.

And then Kendra got called in to sing. When she came out, her face was flushed and she started crying.

"I did awful!"

Cassie and Janice patted her on the back and tried to make her feel better, but Cassie couldn't help the relief she felt. If Kendra did awful, then that was one person down.

Janice went next, and she also came out looking shaky.

"I think I did okay," she said. "My voice wouldn't stop shaking."

"They probably just thought it was extra vibrato," Cassie said.

"Yeah. I hope so."

And then it was Cassie's turn. She took a deep breath to calm her nerves and then went inside the room.

The high school choir teacher, Mr. Cullen, looked up.

"Cassandra Jones?"

She gave a nod and cleared her throat. "Yes."

He nodded at a student in the corner, and the music to her song began playing. Oh! She was starting! She listened carefully and then came in right where she was supposed to. She sang the notes exactly, with precision, although she did forget to do the crescendos she had practiced. There was nothing flamboyant or fancy about her singing, but she felt very good about her performance when the song ended.

"Thank you, Cassandra. Now could you step over to that music stand behind you?"

Music stand? She turned around and spotted one to her side. She took a step behind it.

"Thank you. Please sing the top line."

Cassie's heart skipped a beat . . . Sight reading! She was awful at this! She studied the top line, heart hammering in her throat. She knew middle C, so she found it quickly, then moved her hands up and down with the notes. She couldn't just get the notes right, though; she had to have the right rhythm.

Was the second note a G or an F? She counted on her fingers up to a fourth.

Opening her mouth, she started on the notes. If it was supposed to be a recognizable song, she had no idea what it was. She followed the notes up, then back down, remembering at the last minute to hold the last one for four counts. Then she looked up from the music stand, her face flaming. She had done horrible on that. They wouldn't hold that against her, would they?

"Thank you, Cassandra," Mr. Cullen said, and Ms. Berry smiled at her from behind the table. "You may go. Please collect the next student on the list."

Cassie hardly dared breathe as she walked out. She found the next student and told them it was their turn, then hurried over to where Janice was waiting. Kendra had already left.

"How did it go?" Janice asked.

Cassie clasped her hands. "I think it went really well. I didn't mess up my song any, but the sight reading was horrible." Her heart fluttered anxiously. She might really have a chance of making it.

Janice's mom showed up to get her then, and Janice said, "Call me as soon as you hear anything."

Cassie nodded. "I will. Same to you."

Janice waved, and Cassie sat down on the curb outside to wait for her own mother.

The tryouts finished, and the students began to disappear as parents showed up to collect them. Still Cassie waited.

The back door to the choir room opened, and Ms. Berry stepped out. She shuffled the papers in her hands, a pleased smile on her face.

"Well, Cassie," Ms. Berry said. "That was fun, wasn't it?"

"Yeah." She tried to read Ms. Berry's face. Certainly she knew something.

"I'm so happy," Ms. Berry said. "Two of my freshmen made it."

Cassie's heart lurched. "Who?" she asked with baited breath, not even daring to speculate.

"Kendra and Janice. You did really well, Cassie. Try again next year."

All of the air rushed out of Cassie's lungs. Kendra and Janice made it but not Cassie? This made no sense at all. She had felt so confident with her tryout.

But all she could do was paste a smile on her face and bob her head. "Good for them."

She kept the forced smile on her face until Ms. Berry had driven away. And then she let it drop as the tears gathered. Was there just something wrong with her? Were her days as a prodigy singer over?

She didn't call Janice to tell her. She figured Ms. Berry could do that.

☙ ❧

"Did you hear about Amity going to the movies with Matt over the weekend?" Andrea asked Cassie in first hour.

Nobody else was talking to Cassie because they were too busy congratulating Janice. Cassie lifted her head around and stared at Andrea. "What?"

Andrea nodded. "I'm not supposed to tell you. But he invited her, and she couldn't say no."

Couldn't say no. Yeah, right. Amity did whatever she wanted, not worrying about other people's feelings. Cassie analyzed her own feelings and discovered mostly what she felt was irritation with Amity. Matt was a flirt and a player, and he didn't deserve Cassie.

"Good for them. I hope they're supremely happy with each other for the next week until she gets tired of him."

"Right?" Andrea giggled, looking satisfied with Cassie's answer.

The day was nearly unbearable for Cassie. It seemed like every single person in school came up to Janice and congratulated her, following it up with, "Oh, I knew you'd make it!"

Nobody noticed Cassie. Nobody commented on her. Perhaps they had also known she wouldn't make it.

She sat by Riley in choir and ignored all the praise Janice and Kendra were getting. She pulled out a book and pretended she didn't notice anyone else in the room.

CHAPTER SEVENTY-TWO

The Crap Slide

Turned out a week was too long for Matt and Amity. Cassie's phone rang while she was at the soccer store, helping her dad. It surprised her to see Amity's name.

Was she calling to confess about her date with Matt? Cassie did not want to talk to her about that. She answered the phone with some trepidation. "Hello?"

"Cassie, it's Amity."

"Hey." Cassie sat down on the stool behind the register and waited.

Amity cleared her throat. "I just wanted to let you know I don't like Matt anymore."

"You don't?" Cassie sat up straight. "Since when?"

"Just since the weekend."

Since the movie, she meant. That must've been when Amity realized she didn't like Matt. "It doesn't matter. He's not interested in me, whether or not you're around." Although Amity leading him on probably had not helped the matter. "What are you going to tell him?"

"Oh, nothing. It's not like we're going out. He'll figure it out eventually."

Cassie rolled her eyes. So like Amity. "Of course. You wouldn't want to hurt his feelings or anything."

"Exactly," Amity said, sounding relieved. "See, I knew if anyone would understand, it would be you."

"Oh, I understand, all right. I've got to go, I'm working my dad's store right now."

"Really? You didn't want to come over or anything?"

"Not today. I have to work."

"Oh, okay. Well, I'll see you in school tomorrow. You won't tell Matt, will you?"

"We don't even talk to each other. I'm not going to tell him." Though she wished someone would. He deserved to get his heart broken just like Cassie had.

❧

The last day of school.

The last day of junior high. The last day of ninth grade.

Next year would be high school. Next year Cassie would turn sixteen. She would learn to drive a car, and she would be able to date.

Everything about next year thrilled her and terrified her at the same time.

Yearbooks were handed out in first hour, and Cassie and Janice and Andrea sat in a circle writing in each other's books and giggling.

"Do you think we'll even have the same friends?" Janice asked. "Or do you think everything will change?"

"Of course we'll still have the same friends," Cassie said. "All of us are friends forever. Even when we're mad at each other." Even as she said it, though, Cassie wasn't sure. Sometime she really didn't want to be Amity or Maureen's friend anymore.

Everyone was goofing off in computers also. Cassie left her yearbook at the table and went over to one of the computers to talk with Jaclyn. Out of the corner of her eye, she saw someone pick up her book, and she turned.

It was Matt. He pulled out a pen and wrote something, which totally surprised her. Then he looked up and gave her a smile before walking away.

Cassie stood there, flabbergasted and totally annoyed. Did he think that he could just move from Amity to Cassie and she wouldn't care? She was so not interested in him. She turned back to Jaclyn, feeling a little lighter as they continued their conversation.

High school in a few months. No more of these little boys just hitting puberty. She was certain it would only take a few weeks for her to find a real boyfriend.

❧

Cara sat down at the lunch table with a big grin on her face. "My mom said I could have everyone over after school. Who can come?"

"I can for sure," Maureen said.

"Count me in," Amity said.

Cassie felt a surge of longing. She wanted to go with them, to finish up junior high together. "I ride the bus home. I'll have to see if my mom can bring me over."

"Just ride with me," Maureen said. "We can go to Cara's together."

Cassie gave her a surprised look. "Thanks."

"Janice? Andrea?" Cara gave each of them a questioning look as she opened her chocolate milk.

Janice shook her head. "We've got plans after school. Sorry."

"I think we do too," Andrea said. "But I'll call my mom and ask."

It turned out Andrea couldn't come. Amity's mom would bring her later. Cassie and Cara piled into Maureen's car after school, grateful for the opportunity to hang out with her friends at least this last time before high school started.

Maureen was in a goofy mood, reminding Cassie of the days they spent together last summer when they were still really close. They sang loudly to the songs on the radio and pushed each other around the car as it took the curves.

They were the first to arrive at Cara's house, and Cara promptly handed them each a pair of cut-off shorts and a tank top to put on. "We're walking to the crap slide," she said.

"No," Maureen groaned. "Not the crap slide."

Cara shoved her. "You love it as much as I do!"

"What's the crap side?" Cassie had never heard of it, and she admitted it sounded a little ominous.

Maureen turned to Cassie. "It's at this lake closer to your house. The farmer dams the pond, but there's always a little bit of water that runs down the dam into a small swamp at the bottom. It's covered with algae and all kinds of gross stuff."

Cara giggled. "We've been going there since I was a kid. We always come off the slide covered in slime and gunk. Can't get more hillbilly than that!"

Cassie had a hard time picturing her beautiful, sophisticated friend doing something as back-country as sliding through algae mud on a farmer's run off.

"Hello!" Amity breezed into the room. "I'm here!"

Cara tossed pair of cut-offs and a tank top at her also. "Change your clothes. You don't want to go down the crap slide in that."

"The what?" Amity said, and Cassie and Maureen both laughed.

"The crap slide," Cassie said.

"It's at the white bull. The one you see on the way to Cassie's house."

The white bull. Cassie knew where that was, since it was a landmark used to get to her house, and it was not close to Cara's house. "How are we going to get there?" Neither of Cara's parents were home.

"We'll walk." Cara stopped in front of a mirror and pushed up her blond hair.

"Walk? It must be five miles!"

"If we took the road. But I know the back way." Cara turned around and smiled. "Everybody set?"

The three girls followed Cara out the door. Sure enough, Cara turned left, leading them into the grapevines that lined the countryside.

The sun beat down on them, and sweat dripped past Cassie's eyebrows as they walked.

"We've been walking at least half an hour," Amity complained, voicing Cassie's thoughts.

Cara follow a path only she knew, turning past the grapevines with the little tiny grapes on them into a corn field. The green leaves splayed out above Cassie's head, and she could see nothing except plants around her.

"Not much farther," Cara said. She turned past a few more grapevines, and then the girls spilled out onto the road.

Cassie knew this road. It was the one her family took to get to Cara's house. Janice's land was across the street, where they had had a campout earlier in the year. At the end of the road was the giant white bull, a statue stationed to mark the farmer's ranch.

"Come on," Cara said, and she darted across the two-lane highway. Maureen grabbed Cassie's hand, and they chased after her, Amity right on their heels.

"Do you actually know the farmer who lives here?" Amity asked.

"Yes," Cara said. "He's my uncle." She led the girls over to the big white concrete slide that acted as a run off from the big pond to the little swamp below.

Cassie looked down at the mud and algae that coated the concrete. "I am not going down that."

"Suit yourself." Grinning, Cara sat down on the edge of the dam and pushed herself off.

She didn't fly down it, but slowly scooted past the slippery slime. Maureen didn't hesitate to sit on the edge and follow after.

Cassie exchanged looks with Amity.

"I guess here goes," Amity said, and then she also slid down.

Crapola. Double crapola. How could someone expect her to go down that thing? It had to be ten feet high, maybe even fifteen, and covered in horrible gunk.

The other girls had already crawled off the side. They were laughing, and they hadn't even gotten into the water.

"Cassie, don't be a chicken!" Maureen shouted.

She was the only one who hadn't gone. Cassie would not be remembered as the sissy one of their group. She sat herself down on the edge, took a deep breath, and pushed off.

Like Cara, Cassie did not fly down the slippery concrete. In fact, she moved so slowly that she had to push along the back of the cement to make her body go. She picked up speed as she went over the algae, moving faster until the slide leveled out near the bottom. Her friends cheered, and Cassie stood up, laughing as she made her way off the slide.

Cara started back up the hill. "Let's go again!"

Cassie and Maureen scurried after her, and they went down the slide several more times.

"I'm feeling adventurous now," Cassie said. "I'm going down on my belly." She wiggled her eyebrows.

Maureen laughed. "This I have to see."

"Then watch." Cassie laid out on her stomach and pushed against the concrete. To her surprise, she quickly picked up speed, sliding downward much faster than she ever had on her butt. She lost control as she neared the bottom and squealed when instead of coming to a stop when it leveled out, she flew right over the edge and into the slimy swamp beneath. Her knee hit a rock hard enough to jar her. She stood up, sputtering and gasping.

Amity couldn't stop laughing. "That was hilarious!"

Cara hurried closer. "Are you okay? Did you get hurt?"

Cassie's knee throbbed, and she was certain she would have a horrible bruise. But she pasted a smile on her face and said, "I'm great."

Still giggling, Amity reached out a hand. "Here. I'll help you out."

Cassie grabbed a fist-full of mud and kept it in her hand when she took Amity's. "Oh, that's so kind of you," she said, grinning as she squished the mud between their fingers.

Amity shrieked and jerked her hand away, then flung the pieces of mud clinging to her skin at Cassie. They slid over Cassie's face and hair.

"Oh, no, you don't!" Cassie said. She grabbed another handful of mud and threw it at Amity.

"This is on!" Amity scooped up her own fist-full of mud, and Cassie forgot her aching knee as they slung green and black sludge at each other.

Maureen let out a yelp that stopped them in their fight.

"What is this?" she squealed.

Cassie and Amity turned toward her. Maureen held out the edge of her shirt and stared at something. Cara stepped closer and looked as well.

"It's some kind a little worm." She picked it up and examined it, then tossed it into the water.

"A worm?" Amity lifted her feet and moved over to the grass. She quickly scanned her body, looking for similar creatures. "Ew! I found one!"

Cassie hurried away from the swamp. "Check me!"

Cara and Amity turned to Cassie, and Amity let out a gasp. "You are covered in them!"

"Really? Get them off!" Cassie brushed her hands down her shirt and then looked closely at the tiny wriggling of worms on her fingers. "Oh!" she shrieked.

Her friends stepped closer, but nobody seemed willing to pick the worms off her. "It must be because she went in the water," Cara said.

Cassie bent to examine her shorts. Even her shoes were covered in them. "Oh no. I can't walk in these." She took off her shoes and socks, holding them in her hand. She would've taken off her shirt if they weren't in a public place.

"You can't walk back to my house like that," Cara said. "You'll hurt your feet!"

Cassie grunted. "I'll take my chances." She headed for the road, leaving the others to follow her.

Cara ended up taking her shoes off also, squealing each time she found a worm on her body. The walk back to her house was miserable. Cassie moved so quickly that the bottoms of her feet burned. The hot, black asphalt felt as if it skinned the soles of her feet with each step. Her clothing stuck to her skin, and the thought of those little worms crawling all over her made her writhe with discomfort. She couldn't wait to shed everything and jump in the shower. She broke into a run when she spotted Cara's house, and she arrived before the other girls. Putting her shoes on the patio, she grabbed the door knob and turned. Locked! The house was locked. With a groan, she dropped into a lawnchair and stared out at the tall grapevines, waiting for her friends to emerge.

Finally they did, and Cara gave her a surprised look. "Why didn't you just go in?"

"It's locked," she said. "Otherwise I would have."

"Oh." Cara lifted the welcome mat and pulled out a key. "I thought you knew about the spare. You could've just let yourself in."

Well. Now Cassie felt stupid. "I get the bathroom first!" She pushed past Cara into the bedroom in the back, pausing only to grab the clothes she'd taken off before they left for the crap slide. She turned on the hot water of the shower before she even locked the bathroom door, and then she stripped out of the clothes as quickly as she could. She watched the mud and gunk rinse off her body and run off into the drain. She breathed a sigh of relief as she began to feel clean again.

But even as Cassie stepped out of the shower, the moment she stepped onto the cold tile, her feet ached. They burned as if she were walking on hot coals. She dressed quickly and then padded across the soft carpet, relishing how the material soothed her feet.

Amity had taken a shower in Cara's parents' bathroom, and she waited at the island with her hair wrapped in a towel. Cassie collapsed onto a barstool and stuck her feet straight out in front of her.

"My feet!" she moaned. "They feel like they're on fire!"

Amity opened a bag of chips and stuck it on the island. "I guess you're not used to walking barefoot."

"Definitely not."

Cara emerged from her bathroom several minutes later, dressed in cute shorts and a shirt for pajamas. "My feet!" she said. "I don't think I'll be able to walk again!"

Cassie looked at Amity, and they both laughed. "I guess you're not used to walking barefoot either," Cassie said with a wink.

Clean and dry again, the girls curled up on Cara's couch with glasses of water and soda, reliving their experiences on the crap slide. Then Cara said, "What do you think will happen next year in high school?"

Just like that, the whole mood changed. Cassie stared into her glass, thinking about everything she hoped the next year would be.

"I'm going to be the most popular girl in school," Amity said. "I want to be homecoming queen every year."

Maureen snorted. "You'll be lucky to be homecoming wench."

"You're the wench!" Amity whacked her on the shoulder.

"What do you want for next year, Maureen?" Cara asked.

"To be your best friend," Maureen answered without hesitation. "As long as I can go wherever you go, I'll be fine."

Cara favored her with a smile before looking at Cassie. "And you, Miss Cassie?"

"I want to fall in love," Cassie said. "I want to have a boyfriend who will stick by my side for the next three years. And I want to be blissfully happy with him."

Cara lifted her bubbling glass of soda. "To high school."

"What about you, Cara?" Amity said. "You never said what you want."

A shadow flicked over Cara's face, but just as quickly it was gone. She shrugged. "I want to belong. That's all."

It was a weird sentiment, Cassie thought. Of course Cara belonged. She was the core to their friendship. But Cassie smiled and lifted her glass as well. "To high school." Excitement bubbled up in her chest just like that of the soda in Cara's glass.

It was right around the corner. The greatest adventure yet.